BRIAN FLYNN

BLACK AGENT

Brian Flynn was born in 1885 in Leyton, Essex. He won a scholarship to the City Of London School, and from there went into the civil service. In World War I he served as Special Constable on the Home Front, also teaching "Accountancy, Languages, Maths and Elocution to men, women, boys and girls" in the evenings, and acting in his spare time.

It was a seaside family holiday that inspired Brian Flynn to turn his hand to writing in the mid-twenties. Finding most mystery novels of the time "mediocre in the extreme", he decided to compose his own. Edith, the author's wife, encouraged its completion, and after a protracted period finding a publisher, it was eventually released in 1927 by John Hamilton in the UK and Macrae Smith in the U.S. as *The Billiard-Room Mystery*.

The author died in 1958. In all, he wrote and published 57 mysteries, the vast majority featuring the super-sleuth Antony Bathurst.

BRIAN FLYNN

BLACK AGENT

With an introduction
By Steve Barge

DEAN STREET PRESS
Disclaimer

Any work of fiction whose language is entirely cleansed of the idioms and expressions of its time would rightly be condemned–by that fact if by no other–as being an unfaithful witness to the world it seeks to portray. Therefore, no apology can be considered necessary for the occasional term or phrase that reflects the era of this book's original publication, even if some may now view such words with unease.

It is hoped that modern readers will approach these passages with an understanding of the historical context, and with the assurance that no malice was intended then, nor is any endorsed now.

INTRODUCTION

"Having once constructed my main plot, I sit down to write and permit the puppets to do their own dancing."

Thus wrote Brian Flynn in an article for Crime Book Magazine. They had awarded Black Agent (1949) the Society's Selection for that issue and asked Brian to introduce himself. While Brian had, until recently, been long forgotten as a crime writer, it is unclear how unknown he was when he was writing his fifty-seven mystery novels. From the tone of the article, it would seem that he viewed himself as something of a lesser author—when mentioning *"the distinguished authors who now write detective stories"* and *"the brilliant examples they constantly offer"* he refers to his own *"comparative unworthiness for the fire and burden of the competition."* However, he ends that section on a positive note:

"The stars have always been the most desired of all goals, so I allow exultation and determination to take the place of that but temporary dismay".

At this stage of his writing career, Brian was writing exclusively for John Long, a publisher that focussed primarily on the library market. His first book, *The Billiard Room Mystery* (1927), was published by John Hamilton, as were the next four, and then he moved to John Long for the rest of his career. (For the sake of accuracy, I feel that I should note that the first John Long book, *The Five Red Fingers* (1929), was actually published before the last Hamilton book, *Invisible Death* (1929).)

A selection of books was published in the US as well, the last of these being *The Case Of The Purple Calf* as *The Ladder Of Death* in 1935. A few other titles were translated into French (*The Case Of Elymas The Sorcerer* (1945) as Bryan Flynn), German (*The Mystery Of The Peacock's Eye* (1928), *The Horn* (1934) and Swedish (*The Case Of The Black Twenty-Two* (1928)). There is, according to a comment by Brian in an article, also a Danish translation, but I am yet to discover any evidence of this.

In the UK, there were some paperback reprints, all by John Long. A few appeared in their Four-Star Thrillers series, and some later titles such as *Such Bright Disguises* (1941), *Reverse the Charges* (1943) and *The Swinging Death* (1949) in the company's Pocket Editions, alongside such authors as Edgar Wallace, John Creasey and Frances Durbridge. By the time of *Men for Pieces* (1949), Brian's books were solely being printed in hardback, destined primarily for library shelves. Of course, this is one reason why copies of his books are particularly hard to find . . .

For those of you who are new to Brian's work, the majority of his output, fifty-three of his books, featuring the gentleman-detective Anthony Bathurst. One other is a children's book, *Tragedy at Trinket*, which can be recommended if you think most schoolboy murder mysteries don't have enough schoolboy cricket in them or vice versa (and features Bathurst's nephew, despite being published by a different company, Nelson). The final three are the Sebastian Stole mysteries, written under the pseudonym Charles Wogan. Stole is the exiled Crown Prince of Calorania, but his exploits only last three books. While the first book is quite distinctive from the Bathurst mysteries, the third one, *Cyanide For A Chorister* (1950), could have easily been one of Anthony's adventures with only minor alterations, and perhaps that is why this one, published between *Men For Pieces* (1950) and *Black Agent* (1951) was the final case for Stole and thereafter Brian focussed exclusively on Bathurst.

Writing exclusively for one sleuth might be seen as problematic, but it is notable how the style of the books varies as the series goes on, which may well be a reflection of the times as well. The country house settings of some of the early titles has long since gone by the time *Men For Pieces* (1949) is published, and there have been some changes to Brian's writing style. While Bathurst's character remains constant, there are far fewer books that are narrated by a third party—all of the five books from *Men For Pieces* (1949) to *The Ring Of Innocent* (1952) are written in the third person. As the series progresses, there are some books that veer away from the whodunit element as well.

A case could be made for the first such deviation from the norm being the inverted mystery *Such Bright Disguises* (1941), but there is still a whodunnit element at the end of the tale. The first of the out-and-out thrillers, however, was *The Grim Maiden* (1944), swiftly followed by *Conspiracy At Angel* (1947) and *Where There Was Smoke* (1951), all of which being tales of a criminal conspiracy where the story is more about the puzzle of what exactly is going on, rather than the identity of the villain of the piece. There are earlier examples of these conspiracy stories—*The Case Of The Purple Calf* (1934) and *They Never Came Back* (1940) for example, but these also have an unmasking at the end of the tale.

This is a reflection, though, of Brian's overall style at this point. The third person focus on primarily Bathurst and occasionally his co-investigators means that the focus of the book is on the investigation. Once Bathurst arrives on the scene, there are few scenes depicting suspects discussing things—we are exclusively seeing what Bathurst sees. One local newspaper review made comparisons to Freeman Wills Crofts, the creator of Inspector French, and this comparison is a reasonable one. Of course, that may not inspire some readers, as Crofts is one of the authors who has been in the past dismissed as "humdrum", thanks in part to Julian Symons' critique, but the Inspector French books are another until-recently-lost highlights of the Golden Age and I do recommend that readers who have dismissed him give him another go. Once you've read all the available Brian Flynn books, of course. After all, an entire narrative spent in Anthony Bathurst's company is no bad thing.

As there were no reprints of the titles from *Men For Pieces* (1949) onwards, we are lucky to be able to bring these five books to you. We have to thank Brian's estate for *Men For Pieces* as in my eight years collecting his work, I have never seen a copy for sale on the second-hand market. I can see why, as it's a really fun mystery, with Bathurst himself all but dismissing a dead body as suicide (he clearly doesn't realise that he's in a detective novel) until the victim's sister spots that the plug from the bath is in the wrong place! That's enough for our hero to dive into a mystery involving stolen and returned money, a plethora of suspects and a genuine surprise at the end. The original cover billed it as "Tense and Exciting" and they are not far from being wrong.

Black Agent (1950)—at this point Brian was clearly using his Big Book Of Quotations to find his titles—has a typically odd set-up for a Bathurst mystery. Barbara Marsden disappeared without trace from a New Year's party in her village. The only trace is spotted a month later when the distinctive yellow dress she was wearing is spotted being used as a costume in a play, only for the woman wearing it to also disappear . . . It's an original (if odd) concept and once the inevitable bodies appear, Brian does a great job of ratchetting up the tension. We also get another appearance of Bathurst's sort-of love interest and one of the earliest examples of a female Scotland Yard officer, Helen Repton.

The aforementioned *Where There Was Smoke* (1951) goes even further with the odd set-up. Donald Finney, a chemist, is offered work by the mysterious Mr Rehoboam, only for Donald's body to be discovered with no obvious cause of death. Questions abound however. Why was his skin discoloured? How did he have a printed note with the local Inspector Stire's name on it? And why was a piece of cooked bacon rind hidden in his belly button? A thriller following Bathurst's investigations—and there are some impressive Sherlockian deductions that Bathurst makes just from the crime scene—and a really fun adventure. Oh, and there's the only creative use of Alphabetti Spaghetti that I've aware of in a mystery novel . . .

Another Macbeth quote provides the title for *And Cauldron Bubble* (1951) although a reader hoping for a witch related mystery may be disappointed. Back to the whodunnits, and this time Bathurst is investigating a disappearance and a murder. Lady Blanchflower and her companion Mrs Whitburn left *The Red Deer* together after dinner, only for Lady Blanchflower to be found strangled and of Mrs Whitburn, there is no trace. And under Lady Blanchflower's body is, for some reason, a man's wig. This is one of the books where we see Bathurst being more fallible. With mostly just his intuition to go on, he follows several dead ends until the truth is revealed. This is similar to the later serial-killer title, *The Seventh Sign*, although we don't see Bathurst sinking to the same levels of frustration and despair here.

The final book in this set of re-releases is *The Ring Of Innocent* (1952) and we kick off with that old chestnut, the overheard conversation. Martin Scudamore overhears a mention of four rings and that if a certain Mr Lovelace interferes, "I'll slit his throat—without the slightest compunction or hesitation". Scudamore mentions it to Helen Repton, who promptly tells Bathurst, they arrive in time to hear Lovelace's dying message—the two words "*innocent*" and "*teaspoon*". It's a good mystery and moves along at a rapid pace, and, most importantly, is probably the title where we get the most insight into the Bathurst-Repton "relationship".

It brings me great delight that we are able to continue to bring the adventures of Brian Flynn back to the masses. I need to thank the many people who have helped along the way to revive Anthony Bathurst, but most importantly the late Rupert Heath, without whom Brian Flynn—and many other authors—would still be naught but a memory.

Steve Barge

"Good things of the day begin to droop and drowse,
While night's black agents to their preys do rouse."
Macbeth

CHAPTER 1

1

The little town of Wavering, on the evening of the 24th of January, lay under a mantle of snow. The fall had started just before noon and had kept on steadily for some hours. Much of the snow had settled and except for the main road where the traffic was, the white carpet was everywhere.

The fields on each side of the railway-line looked like large white handkerchiefs spread carelessly on the ground to dry, and the hedgerows in the country beyond the town glistened under their white covering in clearly-defined traceries of white and black.

Wavering, in Essex, less than twenty miles from London, is a small town which might seem to have deliberately, and with mischief aforethought, perched itself upon a ridge. The trees of Wavering are lovely and almost everywhere, and high woods separate its pasture lands. After you leave the main road with its shops and inns and smithy and municipal importances, you find that delightfully tiny houses nestle everywhere and that when you suddenly come upon them, nooked and crannied, they do no more than peep out at you from cunningly contrived hiding-places.

The place is remote and tranquil, its houses and cottages have long, low, red-tiled roofs and from all directions there are charming little lanes which run along flatly before dropping, sometimes gradually, sometimes suddenly, into valleys on each side of the Wavering ridge. In the summer, it basks in the sunshine. In the winter, it faces the weather with courage and confidence.

On the evening of this January day when the snow had fallen, an important event was being held in Wavering. Important, that is to say, from the standards which swayed Wavering. The New Year Social and Dance was being held in the hall of the Institute, attached to the parish church of St Simon. The church, with its Norman tower, stands at the southern end of the High Street, almost exactly opposite the smithy. Actually, the dedication of Wavering's parish church is in honour of St. Simon Zelotes, and a scholarly seventeenth century Rector, in jealous tradition, had caused to be manufactured and placed in a prominent position near the church door, a stone figure of the Saint with a saw in his right hand and a fish in his left—the one to mark the instrument of his glorious martyrdom and the other in allusion to his worldly occupation.

Despite the rigours of the weather, and notwithstanding a strong counter-attraction at the cinema, of *Passion's Entanglement*—featuring Hedy Vine and Derek Van llouten—the screen's fiercest lovers—the social and dance at the Institute had been attended in large numbers. The two churchwardens, Mr. Tidman the butcher and Mr. Vernon Panniter the solicitor, together with the Rector, the Rev. Matthew Hopkins and the curate, the Rev. Frank Cheam, had beamed engagingly upon the number of their guests, among whom reasonably young people abounded, and they had almost reached that part of the proceedings when the time would come to call a halt to the festivities and gradually shepherd the various members of the flock towards their respective homes. The last dance was announced . . . the New Year's Social was over. One by one, and in pairs and groups, the many dancers and the few card-players began to leave the hall. Parents were there—with children and without— bachelors, spinsters, couples definitely attached, about to be attached or merely temporarily attracted to each other, and lastly odd people of each sex—some alone in the world—some not! Some who had come to the social alone . . . and who would be returning home alone.

One of this last-mentioned kind was Barbara Marsden. She was standing by the door watching the people going out. As she stood and watched, a young man turned to her.

"Coming my way, Barbara?"

She smiled at him but shook her head at the question. The question which might well have been an invitation.

"No—Norman—not yet. I'm waiting for somebody." Norman Ferguson laughed, waved to her gaily and went out. A group of people followed on his heels. "Gosh," one of them—a girl—said laughingly as she stepped into the night, "what a perfectly marvellous moon! Look how it shines on the snow. If I fall over I hope somebody'll pick me up."

"Don't worry," came the reply from the background "there'll probably be a scrap for it. Thrills like that don't come every day."

The time at that moment was thirty-three minutes past eleven.

2

At five minutes past one on the following morning, the telephone rang insistently in the Rectory of St. Simon's. It is to be recorded that one of the two people sleeping there failed to hear it. This was Mrs. Hodgson, the Rector's housekeeper, who had served him in that capacity ever since he had been given the preferment of Wavering, some three years previously. Mrs. Hodgson was stout, florid-faced, middle-aged, rather deaf and an unusually heavy sleeper. The fact, therefore, that she slept on when the telephone rang at this unearthly hour, is eminently understandable. It would indeed have been surprising if she had done anything else.

The Rector himself, however, was awakened by the shrill ringing of the instrument. He sat up in bed, rubbed his eyes and frowned. As he did so, the telephone rang again and the thought came to him that his telephone had never before behaved in this manner, at this time of the morning, since he had become Rector of Wavering. He pulled on a pair of slippers, slid his plump shoulders into his dressing gown, switched on the landing-light and padded softly downstairs. The telephone that had disturbed him was in his study. He pushed open the study door, went to the telephone and picked up the receiver from its cradle.

"This is the Rectory of St. Simon's. The Rector speaking. What is it, please?" His voice was sharp with a soupçon of unfriendliness.

There was no delay with regard to the reply. The Rector listened intently.

"Sorry to trouble you at this time of the morning, sir, but it's Marsden speaking. Marsden of Pollards' Farm. It's about Barbara, my daughter. Could you tell me please, what time she came away from the social this evening? Because she's not back home yet—and my missus is in a rare terrible state about it—I can tell you."

The Rev. Matthew Hopkins clucked in dismay. "Dear, dear, Mr. Marsden—the naughty girl! To stay out so long on a cold night like this. It's really too bad of her. Let me see now—what time did she leave? The social finished up just about half-past eleven. I expect your Barbara left about the same time as most of the others. She must have—because when I gave a last look at the Hall just before midnight when Mr. Luck the caretaker was locking up—it was empty. Everybody had gone home."

The voice at the other end of the line came back with intensified anxiety. "That makes it worse, Rector. It does indeed. It's gone one o'clock now—and there's not a sign of her. I tell you, sir—the Missus is almost beside 'erself and I'm so worried that I'm a good mind to get a search-party out."

"Yes, I can understand your anxiety, Marsden. Has Barbara ever been late home before?"

"Never, sir! Never in her life. That's one o' the reasons the missus and I are so worried about it. Always been a good reliable girl, Barbara has. I'll say that for her. Never acted so as to give us a moment's anxiety."

The Rector clucked again. "With whom did she come to the social?" he asked; "is there . . . er . . . any young man in the offing? That may be the explanation of this temporary absence."

"No, sir. That line of argument won't do at all. Nobody took 'er. She went on her own. There *was* a young chap some few months back, young Sidney Rolleston—he and my girl were seein' a rare lot of each other . . . but it all fell through when he was called up and went into the Navy. Since then young Ferguson—the son of old Duncan Ferguson on the Great Coxted Road—has tried to 'ang 'is 'at up but Barbara wasn't having any. She's got ideas a bit above that sort of family. She was on her own to-night. If she *is* with a chap somewhere . . . called in at his house on the way home to see his people perhaps . . . it's someone she's picked up with at your "Social" last night. But even then—I'd lay a hundred to one against it. Knowing my daughter as I do."

By this time the Rev. Hopkins was growing colder and colder. His back, feet, shins and hands were like ice.

"Well, Mr. Marsden," he said defensively, "I really don't know how I can help you—situated as I am here—or even advise you. I don't know *what* to suggest. But you can take it from me that your daughter left with the others—well certainly *before* twelve o'clock. Let's hope you have good news before very long."

"Thank you, Rector. I am sure I hope so too. Well—if that's all you can tell me—I hope you'll excuse me ringing as I did—bringing you out o' your bed. Maybe Barbara'll soon turn up though. I'm fair eaten up with worry."

Marsden rang off and the Rev. Matthew Hopkins returned to bedroom and bed. He shivered as he pulled the bedclothes over him. He tried to settle down to sleep. He was tired—the previous day had not been an easy one for him. Any amount of work for a parish priest in one of these 'Socials'. One of the drawbacks of being a bachelor. But sleep would not come to his summoning. He was cold—standing in his study talking on the telephone to Barbara Marsden's father had chilled him to the bone. Eventually—after several abortive attempts—he gave up the idea of trying to get to sleep and lay there in bed watching the moon. It hung like a great golden lamp, poised over the belt of elm trees at the bottom of the Rectory garden. His eyes were fascinated by it. Then his mind wandered to the people of Wavering. The people of his parish. All of them. Men, women and children. Those of them who came to church—and those of them who did not. He wondered if Marsden had succeeded in getting his search-party to work. How many people were there, who lived in close proximity to the Marsden farm? The Rector tried to count them up. Come to think of it—when you considered it seriously—there weren't a great many. You couldn't expect Marsden to tramp miles across country looking for people at this time in the morning. And then when he had found them, to ask them to band themselves into a search-party.

Then the Rector began to grow introspective. He wondered whether he had done a wise thing in not offering to join the Marsden search-party. Perhaps as Rector he ought to have done. He shouldn't have acted selfishly. His action would be bound to invite criticism. On the other hand—it was a bitterly cold night—and he was no longer a young man. Things of that kind must, surely, be taken into consideration. There was reason in all things. If Cheam knew, he would go like a shot, but the house where the curate lodged wasn't on the telephone. The moon began to go down. His eyes came back to it. The hands of the Rector's watch crawled on towards the hours that marked the morning. He heard the clock of St. Simon's strike two, three and four. Between four and five, after tossing and turning at repeated but irregular intervals, the Rector fell into a fitful sleep, although he knew in his subconscious mind that he must rise early. It was St. Paul's Day—there was a church bell to be rung and a service to be taken—even though few of the faithful might attend it. The services at St. Simon's were conducted with scrupulous regard—the Rev. Matthew Hopkins was his own sternest critic. He allowed himself no latitudes or excuses.

Just before six o'clock he awoke again. It was a cold, clear crystal morning. As he came to full wakefulness out of the haven of sleep, he wondered what had happened to the Marsden search-party. Assuming that one had been formed.

3

The Rector, however, was soon to find out. Early in the morning—as soon, in fact, as he returned from the Church to the Rectory after taking the service—the news, which had at first been whispered, seemed to be all over the town.

Wavering woke up on that morning of the 25th of January to find that Barbara Marsden—whom nearly all of them knew so well—was missing. George Marsden had been to the police. As he had foreshadowed to the Rector on the telephone in the early hours of the morning, he had hastily improvised a small search-party from the three or four farm holdings which were situated close to his, and five men, in addition to himself and his son Rex, had set out somewhere in the region of two o'clock in the morning, to look for the missing girl. Without, as it turned out, any success whatever.

Of Barbara Marsden they failed to discover the slightest trace! Fields, ditches, barns, out-houses, byres, anywhere near the route which Barbara might reasonably have been anticipated to take on her journey home from St. Simon's to her father's farm, yielded absolutely nothing. There was no sign whatever of Barbara Marsden or of anything connected in any way with her.

George Marsden and Rex, worried, anxious and crest fallen, took the alarming news home to Pollards' Farm and the boy broke the sinister tidings to his mother. As a result of the painful interview which followed, George Marsden immediately telephoned to the police. Sergeant Loder was in the charge-room and took the call. He listened attentively and made certain notes with regard to what George Marsden had to tell him. Within a little, these are the details which Loder jotted down.

Missing since about 11.30 p.m. Jan. 24. Barbara Marsden. Address, Pollards' Farm, Wavering. Aged 22. Dark hair, dark eyes, pale complexion. Thin, slim and of medium height. Attended the New Year's Social and

Dance at the Parish Church Hall, High St., Wavering on the evening of her disappearance. Went there alone—not as a member of any party. Not returned home—no news of her—no sign of her. Then followed a brief description of the clothing she had been wearing.

Sergeant Loder tapped his front teeth with the butt of the pen he had used. "Sorry about this, Mr. Marsden. Very sorry, indeed. Very worryin' to you—no doubt. I know your girl well—by sight. Often see her up and down the High Street. Well—leave it to me—and I hope and trust we'll soon have better news. If you can—keep smiling."

George Marsden thanked the sergeant and rang off. He walked back to his wife and son and told them what he had said to Loder and what Loder had said to him. Loder left the desk where he had taken George Marsden's telephone call and made his way into one of the back rooms of the police station. Here he found a uniformed constable by the name of Dyer.

"Tom," said Loder, "I've got a job for you. Not too nice a one, either. Now—it's like this—you listen to me. George Marsden of Pollards' Farm has just been on the 'phone to me. He's in a spot of rare trouble—poor fellow. To do with his girl, young Barbara."

Loder went on and gave Dyer the full position as he knew it.

"Now you get along, Tom" concluded Loder—"and see what you can pick up. There's one thing about it—you can't say the scent's cold. Come back here at noon and report. If there's nothin' doin' by then—I shall have to think things over very carefully. It may mean that very serious measures will have to be taken. On the other hand, you may touch lucky early on. Now you get along, Tom."

Loder broke off and paused to listen. The telephone in the police-station was ringing again. "*More* trouble," said the sergeant. "I'd better go and answer it -I don't quite know what to think of the fellow who invented telephones. One of these days I'll think of something to call him."

He walked back to the main room of the police-station, where the telephone was ringing almost vindictively. At least that was the impression which came to Loder as he listened to it.

"Hallo," he said, as he lifted the receiver. "Wavering Police . . ." Loder listened carefully to the message which was coming through to him.

"It's Tidman speaking . . . that you, Sergeant Loder . . . Owen Tidman speaking . . . the butcher in the High Street."

Loder nodded—unnecessarily. "O.K., Mr. Tidman, Loder here. Go ahead."

"I want to report something stolen from my shop," went on Tidman, "during the night. Or at any rate after I closed up the shop yesterday afternoon."

Loder pulled his note-book towards him. "O.K., Mr. Tidman. What is it you've lost?"

Tidman's reply, when it came, immediately brought him to a condition of acute astonishment, if not incredulity.

"A large basin of dripping, Sergeant Loder. Beef fat. Which I always keep in the back of my shop. I don't doubt you've seen it there yourself, many times, when you've had occasion to come into my shop."

Loder's pencil poised over the page. "Dripping? A basin of dripping? You're not going to tell me, Mr. Tidman, in all seriousness, that anybody would break into your shop to steal a basin of dripping? How did they effect entrance? What's the damage? Are you certain nothing else has been taken?"

Loder knew that Tidman was hesitating at the other end of the line.

"Well, Sergeant—there's no particular damage to speak of from that point of view—the thief came in the back way. Along the mews that runs along the rear of all the shops this side of the High Street. That's as easy as kiss your hand. Forced the lock of the back door. It was none too strong I'm prepared to admit that. And nothing else has been taken—as far as I can see."

Loder pushed away the note-book in which he had been writing with an air of complete resignation. "Right-o, Mr. Tidman. Seems a rare funny business to me. Anyhow—I'll send somebody along to your place to have a look round. Either that or I'll pop along myself. Depends on how much time I get. They say it never rains but it pours."

"How d'ye mean?" came Tidman's query.

"Why—one of the girls that went to the Church do last night hasn't got back home yet. Been reported missing by her father. No sign of her anywhere."

"That's bad. Which girl?"

"Barbara Marsden—from Pollards' Farm. George Marsden's girl. Black-haired, dark-eyed little thing. Expect you know her better than I do. What with her disappearing like this—and your basin of ruddy dripping—"

Loder hung up, as the butcher's reply seemed a trifle on the incoherent side. That was the worst of Tidman, too important by half!

4

Constable Dyer, on his mission, as ordered by Sergeant Loder, made several calls that morning. In turn he called upon Frederick Luck, the caretaker the of St. Simon's Hall and Institute, the Rector of St. Simon's, the Rev. Matthew Hopkins, the curate, the Rev. Frank Cheam, Mr. Vernon Parmiter, the solicitor and the Rector's warden, and finally upon Owen Tidman, the butcher of the High Street, and also the people's warden:

Concerning Barbara, he was able on all his visits to elicit one piece of information of definite value—and one piece only. Which was this. That Barbara had been seen standing close to the exit door of the hall as the people were beginning to leave the Social for home. This piece of news came to the constable at his first call. Luck told Tom Dyer that he heard Barbara speak to somebody round about half-past eleven—but he hadn't been able to hear what was said either by Barbara Marsden herself, or by the person to whom she spoke. He had heard her voice—he knew it well—and it came from somewhere near the door. He had no recollection of seeing the girl after that.

The Rector, at the Rectory, and Frank Cheam, at his 'digs' in a turning off the High Street, each stated that the hall was entirely empty some few minutes before midnight. Each one of them remembered looking into it and noticing the fact.

Parmiter, the next man upon whom Dyer called, and *very much* the solicitor, had but a vague remembrance of having seen Barbara dancing once or twice during the evening, which was the limit of the information he was able to supply.

When Dyer inquired if he could remember the names of any of the people Barbara had danced with, he replied: "I'm sorry, Constable Dyer, but I haven't the slightest idea. Actually I scarcely took the trouble to notice."

As has already been stated, Tom Dyer came eventually to Owen Tidman. The butcher was short, dark and fat—middle aged and in appearance, strongly reminiscent of the Mongolian. His skin was yellowish in shade and a thin, wispy moustache crawled across his upper lip. But he was a generous man, always ready to do anybody a good turn if such a turn were needed—and well-liked in Wavering.

"Morning, Constable," said the butcher, "been waiting for you to turn up—I expected you before this."

Dyer sought appropriate explanation of Tidman's remark. Tidman at once straightened out the matter. Dyer listened to him and nodded. Then he stroked his chin contemplatively. "Ve-ry peculiar," he said, "ve-ry peculiar indeed. It'd be rare strange if the disappearance of your basin of fat was connected in any way with this girl being missin'. It would an' all! If you don't mind—I'd like to ask you one or two questions, Mr. Tidman. With regard to that church Social of yours last night."

"That's all right, Constable," replied Owen Tidinan, "ask away."

Dyer produced his note-book and put the same questions to the butcher that he had put to the other people upon whom he had called that morning. To almost all the inquiries, Tidman shook his head negatively. All that Dyer was able to extract from him was that he had noticed Barbara Marsden 'flittin' about the hall from time to time with various people. Different boys, as a rule, she was dancin' with. She was a bit on the conspicuous side because of the yellow dance frock she was wearing. You know what I mean, Constable Dyer—you could pick her out—easy.

"I see. Now what would ha' been the time, do you reckon, Mr. Tidman, when you last clapped eyes on her? Just about? It don't matter to a few minutes or so, one way or the other."

Tidman considercd Dyer's question. "I should say about eleven o'clock," he answered.

"You didn't see her leave?"

Tidman shook his head. "No. I can't say that I did. Not actually leave the hall. Just about the time they started to break up I was talking to Mr. Gosling about the show the Church Dramatic Society is puttin' on in a week or so for the Organ Fund. Mr. Cheam, the curate, was with us and took part in the discussion. No—I never saw Barbara Marsden leave the hall."

Constable Dyer grunted—if only to express a certain measure of dissatisfaction. But Tidman wondered what the grunt meant. Dyer put away his note-book and pencil.

"Now show me where your robbery took place, will you, Mr. Tidman? Of that basin of dripping you had pinched."

"Right. Come this way, Constable."

Tidman led Dyer through the butcher's shop, through an out-house and into the yard. A mews ran along the back of the shops on this side of the High Street. It began from the wall of St. Simon's Church which stood on the corner and ran as far as the courtyard of Wavering's most ancient inn, The 'Red Cock.' Tidman pointed to the out-house door.

"The chap forced this open. That's how he got in. The lock wasn't strong. A big fellow, with big shoulders 'ud do it easy. Child's play!"

Dyer looked solemn and took note of the facts. "Where was the fat?"

Tidman pointed into the shop. "At the back of the counter there—on the right. I nearly always keep some there during business hours. It was so cold last night I left it there. I was in a hurry when I closed up—what with the social and one or two other things—I didn't bother about it."

Dyer nodded profoundly. "And now you've lost it. Through being careless-like. Can you give me a description of the basin it was in?"

"A big blue and white basin—old-fashioned sort."

Dyer produced his note-book again and made certain laborious entries therein. As he did so, he heard the clock of St. Simon's strike twelve. He remembered what Sergeant Loder had told him with regard to reporting back at the station.

"That'll be all for now, Mr. Tidman," he said lugubriously, "so I'll wish you good morning."

Tidman watched him from the shop door as he made his way up the High Street. The butcher glanced at the place on his counter where his basin of dripping had stood, glanced again up the street at Constable Dyer's retreating figure and shook his head doubtfully. It may be that Owen Tidman was a man of strong opinions. It may even be that he harboured prejudices. Or found it difficult to suffer fools gladly.

CHAPTER 2

1

D ays came and went. Until they made a week . . . and January became February . . . and then another week passed . . . and another. By this time, Sergeant Loder had the assistance of the police from their County Headquarters at Remsford some eight miles away . . . but not a trace was found of either the dark-haired, dark-eyed Barbara Marsden or of Tidman's blue-and-white-striped basin that had contained dripping.

Many of the inhabitants of Wavering grew restive, critical, and even challenging under the police's failure. There was a great deal of talk in the streets. There were several letters to the *Wavering Chronicle*. Some went so far as to say that the local police authorities should have put their pride in their pocket, realized that the job was beyond their compass and at once requested the help of Scotland Yard. But inasmuch as the Remsford Police did nothing of the sort, Scotland Yard remained detached and, perhaps, not too strongly interested. Almost invariably, the 'Yard' has troubles of its own. To say nothing of the fact that young girls are constantly being reported as 'missing' from various parts of England—from more causes, no doubt, than one.

Many suggestions to account for the strange and sudden vanishing of Barbara Marsden circulated throughout the little town of Wavering, among which the most popularly accepted was that Barbara had run off somewhere—'with a chap'. In a town of the calibre of Wavering, romance is ever near the hearts of so many people—especially those of the alleged gentler sex. The position remained thus for just over three weeks. Until a sharp-eyed woman happened to notice something.

On the evening of the 15th February, the St. Simon's Dramatic Society staged a performance in the hall of the Institute (that same hall in which

Barbara Marsden had been last seen just over three weeks previously) of the amusing farce so beloved of Amateur Dramatic clubs, entitled *Nothing But the Truth*. It was a production into which Edmund Gosling, the producer, and also the vital force behind the society, had put much care, all his experience, and no little skill.

During the second act, however, a certain disturbance took place in the audience. Some people, seated near to its centre, described the disturbance as a commotion and several of them approximated indignation. But the lady who appeared to be the cause of this unusual happening, left her seat and the hall at the conclusion of the second Act, walked straight along to the police-station at the end of the High Street and requested to be allowed to speak to Sergeant Loder immediately. Loder, who happened to be on duty, came into the charge-room directly he heard that he was wanted.

"Who is it wants me at this time of night?" he enquired as he entered the room. His face looked worried and anxious—and his hair might have been tidier. Life hadn't exactly been a bed of roses for Sergeant Loder during the three weeks that had just passed and although he was unaware of the fact when this summons came for him, the next three weeks were going to be even worse.

"Who is it enquiring for me?" he repeated, as he came to the desk.

A stout, florid-faced, quick-eyed woman rose from a chair and confronted him. Her manner was bustling and business-like.

"Good evening, Sergeant Loder," she said. "I know you—even though you may not know me. I'm Wavering born and bred, I am—all my forty-two years. Miss Wilkes the name—dressmaker—of Shelford Row—that's a turning off the High Street—in case you don't know. Yes—I'm Julia Wilkes—and I expect you're wondering what it is that's brought me to a place like this at this time of an evening. You wouldn't be human if you didn't." Julia Wilkes looked round the police-station with something like a disapproving eye. "First time I ever stood in the realm of the law—and that's a fact. Though I've often been curious as to what these places were really like when you got inside 'em. Now I know—I don't think much of 'em."

Her tone suddenly changed and she looked straight at Loder.

"I take it, Sergeant Loder, that you're still interested in what happened to Barbara Marsden on the evening of the New Year Social?"

The unexpected remark took the Sergeant with swift surprise and he shot Julia Wilkes a quick, sharp, critical glance. At the same time he took a step forward.

"What do you know about Barbara Marsden?" he asked.

"Nothing," replied Julia Wilkes, "nothing whatever beyond the fact that she's missing—but what I've come to tell you is this. Down the High Street in the Church hall, the St. Simon's Dramatic Society is giving a show. A dramatic performance. Don't get me wrong, Sergeant. It's giving a show *now*—at this very moment—while we're talking—the *show's going on*! See what I mean? Well—in that show—just a few hundred yards down the street—one of the girls is wearing the very frock that Barbara Marsden wore the night she disappeared. Yes—*you* can look! I know it all right—I ought to—you see I happened to make it for her."

Miss Wilkes set her lips primly and waited for the sergeant's reaction. Loder stared at Julia Wilkes incredulously. When he found words he said: "You're absolutely certain of what you've said?"

"I am, Sergeant Loder. Shouldn't have come here otherwise. I know the frock too well not to recognize it when I see it. I made it specially for Barbara for the New Year's Social. I've made her frocks for years. I recognized it by its shade of colour, by the cut of the sleeves and by the way the sequins are sewn on it. On the 24th of January it was on Barbara's back—now it's on another girl's back and appearing in *Nothing But the Truth*. Where it's been in between—ask me another. When I saw it come on the stage and knew it for what it was—I could hardly believe my eyes, but I thought it was my duty to come along to the station here immediately and have a word with you about it."

Loder still stared. "What did you say the name of the play was?"

"*Nothing But the Truth.*"

"Blimey," said Loder, using his handkerchief on his forehead—"I'll hand it to 'em—they couldn't have picked a better title. Somebody must have known something!"

2

Julia Wilkes made a noise that resembled a snort. She was an outspoken woman and she prided herself thereon. Moreover, she liked people to return to her much of her own coin. At this moment, Loder was a source of acute disappointment to her. For one thing, this was, in her opinion, scarcely the time for feeble attempts at humour. She must bring this sergeant who faced her, staring and still semi-incredulous, to his official senses!

"Well?" she inquired tartly, "what do we do? Stand here like a couple of ninnies, or—"

Loder pulled himself together and was himself again.

He had noted the use of the plural pronoun.

"We do not stand here, Miss Wilkes," he replied with an impression of dignity; "on the other hand, we make our way to the St. Simon's Church hall. To this play that you say is still going on. You and I! I must see this young lady that's wearing this frock. Have you any idea what time the performance is likely to be over?"

"If you're asking me for the exact time, Sergeant Loder, I can't help you. But if you're asking me for 'somewhere roundabout', I should say about half-past ten. Say, half-past ten till a quarter to eleven. That's about the usual time for a play to end. I've seen 'em do several in my time."

Loder looked up at the clock on the wall in the police station. "Right. We've got tons of time, then. We'll stroll up there. This job, you know, Miss Wilkes, will require careful handling." Loder scratched his chin reflectively.

"It will and all," replied Julia Wilkes brightly. "Do you think you're quite up to it?"

Loder coughed. He wasn't at his best or brightest. For the reason that he found Julia Wilkes disconcerting.

"I'll do my best," he returned dryly—"after all, I shall have the benefit of your assistance."

Julia Wilkes threw it back at him without ceremony or hesitation. "You can pack up the sarcasm, Sergeant, as soon as you like. It's entirely uncalled for. I haven't come on this journey because I like it—I can tell you. Another thing—I paid half a crown for my ticket. Saw only half the show. Don't think much of *that*, as a business proposition. No more would you. Fortunes aren't made that way."

"I quite understand how you're feeling, Miss Wilkes," returned Loder, "and I had no intention of being sarcastic as you seem to think. Please forget it. I think we're just about at the hall."

"We are, Sergeant Loder. Here's the entrance. I suggest we go in the back way—the dressing-rooms are at the back and then you can get hold of somebody like Mr. Gosling. He's the producer of the show and he's really the . . . er . . . head of the Dramatic Society, if you know what I mean."

Loder nodded and said that he did. "O.K., Miss Wilkes that's a very sound suggestion. Let's try this door here."

He rapped smartly on the wooden panels. There was no answer. "Nobody there," said Loder.

"Try the handle," essayed the practical Miss Wilkes. "It may be open."

Loder tried—and turned the handle. Miss Wilkes and he entered. The lady smiled with satisfaction. The room was empty—but the electric light was on. Evidently it had been in recent use. Julia Wilkes could see from the open communication door that the dressing-rooms were adjoining.· She pointed them out to the sergeant.

"The play isn't over yet . . . the dressing-rooms are empty . . . look! But I shouldn't think the curtain'll be very long. Can't be, judging by the time it is now. Suppose we walk through . . . we may meet somebody who can put us in touch with Mr. Gosling. That's what you really want, isn't it? He's the best man to see."

"That's the idea, Miss Wilkes. We'll go along—as you say."

As he spoke, he noticed that she was fumbling with a programme. Julia Wilkes spoke. "I just want to make sure what the girl's name is. She was a stranger to me. The one that's wearing Barbara's frock, I mean. Now—where are we?"

She ran her finger down the list of names. "Here we are. Here's the cast. Vera Ferris. That's funny. Don't know her. Not a name I know at all. Not in Wavering. May be new people in the place. There are all those new houses up there by—"

Julia Wilkes was interrupted by a loud and sustained burst of clapping. She looked significantly at Sergeant Loder. "There you are," she said, "that's the curtain—depend on it. Wait for 'The King'—then you can pop out and do your stuff."

Loder looked round the room as though assessing the conditions. "There'll be a clattering horde down here in a few minutes if I'm any judge—I've been behind the scenes once or twice—I know what it's like just after a show finishes. Like Bedlam let loose. I'm wondering the best thing I can do to get a bit of comparative privacy. I know—you stay in here, Miss Wilkes—and I'll get hold of Gosling and this girl, Vera

Ferris—and I'll bring them in here to you. Then we can talk things over more or less amongst ourselves. Just the four of us. I'll tell Gosling not to let anybody else in here. How does that strike you?"

"Sound idea, Sergeant Loder. Couldn't be better. Hark! There's the orchestra for 'The King'. You get along and button-hole Gosling as soon as he shows up. I'll wait in here, as you said. Tell Gosling it's serious directly you get the chance—otherwise he'll want to argue . . . don't bandy words with him . . . you may want to interview certain people before they dash off home."

"You certainly do think of things, Miss Wilkes," said Sergeant Loder as he made for the door.

"Cut that," came the reply, "once and for all! All balsam! Told you that just now. Otherwise you'll find *me* missing when you come back."

Loder relinquished the unequal struggle, took a few steps forward, closed the door of the room behind him and found himself in the path of a merry company of young men and young women. Most of them were laughing excitedly . . . many of them were breathless . . . a great number were talking . . . and they all seemed to be saying . . . 'oh I say—jolly good show . . . jolly good show'.

3

Sergeant Loder had a few quick, grave words with Edmund Gosling. Gosling, visibly affected at Loder's presence, spoke sharply to the members of the cast, found Vera Ferris and brought her, nervously trembling, to Loder. The three of them joined Julia Wilkes in the adjoining room. When they were all inside, Loder, rather ostentatiously, closed the door. "Sit down, will you, please?" he asked quietly. He indicated chairs with his hand . . . rather vaguely.

Julia Wilkes and the young actress, Vera Ferris; still with her make-up on, sat down. Edmund Gosling didn't. He stood there facing Loder, carelessly and nonchalantly, with his back against the wall. He was middle-aged, short, plump and fair. His face was wholly benevolent . . . almost cherubic. He wore rimless glasses over light-brown eyes and his fingers toyed with a gold chain that he wore loosely from his waistcoat. On the chain hung a plain gold cross. The St. Simon's Dramatic Society was a large part of his life . . . it had been for some years. He had founded it . . . and he had fostered it. As he looked down at the scene in front of him he felt that the first thing needed of him was protection for his young protégée, Vera Ferris.

"Miss Ferris," said Sergeant Loder, "I'm sorry to give you this trouble. But it's so serious that I've no option. But you wore a frock earlier in the play this evening—a yellow frock—with sequins on it." To Edmund Gosling's profound astonishment, the girl addressed paled perceptibly when she heard what Loder had said. She half-nodded to Loder's question.

"Yes . . . yes . . . I did . . . er . . . wear a yellow frock in the second act. That is quite right. Why do you ask?" She folded her hands in her lap and looked almost imploringly in the direction of Edmund Gosling. But Loder was in again before Gosling could venture anything.

"Will you please tell me, Miss Ferris, just where you got that yellow frock you wore this evening? And also, where that same yellow frock is now?"

Gosling broke in . . . almost with hostility . . . certainly with challenge. "What's the idea, Sergeant Loder? What is it that you're really—"

Loder silenced him with a wave of the hand. "Please keep out of this, Mr. Gosling, for the time being—and let Miss Ferris answer my questions. Later on, you'll be hearing more."

The girl herself appeared to have somewhat recovered from her early shock and to be in slightly better heart. Julia Wilkes thought that Gosling's intervention, fruitless though it had been, had given her courage.

"It's quite simple, sir," said Vera Ferris, "and I'm sure I don't know what all the fuss is about—I don't really. But when I was dressing this evening to go on for the second act, careless-like I put my arm through one of the sleeves of my frock—and tore it all the way down. It was a shocking tear—it was, really—ripped right up—and I was in a terrible state about it. I could have cried my eyes out—I could really! There was no time to mend it—even if I'd had everything to hand—which I hadn't. I couldn't make up my mind *what* to do for the best. You see, my other frocks I was wearing in the play weren't suitable for the second act. Well— there I was worrying . . . until one of the other girls in the dressing-room, Nina Crump it was, said there were some dresses in one of the Dramatic Society's 'skip's. She said she'd seen them. That one over there."

Vera Ferris pointed to the smaller of two 'theatrical' baskets standing by the wall near where Edmund Gosling was still leaning.

"Go on, please," prompted Loder with grim persistence.

The girl who had been explaining shot a scared glance at him. Loder was so tight-lipped . . . so altogether uncompromising. He had neither kindness nor sympathy. There was something about him which frightened her.

"Well . . . I went out and turned the 'skip' out . . . when Nina Crump said that . . . to see what I could find . . . and true enough, there *were* some old frocks and costumes in there amongst a lot of other things. And, as it happened, one really nice new frock as well. Somebody, I expect, has recently made a gift of it to the Dramatic Society . . . perhaps it didn't fit the person it was made for too well. People do do those things. Make presents to the Society, I mean. As Mr. Gosling will tell you . . . it frequently happens. Well . . . there isn't much more for me to say. I took the frock as it was . . . proper corn in Egypt to me it was, I can tell you . . . it didn't fit me too badly . . . considering how I'd come by it . . . and I wore it on the stage. It wasn't suitable for the next act . . . so I didn't wear it any more. There was no need for me to do so. I'm sure I didn't know I was committing any crime," concluded Vera Ferris bitterly and semi-defiantly.

"If I may be permitted to interrupt," the words came frigidly from an acidulated Edmund Gosling, "Miss Ferris told me about the incident at the first opportunity which occurred to her and I endorsed her action. She told me exactly what she has just told you. And now, Sergeant Loder, will you please explain to us what this is all about? I think that you owe *that* much to us, at the very least."

Loder looked with significance at Julia Wilkes. She nodded to him almost imperceptibly.

"O.K., Mr. Gosling," said the sergeant, "and I won't waste words, either." He swung round on to Vera Ferris. "That frock, Miss Ferris, the yellow frock from the 'skip'. Get it please, will you, and bring it here."

"Certainly. I haven't replaced it yet. But I should have done if you hadn't pounced on me as you did. It's in the girls' dressing-room next door. Won't take me two ticks."

There was a silence as Vera Ferris went out, pale . . . and rather sullen . . . and the silence continued until she returned, carrying the yellow frock on her arm.

"Give the frock to this lady, will you please, Miss Ferris?" said Sergeant Loder.

The girl obeyed the instruction. Julia Wilkes took the frock from her, turned it over and nodded decisively. "As I said, Sergeant Loder, not a doubt about it. The answer is in the affirmative. I know it too well to make any mistake."

She spoke primly and emphatically, like a quarrelsome woman who has succeeded in obtaining the triumphant last word.

Loder's jaw was firm and rigid. "Thank you, Miss Wilkes. That's definite—and settles it for me." He turned sharply to Gosling and the girl who had worn the frock. "The point is this," he declared forcibly, "that yellow evening frock which Miss Wilkes is holding and which Miss Ferris wore on the stage this evening is not just an ordinary frock. It was made by Miss Wilkes for Barbara Marsden."

Loder paused, but the silence was so intense that he continued almost immediately. "Barbara Marsden was wearing it at the Church Social on the evening . . . three weeks ago . . . when she disappeared. And now it turns up in the St. Simon's Dramatic Society's 'skip'. It certainly seems that there will have to be explanations from somebody."

Vera Ferris looked like chalk. She turned as though for aid to Edmund Gosling. Gosling blinked through his glasses. Neither of them spoke. Loder, rather inconsequently, added words.

"Miss Wilkes here happened to be in the audience at your performance this evening, Mr. Gosling. Directly Miss Ferris came on the stage wearing the frock Miss Wilkes recognized it as the one she had recently made for Barbara Marsden."

As Loder said this, Gosling seemed to recover himself and began to move towards the 'skip' at which Vera Ferris had pointed at the beginning of the interview.

"We must look in the 'skip'," he said impulsively; "that's obvious . . . there may be . . . "

"Oh—what?" cried Vera Ferris, "what do you mean?"

"There may be," repeated Edmund Gosling, "other things in there. Who knows?"

"Just a moment," said Loder somewhat impulsively. He placed himself between Gosling and the 'skip'. "This is a job for me," he said, "and for nobody else."

Gosling turned away and shrugged his shoulders. "Please yourself," he muttered.

Loder walked to the smaller of the two 'skips' and flung back the lid. As he did so, a smothered cry came from Vera Ferris. But Julia Wilkes bent forward. She was made of sterner stuff.

4

As it happened, however, Vera Ferris need not have cried out. When he threw back the lid, Loder saw clothes, costumes, various specimens of uniform, curtains, cushions, various small 'hand-props' such as glasses, cups and saucers, plates, brushes, table-mats, ink-stands and a number of small wooden trays. He found nothing in the 'skip' from which Vera had taken the yellow frock which had belonged to Barbara Marsden. Loder was looking for underclothes or stockings, or shoes . . . or personal ornaments . . . Vera had dreaded the appearance of Barbara's nude and dead body . . . Julia Wilkes . . . alert and watchful . . . had maintained an absolutely open mind . . . and it would be difficult to record with any clarity or accuracy, the conditions for which Edmund Gosling had prepared and steeled himself. Loder made a perfunctory sorting-out of the various articles which his hands had tumbled from the 'skip'. He heard Gosling's voice speak over his shoulder.

"All St. Simon's stuff, Sergeant, that you've got there . . . every scrap of it. What a relief!"

Loder turned and looked at him. "Sure of that?"

Gosling took out his handkerchief and nodded with slow confirmation. "As good as—from what I saw. Without turning every article over separately."

"H'm!" Loder straightened himself. "Comes to this, then. Who has charge of this basket? In the ordinary way?"

Edmund Gosling fingered his chin reflectively. "Well I'm afraid there's more than one way of answering that. It's *really*—according to the Society's rules—the responsibility of the Property and Wardrobe Mistress—that's Mrs. Parmiter, wife of Parmiter, the churchwarden. But as it works out as a practical issue, I should say that this is the normal place for it . . . that it's constantly left unlocked and, of course, while it's unlocked, plenty of people would have comparatively easy access to it."

Loder growled at what he heard. "That's not going to help me much."

"Sorry, Sergeant—but that's the way it goes."

Loder turned away from him with a gesture of impatience. As he completed the movement, he caught the eye of Julia Wilkes, who was still sitting in her chair with Barbara Marsden's yellow frock lying across her lap. Loder saw that Julia was endeavouring to attract his attention. Loder at once went over to her.

"Did you want me, Miss Wilkes?"

"What about that other 'skip'?" asked Julia, pointing to the larger basket, "that one over there in the corner? How about your having a peep in there? It *might* have something in it."

Loder looked at her and then at the 'skip'. "Why?" he inquired—"what's on your mind?" He stopped suddenly on the question. Her meaning had dawned on him. "Yes. I should! You're right about that, Miss Wilkes."

Edmund Gosling looked across and saw Loder on his way to the second basket.

"That one's empty," he called out; "hasn't been used this season at all."

Loder saw that the 'skip' was unpadlocked and opened the lid. He saw, too—at once—that Gosling was right. This bigger 'skip' was absolutely empty. And then . . . quite suddenly . . . as he looked down into the empty space . . . Loder uttered a sharp exclamation.

"What is it?" cried Edmund Gosling with fear in his voice.

Loder turned and beckoned to him and then pointed to the bottom of the 'skip'.

Gosling peered vaguely and uncertainly at a large, irregular stain.

"Blood," cried Loder . . . "that's blood down there, if ever I saw it."

CHAPTER 3

1

"There are other marks, too," pointed out Edmund Gosling, "on the sides there. Notice what I mean. Look there and there."

Loder dragged the 'skip' out of the corner where it had been standing. He looked long and carefully at the marks which Gosling had pointed out. Julia Wilkes came and stood by the two men, but the girl, Vera Ferris, stayed behind on the chair. Every now and then she trembled and her fingers worked convulsively. Julia shot a quick glance at her and saw that she was perilously close to tears. Loder spoke.

"Those marks on the side aren't blood. At least that's my opinion. They're quite different to the big stain at the bottom."

Gosling took another look at the interior of the basket. He saw immediately that, in one respect at least, Loder was right. The marks on the side of the 'skip' *were* different from the large irregular stain at the bottom. There was no doubt about it whatever. If Loder had looked worried when Julia Wilkes's arrival at the police-station brought him into action he looked a thousand times worse now. He felt that his best plan was to 'phone through to Remsford headquarters at once and report his findings. He turned rather hopelessly to Gosling again.

"Many people—other than those connected with your Dramatic Society—would have access to this room and these 'skips', I take it? That is so, isn't it?"

Gosling was quick to confirm. "Oh—undoubtedly. And it's quite a simple matter to get *in* here—that's another thing. I should say that the door of the main hall is constantly open. All day, probably, when there's something on in the evening. People going backwards and forwards—you know the kind of thing I mean."

Loder rubbed gloomily at his top lip. "Take the night of the "Social," the night Barbara Marsden was last seen, anybody could have got in here then? From the "Social"? Yes?"

Gosling nodded—"I should say so—yes. Although—of course—"

Whatever it was that Gosling had been about to say, was lost. For the reason that Vera Ferris came into the conversation with a rather surprising interruption.

"Why—yes, Mr. Gosling, you were in here yourself! On the evening of the New Year Social. Don't you remember? You were in here with Mr. Cheam and Mr. Tidman. The three of you. Don't you remember my coming to you with a message from the Rector?"

Directly Vera Ferris had started to speak, Gosling paused as though he were considering something. Then he smiled at the girl who had put the question to him. The half-frown he had worn cleared from his features and he nodded.

"That's quite right, Vera. That's absolutely right. Full marks for an excellent memory. I *was* in here that evening with Tidman and Mr. Cheam. We were discussing this evening's show—and its prospects. I'd clean forgotten the incident until your mentioning it brought it back to me." He turned and addressed Loder. "Miss Ferris is right, Sergeant. The three of us, Tidman, the Rev. Cheam and I were in here discussing the show that we put on this evening. Peculiar sort of coincidence—eh? All the same, it certainly supports your point, Sergeant—plenty of people *could* have got in here, who wanted to."

Loder said nothing—but his apprehension was growing apace. Try as he would, his thoughts refused to be harnessed into control. Gosling came at him again.

"By the way, Sergeant—the others in the dressing-room? It's getting late. Can they go—or will you be wanting to speak to any of them?"
.

Loder thought quickly. "Well—it's a little awkward, I suppose, whichever way you choose to look at it—and as you say, time's getting on. They can go, I think—with the exception of that young lady Miss Ferris here mentioned—what was the name—Crump? I'd like a few words with her."

Edmund Gosling motioned to Vera Ferris. "Ask Nina to come in here—will you, Vera?"

But again Loder took it upon himself to intervene. "Just a minute. *If* you don't mind. I'd much prefer to deal with this in my own way. Perhaps, Miss Wilkes, you wouldn't mind obliging me by asking Miss Crump to come in here for a few minutes?"

Gosling tossed his head as though he desired no more to do with the matter. Vera Ferris made no attempt to conceal her indignation at Loder's unspoken innuendo. The look on her face was eloquent. Julia Wilkes, however, jumped up briskly to do Loder's bidding, tossing the yellow frock, as she did so, upon a near and vacant chair. Not a word was said while they waited for Nina Crump.

Julia, however, was back in a few minutes. She was accompanied by a fat, rosy-cheeked, dark-haired, hard breathing girl in a red frock that was distinctly on the tight side.

"Miss Crump, Sergeant Loder," announced Julia Wilkes. "At your service."

Loder nodded. "Good evening, Miss Crump—sorry to trouble you, but something serious has turned up here this evening—and it's just possible you may be able to help me. But first of all, I'll tell you what it is."

Loder gave a brief account of the incident of the Marsden frock as it affected Julia Wilkes and Vera Ferris. Nina Crump's round eyes grew rounder than ever and she breathed heavily. "Now, Miss Crump," went on Loder—"the point is this—you remember suggesting to Miss Ferris when she tore the sleeve of her frock that she looked in the 'skip' to see if she could find something else that she could wear for the performance?"

"Yes. Certainly I do." Nina was flushed but full of fight.

She nodded her head vigorously.

"And you're aware that she found this frock in there?" Loder took the yellow frock from the chair and held it up in front of her.

"Yes. Perfectly aware. And I know, too, that Vera wore it on the stage. It may save time if I tell you that."

"Thank you," returned Loder primly, "which then brings me to another question. Did you *know* when you suggested that Miss Ferris should look in the 'skip', that this particular frock was in there?"

"Oh—yes. I'd seen it there previously." More vigorous noddings from Nina.

"Previously? When did you *first* see it? I'd very much like to know. Can you remember that?"

Nina was still going strong. "I can, Sergeant Loder. Very well indeed. I first saw it about five minutes before I spoke to Vera. Not more—

and perhaps even less. You see there was a reason for that—I'd been turnin' the things over in the 'skip' looking for some drawing-pins for Mrs. Parmiter—and I suddenly came across the frock. That was why I mentioned it to Vera when she tore hers."

"Where exactly was it when you first saw it? On the top of the things in the 'skip'? Or near the bottom?"

Nina Crump shook her head. "Oh—no! Neither at the top nor the bottom. I came across it some way down. It was nowhere near the top."

"Thank you, Miss Crump—I'm inclined to think that's important."

Loder pushed his fingers through his hair. He looked at Julia Wilkes meaningly and then he transferred the glance to Edmund Gosling.

"What I've got to do," he said, "is to find Barbara Marsden. Finding the frock she wore's only a step. Seems to me that the chances are she isn't very far away from where the frock was."

Nobody in the room made any answer. Each of them was thinking, probably, in the same, unpleasant terms.

2

A week passed. Loder and the Remsford police put nearly everything else on one side and concentrated on the task of finding the missing Barbara Marsden. All their efforts, how ever, came to failure. The weather remained bitterly cold, snow fell persistently, the ice held on almost all stretches of water, and the countryside generally slipped back into the relentless grip of King Winter and his henchman Frost. For day after day the roads were iron-rutted and the grass rimed with hoar.

At a quarter-past eleven, however, on the night of 22nd February, a telephone-call was put through to the Wavering police-station. Constable Tom Dyer was on duty and he walked sluggishly towards the telephone to answer it.

"Wavering Police," he said, as he lifted the receiver. "Tidman speaking," came the reply. "Owen Tidman. Butcher—High Street. Yes—it's me again. Is that Sergeant Loder speaking?"

"No—it's not. It's Constable Dyer this end. What was it you wanted, Mr. Tidman? Anything I can do for you?"

"Well—you can—and yet in a way I suppose you can't. Anyhow, Constable Dyer—the trouble's this. I've had a second basin of fat pinched from the back of my shop this evening—just in the same way as I lost that other one about a month ago. I've only just missed it. And you know what happened in Wavering the night the *first* one was took! Reckon you of all people don't want me to remind you. That's what's made me ring the station at once. As soon as ever I found the basin was missing."

It is true to say that Constable Dyer was shaken out of his normal equanimity. And, to make matters worse from his point of view, Loder was absent and had been absent for some hours. Dyer wasn't quite sure where the sergeant was. Then what he took to be his sturdy common sense asserted itself.

"Reckon you're *lookin*' for a coincidence, Mr. Tidman, when you talk like that—still I'll make a note of what you've reported. Darned peculiar thing—I'll agree to that. I've been in the Force a good many years now but I never knew a feller before with a mania for pinchin' basins of drippin'! Still, these days there's no accountin' for anything these 'baskets' 'll get up to. What's that? . . . O.K. I'll tell the sergeant what you say directly he comes in. Good evening, Mr. Tidman . . . yes . . . I'll see to that for you. Don't you worry."

Tidman rang off and Tom Dyer hung up thoughtfully.

As he turned away from the telephone, Sergeant Loder walked in. Dyer, immensely relieved to see his superior officer, threw the Tidman news at him immediately. Loder listened and stared. Then Dyer noticed that his face and his lips . . . particularly his lips . . . had gone strangely white.

"Why," said Dyer, his voice frothing with anxiety, "what's the trouble, Sergeant? Surely you're not thinkin' on the same lines as Owen Tidman? Don't tell me that. I never reckoned you had time for such things as superstition and er—old wives' tales? Why—man—"

"Shut your mouth, Tom," snapped Loder—"you don't know what you're talkin' about. Superstition—my foot! If *you* knew what I know—you wouldn't be talkin' as you did just now."

"Why—Sergeant," returned the constable, "what is it that you know that you ain't passed on to me?"

Loder hesitated before he answered. "Tom," he said slowly, "I've just come back from Remsford. Been on the Marsden case." Again the sergeant hesitated. Dyer's eyes searched Loder's face . . . for the second time since the sergeant had entered. "Yes, Tom," went on Loder, "I've had a long consultation over at Remsford—been there since three o'clock this afternoon. The Marsden affair all the time. Been discussing what we can do that we haven't already done. And it doesn't add up to much, as you yourself very well know. It's the Press—and the letters to the Press that have caused so much heat to be turned on. That's where the trouble lies. But there's this, Tom, and this is what's worryin' me. I've been chewin' it over all the way back. Amongst other things this afternoon, we've had the analyst's report. You remember those stains or marks—if you like to call 'em that—that I spotted on the sides of that theatrical basket? Not the bloodstains—the other marks."

Dyer nodded. "Reckon I do, Sergeant. Very well indeed. Had 'em in my mind scores of times. What about 'em?"

When he replied, Loder spoke slowly and quietly, "The analyst's report on those marks, Tom, is that *they were caused by beef fat*. According to him minute portions of beef fatty substance were found adhering to parts of the wicker of the basket. *Now* you know how I felt when I came in and you gave me that news *re* Tidman. *And*—why I felt like it."

Dyer whistled at what Loder had told him. "My God, Sergeant—I see what you mean. But . . . but . . . "

Words refused to come to his aid and Constable Dyer paused for lack of them. Loder shook his head.

"I'm frightened, Tom. I'll admit it. It's no good sayin' I'm not. Your news has put the lid on it for me. We've got to face up to the fact that there's a killer abroad in Wavering—that's how it works out to me. A killer who kills when the mood takes him. Without motive—or at least without any motive that's apparent. Which doesn't make things easier for the likes of you and me."

Dyer stared at him . . . almost open-mouthed. Loder turned away from him and walked towards the fire-place. He put his hands to the comfort of the blaze. For some seconds he stayed there—the warmth pleased him and smoothed out some of the awkward and uncomfortable ridges of his tiredness. Dyer saw what Loder was doing. He walked to the corner of the fire-place and lifted up the coal scuttle to feed the fire. As the first pieces of coal fell into the lick of the flames, a crisp footstep sounded outside the door. Loder and Dyer turned to see the door opening. A man entered the room as Dyer replaced the coal-scuttle in its corner. He was a short, thick-set man with heavy shoulders and a lurching gait. Loder thought directly he looked at him that there was a strange look in his eyes as he came forward to the two policemen.

"Good evening. I know it's over-late," said the man who had entered, "but my name's Ferris—James Ferris of Spencer Street. I've come about my girl—my girl Vera. I'm worried about her—more worried than I can say. She went out this evening—just after tea . . . said she wouldn't be more than a few minutes . . . and she's never come back. My missus is almost beside 'erself . . . you see . . . there was Barbara Marsden "

Loder's hands began to tremble. Dyer could see them plainly.

3

Anthony Lotherington Bathurst and Chief Detective Inspector Andrew MacMorran of Scotland Yard, sat with the Chief Constable of the County, Sir Nigel Kempton, Inspector Steadman of the Remsford Police and Sergeant Loder of Wavering. The venue was Steadman's room at Remsford. Sir Nigel Kempton brought his speech to a conclusion.

"There you are, gentlemen," were his final words, "there you have the full facts as we know them. I hope I've covered everything. Both girls have disappeared. Not a trace of them has come from anywhere. Clean vanished. Together with the two basins of fat from the local butcher's. If it weren't tragic—"

Sir Nigel shrugged his broad shoulders and paused abruptly. There was a silence of some seconds after the Chief Constable had finished.

"And you've searched everywhere, you say," said MacMorran eventually.

"Within the limits of our powers—yes. Fields, barns, undergrowth—ponds have been dragged where the ice has broken, ditches cleared—damn it all—we can't dig up the whole ruddy countryside."

"H'm," said MacMorran dryly, "as you say."

Inspector Steadman leant over to his visitors and passed round two photographs. "These are two fairly recent photos of the two missing girls."

MacMorran looked at them and without comment handed them on to Anthony. Anthony took them and examined them with some care. Suddenly he put a question to Loder.

"Any relationship that you're aware of between these two girls, Sergeant Loder?"

Loder looked somewhat surprised at the question.

"Blood-relationship—I mean," added Anthony.

"Not that I know of," replied the sergeant from Wavering; "if there is, it hasn't been mentioned to me."

"Really? Well—*you* should know! But there certainly seems to me a strong physical likeness between them—that is to *my* eye. What's their colouring—or their respective colourings? Any idea?"

Loder looked across to Inspector Steadman. "I fancy that you have the descriptions that were issued, Inspector. Perhaps you'd let Mr. Bathurst know."

Steadman raked out two documents from a heap of papers in front of him. "Here you are, Mr. Bathurst. Here are the two official descriptions of the missing girls. You can read them for yourself."

The inspector put the two sheets of paper into Anthony's hand. Anthony read the details with care. Then he pushed the two papers in front of MacMorran.

"Have a look at these, Chief—will you? And then tell me what you think about them. Take your time."

MacMorran read the two descriptions as Anthony had. "H'm," he said eventually. "I think I can see what you're getting at, Mr. Bathurst. There are certainly—on paper—*some* points of resemblance. For instance—the respective heights are much the same. The first girl, Barbara Marsden, five feet five inches, the second just half an inch taller. Dark hair in each instance—also dark eyes. I should say there's no doubt they're similar types. Colouring's the same. I take it that's what you meant, isn't it?"

Anthony nodded. "That's the idea. That's exactly what I did mean. It struck me they might almost pass for sisters. The killer, whoever he may happen to be, seems to be allergic to brunettes."

Steadman fingered his chin. "Funny you should say that. Something of the kind occurred once in the States. Not so many years ago, either. Only it was blondes there, if my memory serves me correctly."

Anthony studied the case-papers which Steadman and Loder had prepared. "This 'fat' business—these two stolen basins of dripping—I see that your analyst asserts positively that the marks inside the 'skip' in the dressing-room at the Church hall are definitely connected with a 'fatty' substance of some kind. I find that point unusually interesting. These smears on the wickerwork were found in a different basket from that in which Miss Marsden's frock was discovered, I understand?"

"That's so, Mr. Bathurst," answered Sergeant Loder.

"May I see the notes?" said MacMorran.

Anthony handed over the case-papers. MacMorran examined them in detail.

"Most extraordinary," he commented when he had finished reading them; "two basins of ordinary dripping-fat stolen from the same butcher—one according to what I read here—a blue-and-white-striped basin and the other a basin of yellow colour. And why should marks of this fat turn up again inside an empty basket? Nothing like anything I've ever come across before."

MacMorran rubbed the ridge of his jaw. Anthony turned to Loder. "I also understand from what the Chief Constable said some little time back, Sergeant, that Barbara Marsden's frock was *recognised* by a Miss Wilkes when Vera Ferris borrowed it during a dramatic performance and wore it? That is so, isn't it?"

"Quite correct, Mr. Bathurst," returned Loder. "Miss Wilkes is the dressmaker who actually made it. She's a local woman. Directly she saw Vera Ferris make her entrance on the stage wearing it, she recognized it. As you would expect her to."

"I see." Anthony spoke slowly. "So that it's quite a likely contingency that if Miss Ferris *hadn't* worn the frock when she did, it might have remained in the dramatic society's 'props' basket for some considerable time? Undetected, unhonoured and unsung?"

The Chief Constable took it upon himself to answer the question. "It would seem so—yes. According to the evidence."

"Curious," continued Anthony, "or perhaps even 'curiouser', that the very girl who wore the missing girl's frock, should herself be missing within a week. Altogether—a pretty problem, gentlemen."

Another period of silence ensued. "There is this about it," contributed Loder eventually, "Vera Ferris wasn't the first girl to come into actual contact with the yellow frock. As a matter of fact—her attention was called to it originally by another girl. A girl in the dramatic society named Nina Crump. I don't think that that fact should be overlooked. Because it may very well be important."

"Tell me," said Anthony. Loder supplied the details. "I see," remarked Anthony when the Wavering sergeant had finished, "so Miss Ferris was the *second* girl that evening as far as the frock was concerned—not the first. From which it comes to this, *but* for the frock which was torn, followed by the frock which was worn, things might certainly not have progressed as they have. Extremely interesting! I commend these rather extraordinary facts to your notice, Chief."

MacMorran nodded and turned to address the Chief Constable. "With your agreement, Sir Nigel—"

Before he could complete the sentence there came a sharp tap on the door. Inspector Steadman looked enquiringly at Sir Nigel Kempton. The latter nodded with understanding.

"Better see who it is, I think, Inspector."

Steadman rose and went to the door. The others heard him in conversation. Steadman closed the door and returned to the circle.

"There's a telephone message for you, Sergeant Loder, from Wavering police-station. According to what I've just been told—it's urgent. I don't know whether you'd like to—"

"See what it is, Sergeant," added the Chief Constable. "Very good, sir." Loder rose and made a quick exit. "May be some important news," remarked Steadman; "rather fancy it is myself from the tone of the message. My chap that answered the 'phone has the same idea. That's why he brought it along to me at once. Shall we wait till Loder comes back?"

Sir Nigel nodded his confirmation of the inspector's suggestion. The waiting period was not of long duration. Loder was back in less than five minutes. All eyes searched his face as he entered. He took his seat and began to speak with quiet gravity.

"That was Constable Dyer at Wavering, sir," he said, addressing the Chief Constable, "he had something to report which he considered was of extreme urgency and importance. It's this. About half an hour ago, a youth named Albert Barker went into the police-station at Wavering. He asked for me, but Dyer told him that I wasn't there and dealt with him in my absence. This boy, Barker, produced two broken halves of a basin—a large blue-and-white-striped basin. His story was as follows. He told it to Dyer and Dyer has just given it to me. Young Barker states that he was crossing the allotments on the Remsford side of St. Simon's church, when his foot accidentally kicked against a heap of refuse. It's a kind of old compost-heap left by the allotment-holders—been under snow for some time now. When he looked to see what it was exactly that he had kicked against, he saw two pieces of a broken basin. Now Barker's a Wavering lad—and he was fully aware of the circumstances that have been published concerning the disappearance of the two local girls. He knew, too, all about the theft of Tidman's basins. His intelligence told him to report the facts to our people at once. So he went along to the station, taking the broken pieces of the basin with him."

Steadman showed signs of interrupting. Loder checked him. "Just a moment, Inspector—if you don't mind. Then you can have your say. I haven't finished yet. Dyer, my constable, at once got into touch with

Tidman, the butcher. Tidman went along to the station. He has identified the pieces. They are parts of the basin which was stolen from his shop on the night of the 24th January."

4

The significance of Loder's words was plain. There was a silence of some seconds. Sir Nigel Kempton broke it. He spoke with a certain amount of asperity.

"Evidently *something* you missed, Inspector! I understood from you that practically every inch of ground had been thoroughly gone over. From what we've just heard, it would appear that that is not so. I confess I find it rather disturbing." The Chief Constable moved irritably in his seat. Steadman's annoyance showed on his face. He turned to Sergeant Loder.

"Where exactly are these allotments, Sergeant? At the moment I can't place them."

Loder supplied the necessary information. "St Simon's Church is on the corner. If you take the turning by the church and go down it for about two hundred and fifty yards, on the Remsford side, you come to an old hockey pitch. Years ago it used to be played on by the Wavering Town Hockey Club. In fact, the partly-dismantled pavilion that in those days belonged to the club, is still standing. But the actual ground, for some years now, has been used for allotments. That's the place, according to Dyer, where this lad, Barker, ran across the broken pieces of basin. To the best of my knowledge and belief, an intensive search was made all over that ground. And, of course, with all respect to the Chief Constable, when that search was made, the basin pieces may not have been there. I should say that it's quite on the cards that they've been dumped there subsequently."

"That may be so, of course," added Inspector Steadman, for the especial benefit of Sir Nigel Kempton. Anthony Bathurst looked up before coming in with a question.

"This old, dismantled hockey-club pavilion you mentioned, Sergeant Loder, I presume that that's been looked at?"

"Oh—yes, Mr. Bathurst. There's not much chance of hiding a body there—if that's what you're thinking of. There's only the skeleton of the building standing as it were—and the floors are bare absolutely. Just the wooden boards. And at the rear of the pavilion there's an old rusted tank which used to hold the water for the baths and the 'shower' when the game was over. And there are other old broken parts of the same outfit. You must understand that the place is devoid of anything like furniture."

"I see. Thank you, Sergeant."

"All the same," contributed MacMorran, "whatever may or may not be there—it comes to this. From what we've just heard, the whole of this allotment set-up can do with another close examination. In my judgment that fact sticks out like a sore thumb. Don't you agree with me, sir?"

The Chief Constable, to whom the question had been addressed, gave quick concurrence. "Undoubtedly. As I hinted just now, I find the whole business unsatisfactory and unsettling. If you hadn't made the suggestion, I should have made it myself. And, in addition—it must be proceeded with without delay, Inspector Steadman. Please understand that. See to it, will you?"

Sir Nigel Kempton looked at the clock on the wall. "And perhaps, gentlemen, we've now reached a stage where we can profitably adjourn the conference."

Without waiting for a reply, the Chief Constable rose from his chair.

CHAPTER 4

1

Anthony and MacMorran, with the two local police officials, came to the five-barred gate which yielded entrance to the allotments that now held the field which had once been the home of the Wavering Hockey Club.

"It's beginning to thaw," said Steadman; "look."

The ice on the gate had started to drip and the snow on the ground gave certain evidences that before long it would become slush.

"Show me, first of all, please," said MacMorran, "where the lad, Barker, found the broken pieces of basin."

Loder led the way to an old pile of refuse on the top of which the layer of snow was melting fast. He indicated the bottom of the heap nearest to the path.

"That's where he kicked against it. The basin-pieces were lying just about there." The sergeant gestured with his hand.

Anthony looked down and spoke to Andrew MacMorran. "From which it may be inferred, that there's a strong probability that the person who stole the basin from Tidman the butcher, has at some time passed this way. A probability but not a certainty."

"Quite," said MacMorran.

Anthony looked round at the thawing snow and measured distances with his eyes. "Foot-prints would have shown here before the thaw set in. Might have told us something. Pity we didn't get here, say a week ago." He pointed to the eastern end of the field. "That building there, I take it, is the old pavilion you spoke about, Sergeant?"

"That's right, Mr. Bathurst. That's the place."

"I'd like to have a look at it," replied Anthony; "after all, don't suppose *many* people would go near it at this time of the year—and in the weather we've just experienced. At least, that's how it appeals to me."

"We'll go along there now," said Steadman, "although it's already been inspected by our people. Still—I agree with you, Mr. Bathurst—to-day isn't yesterday and lots of things can have happened since."

"Neither yesterday nor the day before, Inspector Steadman. That's the fact we mustn't be tempted to forget."

The four men made their way through the part-snow part-slush to the old hockey-club pavilion. Anthony saw that it was an entirely wooden structure and that the door was ajar. The floor was bare except for patches of drift-snow which had been blown in through the open door. It was obvious that originally there had been two compartments—one, naturally for each of the teams—the home and the visiting. The back of the pavilion had been badly damaged, but the remnants of washing-basins and 'showers' were still to be seen with some of the fittings intact.

"Rocket," said Loder curtly, "February, 1945. Caught it bang-on. Come and look round here."

At the rear of the building, only partly covered by roofing, lay the remains of a large water-tank and next to it a normal sized bath. One side of the tank had been twisted and warped by the blast into a shape which bordered on the grotesque, but the old bath seemed to be almost intact. It lay propped against that side of the tank which had received but minor damage. The bath was piled with old bricks, broken slats of wood, bits of tank, lengths of rusted iron and miscellaneous debris generally. It seemed that somebody, some time after the rocket had fallen, had made an attempt to 'tidy things up'.

The four men, after surveying the wreckage, returned to the shell of the pavilion again, and entered the building. Anthony looked carefully round the interior. He walked from one compartment to the other.

"I should say," he remarked, "that nobody has been actually inside here for some time. In all probability since the bad spell of weather began. Look at the floor, for instance, where the powdery snow has drifted and been blown in. The only marks visible are those that we've just made. There are no others that I can see."

The others concurred. "I don't think there's any doubt about it," added Steadman, "which is another way of saying that we're wasting our time by staying in here. Isn't that so? The place is bare. Bone empty! Look at it. Not a stick or stone left in it. The last place in the world to conceal anything. Don't forget it's been derelict like this for some years now."

"And yet," returned Anthony, "that broken basin found only a few yards from here, *will* persist in my mind. It keeps on coming back to me. Now I wonder why that is."

For the second time he looked carefully round the interior of the pavilion. Leaving the dressing-compartments in the front, he wandered off on his own, skirted the wash-basins and came again to the rear of the edifice where the water-tank and the old rusted bath lay on the rimed grass. For some seconds he stood gazing at them, apparently lost in thought. Suddenly, he came to a decision. He called to the others.

"Come here, gentlemen—will you, please?"

MacMorran, Steadman and Loder joined him at the back of the pavilion. Anthony pointed to the collection of junk that filled the bath.

"What is that, gentlemen, lying just underneath those three broken bricks—at the head of the bath? If you look at it carefully you can just discern the edge of something. Something, I think, which may prove to be distinctly interesting."

Loder was the first to move towards the bath. Darting forward quickly as Anthony spoke, he moved the bricks aside. To reveal a large yellowish basin, firmly wedged between them. MacMorran and Steadman were with him almost immediately.

"The second of Mr. Tidman's missing basins I rather fancy," said Anthony quietly, "and now I suggest, gentlemen, that between us we empty this bath of all its debris. Preparing ourselves at the same time, for the worst."

Loder was already at work tossing the various articles on the grass and some seconds later the whereabouts of Barbara Marsden and Vera Ferris was a mystery no longer. In addition to a brown-paper parcel, two nude bodies lay at the bottom of the bath. That of Barbara Marsden lay underneath the other. On her right-hand cheek was a dried lash of blood. A similar mark was visible on the left-hand cheek of Vera Ferris. As though, it seemed to Anthony, each girl's face had been fiercely clawed by a large animal. Steadman swore with profane abandon.

"It looks," said Anthony, "as though we haven't wasted our time after all. Undo that parcel, will you, Sergeant?" Loder, white-faced, hands trembling, glanced at Steadman and obeyed. The parcel disclosed a light-blue knitted jumper, a dark-blue skirt, underclothes, stockings and shoes.

The oratory of the inspector from Remsford continued in full spate for some moments. Even MacMorran listened to it with a degree of awe.

2

The autopsy, carried out by Doctor Crompton at Remsford, revealed the fact that in each instance, the victim had been strangled. The cheeks had been slashed before death and there were distinct traces of fat on each of the bodies—particularly on the feet and on the shoulders. But there had been no attempt in either case at any sexual violation although the strangulation had been manual. The clothing was identified by Mrs. Catherine Ferris as having been worn by her daughter Vera on the evening of her disappearance.

Anthony and MacMorran conferred with the Remsford Police officials in the same room in which they had sat before and discussed at some length the findings of the doctor. Sir Nigel Kempton, as on the previous occasion, controlled the conference.

"It would appear to me," he concluded after several of the people present had had their say, "that we must look for the killer of these girls amongst the people who attended the New Year's Social at the St. Simon's Church hall on the evening of 24th January."

There was a silence as Sir Nigel's words were considered. "Because of the incident of the yellow frock, I take it?" queried MacMorran.

The Chief Constable nodded. "Mainly because of that, Inspector MacMorran."

"Sir Nigel's is a good point," contributed Anthony, "*but*—if he will allow me to emphasize it at this stage in the proceedings—we mustn't overlook the fact that as far as we have been told, the hall in question is comparatively easy of access to almost anybody. Even to members of the general public who might be no more than mere passers-by."

Sir Nigel demurred from Anthony's suggestion. "Passers by wouldn't know that the Dramatic Society's 'skip' was in the dressing-room."

"That's true," countered Anthony, "but they'd find it directly they *entered* the dressing-room. According to my information they couldn't very well miss it. I agree, though, that the balance of probability is on your side. All I say is that we can't rule out my possibility altogether."

"How many people were there—who actually attended this New Year's social?" The question came from MacMorran. Steadman leant forward and reached for his papers.

"I have the figures here somewhere. I got Loder to compile the list for me. Took him some little time, too. We've got both the names and the addresses. Let me see now—ah here it is. Two hundred and thirty-three. In almost every instance, the people came from Wavering itself or just outside. Which is just what you'd expect—seeing the kind of night it was. Where the address isn't a local one, it belongs in every case to somebody who was actually staying in Wavering that night with either a friend or a relation. Which again, is quite a normal happening. There you are, Inspector. The other list is in relation to the audience at the play."

Steadman handed the papers to MacMorran. The latter looked down the columns.

"Some little investigation," he commented.

Steadman shook his head. "Not *so* bad! Not so bad as it looks by a long way. Many of 'em there are just kids—or almost. Can be ruled out from the start. Not a killer amongst 'em."

MacMorran returned the list to Loder. Anthony passed round his cigarette-case and spoke again.

"There's one thing I would like to say—and that's this. So far none of us seems to have touched on it. But to my mind its significance is extraordinary—and may be vital. How are we to regard the issue of the stolen fat? In two separate basins! From the counter of the local butcher? I confess I find it extremely interesting. Mainly, I suppose, because I *can't* explain it."

"Maniac," replied the Chief Constable tersely—"complete maniac. You often find a particular form of mania working out in some extraordinary manner such as in this case. A psychological trait arising out of pure sadism. One maniac squirts ink on ladies' dresses, another slashes clothes, this beast that we've got to trap goes for fat. Don't think we need worry about it—to any great extent. Probably means nothing at all—beyond the expression of the mere sadistic tendency."

Anthony knocked cigarette-ash into a tray. "You may be right, sir, but I don't know that I agree with you. I think there must be a certain significance attached to it which at the moment is eluding us. Anyhow—time will tell. Then there's a second point. I'm by no means so convinced about this—but I feel that I must mention it. And that's the yellow frock. Please note that Barbara Marsden wore it on the night she disappeared. Almost certainly also on the night she was murdered. Probably the same night, possibly not. Vera Ferris also wore it—three weeks later. And *Vera Ferris* becomes the second girl to be murdered. Please note that. Now the query which arises in my mind is just this. Was Vera Ferris definitely selected as the second victim because *she had worn the yellow frock*? Or because *she was Vera Ferris*? Personally, at the moment, I'm inclined to the first idea."

There was a silence which was eventually broken by the Chief Constable. "Now let's see where we are. Does that mean," he asked, "that you're of the opinion that in some mysterious fashion, the killer is allergic to the colour yellow? Or that the sight of the yellow frock arouses the blood-lust in him? Am I to take it that you're thinking on those lines?"

Anthony shook his head. "Not altogether. You've gone rather farther, sir, than I intended. I was merely going part of the way. Whereas, you've completed the journey. As I see things, the sight of the yellow frock on the second girl probably *reminded* the killer of his first crime. With the result—that the lust came on him again and he killed for the second time."

Steadman came in with an intervention. "But do you think," he asked, rather tentatively, "that a man of his mental calibre would recognize a woman's frock? Candidly, I doubt whether I should. I'd say this. *Some* men would—but on the other hand, very many men *wouldn't.*"

"You forget, Inspector Steadman," replied Anthony quietly, "that this person had but a few days previously murdered a girl *who was wearing the frock*. Such a thing would surely impress the mind of the murderer? Personally, I think that can be taken for granted."

"I agree with Bathurst," said Sir Nigel, "provided we can be assured that the killer is ninety per cent normal. With a mind capable of receiving normal impressions. Supposing he's not? Supposing he's a complete loony. Utterly 'bats'? Who at some previous time in his life has actually been in a nut-house? What then? It's quite on the cards, in that case, as *I* see it, that his mind would take no impressions at all. Do you see my point?"

Anthony nodded and then steered the ship again to the course he wanted. "I think we're beginning to get somewhere, Sir Nigel. Let me explain what I mean. Concede to me, for the sake of argument, that my premises are sound. With regard to the *sight* of the yellow frock on the second girl, reminding the murderer of his first crime and at the same time providing him with the idea for the second murder. If I *should* happen to be right over that and I'm confident I am—it gives us a splendid jumping-off place. Do you follow me?"

"I do" intervened MacMorran quickly, "because it means this. That the killer was not only at the New Year's Social on the evening of the

24th of January—*but also was present at the performance given by the Dramatic Society*. Because that was the one and only occasion when Vera Ferris wore the yellow frock and therefore the only occasion when he could have seen it. I agree with Mr. Bathurst. We certainly *have* got somewhere."

"And going on from there," continued Anthony, "it looks as though Sergeant Loder's list can be narrowed down very considerably."

"Not so much as you might be inclined to think," parried Steadman, "let me sound a warning—for the simple reason that the people at the New Year's Social and the audience at the play, were—very largely— drawn from the same circle. Namely—the congregation at St. Simon's. Plus their friends, relations and acquaintances. Still—it will mean some eliminations no doubt."

"I think, then, that we can safely assume this," said Anthony, "that the killer was almost *certainly* at the dramatic performance and *probably* at the New Year's Social. I think they're the safest terms we can employ. I wouldn't go beyond 'probably' in the latter instance. In the case of Barbara Marsden—she may have been encountered in the street—on her way home from the Social. We don't know."

MacMorran turned to Sergeant Loder. "Let me have those names and addresses, Sergeant—of the people present at both functions. I'd like to have another look at them."

"O.K., Inspector, but I think the best thing I can do is to make out a separate list for you and let you have that. At the moment the 'double attendance' names haven't been extracted separately. I'll make it my first job."

"Thank you, Sergeant—the sooner the better as far as I'm concerned."

Anthony spoke to Inspector Steadman. "There's no previous record, I suppose, in the village of Wavering or its vicinity of anything abnormal? Fairly recently? Assaults on, or interference with women? Nobody in the place with blots on the moral escutcheon?"

The Remsford inspector shook his head. "Not that I'm aware of. Can't think of anybody. Loder, though, could probably answer that better than I'm able to. What do you say, Sergeant Loder? You heard what Mr. Bathurst asked me?"

The sergeant shook his head as Steadman had. "We don't get a great deal of real crime in Wavering, Mr. Bathurst. Pretty clean sheet as a general rule. Few drunks—the beer's not that strong these days—motoring offences are the most frequent I should say. Very little housebreaking—no—Wavering's a well-behaved community taking it by and large! Why—during the six months to Christmas last there were only—"

Sergeant Loder stopped rather abruptly in his recital. "That's funny," he remarked, "I've just thought of something."

"Oh—what is it?" questioned Anthony.

"Well," proceeded Loder rather shamefacedly, "now I come to think of it, we *did* have a bit of a shemozzle in the High Street some time in November. It's just come back to me. Late in the afternoon it was. Just as it was beginning to get dark. A couple of those wandering Poles that go about with a performing bear had a row in the High Street with a motorist—just in front of Tidman's shop. They swore that the car had hit the bear in the side. The motorist swore he hadn't touched him. In the end there was a proper scrap with the result that they were fined forty-bob or something like that the next morning for a breach of the peace. That's about the only unusual incident we've had in Wavering for months that I can think of."

Anthony furrowed his brows. "Certainly an unusual occurrence, Sergeant. And in front of Tidman's shop—eh? I think I'd like an official account of the incident if you could supply me with one."

Sir Nigel Kempton, who had been listening to the exchanges of conversation between Anthony and Loder, had something to add to the narrative.

"Those two fellows you're speaking of, Sergeant, have been going the rounds of the countryside for some months now. I've actually passed them several times when I've been in the car. I can tell you that. On Christmas Eve they were on the outskirts of Remsford—I actually saw them. And early in the New Year I ran across them again near Great Coxted. Their bear's a remarkably fine animal—a really magnificent specimen—usually muzzled. I don't think I've ever seen a finer. *But*—and this is what I really wanted to say—I don't fancy they're Poles. Their appearance didn't suggest so to me; l should have put them down as Savoyards—or something of that sort."

Loder nodded. "I remember the bear well," he remarked, "if it had been stuffed with gold and lined with diamonds those two fellows couldn't have made a bigger fuss of it. A jolly sight more concerned about the perishing animal than they were about themselves."

"There's a reason for that, Sergeant—and an excellent one at that," said Anthony, "you must remember that that bear represents their one and only capital asset—they get their food and lodging out of it—no wonder they look after the animal. Wouldn't you? To say nothing of the possibility of it being nationalized in the near future."

"I suppose I would," replied Loder ruefully, "in that case. All the same, I'm not so partial to bears as some people—a good old tomcat asleep on the rug in front of the fire's more in my line."

The Chief Constable laughed. "Well," he said, "these two fellows with their performing bear are still knocking about the country—take it from me. It's more than likely, Bathurst, that before you're finished with this case, you'll run into them."

3

Anthony and Andrew MacMorran put up at the 'Nag's Head'—a little public house about half a mile out of Wavering, and on the Remsford Road. To reach Wavering from where they were staying, Anthony and the Scotland Yard inspector were called upon to pass the allotments where the bodies had been found, St. Simon's Church, and the hall of the Institute. The 'Nag's Head' faced Wavering Green upon the square of which, in due season, the village side played its cricket. It was a mediaeval house reputed to have been built on the site of an important Roman dwelling. It is claimed that a portion of Roman mosaic pavement has been found beneath the inn. Frankly, the 'Nag's Head' was a museum specimen. Beyond the entrance archway, there remained the original two-storeyed hall of timber, wattle and daub which dated back to the year 1470. Wherever Anthony went in his exploration of the 'Nag's Head', he found magnificent oak carving and tracery and on the spandrels of the entrance archway were figures of St. George and the Dragon carved in the reign of the seventh Henry. Anthony was delighted by all that he saw in this ancient inn and that included what was brought to him on plates and also in tankards and glasses.

After their first dinner in the 'Nag's Head', Anthony and MacMorran adjourned upstairs to the Oak Lounge with its beautifully-moulded beams—timber which, unhappily, had been hidden for generations. Anthony smoked cigarettes and MacMorran his ancient pipe.

"To-morrow—while you're at work, Andrew, on Loder's list, I fancy I'll pop into Remsford and have a word or two with a certain Doctor Crompton. Same gentleman that performed the P.M.s. I've a feeling in my bones that I'd like some rather more detailed information than he supplied to Steadman." MacMorran puffed serenely at his pipe and nodded.

"Hunch?" he queried curtly.

"Have a heart, Andrew! Haven't covered the first furlong yet. No—just curious for certain details—that's all."

"Well—if you're curious—I'm curious as well. What are you after—exactly?"

Anthony tossed his cigarette-stub into the flames of the fire. "Condition of the two bodies, Andrew. Medical details rather than the vaguely general stuff that's been dished out so far. Manual strangulation—no sexual interference—wounds on the cheek—fat on the bodies! I'd like more details than that. Actually—I have one or two questions I desire to put to our friend Doctor Crompton. Questions which I don't want to leave unanswered for too long. My feet are sensitive, my dear Andrew—don't care at all for growing grass."

MacMorran grunted. "I'm inclined to think," he said, rather solemnly, "that the Chief Constable's got the right end of the stick when all's said and done. We're up against a genuine case of sadism. And the use of the fat by the killer means no more than just a mental kink. In fact—I feel pretty well convinced about it. To my mind it's the only possible explanation—because otherwise there's neither rhyme nor reason about it."

He looked rather cunningly at Anthony to see what the latter's reactions were and then carefully examined the bowl of his pipe. But Anthony was giving nothing away. At this stage of the case, his own mental pockets were by no means full enough to be emptied for sharing.

"Andrew," he said gravely, "there's one thing that we must not overlook. It's been on my mind all day. Even when we were with the Chief Constable and the others at Remsford. No matter how often I get away from it—it always returns to me. You know what I mean, don't you?"

"I may do," replied the cautious MacMorran, "but you tell me."

"Why, this. The killer has already killed twice—it's well on the cards he may strike again. It will be terrible if he does—with us here on the spot, as it were, for the express purpose of capturing him. Means that we've got to work fast, Andrew. Means a race against time. I can't visualize any other possibility."

"I'm rather optimistic," rejoined MacMorran, "quite confident in fact. In a village of this kind, I don't feel that we should have *too* much difficulty in getting our man. A very different proposition from London. Neither needle nor haystack in a country place like this. Bound to make a big difference."

Anthony shook his head. "There's another possible issue, Andrew, that you haven't even contemplated. Supposing the murderer hasn't yet killed his *real* victim? Thought of *that*? Seems to me there's the possibility."

MacMorran was puzzled by Anthony's remark. "How do you mean?" he asked—"I don't know that I get you."

"Why—this. Supposing the killer is out to kill a *third* girl—for what we'll call a normal reason—that the third girl's the *authentic* victim—and that he's killed these other two in order to establish an absolutely false trail? To put the police on an entirely wrong scent? How about it then, Andrew?"

MacMorran nodded slowly. "You mean a murderer who's an absolutely normal person, but out to foster the idea that there's a mad killer at large? In order to obscure the true motive of the *real* murder when it comes?"

"Exactly, Andrew. That's just what I do mean."

"I think the chances are well against it."

"So they may be—but it nevertheless still remains a possibility." Anthony drew his chair closer to the fire and put his hands to the blaze.

"All the same, I hope to have that interview with Doctor Crompton sometime to-morrow morning."

CHAPTER 5

1

Anthony telephoned to Doctor Crompton from the 'Nag's Head' immediately after breakfast on the following morning and arranged to meet him in his surgery at Remsford at eleven o'clock. Anthony drove in. The roads were really bad—the thaw by now being well advanced. Crompton was a burly, thick-necked man with fair hair, brown eyes, freckled face and prominent teeth.

"You're punctual," he said genially, as Anthony was shown into the surgery and at the same time he held out his hand. "Delighted to meet you, Bathurst. Know your reputation of course. Take that chair over there and make yourself comfortable."

"Thank you, Doctor. Good of you to see me like this. And I sincerely hope that I shan't take up too much of your time. Kick me out the very minute you want to."

Crompton glanced at the clock on the mantelpiece. "I can give you half an hour—comfortably. Will that do?"

"Admirably. It may even come to less than that."

"Now tell me—what is it you want of me?"

Anthony crossed his legs. "You did the P.M.s on the two girls?"

"I did. Steadman's had my reports some days now. Doubtless you and MacMorran have seen them?"

"We have, Doctor. It's with regard to those two reports that I've come to see you this morning." Anthony paused. To proceed again almost immediately. "Now—how shall I put it—so that you can see exactly what's passing through my mind? Let me say this. From one or two points of view, they're general rather than particular."

Crompton smiled. "There's safety in numbers—it's commonly reputed—and equally so in generalities. You don't need me to tell you that."

Anthony returned the smile. "No. I don't. And thanks for the frankness. Nobody appreciates the point more than I do."

Crompton was in again. "Tell me exactly what's troubling you, Bathurst." He smiled again. "Or in other words—come to the point. Then perhaps I shall be able to help you."

"Well—there are two main points as I see the two murders. I'll take them in what I consider is the order of their importance. First of all—the fat. The fat that to all appearances and from all accounts was stolen from the local butcher's in his basins. Tell me all you can about that fat, Doctor. I promise you I'll listen to all you say with acute attention."

Crompton frowned. "Wasn't my report to Steadman plain with regard to that. I certainly thought it was."

"It was admirable, Doctor—but please amplify it for me. As an investigator, groping in the dark, I thirst for details, details—and then more details."

There was a pause—before Crompton looked up and said suddenly: "Look here! Ask me questions—the questions that raise themselves in your mind—and I'll do my best to answer them. That occurs to me as being the best way to furnish you with what you want."

Anthony nodded eagerly. "Very good, Doctor. That will suit me splendidly—if it suits you. The fat! Where was it exactly on the bodies?"

"The traces of the fat were mainly on the shoulders and on the feet. All round the fleshy parts of the shoulders—front and back—down to the dorsal muscles. In the case of the feet—I should say that the greater part of the fat had been placed on the soles. Round the balls of the big toes."

"I see. Had any other parts of the body been treated in this fashion?"

Crompton shook his head. "That's not so easy to answer bearing in mind the lapse of time—especially in the case of the girl, Barbara Marsden. And remembering, too, that the bodies had been placed at the bottom of that old bath. But I should say—in answer to your question—no."

"Thank you. Now—Doctor—here's a sticky one for you. What, in your opinion, was the fat used for? In other words, why did it have to be stolen and put on the bodies?"

Crompton shrugged his shoulders. "My dear chap! Search me!"

Anthony grinned at Crompton's grimaces of denial. "Well—try it this way—ever encountered anything of the kind previously?"

"Good lord—no. Never. Nothing remotely similar. In the entire twenty-two years of my professional career!"

Anthony persisted. "If you *had* to give a reason—assume, say, definite compulsion—what would you say then?"

"As to the reason for the fat being on the bodies? Well—surely there's but one possible explanation—the chap that did the jobs is 'nuts'. Absolutely and utterly—'nuts'. What other answer is possible?"

"Thank you, Doctor, again. Then I'll take that as read. I won't worry you any more with regard to the fat. I'll go on to point number two. The wounds on the cheeks. Will you please describe those to me in detail? I saw them, of course, in the first instance on the allotments when the bodies were discovered. At the same time, however, I feel now I'd like an expert opinion on them."

Doctor Crompton put his finger-tips together. "The two wounds were almost identical. Barbara Marsden's was down the right cheek—Vera Ferris's down the left. Each, I should say, was between two and three inches in length. Perhaps two and a half inches would be the nearest estimate. Probably inflicted I should say, by the point of an extremely sharp knife. Neither however, by any stretch of imagination could be called a deep wound. They were more slashes than anything else." Doctor Crompton paused.

"A dagger? Or a pocket-knife?" The questions came from Anthony.

"Either," answered the doctor—"that means either—possibly."

"Or even," continued Anthony, "by a sharply-pointed finger-nail? Yes?"

Crompton hesitated some time before he replied. "Perhaps . . . a finger-nail . . . shaped as you suggest *might* have caused the slashes. But I should incline more to the knife theory."

Anthony nodded and came again. "At any rate, Doctor; whether the marks were caused by a knife or by a finger nail, you would agree that the method of marking the cheeks was *deliberate*?"

"Oh—undoubtedly. The beast was out to mark his victims—and did so."

"Your mentioning the word 'beast' has given me another train of thought. Could an animal have caused the marks?" Crompton looked startled at the suggestion. "An animal? I . . . er . . . hadn't considered the possibility. What kind of animal were you thinking of?"

"Any animal that possessed a sharp claw."

Crompton brightened. "Ah—a sharp claw. You're postulating *one*. With an animal—there would be *claws*—surely? In other words, more than one claw-mark. Almost a certainty, don't you think?"

Anthony considered the matter. "I suppose—in normal circumstances I must agree with you. But I *can* visualize certain conditions—abnormal, of course—under which there might be but a single claw-mark. However, it can pass for the time being. I'll move on to my last point. My time of worrying you is nearly up. You'll probably be pleased to hear that."

Crompton waved a sympathetic hand. "That's all right, my dear chap. I'll tell you when you've had it. Go ahead with your third point."

"Thank you, Doctor. Cause of death! To quote your own words in your report to Steadman—'manual strangulation'. Any interesting details to add to that? That might interest me?"

Crompton looked up. "Before I answer that one, Bathurst, I'd like to turn up my own notes on the matter. I mean the notes I made immediately after I'd finished the P.M.s. I'll pop in the other room and get them. Stay put—I won't keep you waiting longer than a few seconds. I know exactly where they are."

Crompton slipped out of the room and was as good as his word with regard to the quickness of his return. "I've got the notes here," he explained, "they were in a drawer in the next room. They're pretty full too. Now just give me half a sec. while I run over them."

The doctor flicked over a file of papers. Some seconds elapsed before Crompton spoke again. "Here we are. This is the lot. Now just permit me a second or so while I refresh my memory. Er . . . um . . . h'm . . . er . . . I'll read to you the impressions I formed immediately following the P.M.s. That should give you what you want. Both girls were undoubtedly strangled by the hands of the killer, using fingers and thumbs. There was extensive bruising round the trachea in each case and there were clear traces of three finger-marks and a thumb-mark on the skin of Barbara Marsden. In the case of Vera Ferris, the second girl, there were but two impressions. One of a finger and the other of a thumb. There isn't the slightest doubt, Bathurst, that each girl was strangled deliberately by the strong hands of a murderer. And I say 'strong' advisedly—because I should assert it's pretty conclusive that the killer has physical strength well above the average."

"Tell me, Doctor, why you think that."

Crompton's answer came without the slightest hesitation. "From the severity of the bruising and from the extensive nature of the bruised areas. I know what you're thinking but you must remember this. Putrefaction normally sets in within two or three days after death. Very seldom later than that. You get a greenish tint over the abdomen. In from, say, two to three weeks the body becomes greenish-brown throughout, the skin begins to give way and the features gradually become more and more unrecognizable. But don't forget also that in the bodies of these two girls, exposed as they had been to conditions of severe frost and extreme cold, the ordinary course of putrefaction was to a degree arrested. They were something like carcases in a refrigeration chamber. In other words—they were frozen stiff."

Anthony nodded. "Which seems to indicate, Doctor, that in the case of Barbara Marsden's body it must have been taken to the allotment very soon after her death."

"I agree with that, Bathurst. According to my findings, I should say that there's every indication that way."

"Let's go on from there, Doctor. Not too far. Just a little way. You'll see what I'm getting at. How was the body moved? Car?"

Crompton nodded. "That, I should say, is the most likely proposition. Unless . . . of course . . . I think you may be overlooking the possibility . . . the murder actually took place on the allotments. Have you thought of that as at all likely?"

Anthony countered at once. "*Both* murders?"

Crompton's face changed. "Yes. That's a point to you, I admit. In concentrating on Barbara Marsden I was tempted to forget the second girl, Vera Ferris. Certainly looks as though there were a car on the horizon."

"That's a help, you know, Doctor. A considerable help."

"You mean—it narrows the circle?"

"It certainly does. Brings us definitely close to the 'owner-driver' category."

Crompton stroked his chin as he took in what Anthony, had said. "Suppose it does. Still—all the same—it leaves the door open fairly wide even then. There are plenty of people who answer to that description you've just given."

"Would there be—in a small place like Wavering?"

"Well—there's not only Wavering itself to consider. There are the adjoining districts as well. They must come into the argument. Take this place for example. Remsford. Population—over thirty thousand. Pretty good size, you know, and reasonably close to Wavering."

Anthony at once thought of the list of names and addresses which MacMorran had received from Loder. How many car 'owner-drivers' were there, he thought, in the St. Simon's list connexion? It would be decidedly interesting to find out. But Doctor Crompton had gone on.

"Don't envy you fellows your job in this case. Not one little bit. Seems to me that apart from what we've just been talking about, the two crimes are almost clueless. And on that account I don't see quite where you can make a reasonable start."

Anthony demurred. "No—I don't think myself it's too bad. Not as bad as you make out. I can truthfully say I've faced much bleaker prospects in the past. Actually, Doctor, I'm more afraid of something else."

Crompton sensed the gravity in his voice and regarded him curiously. "What's that—may I ask?"

"A third murder *before* we get our man," replied Anthony quietly, "hadn't you thought of that possibility yourself?"

Crompton's fingers again went to his chin. "Perhaps I hadn't. It's hardly my province, I suppose, to look ahead like that. I *see*—you're afraid this killer may strike again." The doctor shook his head sadly. "That's bad. For everybody. Both in Wavering and in the towns and valleys roundabout. What makes you so . . . er . . . pessimistic?"

"The particular type of crime, Doctor. Apparently motive-less, apparently meaningless. No real threads about it that can be got hold of. Committed, as you yourself fear, by a madman. You see—*anybody* may be a madman without raising the slightest suspicion. That's what makes the task of the police so difficult. You don't know that *I'm* not. Equally—I don't know that *you're* not. And we're both similarly placed with regard to the man next door. Sane for eleven months of every year—but bats in the belfry every November."

Crompton looked a trifle perturbed at Anthony's remark. "But this is February," he said surprisingly.

"As you say, Doctor," said Anthony as he rose to take his departure—"this is February—and last month was January—when Barbara Marsden died."

2

When Anthony arrived back at the 'Nag's Head', he gave MacMorran a résumé of Crompton's advices.

"H'm—doesn't get us very much farther that I can see," growled the inspector, "in a way he's only told us what we already knew. That the girls were strangled."

"By an unusually strong pair of hands."

"Go on," said MacMorran with heavy sarcasm. "Shouldn't have thought it! Should have looked for one of the local pansies."

Anthony grinned at the iron in the inspector's voice. "All right, Andrew—all right. Crompton may not have told me a lot more than we knew—but he has given me some extremely important details. And after all—it's details which count."

MacMorran was looking as pleased as a lizard in an ice-cream parlour. Anthony noticed the ominous signs on the inspector's face.

"Oh," he said, "I see! I was slow! What's the real trouble, Andrew?"

MacMorran grunted. "No trouble. But just look at these lists of Loders. He sent them up to me this morning. According to his statistics, no fewer than one hundred and seventy-one people were present at both the St. Simon's New Year's Social *and* the dramatic performance. Not five! Not even fifty! Just a little matter of a hundred and seventy one. Never absent—never late."

"How many children are included in that figure?"

MacMorran wagged his head with pompous denial. "Oh—no. You can't have that. They've already been weeded out. There'd have been an odd million or two if you included them. This is the pukka figure. I'll give it to you again. No fewer than one hundred and seventy-one adults (or near adults) went to the New Year's Social and also supported the Dramatic Society's effort on behalf of the finances of the Church Organ Fund. St. Simon's is the Parish Church of Wavering and it has a surprisingly large congregation for these days. And, of course, these country places are different from the suburbs and the dormitories. Very different. Their church means much more to 'em and they attend the services and support the various functions which come along during the year with a good deal of enthusiasm. No—one hundred and seventy-one it is! No decrease on one-seven-one."

Anthony held out his hand. "Chuck those lists over here, Andrew—let me have a dekko—do you mind? I fancy that I may have a measure of balm for your stricken soul. Balm, my lad! Balm in Gilead."

MacMorran tossed over Loder's lists. "How do you mean—balm ?" he asked suspiciously.

Anthony gazed down the lists of names and addresses. Why," he said, "Crompton is of the opinion that the bodies were taken to the old pavilion by car—and I must say that by and large I agree with him. With that fact in mind—"

MacMorran nodded and interrupted. "Yes—I know. I'd considered the point about the car myself. You mean 'owner-drivers'?"

"That's the idea, Andrew. That'll play merry hell with your hundred and seventy-one. They'll melt like chocolate in a baby's hand. Let me have another squint down these lists. If I'm any judge—you'll be down among the twenties. Or perhaps even less than that. Bit different—eh? Get Loder to it for you as soon as possible. Pick out all the owner-drivers. And when it's done—I'd like to have another dekko at the fresh list myself. *That's* the time it'll begin to look interesting."

He passed the lists back to the inspector. MacMorran folded them carefully and tucked them away in his breast-pocket.

"Let's hope you're right," he remarked dolefully. "I'd appreciate something on the bright side. I might begin to think Life was worth living again."

"Andrew," said Anthony, "let me have a look at you. You sound to me as though you're in a bad way."

He went through the procedure of examining the inspector's face with extreme care. "You are in a   bad way, Andrew—you want some beer—badly. Beer from the head of the Nag. I'll see that it's supplied within five minutes."

"Ay, Mr. Bathurst," returned MacMorran. "I'm thinkin' that perhaps you're right. lt *might* brighten me up a bit."

3

As Anthony had vaticinated, Loder's list of 'owner drivers', who had patronized both the New Year's Social and the Dramatic performance by the St. Simon's Church Dramatic Society, was meagre in the extreme. Even Anthony's calculation of *circa* twenty was found to err on the side of generosity. For, when Inspector MacMorran received the new list from

Loder, he found that it contained five names, and five names only. One hundred and sixty-six had fallen by the way. These five were with their respective addresses, and in alphabetical order: Duncan Ferguson, 17, Great Coxted Road; Edmund Gosling, 5, Geddy Way; Vernon Parmiter, 'The Heritage', Remsford Road; Owen Tidman, 37, High Street; and Leonard Shapscott Unwin, 'Pitchcroft', Cheyne Avenue.

MacMorran saw the meagre proportions of the fresh list, rejoiced and rubbed his hands. This was better! This was decidedly better! He looked down the list of names carefully before tossing the paper over to Anthony.

"Congratulations. You were right. In a way perhaps too right. Can't help thinking we may have jettisoned too many. It's very much like the servant's baby."

Anthony took a quick glance at the five names. "H'm," he said—"we move now—in rather exalted company. That was, of course, bound to happen more or less—seeing what we were looking for. But this is much 'more' so than 'less'. For, if my memory serve me correctly, in these five names we have two churchwardens of St. Simon's and the 'big noise' behind the Dramatic Society. The other two leave me cold—I've never heard of them."

"You will do," said MacMorran, pocketing the list with a grin—"and before many hours are out."

"O.K., Andrew," Anthony grinned back. "You've said it—which ones would you like me to call on? If I can help you—I will. And the more absolutely authentic local colour I can get from them, the better I shall be pleased."

"You can do the lot," replied MacMorran, "then I can concentrate on the pavilion for a couple of days or so. I've an idea that it may pay dividends. If the murderer were there—and it's as certain as daylight that he must have been—"

"Yes, Andrew. Excellent idea on your part. And I'll get to work on this little bunch of Loder's. The motoring five. I'll start on 'em first thing to-morrow morning. That suit you?"

MacMorran nodded. "Good! There's one thing—with a motiveless murder, you don't get a headache looking for the motive."

Anthony heard—and then remarked with a shake of the head: "Say that again, Andrew—will you?"

MacMorran repeated his original statement. Mr. Bathurst rubbed the end of his nose with the tip of his finger. "As a statement embodying profound wisdom, Andrew—"

But MacMorran sensed what was coming. "Nuts," he replied crudely, "you ruddy well know what I mean."

CHAPTER 6

1

To begin with, Anthony stuck to the alphabetical order of his visiting. That is to say, his first call on the morning of the morrow was on Duncan Ferguson of number 17, Great Coxted Road. Anthony was lucky first shot. Duncan Ferguson was at home. A board erected in front of the house informed Anthony and anybody else of the general public who cared to read it, that Messrs. D. Ferguson and Son were builders and decorators, prepared to give estimates whenever and wherever either repairs or redecorations were needed by householders, clubs, councils, corporations, etc., etc.

The man who answered Anthony's ringing of the bell and who now faced him in a large apartment, semi-room, semi-office—was broad, thick-armed and powerful. His face was heavy and on the coarse side. His skin was ruddy-tanned by constant association with the open air, wind and sun. It was seared and seamed, too, both by exposure and experience and Anthony could see at once that the man standing opposite to him was a man who was prepared to take rough buffets from Fortune and at the same time hand something similar back—with compound interest more likely than not.

Duncan Ferguson wore a battered, brown, soft felt hat and the number of days' stubble-growth that straggled over his cheeks and chin was problematical. His eyes were dark and brooding, the same colour as his hair and there was no quality of kindness in them. They were hard, determined and challenging. He smiled at Anthony after the latter had introduced himself and stated his business. It was not a cheerful smile or a genial one. Because there was spite in it. Spite and resentment and malice and hostility—all four. And after he had smiled, Duncan Ferguson nodded his head as though he were confirming something to himself.

"Yes," he said truculently, "I know why you're here, mister. I know why you've come. I know it very well indeed. Nosin' round—askin' questions. Of honest folk who mind their own perishin' business and don't want the police on their private premises. Well—just make a note of this, will you—I've nothin' to tell you. Nothin' at all. So *you* won't waste *my* time—and *I* won't waste *yours*." Ferguson thrust his hands into his pockets and surveyed Anthony defiantly.

"I'm sorry, Mr. Ferguson," replied Anthony—"I'm sorry you look at it like that. After all—two girls have been killed—two decent Wavering girls—who had a normal right to many years of Life and the good things that Life brings and for all we know, those two girls may even yet be followed by a third. Might perhaps be your daughter—might be somebody else's. We can't tell. All that we can do—is our best prevent it. And to do that best—we need help. All the help we can get in Wavering—from everybody."

Ferguson laughed loud and long. "Help," he repeated—and there was unmistakable contempt and scorn in his voice "I told you just now I had nothin' to tell you. So I *can't* help you. That's pretty well Gospel, isn't it? I went to the New Year's Social—but only in a manner of speakin'. I took my son up there in the car—and came away myself very soon after I'd dropped him there. Socials aren't much in my line. l guess you can see that by just half a glance in my direction. With regard to the play-acting, it was pretty much the same set-up. I took the missus up to the 'all in the car and fetched 'er 'ome again when it was all over. Plays ain't any more in my line than ruddy Socials. So if you want information about what went on at either of them church do's, you're barkin' up the wrong ruddy tree. And I can't say fairer than that."

Ferguson spat with superb adroitness and judgment between his own two feet. He had spoken all the time with an easy and most disquieting assurance and Anthony wondered whether further persistence would yield him any reasonable profit. He was watching Ferguson's face and suddenly he saw it change. For some reason, not evident to Anthony, the man appeared to be attempting to master his anger . . . to control his natural truculence, and then Anthony heard a step outside the door. A step which Ferguson had already hear—*that* fact was obvious. The door opened and a young man entered the room. When he saw that the room was occupied, he stepped back with an apology on his lips. Anthony heard the words "Sorry, Dad." But Duncan Ferguson would have none of it and called to his son.

"Come in here, Norman. You won't be in the way."

The strange thing was, that the elder man had spoken to his son in a perfectly quiet voice, which contrasted so strangely with the fiercely vehement tones he had used before. His face, too, had found repose—a condition entirely different from the previous convulsion which had held it.

Norman Ferguson heeded his father and stepped back into the room.

"Come here, son," said Ferguson—"this man here's from the police. Enquirin' *re* these murders in Wavering. Maybe you can tell 'im more than what I can. But—take an old man's advice—don't open your trap unless you feel like it. And if you do—well—in that case tell the truth, the 'ole truth and nothin' but the truth."

Duncan Ferguson stood back—and Anthony looked at his son, Norman. He saw a tall, slim, rather good-looking lad in the early twenties. With blue eyes, well-cut features, well trimmed hair and— Anthony then caught him in profile. The nose was too big for the other parts of the face—it spoiled him—it was almost predatory. Nevertheless, thought Anthony, Norman Ferguson was a presentable young fellow and, remembering his sire, of a surprisingly good type.

Anthony smiled at him. "Good morning. So your father thinks that you can tell me more than he can? Actually—I've come to see if I can pick up anything. Any crumb or any morsel that may be here waiting to be picked up, as it were and which, when it has been—may well put me on the road to discovery. It's not a good thing, you know, when killers are at large in a place like Wavering. One doesn't know what's going to happen next. Killers are best behind bars. And if you can volunteer anything . . . "

Norman Ferguson nodded as though he were in thorough agreement with what Anthony had just said. But his face had paled at the words he had heard and it was clear that he was under the influence of a strong emotion.

"As it happens," he said in a pleasant voice, "I *can* tell you something. Not much—very little actually—but *something*." He paused.

Anthony regarded him curiously. The emotion was even more disturbingly active than it had been previously. Norman Ferguson cleared his throat and began to speak again. Anthony listened to what the young man had to say with acute interest.

"It's true I was at the New Year's Social in the Church hall on the evening of the twenty-fourth of January. That's what my father means. My father took me up there in the car. He offered to. The weather was terrible—it had snowed all the day and the car from here to the hall was a godsend for me. Walking up there in what passes these days for glad rags was the very last thing I wanted. My father left me there and came away almost at once." Norman Ferguson smiled ruefully. "Affairs of that sort don't make much appeal to him as you may well guess. He's tough, you see, it's his upbringing—mine's been a bit different. Also—what he's been through in his time."

He glanced in his father's direction to see how the old man was taking it. Duncan Ferguson stood there with a grim look on his face—but the look was enigmatical—it might have meant anything. He said nothing, however, so his son proceeded.

"The real reason I went to the New Year's Social was to see Barbara Marsden. I knew that she would be there—because she had told me two or three days previously that she was going. If she hadn't been going—I shouldn't have gone believe me."

Norman Ferguson wasn't looking at Anthony now—he was looking ahead of him—into the distance. But for the manner of his speaking, he might have been alone.

"I was keen on Barbara. Always had been—from my school-days. If you like it better—I suppose I was in love with her. I wanted her to be my girl. And, later on, when my position had bettered itself, I should have wanted to marry her. I should have asked her. But—well—that's all over now—the kid's had it."

Norman Ferguson stopped. But Anthony did not interrupt. He waited patiently for the young fellow to go on again. Norman went on.

"I don't know whether Barbara returned any of my affection for her. I couldn't tell. Now—I shall never know. Probably she didn't. She'd been keen on another chap. I knew that. Sid Rolleston's his name—he's a matelot. He joined the Navy about the same time I was called up for the R.A.F. I fancy that lark, though, had fallen through . . . some little time ago. I'm not sure—I just think so. Perhaps if I'd kept on peggin' away I might have got somewhere with Barbara in the end—perhaps not. More likely not. She wasn't everybody's cup of tea. I'll say! Bit too superior for most of the village stuff. That's where Sid Rolleston came in —she'd told me he was a very well-educated chap. College or something like that. Well—I'll give you the gen—I went along that evening in January and Barbara and I had a lovely time together. I'll say we did. I had several dances with her—more than anybody else had—and she looked smashing. In the now famous yellow frock."

The bitterness in Norman Ferguson's voice was distinctly audible He paused again. And again Anthony waited for him. On this occasion, however, the period of pause was longer and the far-away look in the younger Ferguson's eyes was more noticeable. He began to speak again. His voice softer.

"As I said, I had several dances with Barbara that evening. She was a lovely dancer and I'm not so dusty myself—although they say self-praise is no recommendation. I reckon I danced with Barbara twice out of every three dances that evening although I'm ready to admit that several other fellows danced with her. Four or five, I should say. Well—the evening wore on to its close—and I'm coming to what I think from your point of view, sir, is the important part. I'd been watching points for some little time on my own so that I could see her home. When the last dance was over, I buzzed off to the cloakroom like whizzo, shoved my hat and overcoat on and got into a position in the hall itself where I would be bound to see Barbara come out. She must pass me. When I did eventually see her, to my annoyance she hadn't put her out-of-door things on. I was standing by the door. And she came along and stood close to me. I was ready to go. She wasn't. I couldn't quite make it out. Why this was so. All the same, I wasn't going to let her see I was disappointed so I called out to her from where I was standing. Something about was she coming along. I can't remember the exact words I used. Anyhow she shook her head and said 'no'. And then she said she wasn't coming home yet—because she was waiting for somebody. When she said that, I knew I'd had it—as far as seeing her home was concerned—so I waved, grinned at her, and shoved off home on my own. That's my way—I never let 'em see when they get me down. Doesn't pay dividends. Tells 'em too much. And I don't believe in doing that—ever."

Norman Ferguson's jaw jutted out with resolution and determination—and Anthony saw, for the first time, with something of a shock that there was a strong physical likeness between father and son. It took you sometime to find it but it was there all right. Heredity will out. But Anthony quickly disposed of this Ferguson physical complex and turned his mind to the undoubted importance of what the younger man had just said. That Barbara Marsden had not left the dance hall with him because 'she was waiting for somebody'.

"Any idea for whom Miss Marsden was waiting?" he asked Norman Ferguson quietly.

"No," came the steady reply—"not the slightest. Wish I had. I saw nothing during the evening that had just passed which would justify me in putting a name to anybody. I've already told the police that."

Anthony nodded. "I see. That's a very fair reply. Then I'll ask you something else. When Miss Marsden spoke to you like that near the door of the hall, were you of the opinion at the time that she was telling you the truth? That she *was* waiting for somebody? Or did you think that she was just giving you the air?"

"I think," said Norman Ferguson as steadily as before, "that she was telling me the truth."

"What makes you think that?"

Norman chose the words of his next reply carefully. "Because of her manner and her general demeanour. Of the way she spoke. Her tone of voice. The way she looked. Everything about her. I should say—I knew her pretty well, remember—that she was 'quietly excited'."

"You mean," amplified Anthony, "that in your opinion, she was anticipating something? Looking forward? To something which she regarded as probably pleasurable?"

For some reason Norman Ferguson flushed. "Yes," he said, "that's exactly what I do mean. I am glad that I was able to make myself so clear."

Duncan Ferguson, who had been listening stolidly to the conversation, turned towards his son.

"Reckon you've said enough, son. Or maybe—more than enough."

"That's O.K., Dad. I know what I'm saying—and there's no need for you to get fussed up about it."

The elder man shrugged his shoulders and turned away. It was clear that he was annoyed. Anthony cut in again.

"Perhaps you'd be good enough to let me ask you one or two questions. Would you mind?"

"Certainly not. O.K. by me. Go ahead. Ask as many as you like. What are they?"

"You say you danced with Miss Marsden several times?"

"That's right. More than a dozen times—at least. Perhaps even more than that. Right from the kick-off. Let me see now . . . "

"That's good enough. If you danced with her so frequently as you say—then you saw quite a lot of her during the evening."

"I did that. As I said to you just now—more than anybody."

"So that *you*—better than anybody—were able to observe how she was? Now tell me, Mr. Ferguson—was this mood of pleasurable anticipation that you described to me just now—this mood that was hers at the finish of the evening—when you were thinking about going home with her—in any way noticeable *during* the evening? When you were dancing with her at any time, for example?"

Norman Ferguson was a little slow in replying. "Do you know," he said at length, "I've asked myself that question more than once as I've brooded over things since she died—and even now, I don't feel certain as to how I should answer it. You see—*I'm not certain*. I can't *feel* certain. I wish I could. It would clear my mind and help matters if I could." He passed his hand across his forehead.

"'Try," prompted Anthony gently, "think of little indications that she may have given, mannerisms, things that were actually said, or even perhaps merely hinted at, words she used, phrases she employed, the way she laughed, or didn't laugh, the manner in which she replied to something you said, the look on her face—"

Norman Ferguson interrupted him. "Thanks," he said bitterly, "thanks for the memories."

"I'm sorry," returned Anthony quietly, "but sometimes one has to be cruel to be kind. The lanced carbuncle is worth it—in a day or so. Try to think—on the lines I suggested."

There ensued a silence of some moments. Eventually Norman Ferguson began to speak again. "I think," he said, weighing every word with care, "that Barbara—taking everything into consideration—*did* begin to show that feeling I spoke about, late in the evening. By late, I don't mean at the very end, but late as compared with early. Yes—the more I think it over, the more certain I am of that."

Anthony nodded slowly. "Good," he said—"you see what we can deduce from that, don't you? That gets us somewhere."

The young man stared at him. "Why—what?" he demanded.

"Why—that something happened to Barbara *during* the evening. Something—it may be—which she didn't expect but which, when it came along, pleased her and gave her that state of mind which you have described. And I can't help thinking," concluded Anthony, "that it must have been something to do with her affections. It seems to me that everything points that way. This fellow, Sid Rolleston, couldn't have turned up at the Social by any chance, I suppose?"

Norman Ferguson shook his head. "Not that I know of. Certainly I never set eyes on him. I couldn't have missed him. He'd have been in uniform."

Anthony began to consider possibilities. "Did she leave the hall at any time during the evening—do you know? Can you answer that?" -

Norman Ferguson was ready with denial. "Not that I noticed. And I had my eyes on her best part of the time. I should say she was in that hall all the time."

"Did you see her in conversation with anybody?"

The answer came with a certain amount of impatience. "Well—what do you think? From half-past seven till about half-past eleven? A four-hour do? Have a heart, guvnor. It would ha' been ruddy funny if I hadn't! Barbara wasn't dumb—I'd say she wasn't."

Anthony hastened to apologize. "I'm sorry—I framed my question carelessly. I should have asked you—did you see her in conversation with any one person in particular'?"

"Come to that—I don't think I did. Nobody more than anybody else. I should say, if it came to the pinch—that she spoke to yours truly much more than she did to anybody else."

"In that case, then, Mr. Ferguson, it comes to this—you can't help me."

Norman Ferguson shook his head. But it was in corroboration of what Anthony had just said. "No," he remarked—"I don't think I can. Honestly, sir. I saw nothing that evening—in connexion with Barbara—that I can justifiably regard as the slightest bit suspicious. I only wish I had—and you can believe, or disbelieve that—just as you please."

Again came the jutting out of the Ferguson jaw. Anthony saw Duncan Ferguson nod to himself as though he were entirely approving both his son's final statements and general conduct. Anthony wondered whether he would do any more good by remaining. After all—he hadn't altogether wasted his time—he had picked up something. A trifle? Perhaps you never knew for certain when you were investigating a case of murder.

"Well, gentlemen," he said, "I won't take up any more of your time. Thank you very much for your assistance. Maybe—I'll come and see you again."

"Maybe you won't," said Duncan Ferguson dryly—from the corner of his mouth.

Anthony heard the remark. "Wait and see, Mr. Ferguson," he said quietly as he walked away.

The elder Ferguson turned on him in a flash and there was enmity and hostility plain to see in the dark eyes.

"Oh—get the hell out of here," he cried savagely. "I hate your guts—and that goes for all your ruddy kind."

Again, Anthony had no difficulty in hearing what Ferguson had said. "Really, Mr. Ferguson," he said to himself on his way out, "not *quite* the perfect host! Now I wonder why that is? Is it likely that a remnant of a skeleton *does* still hang in the Ferguson cupboard?"

2

It is to be recorded that Edmund Gosling, of number five Geddy Way was passing through a most unhappy time. He was a bachelor with a private income of moderate proportions which had come to him comparatively early in his life. The only work he had ever done since he came down from Cambridge had been in connexion with the stage. Actually he had been a professional actor for a period of eleven years. The events which had brought that about were these. In his second year at Cambridge he had made the acquaintance of no less a person than Martin Hartley, then at the zenith of his professional career. Martin Hartley, touring East Anglia at the time, saw that Edmund Gosling had both aspirations and ability and he persuaded him to join his company as a professional actor within a fortnight of his going down. The task of persuasion was by no means difficult. For these reasons. Hartley was about to undertake a tour in the Antipodes with Shakespeare as his principal offering. The dual temptation proved too much for the young undergraduate to resist and at the end of the July of the summer in which he had come down, he found himself signed up and sealed down as a member of the famous 'Martin Bartley's No. 1 Touring Company'.

And then, one Boxing day, when they were playing Melbourne in *The Tempest*, the news had come to Edmund Gosling that an uncle on his mother's side, a widower with no children, had died suddenly of double pneumonia and left him an estate producing an income of about £600 per year. By this time, Edmund Gosling had been under the Martin Hartley banner for over five years. He had reached the age of twenty-seven and the glamour of the footlights, so dazzlingly bright and beckoning at the age of twenty-two on the banks of the Cam, had most definitely begun to dim. It must be conceded as well, that his histrionic ability had remained much where it was at the time when he signed on the dotted line and thereby attached himself to the Hartley allegiance. It is true that he had gained considerably in experience but apart from this one direction, there had been no histrionic giant strides made by Edmund Gosling.

At the time of the Wavering murders, Gosling was middle-aged and distinctly inclined to the spread thereof. He was usually smiling. He was always pleasant-looking. His face was round and pink—rimless glasses over a noticeable pair of big, light-brown eyes. His walk was odd. Very few people walked as Edmund Gosling walked. His steps were jaunty—but at the same time—measured. Martin Hartley, when he had first seen Edmund Gosling walk, had said of him in the words of Wilde, 'with the pirouette of a marionette, he trips on pointed tread'. Indeed, to many discerning eyes, it seemed when watching Gosling walk that he was endeavouring to keep time to the strains of an unusual tune which only he was hearing.

When he had come to Wavering to reside some few years previously, it had been a natural concomitant to his normal habit of thought, for him to found the St. Simon's Dramatic Society. After all, the theatre, if not in his blood, was in his oesophagus and in addition to the inclination, he now had the time and the money. When the Rev. Matthew Hopkins had become the Rector of St. Simon's, he had taken at least part of Edmund Gosling to his sacerdotal bosom and in a comparatively short time the two had become firm and faithful acquaintances. The deaths of Barbara Marsden and Vera Ferris—the *murders* of these two girls—had affected Edmund Gosling profoundly. He knew Barbara Marsden by sight and he knew Vera Ferris almost intimately, by reason of her membership of the Church Dramatic Society.

Since the death of Barbara Marsden it would be true to say that Gosling had scarcely slept. Geddy Way—the road in which he resided— was close to the Wavering railway station, and for weeks now, Edmund Gosling, lying in his bed, had heard the last train come into the station and the first train leave it. This second contingency occurred at 5.10 in the morning, so the acute nature of Gosling's insomnia may be appreciated. He lay in bed vainly pursuing the sweetness of fugitive slumber, and hearing the church clock strike the hours, night after night and morning after morning with his plump, pink hands passing repeatedly through his pillowed hair. Hair which he wore much longer than the conventional cut. Many anxieties assailed him. He had a shrewd, calculating brain, allied to an intelligence which grasped most things much quicker than many. His eyes had been made for seeing—and often for admiring. And one thing which he knew for certain—was this. That the murders of these two girls in Wavering, would undoubtedly strike a shrewd blow at the success of the St. Simon's Dramatic Society. Especially considering that

Vera Ferris, the second victim, had been a playing member thereof. It was an assured thing that the iron hand of stricter parental control would descend upon the adolescent life of Wavering and institute something in the nature of a curfew—particularly with regard to the girls. And Edmund Gosling liked girls!

For, in his plump, pink manner, he invariably did his best, when in the company of members of the gentler sex, to be debonair, vivacious, and virile even though a completely satisfying acquisition of the last-named quality consistently eluded him. He had always delighted in the company of the ladies and it would be entirely fair to say of him that he was a ladies' man.

During the morning of the day on which he was favoured with a call from Anthony Bathurst, Edmund Gosling had sat moodily in his living-room for most of the time since breakfast. What else, he said to himself, was there for him to do? The weather, although progressing in slow stages of improvement, was still much too cold for most things, and Gosling's mind was as cold and cheerless as the weather. Actually he saw Anthony cross the street and come to his door. He had been standing gazing apathetically out of the window, churning crises in his mind when this had happened, and for some reason best known to himself he was inclined to resent what he considered was nothing less than an intrusion. Some seconds later he stood on the threshold and looked silently at the tall, well set-up man whom he saw facing him. Secretly, Edmund Gosling at once fell on envy. For Anthony, let it be whispered, was in appearance, much that Edmund Gosling had always desired to be. With quick mental alertness, Gosling took in his height, his slimness, his grey eyes, his brown-tanned skin, his well-cut features and more perhaps than anything else—Anthony's general air. That general air of efficiency, of whimsical competency, of complete poise, of superb self-confidence. Anthony's clothes too, bespoke both the expert hand and the discriminating taste. Edmund Gosling saw all these things only too clearly—and the iron of lost endeavour entered into his soul.

Anthony spoke to him. "Pardon me—have I the pleasure of addressing Mr. Edmund Gosling?"

"That's right," returned Gosling—"I'm Edmund Gosling—what is your business, may I ask?"

Anthony explained in a few words. Gosling at once became the victim of confused emotions. "In that case," he said grudgingly—"I suppose you'd better come in. We can't very well talk like this."

"Thank you," returned Anthony.

Gosling conducted him into a room of warm-hued rugs, many shelves with many books, wicker chairs and small tables. Gosling, leading the way, motioned towards a chair.

"Hadn't you better sit down?"

"Thank you," said Anthony again.

Gosling took a rather ornamental cigarette-box from one of the tables and pushed it towards Anthony. "Smoke?" he said with curt invitation.

Anthony thanked him again for the courtesy, opened the box and took out a cigarette. He saw that it was of unusually good quality. Gosling watched him carefully as he struck the match to light it. The inspection was more critical than anything else.

"What . . . er . . . can I do for you?" eventually asked Gosling.

Anthony smiled and waved away smoke. "Forgive me if I'm a nuisance. But needs must—you know! As I told you just now—it's about those two girls of yours. It's like this. The police are very much afraid that the two may become three—or even more than that. Not very pleasant for Wavering. And as you know—apart from the basins stolen from the butcher and the yellow frock business—the crimes are almost clueless. Which means that we're on a very sticky wicket. For that reason I'm hunting in all the places I can think of. That's why I'm here, Mr. Gosling."

Edmund Gosling listened and shook his head. "I'm sorry—but you're wrong. I mean—something you said. And I must correct you. About two girls of mine. That's not true. Vera Ferris belonged to the Dramatic Society—but Barbara Marsden, the first girl who was killed, didn't. She was nothing whatever to do with it. In fact—I scarcely knew her. By sight—perhaps—but I assure you no more than that. Certainly not to speak to."

Anthony nodded. "I see. I apologize. Tell me, please, then, about Vera Ferris. Anything that you think important." Gosling took a cigarette and shook his head for the second time. "There you are, you see. You're asking too much of me—you are really. As far as I am concerned, she was just a rather undistinguished member of the Dramatic Society. By no means one of our star players. She joined us, I suppose, about two seasons ago. I think I'm right in saying that the part she had in the last production was the first time she'd been cast. Previously she'd merely understudied. Just an ordinary, commonplace sort of girl—like many hundreds of others in this country of ours—not bad-looking according to her type—beyond that I've nothing whatever to say."

Anthony could see that Gosling was looking far from pleased. "Any attachments?" queried Anthony. "As far as you know?"

Gosling was stiff. "*Not* as far as I know. Which unfortunately may mean very little. I don't concern myself—unless I'm forced—with the private affairs of the members of the Dramatic Society. I'm on the committee of the Society, I usually produce their plays, and I'm in the chair for most of the auditions, but the personal, private side doesn't come my way. My interest is entirely confined to the artistic side."

Gosling was holding off now—at arm's length. Anthony harboured no doubts with regard to that. He resolved to change the ground.

"The finding of Barbara Marsden's frock in the 'skip' belonging to the Dramatic Society—what are your views on that, Mr. Gosling? Do you attach much importance to it?"

For the first time since the interview had started, Gosling seemed completely master of himself. "No—I most certainly don't. That 'skip' of ours is far too easy of access. In that dressing-room there—you've seen the place, perhaps—well anyone can walk in—it would be preposterously easy for *anybody* to conceal anything in the 'skip'. The outer door of the hall is often unlocked—and I'm afraid the 'skip' itself is seldom fastened up. Actually I'm raising that particular matter at the next Committee meeting of the Dramatic Society. The matter will then be thrashed out. I'm afraid I shall be upsetting Mrs. Parmiter—but that can't be helped. There *are* times when one *has* to put one's foot down. And this is going to be one of them."

"Mrs. Parmiter?" queried Anthony—"I don't think I'm in on that one."

Edmund Gosling shrugged his shoulders rather petulantly.

"And yet," continued Anthony, before Gosling could say anything, "the name seems to strike a chord somewhere." Gosling realized that it was up to him to supply the explanation. "Mrs. Parmiter," he said, "is the Property and Wardrobe Mistress to the St. Simon's Dramatic Society. I don't know whether you have any knowledge of the stage. If you haven't—"

Anthony cut in. "O.U.D.S.," he said laconically.

"Really?" exclaimed Gosling with surprise, "now that's most interesting—I'm a 'Tab myself. 'Footlights.' Really—I had no idea." He paused as though at a loss for words and then quickly collected himself. "Well—then—that explains the position of Mrs. Parmiter—from the angle of the Dramatic Society. Incidentally, she is also the wife of one of the churchwardens."

Anthony nodded. "That's it. It's clicked! That's the connexion in which I'd heard the name. But go on, please."

"Her husband is Mr. Vernon Parmiter—besides being a churchwarden he's the only solicitor of which Wavering boasts."

"And what is it exactly, Mr. Gosling, that you intend to put your foot on?" Anthony's smile was like that of the Heathen Chinee—childlike and bland.

"Mrs. Parmiter's irritating carelessness," replied Gosling. "For after all, be as generous as you like, it *is* carelessness. You can't call it by any other name. She should have seen that all the 'skips' belonging to the Dramatic Society were properly locked up. If for no other reason than to safeguard the Society's finances. Nothing frightfully valuable in them perhaps—but taking all the stuff, by and large—there's a good few quids' worth in those 'skips' of ours. Especially these days. And it should be properly looked after."

Gosling had coloured with indignation as he launched his indictment against the absent lady and he finished up by saying: "The fur will fly all right, when I get going. No doubt about that. The Parmiters are big noises in Wavering—and used to getting their own way—not that I care a tuppenny damn about that."

"Wish you luck," said Anthony. "The under-dog's interest has always appealed to me. Now—just one or two questions, Mr. Gosling, before I take myself off and leave you to your leisure. You needn't answer them unless you like—I hope you will like. You were present, I believe at the New Year's Social on the twenty-fourth January?"

Gosling hesitated over his reply. "Well," he answered eventually, "I suppose you'd call it that. I was certainly there on the premises, although I took no part whatever in the general proceedings. I'm not a dancer—never was—and there wasn't much else going that evening."

"And yet you went?"

Gosling flushed. "Well—Wavering's pretty dead in the winter—you know—and anything's better than nothing. I just floated round here and there—chatting from time to time with various people. I saw Cheam—he's our curate—and Tidman. You've heard about him, of course. He is the other warden. Parmiter, too, in the early part of the evening. I didn't actually speak to the Rector himself although I saw him there. Oh—and I spoke to Luck, the caretaker."

"Did you notice Barbara Marsden at all?"

Gosling pursed his lips. "Scarcely at all. But as I told you just now—I hardly knew the girl. I doubt very much whether I've ever spoken to her." Anthony was silent and Gosling went on. "I can tell you something, though, with regard to that evening. Strangely enough, it's in connexion with the second girl—Vera Ferris. The girl that I knew through the medium of the Dramatic Society. *She* was present. I know that—because during the evening the Rector sent her along to me with a message. She actually came up to me and delivered it while I was chatting with Cheam and Tidman."

Anthony shook his head. "Seems to me that Vera Ferris, on the evening of the New Year's Social, is comparatively unimportant. She didn't enter the murder picture until a month later. It's Barbara Marsden that's the significant proposition on the evening of the Social."

He watched Gosling closely to see the effect of his remarks.

Gosling, however, concurred at once. He was emphatic in the acquiescence.

"Oh—yes—that *is* so. I agree with you entirely. I merely happened to mention the Ferris incident to you because it suddenly came into my mind. I'm sorry I can't help you at all with regard to Barbara Marsden."

"No—pity! Still—that's the way it goes sometimes and when it does go like that there isn't much we can do about it beyond putting up with it."

Anthony rose from his wicker chair which creaked rather alarmingly as it shed his weight. Gosling suddenly seemed to become more genial.

"Have you met either of our clergy yet, Bathurst? The rector—or the curate, Frank Cheam?"

Anthony shook his head. "No. Not yet. I've scarcely had the time. It's been work ever since Inspector MacMorran and I came into Wavering. That fear I mentioned just now which the police have—that there may be a third murder was no idle statement, I assure you. We all feel that we must get to grips with this killer with the least possible delay—in case."

"I see. And I can understand your difficulties. Matthew Hopkins, our Rector, is a very decent chap indeed. He and I got on, right from the time he came here. You'll like him. Oxonian, too."

"Oh—what college?"

"I think—Corpus Christi. Yes—I'm pretty sure of it. In the few years he's been here he's pulled St. Simon's round splendidly. When he came, there was a considerable amount of apathy in the parish. Congregations were small in the extreme. Now—the church is healthy and active."

Anthony stood and faced Gosling. "Coming back to the murders, you're positive you can think of *nothing*, likely to help me? Any odd thing you've noticed recently, overheard, remembered—"

Gosling waved the idea into non-existence. "Absolutely positive, Bathurst. Nothing whatever."

"In that case, then, I'll thank you for the interview and leave you to the devices and desires of your own heart."

Anthony walked over to the shelves and looked at the long lines of beautiful books. Books that were well-cared for but which, obviously, had also been read. Carlyle's *Sartor Resartus*, Dexter's *Cornish Crosses— Christian and Pagan*, Watson's *Translation of Valentine and Orson*, Bell's *Castilian Literature*, rubbed corner-edges with complete editions of Anatole France, George Meredith, Zola, Aldous Huxley, Mark Twain, and a copy of Dr. Matthew's *Cockney Past and Present: A short history of the Dialect of London*. Anthony saw that Gosling was a reader of unusually discriminating taste and widely-varied interest. His eyes wandered to the shelf directly above that at which he had first looked. He read the names of the authors represented on this second shelf— most of them were familiar to him as he had expected they would be. Priestley, George Eliot, Bernard Shaw, H. G. Wells, Walter Pater, Robert Graves, Coventry Patmore, G. K. Chesterton, Laurence Housman—he paused summarily at the next name in order to grasp at a fugitive wisp of reminiscence. Simultaneously, the voice of Edmund Gosling broke in upon him, disturbed his train of thought and the fugitive wisp for which he had been clutching, ran to the top of a hill—and disappeared down the other side. Gosling's words came to him and he looked down to see Gosling's extended hand.

"Don't forget to come again—if you feel there are other questions you'd like to ask me."

"Thanks," replied Anthony. "It just depends on how things go during the next few days. Maybe I shall need you. Maybe I shan't."

Gosling went to the front door with him and saw him off.

3

When he had walked a few yards and looked at the time, Anthony decided that he would have lunch somewhere before he proceeded to his next port of call. None of the 'pubs' in the vicinity of Wavering High Street seemed to offer anything in the shape of a lunch and after several abortive enquiries at different hostelries, Anthony was compelled to fall back upon a small bakery. As he waded through an unappetizing meal he reviewed his general position and decided to call next on Owen Tidman, churchwarden and butcher.

Tidman's shop was but a few yards distant from where he was and if he called on the butcher soon after lunch, he would find the man in almost for a certainty. From Tidman's he could then move on to Unwin in Cheyne Avenue—leaving Parmiter, the solicitor, for the last call on the list.

By two o'clock he had finished his lunch off the rickety table in the baker's, paid the bill to a sullen-looking waitress whose ideas concerning her physical appearance and sartorial distinction were optimistically unsound, and was on his way to the butcher's shop of Owen Tidman which he knew was past St. Simon's Church on the other side of the High Street. Tidman himself was behind the counter when Anthony entered the shop. Anthony wasted no time.

"Good afternoon, Mr. Tidman. There's my card. You'll guess at once why I've come to see you."

Tidman took the card, read it and smiled. Anthony saw old Cathay in the smile . . . jade . . . and the Ming dynasty. Tidman laid the card on the cracked wooden counter.

"Good afternoon to you. And I should say from what I can see of it that this job's going along in stages. Sort of harmonic progression. First old Tom Dyer with his walrus moustache—silly old blighter—too slow to be last—then Sergeant Loder full of his own importance—and now you. In other words, we're on the up and up."

Anthony saw again the yellowish tint of skin, the distinctly slanting eyes, and the thin wisp of hair which decorated Tidman's top lip.

'If he can't talk Mandarin,' he thought, 'he jolly well ought to.' Aloud he said. "These two murders in Wavering are horrible, Mr. Tidman! A ghastly business. The police are properly up against it. We know that—and we don't attempt to deny it. It's because of that—"

Tidman interrupted him. He placed a chopper on the counter, turned it up and leant on the handle. "It's no good coming to me, mister. You won't get any help in this shop. For the reason that there's none to be had. I sympathize with you in your troubles and difficulties . . . but it's your job and it's just too bad. I told Loder the same thing when he came. I'd have told Dyer, too—but you waste your breath when you talk to that old flannel-foot. I've never found out yet what keeps his ears apart."

"And yet," said Anthony almost meditatively, "it would seem from one of the few pieces of evidence we have that the killer has visited these premises of yours at least twice. Leaving you short of two basins of fat. You *are* remotely implicated, you see, in the crime."

He smiled encouragingly at the butcher. Tidman studied the lines of his chopper. "Yes—I know. Queer thing—that. Coming in here for that fat. Can't understand it. Got in the back entrance, too. As you've no doubt been informed, there's a sort of mews runs along the back of this row of shops—and I've never troubled a lot about bolts and bars. For one thing I bank all the cash regular so that there's never a lot here on the premises. No more than there are customers at this time of the day."

"All the same—there's one thing that's clear," replied Anthony, "the fellow we're after *must* have known the fat was there for the taking. That's an absolute certainty. He wouldn't have broken in on chance."

Tidman shook his head at Anthony's statement. The gesture that accompanied it was a trifle contemptuous. "There's nothing in that, Mister, take it from me. Everybody in Wavering that ever walks into this shop, man, woman, and child, knows full well that Owen Tidman's always got a basin of dripping on his counter. It may be a relic of the old days—but there you are, my old dad always did it and because of that, I've followed his example. With me . . . and my family . . . customs die hard. So don't set any store on what you've just said."

The butcher laid the chopper flat on the counter and his hand went to the steel hanging by the side of his blue apron. He began to jerk the steel up and down nervously.

"The trouble is," went on Anthony, watching Tidman closely, "that there may well be a third murder. The police don't rule out that possibility by any means. In fact, I'm not giving any official secrets away when I say that they rather anticipate it and that the belief's giving them a considerable amount of anxiety. It's no easy job, you know, with twenty four hours in every day, to safeguard the lives of several people. Which is what it may eventually come to."

"Does that mean, mister, that I'm going to be robbed of a third basin of dripping. Because—in that case—"

Anthony intervened. "It *may* do—what do you think?"

"What do I think? Here—come—I can't have that. It's not for the likes of me to think—in an affair of this kind. That's your job, guvnor, and the job of those that work with you. You can't come that on me."

Anthony was grave-faced when he replied. "Because I come to you, Mr. Tidman—in the hope that you may be able to help me—that doesn't mean for one moment that I'm desirous of transferring any responsibility from my shoulders to yours. I assure you that nothing could be further from my desires. It isn't everybody that holds your place in Wavering. You've got to remember that. Not only are you one of the oldest inhabitants—you're also a churchwarden at the Parish Church. Your opinion on most matters to do with Wavering *should* be valuable."

Tidman dropped his steel and played with the weights on his scales. "Sounds very nice and all that. But it's just plain bullsh—I mean—nonsense. If I *could* assist you, I'd be pleased to. None more so. But I can't—and that's that." Tidman turned away as though to terminate the interview.

"One more question before I go," said Anthony.

"What may that be?"

"Will you please take your mind back to last November?"

"Three months ago? Right you are. What about it? Do you want to know where I was on Guy Fawkes night? Because if so—"

Anthony grinned. "It's not as bad as that. What I was going to ask you was this. Do you remember a rough house outside your shop here one afternoon last November? Round about four o'clock?"

Tidman nodded—but there was strong curiosity showing in his eyes. "I'd say I do! But what's that got to do with this other job? And another thing—you and your Scotland Yard pal weren't in on that. How did you come to know about it?"

"Scotland Yard—since you introduced it, Mr. Tidman gets to know most things. You'd be surprised. But do me a favour. Tell me exactly what took place here, will you?"

"Funny you should have harked back to that," said Tidman reflectively, "because it was a rare to do for the streets of Wavering—I can tell you! It *was* about four o'clock, as you said. Just about the time the lights came on. There were a couple of 'Wops' in the middle of the High Street with a performing bear. The biggest bear, I think, that I've ever seen."

"Wops!" interrupted Anthony, almost involuntarily.

"Yes. You know—'Eyties'. This bear was doing a sort of lumbering dance in the street and was holding a couple of wooden poles across its arms—in its paws I suppose they were. You know the idea—I expect you've seen something similar in your time. Well—when the show got just outside here, a car came up behind them. It wasn't going fast—

there wasn't much room with those Wops holding the road with their performing animal—and before you could say 'Jack Robinson' the fat was in the fire. I'll say it was. One of the 'Wops' swore blind that the car had struck the bear. Went off the deep end I can tell you—flared up in a second. There was a proper scuffle—there were two people in the car—the man that was driving and a lady passenger in a kind of yellow mackintosh affair. One of these new plastic jobs. I can see her now because she got out of the car and stood on the pavement just outside the shop here. She was a very attractive woman too. The chap with her wasn't standing for any nonsense, though, and after a lot of shouting and swearing and general pushing about, he poked his left into a 'Wop' chin and then the band began to play. I'll say it did. The other 'Wop' flourished a knife, the motorist caught him by the wrist and it ended with the police coming up and the 'Wop' outfit being marched off to Remsford Gaol. Bear included." Tidman concluded his narrative with a smile of pleasure.

"I had a ring-side seat of the whole affair—saw absolutely everything—and believe me, it was a good show while it lasted."

For a fleeting second, Anthony smiled with him. But his face changed quickly. "Tell me, Mr. Tidman, if you can, was the bear muzzled, can you remember?"

Tidman repeated the question after Anthony. "Was the bear muzzled? Well now—let me think—yes, I rather fancy it *was*. But why—what's the point?"

"Merely that I like to get as full a picture as I can of an incident such as the one you've just described. You think the bear *was* muzzled?"

"I do that," reaffirmed Tidman. "Now you've asked me—I'm pretty sure of it."

He was on the point of adding to his statement when a car drew up outside the shop and the driver, a woman, alighted from it. She entered the shop obviously as a customer, and Anthony stood back from the counter to give her the right of way. Tidman greeted her genially and Anthony heard her answer back brightly and briskly. The order completed, the woman put her purchase into a bag, went to the car again and drove off. Tidman rang up the cash register and threw the coins that had been left on the counter into the appropriate till-compartment.

"Now I should have thought you would have known her," he said rather provocatively, so Anthony thought, "seeing that you're down here on a sort of special investigation into the murders. I was rather surprised when I saw you didn't."

"Why?" queried Anthony, "*should* I know the lady? Is she a Wavering celebrity or merely an ordinary descendant of the British Warrior Queen?"

"You want to wake your ideas up," continued Tidman even more provocatively, "that was Julia Wilkes, the dress maker. Lives in Shelford Row. I oughtn't to have to tell you this, but Julia Wilkes was the woman who—"

"I get it," intervened Anthony, "the woman who spotted Barbara Marsden's frock when Miss Ferris wore it. At the performance given by the Dramatic Society."

Tidman was a little late in hiding his disappointment. "That's it," he assented. "You've rung the bell at last."

"That's the first time," said Anthony, "I've ever seen the lady. Plenty up top—I should say. On first impressions."

"And you'd say right, mister. No doubt about that. . . Julia's no stick-in-the-mud. A remarkably astute business woman in every way. Gets her brains from her old father old Ernest Wilkes—used to do a fine business there in the corn-chandler line. Till he went funny with some sort of religious mania and they shoved him in the nut-house." Tidman tapped his forehead significantly. "When he died," he continued, "his money went to Julia. The mother was dead, too, and Julia was the only child. She started her dress making business with the cash the old man left and since then she's never looked back."

"l wonder," said Anthony, "in fact I've been wondering while you've been talking—would Vera Ferris be alive to-day if Miss Wilkes *hadn't* spotted she was wearing the first dead girl's frock? Do you know, Mr. Tidman. I'm inclined, myself, to think it's a very moot point."

There was a strange smouldering glow in Tidman's eyes. He stared across the counter at Anthony curiously. "What makes you think like that?" he asked.

Anthony parried the question by asking another. "Well what do you think about it yourself?"

Tidman shook his head slowly. "I haven't thought about it. And I don't intend to think about it. It's not my job as I said to you when you first came into my shop. All I can say is—that I never thought I'd live to see such dreadful doings in Wavering. I was born and bred here—and my father before me. That sort of makes me love the little place and I hope I'm never called upon to leave it, because my roots are in it."

Anthony turned towards the door of the shop. "Maybe you'll think differently one day."

"Maybe I shan't," retorted Owen Tidman with emphasized assurance—"I'm a man that knows his own mind. Anybody in Wavering 'll tell you *that*."

4

Upon reaching the house named 'Pitchcroft', in Cheyne Avenue, Anthony encountered a surprise and something, too, in the nature of a small set-back. He rang the bell and his summons was answered by a middle-aged woman with fair hair and florid cheeks. Anthony enquired for Mr. Leonard Unwin. It was then that the surprise materialized.

"He's not in," said the rosy-cheeked lady—"he's at the offices."

"I'm sorry," returned Anthony—"the offices? In Wavering, are they? Could you tell me?"

The lady stared at him as though he were some strange object whose spiritual home was a museum. "Certainly," she replied, "where else would you expect them to be?"

Directly she had spoken she could see that Anthony was out of his depth.

"My husband," she said dryly, "happens to be the editor of the *Wavering Standard*. I thought you would know that. The offices of the paper are in the High Street, two doors from the police-station. I thought everybody in Wavering knew that."

Anthony smiled at her and made excuse. "I'm sorry again. I *didn't* know that. You see—I'm new to Wavering. I'll get along there at once. And please forgive me for the inconvenience I may have caused you."

Anthony raised his hat. The lady returned his smile and closed the door. Anthony made rapid tracks for the same High Street which he had so recently left. He had no difficulty in finding the offices of the *Wavering Standard* and flicked his card at a tall, thin, long-haired, scraggy boy who sat at a high desk in the outer office.

"Your editor, if you please," said Anthony, "and I don't mind how soon it is."

The tall boy shook a diffident head at the proposition. "Can't see him now. Not a hope. He's too busy. This afternoon's our—"

Anthony promptly closured him. "Look at the top of that card, sonny—if you don't mind making the necessary effort and then take it straight in to Mr. Unwin."

The tall boy wavered, read the card as he had been ordered and his eyes almost popped from his head.

"Yes, sir," he said impulsively, "very good, sir, please to wait a minute, sir."

Anthony waited and his patience was not tried. The tall boy was quickly back.

"This way, sir—if you please, sir."

He bent his head and tapped on a door covered with green baize. Then he pushed the door open and Anthony slid into the room. The boy vanished. There was a man seated at a table strewn and untidy with many papers. His appearance was unusual—to say the least of it. His head was completely bald, his nose which sustained a pair of old fashioned pince-nez, was large and curved and his cheeks were thin and bloodless. 'The authentic secretary-bird at last,' thought Anthony, as he faced this anaemic apparition.

"Sit down," said the specimen at the table. Anthony smiled and sat.

"Mr. Unwin, I presume?" he asked at the same time.

"Unwin it is." The voice was thin, piping, and reedy.

Seldom, thought Anthony, has a voice so beautifully matched its possessor. It continued to function.

"I've looked at your card. I wasn't born yesterday. I can guess why you're here. The *Wavering Standard* is honoured. What . . . er . . . *specially* can this humble local paper do for mighty Scotland Yard?"

Anthony opened much as he had opened to Ferguson, Gosling, and Tidman. "Frankly now, Mr. Unwin," he concluded—"I'm wondering whether you can help us at all. The editor of a local paper in a place like Wavering—and it's the only local paper, I believe, in the district—usually has his finger on the pulse of most local activities. In other words, he's a person of rare influence, definite importance, and considerable knowledge."

"Can we put that in our next editorial?" The question came in the reedy voice from the other side of the table. The pince-nez was off the nose now and being subjected to violent polishing with a silk handkerchief.

"With pleasure, Mr. Unwin, with as much added local colour as you please."

The pince-nez was replaced on the bridge of size. The handkerchief was pushed back into pocket.

"May we hint also, at something else. That the police anticipate more murders?"

"Wrapped up well—in a general warning to the public yes. As a stark incitement to terror—no. There are the women and children to be considered."

Unwin took a pencil, unscrewed it and made marks on a piece of paper. Then he looked up at Anthony.

"I'm interested, Mr. Bathurst. What did you imagine we might be able to do for you?"

Anthony put his arms on the side of the table and leant on them. Almost imperceptibly he shrugged his shoulders before beginning to speak.

"Let me put it to you like this. A girl was murdered on or about the twenty-fourth of January. Strangled. By some means of transport, her body was taken to the old Hockey Club pavilion on the allotments at the back of St. Simon's Church."

Unwin was about to speak but Anthony's slightly upraised hand checked him.

"Give me just a moment or two longer, Mr. Unwin please. On the twenty-second of February—or thereabouts—a second Wavering girl was strangled and her body was disposed of in a precisely similar manner. The police think it looks like a car in the picture somewhere. There's another point for your next column on the murders. You can work that up as much as you like."

Unwin frowned at the suggestion. "Maybe—maybe not. There *are* other means of transport, Mr. Bathurst. I can't see myself that a car is anything like certain."

"What else then, would you suggest?" Anthony seemed guileless as he put the question. Unwin puffed out his cheeks in an attempt to achieve importance.

"Surely—there are several possibilities? The killer could have walked to the allotments with the body . . . say, in a trunk? Or even in a sack?"

"Heavy," countered Anthony lazily . . . "strain on the muscles of the arm."

"Oh—I don't know. I couldn't have done it"—Unwin felt his meagre biceps—"but I wouldn't put it past everybody."

Anthony suddenly changed his subject. The transition was so abrupt that Unwin was somewhat taken aback.

"Leaving the subject of the actual murders—if you feel that you can't help me overmuch, Mr. Unwin—have you any memory of the strange case of the performing bear? I refer to a disturbing little escapade which took place outside Tidman's, the butcher's, some time last November. One afternoon."

Unwin nodded. "Certainly I remember it. Good copy—that. We reported it. But why bring that up? I don't think I—?"

"Of what nationality were the two men concerned? Can you remember that?"

Unwin knitted his brows. "Let me see now. Er . . . Bretons, I fancy they were."

"Bretons ?" Anthony considered the answer Unwin had given him with some degree of amusement—Poles, Savoyards, Italians, and now at last Bretons. A beautifully mixed bag, to be sure. He heard Unwin address him again.

"I can turn up the case if you like. If you really are concerned about it. Won't take me very long."

"Ah—that's an idea. Thank you, Mr. Unwin. I'll take advantage of your offer. Many thanks."

"No trouble at all," said the editor of the *Wavering Standard*, rising from his chair. "Stay put for a couple of minutes or so—and I'll be back with the gen."

Unwin opened the door of his room, made several strange noises in the region of his throat and disappeared. Anthony waited patiently for his return. Suddenly the door opened again with a flourish of handle and hinges and Unwin was back in his chair again. He placed a large volume in front of him. Its size was such that Unwin himself was rendered almost invisible.

"This is our official volume for last year," he explained, "we have it bound up in this form—annually. As a matter of fact—if you only knew it—you're in luck's way. It's only been back from the book-binders a matter of a few days."

Unwin began to flick the pages with his fingers with the tempo and touch of the expert. "November—that's what I want. I fancy it was towards the end of the month—your little spot of bother. Trouble 'Bruin'—eh?" Unwin chuckled in his throat at his witticism. It sounded to Anthony as though the man's demise was imminent. "That's not so bad," said the editor of the *Wavering Standard*—" though I says it myself. Let me see now—I'll try the third week of November. I know exactly where to put my finger on it. The particular part of the page, I mean. I've got a visual memory, you know. Once I've read anything in our columns I know exactly where to look for it. Ah—this is about the right issue l fancy . . . let me see . . . yes . . . November the twenty second . . . now just about here it should be . . . and here it is."

Unwin swooped on his prey-paragraph with a squeak of supreme satisfaction and a twitter of triumph. He began to read . . . in a kind of meaningless mumble-jabber . . . of the kind that one hears in local Council chambers or at Committee meetings (assorted). Anthony could catch but an occasional word here and there. Then, eventually, Unwin emerged from his word-bath, his lips dripping with syllables . . . and Anthony heard certain sounds which he ultimately recognized as names. "Max Donck and Dirk Brelonde . . . of Belgian nationality." Unwin paused for breath and looked at him.

"May I glance at the printed paragraph?" he asked of the editor.

Unwin, rather ungraciously, turned the big volume round and pushed it over to him. Anthony read what the *Wavering Standard* of the 22nd of November had to say concerning the disgraceful incident in the Wavering High Street. It puzzled him that Unwin in reading should have made so much of it. The report, actually, was extremely brief. There were but references to the men, the nature of the alleged offence, and the consequent infliction of the fine. In addition to these somewhat meagre details, Anthony noticed that the names of the other people implicated in the incident were Mr. and Mrs. Oscar Hammersley of Regency Mansions, Finchley, Middlesex. He tucked the names of the four principal participants in a brain pigeon-hole, for future reference. They *might* come in handy in God's good time. You never knew when you got your nose on the grindstone of crime.

"Satisfied?" broke in the voice of Unwin—"it seems that according to this the two fellows were Belgians. I knew it was something like that."

Anthony handed back the bulky volume with its annual chronicle of the vices and vagaries of Wavering. "Many thanks," he remarked.

Unwin coughed and looked at his watch rather significantly. "Is there anything else you wanted to know?" he queried, "because if not—"

Both implication and inference were obvious. "Many things, I'm afraid," returned Anthony with a shake of the head, "though I doubt if the answer is here."

Unwin seemed completely impervious to the shaft. "In that case, then—" he said. His head went up in interrogation. "I agree entirely," replied Anthony. He smiled genially at the editor of the *Wavering Standard* and took his leave.

5

'This leaves me only Parmiter,' thought Anthony as he left the offices of the *Wavering Standard*. He checked his pace and looked at his watch. The time was ten minutes to four and it was a dark afternoon, even allowing for the time of the year. He considered his immediate problem. Where would he be the more likely to catch Vernon Parmiter—at his offices in the High Street, or at his home in the Remsford Road? Doubtful, thought Anthony—pretty well a fifty-fifty proposition. The sight of a telephone kiosk in front of the building which did duty as the general post-office decided him. He would telephone to Parmiter's office and find out if the man were there and at the same time available for consultation.

Anthony stepped briskly into the kiosk and telephoned to the Parmiter office. His inquiry was answered without delay. Mr. Vernon Parmiter was there and would be pleased to see Mr. Bathurst at four o'clock precisely. Anthony gave appropriate thanks, confirmed the time of interview, which from his point of view couldn't have been better, and hung up. The clock on Parmiter's mantelpiece was striking four as Anthony was shown into the solicitor's room. Parmiter was seated at his table, evidently prepared and waiting for him. "Good afternoon, Mr. Bathurst. Sit down, will you?"

The voice was both cultured and precise.

"Thank you," said Anthony and looked carefully at the man who had received him. Probably in the early fifties, Vernon Parmiter had a long, prominent jaw, pointed chin, and rather hollow cheeks. There were wrinkles across his forehead, his eyes were a watery blue and he had a little trim, white moustache well brushed up from the corners of his thin, primmish lips. He was most certainly "very much the solicitor." The back of his head bulged into something like prominence above the lines of his lean neck. His shoulders were high and sharp and his white hair was cropped close to his head. Anthony, as he sat opposite to Vernon Parmiter, thought of three appropriate adjectives, quiet, undemonstrative, patrician. He looked up and saw that Parmiter had a faint smile playing round the corners of his lips. The man seemed entirely free from all self-consciousness.

"Now, Mr. Bathurst," he said, "tell me the worst. I've always hated anything in the nature of suspense." The smile remained on the corners of his lips.

Anthony submitted his usual explanatory overture. Parmiter sat and listened and the corners of his lips tightened. His eyes conveyed a hint of restlessness and his fingers tapped rather impatiently on the edge of his table. When Anthony had finished Parmiter said: "I shall be only too pleased to help you—if I can. But I doubt very much if I have anything whatever to offer you of any real value. I saw Barbara on the evening of the New Year's Social. I saw her often during that evening . . . from time to time. I thought she seemed in excellent spirits. But there—she usually did that. So that there was nothing extraordinary about it."

Anthony had noted the use of the Christian name and Parmiter's latest remark presented him with an opportunity to intervene with a question thereon.

"You knew Miss Marsden then?"

"Oh—yes, I knew Miss Marsden."

Parmiter became suddenly prim again. He dropped his eyelids and one of his hands went to a sharp-edged paper-knife that lay on the table in front of him. Although he had answered Anthony's question precisely, the latter felt that Parmiter would almost certainly amplify his reply. He waited, therefore, for the anticipated addition. But none came. Anthony was tempted to probe deeper and succumbed to the temptation.

"You knew her well? That is to say—fairly intimately?"

Parmiter's fingers went from the paper-knife to his white moustache-ends. His cheeks flushed a little and a brightness came into his eyes. Anthony wondered why this should be. Parmiter pursed his lips as he began to speak.

"Well—how can I put it? So that you don't go away from here, Mr. Bathurst, with anything like a false impression. That's the very last thing I should like to happen. The Marsdens are an old Wavering family. And as far as I am concerned my grandfather founded this business at the head of which I now am. Wavering—as you know—is far from being a large place. Indeed—one could call it 'small'—and one wouldn't be far out. I mention these facts so that you may get the right perspective. People who live in large towns, or who are used to large communities, often experience great difficulty in their accurate assessment of life in the country. They fail to understand the exact nature of relationships. There you are then—you have two families—the Parmiters and the Marsdens—each with its roots in Wavering. When I add to that, the information that Barbara was my wife's general help in the house for say a couple of years when Barbara was in her middle 'teens—you can tell how well I knew her."

Parmiter sat back a little, smiled at Anthony and closed his eyes. Anthony tried to remember something—something that Norman Ferguson had told him, but the reminiscence was fugitive and the endeavour unsuccessful. As a result, he found himself asking Vernon Parmiter a question which originally he hadn't intended to ask him.

"What is your own theory of the murders, Mr. Parmiter? I take it, you didn't know the second girl, Vera Ferris?"

Parmiter opened his eyes. "Merely as a member of the Dramatic Society. The Ferris family is *not* of old Wavering stock. They are comparative new-comers to the place." Parmiter paused before going back to Anthony's first question. "What is my theory of the murders? Well—that certainly isn't an easy one for me to answer. I've a legal mind. My mind has been trained to legal matters. I sincerely hope that the training has taught me to think logically and to analyse with some degree of care. Murder! From the envisagement of the crime itself we turn to the contemplation of possible motive. What motive could there possibly have been for the murder of these two innocent girls? As far as we can see you and I—and all the rest of us—there could be no real motive for such a dreadful crime. Certainly *not one* of the conventional motives—that you and I are so well aware of. Revenge, greed, fear—not one of them applies to these murders in Wavering. And—the medical evidence tells us also—that there was no question either of sexual lust. I understand that neither of the victims had been violated in that way. What then remains? A homicidal maniac—the only possible answer, Mr. Bathurst, to the problem that confronts us."

Parmiter shrugged his spare shoulders and became primly precise again. Anthony was silent. He was still vainly questing for the Ferguson reminiscence. Parmiter seemed a trifle impatient with the silence.

"Am I to take it, Mr. Bathurst, that you find yourself in disagreement with me? Surely not?"

"Not at all, Mr. Parmiter. All the same—putting it as you did is rather frightening. Don't you think so? How shall we know him—this maniac killer? Don't you see—*he may be anybody*? How shall we recognize him? That's the anxiety that gnaws at me constantly. It's not a job for one investigator as much as it is a job for a complete organization. A posse of people. When you can't hit on a motive—when you know that there damn well *isn't* a motive—and that you're faced with some form or other of sadistic killing—you know at the same time that you can kiss your hand regretfully to the science of deduction; It can be eliminated altogether. So that your job comes to this. You've got to put your hand on a sadist-killer who in all probability, on the surface at least, is an ordinary respectable citizen, at most times going about his everyday business and looking exactly like the man in the street. And to put your hand on *that* person—out of the great mass of citizens—well—I'll leave you to calculate the odds, Mr. Parmiter."

"I appreciate your difficulties to the full, Mr. Bathurst," returned Parmiter, toying with the paper-knife again, "you've presented the case to me exactly as I see it myself."

Anthony nodded. "Thank you. The job's got to be done by a cleverly-directed scheme of operations. At least—that's how I see things at the moment. Otherwise, the number of girls who have met an untimely end will most certainly become three or even four."

"You mentioned 'a scheme of operations'. What exactly had you in mind when you said that? You've got me interested."

Anthony laughed. "No details yet, I'm afraid. They're nothing like ready. The idea only came to me to-day. But something on the lines of enrolling citizens of Wavering to patrol the streets during the hours of darkness. Ancillary, of course, to the police. Because it all boils down to this—you've got to remember that a couple of bobbies can't be everywhere."

"No. I quite see that. In a way—it makes me rejoice that Wavering *is* such a small place after all. There won't be so much or so many to guard. A distinct advantage."

Anthony seemed to be thinking matters over. "Of course," he said, "harking back to where we were just now, the trouble with those citizen enrolments is this. You stand such an excellent chance of enrolling the killer! So that you put him in the position of watching the watchers—all the time! When you're actually engaged in looking for *him*, he's actually rubbing shoulders with *you*. That state of affairs must be avoided at all costs."

Parmiter nodded agreement. "Yes. I see your point. Something like that marvellous yarn of Gilbert Chesterton's. I can't think of the title for the moment."

Anthony rose. He saw that no good would accrue from prolonging the interview. Parmiter rose simultaneously and shook hands.

"If I think of anything after you've gone, likely to be of assistance to you, I'll 'phone you at once. I presume I can get you that way. Where are you staying?"

Anthony told him. Parmiter scribbled in his diary. Anthony walked to the door. Parmiter accompanied him—a step or so. "By the way," said Parmiter, at the door, "it's just occurred to me—what do you make of the stolen fat? The two basins from the butcher's?"

Anthony smiled and shook his head. "I think there's a great deal more in that, Mr. Parmiter, than meets the eye. And that's to one churchwarden about another."

"Dear me," said Parmiter—"do you know—I hadn't looked at it in that light."

"No," returned Anthony—"it's strange, when one comes to think of it, how easy it is to miss certain aspects. May be a question of angles. After all you know—'Man's a fool. From all his thievings, God gets left and God's the leavings. Bread of life be in the baking. Man's the meal and God's the making. On the Fire which hath no dying, Man's the fat and God's the frying'."

The solicitor cocked his head to one side and stared at him. There was a pause. "Er—yes. . . . I suppose that is so," murmured Parmiter valedictory.

CHAPTER 7

1

Anthony sat with MacMorran in the tiny lounge of the 'Nag's Head'. The occasion was post-prandial. The inspector filled his pipe, applied the match (supplied by the inn) and got the tobacco (furnished by Anthony) burning. The arm-chair was comfortable and Andrew MacMorran for the first time that day felt at ease. Save for the solving of the problem of the Wavering murders, he felt that he was minus care, plus comfort, and that the landlord might very well pass the flowing howl.

Anthony was opposite to him. He knew his MacMorran, which meant that he knew pretty well that the inspector was thinking. Especially with regard to the vessel and its amplitude. Eventually, the inspector broke the tranquillity.

"Well," he said, "I haven't worried you. My telegraphic address has been 'Patience'. Left you to tell the tale in your own time. Nursed you like a mother. What happened to-day ? Did you pick up anything on your wanderings?"

Anthony knocked the ash from his cigarette before he replied. He shook his head as he started to speak.

"If you ask me, Andrew," he said, "not a lot. More like precious little. I'm certainly disappointed. I had hoped for much more than I actually got."

"Tell me about them," said MacMorran simply, "all of them."

Anthony grinned at the inspector. "Pen-pictures from our observer—translated into words—eh? That the idea behind the request?"

"Something like that. What was Ferguson like? You went to him first—didn't you?"

"That's so, Andrew. I met two Ferguson's. *Père et fils*. The boy struck me as a very decent lad. I should say considerably above the local average. Also, genuinely fond of the dead Barbara Marsden."

MacMorran was quick to interrupt. "Well—there you are —suppose he'd been fond of her—and they'd quarrelled. Love's young dream become a nightmare. That's an old story."

"I know, Andrew. There is that possibility, I admit. If Barbara Marsden were the one and only. But what about Vera Ferris? Doesn't she wash out your idea?"

MacMorran grunted. "H'm—I'd overlooked that for the minute. Suppose she does. Unless it's the 'blind' again. What about the father, though? Ferguson senior?"

Anthony shook his head again. "Not so good. Bit of a scallywag, I should say. Been most places in his time. Rough-tongued and coarse generally. Certainly a lewd fellow of the baser sort. From one or two remarks he dropped towards the conclusion of our interview I should hazard the opinion that he's been a guest of His Majesty at some time in the dim and distant past. I gathered he hadn't an overwhelming passion for the guardians of law and order."

MacMorran spoke through the tobacco-smoke. "We can look into that, of course. Simple matter to check it. I think we will—from what you say it may be worth it. But anyhow—go on. Let's hear the rest of the story. How did you find the next chap—Gosling?"

Anthony caressed his chin. "On the whole, Andrew, I think he impressed me favourably. But there's no disputing the fact that he's of an unusual type. And it's rather difficult to understand why a man of his particular calibre should be content to live in a place like Wavering. He has strong theatrical interests—been an old 'pro' I hear—and he has literary inclinations as well. From what I was able to see of him he certainly didn't strike me as a murderer—far from it in fact—oh curse it, Andrew—can't you see what we're up against?"

Anthony rose from his arm-chair and began to pace the lounge.

"What's the sudden excitement ?" commented MacMorran.

Anthony turned to him impulsively. "Why—can't you see, Andrew— that it's a hundred to one *on*—that the man we're looking for looks ordinary, commonplace, just respectable, like thousands of others, *and nothing whatever like a murderer*? That's why I'm worried—and as each day comes and goes—more desperately anxious. Because we've got to pick this chap out, Andrew—this killer who doesn't in any way suggest that he *is* one. Pick him out from all the citizens of Wavering."

Anthony went back to his chair, sat down in it and crossed his legs. "From Gosling I went to Tidman—churchwarden and butcher."

Anthony paused suddenly. MacMorran watched him carefully. To him, listening as he was, the pause was significant.

"Well—what about Tidman? He's in the clear, surely?"

"He's the man who had his fat stolen from his counter—and who reported the thefts to the police. Let me remind you of that, Andrew. Been in the district some time. Generations of Tidmans. An interesting character, Owen Tidman. Something of a personality, too. Especially in a small place like Wavering."

MacMorran came to the point. "Nothing, I suppose, you could pin on him?"

"Nothing at all, Andrew. Haven't even got the pin itself."

MacMorran grunted. "What about Parmiter?"

"Leave him until last—if it's all the same to you. I'd prefer you to. I went to the editor bloke after I left Tidman. Unwin. Did you know—were you aware when you gave me his name in your list that he was the editor of the local rag—the *Wavering Standard*?"

MacMorran grinned pleasantly at the question. "I made it my business to find out. What do you think I've been doing all the time I've been here? Playing snakes and ladders? Or increasing the consumption of alcoholic liquor? What did you think of him?"

"Not a particularly gallant specimen, Andrew. A good cock linnet with a sudden rush of blood to the head would knock him for six. It's a good job for him that the pen is mightier than the sword. Otherwise he'd click for an atrociously lean time."

"He didn't impress you, I take it?"

"He did not. In any eleven of mine he'd be next to the roller. And yet "

"And yet what?"

"Well—there you are—think of what I said just now when you accused me of undue excitement. Unwin's as likely a killer as the next man—or as unlikely! And that's an epitome of the problem."

"That only leaves Parmiter, the solicitor."

"Ah—Parmiter. Vernon Parmiter Esquire. Now Parmiter's by way of being a different saucepan of salmon. Very different."

"In what way—exactly?"

"Solicitor. Legal mind. Trained mind. Neither butcher nor editor. Neither house-decorator nor house-filler. Old-established Wavering family. Same like Tidman of the stolen fat. Known Barbara Marsden and her family from time immemorial. You get some of the picture, Andrew? Very charming. Cultured man. Absurd to think of such a man as killer of two girls. Insult to one's intelligence."

"Eh—what's this?" cut in MacMorran—"why, man—you're going back on your own statements. Where's your sense of consistency? You said just now that anybody—"

Anthony cut him this time. "Well—what if I did? What about the exception that proves the rule?" Anthony stood up.

"I don't get that. I don't see where you're going to. If you—"

"Bed, Andrew—bed. That's where I'm going. The place where the worry of every problem gently and gradually diminishes. Even the problem of the Wavering murders. Good night, Andrew."

2

The Rector of St. Simon's, Wavering, the Rev. Matthew Hopkins, M.A. (Oxon), had expected that the police, or one of their emissaries, would favour him with a call. Tidman had told him of Bathurst's visit to the butcher's shop in the High Street. Parmiter had confided to him that his offices had also been visited.

"That means," said the Rector, "that they'll be coming to see me. As they *should* do. Such a procedure would be only fit and proper."

The Rector went into his living-room and looked round. Mrs. Hodgson wasn't in there. So the Rector looked in the mirror. It must be confessed that this was a well-established habit of his. When he looked, he saw an elderly man, heavy in body and with an excess of chin. If he could have seen his legs reflected at the same time, he would have noticed that they were too short for the proportions of his trunk. His face was florid—not red exactly—but getting on that way. His hair was black. It was also thick and straight. His cheeks were full—almost fat—and the heavy, rather gross mouth, was pursed like that of a man engaged in an exercise of meditation that was both constant and painful. Other people, when they saw the Rector of Wavering for the first time, considered that he looked more farmer than parson, but it was as well for the Rev. Matthew Hopkins's peace of mind, that he remained unaware of these eminently sound opinions. His eyes, however, were the most remarkable feature of his face. They were reddish-brown in colour and their pupils were unusually large—and they were seldom restful. They flickered and danced . . . the Rector had often been fascinated himself by the capricious restlessness of his eyes.

As he looked in the mirror on this particular morning, the Rector noticed with some degree of annoyance that a hair had sprouted from a small mole on his left cheek—and that the hair in question was grey. He turned quickly from the mirror, coughed in the manner of a chiding headmaster and went towards the back of the house. He desired to find Mrs. Hodgson and have a word with her. It was an annoying thing, he reflected, that his housekeeper was never where he wanted her to be. He ran her to earth eventually in the kitchen. Mrs. Hodgson was peeling potatoes—a daily occupation which she loathed beyond description. Her loathing was magnified by the fact that the Rector was inordinately fond of potatoes and insisted on many more than his fair share. The Rector peered into the basin into which Mrs. Hodgson was dropping the potatoes when they were peeled.

"Ah, Mrs. Hodgson," he said, "the kindly fruits of the earth—eh? What are they—Majestic?"

Mrs. Hodgson's feelings outran her discretion. "I could think," she replied viciously, "of much better names than that for them."

She threw a misshapen tuber into the basin. The Rector coughed. He pretended not to hear what his housekeeper had said. It was a subterfuge in which he was remarkably proficient.

"Er . . . Mrs. Hodgson," he opened, "I rather wanted a word with you. An extremely important word. Come into my study . . . will you? And please dry your hands before you come."

Mrs. Hodgson glared into space and then remembered that there were definite points about a respite from potato-peeling—Majestic or otherwise. She dried her hands and followed the Rector into his study. As the Rev. Matthew Hopkins closed the door of that room behind his house-keeper, his thoughts reverted to that most unpleasant occasion . . . some weeks ago . . . when he had come from his warm bed to take Marsden's telephone call . . . the potency of the thought was such that he almost forgot for the moment that Mrs. Hodgson was in the study with him. The Rev. Matthew Hopkins pulled himself together and looked in the direction of his housekeeper. He waved a hand—vaguely.

"Take a seat, Mrs. Hodgson—by all means. Er . . . make yourself comfortable."

Mrs. Hodgson selected an austere-looking chair in the corner of the study. The Rector was quickly into his stride and took the thin end of the wedge.

"What I wanted to say to you, Mrs. Hodgson, was this. It is quite possible—nay, almost probable—that we shall have a visit from the police. At the Rectory here. With regard to those two poor girls who have . . . er . . . died in such distressing circumstances. Er . . . any moment now. In fact—I'm actually expecting something of the kind. I happen to have heard what the police plan of campaign is. There's a man going round Wavering making all sorts of enquiries of a number of people. Some sort of special investigator—I suppose he'd be called."

The Rector paused. Mrs. Hodgson seized the opportunity to rid herself of her question.

"But what's any of it got to do with me?" she asked of her venerable employer. The Rector beamed at her.

"Nothing, Mrs. Hodgson—nothing whatever! That's just the point I was about to make. You've saved me coming to it by laborious degrees. If I *should* happen to be out when this fellow arrives—have nothing whatever to do with him, Mrs. Hodgson. Don't forget now. Tell him if he wishes to see me that he must come again when I'm at home. Don't argue with him in any way. Don't discuss the matter with him at all. Don't show him over the Rectory—and above everything else, Mrs. Hodgson, *don't* answer any questions that he may put to you."

Mrs. Hodgson nodded. "Very good, sir, I understand. May I go back to the kitchen? It's your potatoes."

"Not yet." The Rector was severe. "I haven't quite finished yet. I desire to emphasize that last statement I made. Don't answer *any* questions! No matter how simple the question may appear to be. On the . . . ahem . . . surface. Leave all that to me."

"Yes, sir," said Mrs. Hodgson, "I understand perfectly, sir."

But the Rev. Matthew Hopkins was not done yet. By any means! He grasped his lance more firmly and charged back to the fray.

"You may not be aware of it but the police have a habit, Mrs. Hodgson, of making a highly important question sound extremely innocent. Especially to a person such as yourself. Then, before you know where you are, they pounce on you and . . . er . . . get you all confused . . . and make it appear that you said something which all the time you know you didn't. And . . . er . . . the fat's in the fire."

Mrs. Hodgson, however, resisted sturdily. "They can't upset the truth, Rector. You should know that as well as me. No matter how clever they may be at twisting things."

The Rector felt a sense of shock. "Er . . . what's that?" he inquired.

"I said they couldn't upset the truth, Rector. And no more they can't."

Mrs. Hodgson folded her hands in her lap and tossed her head with frustrated defiance. The Rector coughed for the third time that morning.

"Perhaps not, Mrs. Hodgson," he asserted stiffly. "Er—I think that's all for now—thank you."

"And thank *you*, sir," responded Mrs. Hodgson on her way out.

3

As the Rector of Wavering dismissed his housekeeper in the fashion that has been described, he heard the front door-bell ring. Inasmuch as Mrs. Hodgson was already well on her way to the kitchen and to the basin of water which held a number of peeled potatoes (that might or might not have been Majestics), the Rector (in his opinion both generously and magnanimously) decided to answer the door himself. It might even be the anticipated visit of Scotland Yard's special investigator—in which case it would be just as well if he answered the summons in person. The Rector, therefore, made a quick way to his front door and opened it. A surprise awaited him. It *shouldn't* have been a surprise—because nothing could have been more normal—the caller was Cheam, his curate.

"Oh come in, Cheam," said the Rector—"I don't know why exactly, but I wasn't expecting you."

The Rev. Frank Cheam laughed as he crossed the threshold and pushed his fingers through his thick, black hair.

"Oh—why not? I have been known in the past to call upon you at this time."

The Rector laughed with him. "Too true. But actually I had the idea when the door-bell rang that it was this Scotland Yard fellow that's going the rounds. I expect you've heard about him as well as I have. Come into the study, though, my dear chap, and make yourself comfortable."

Cheam followed the Rector in response to the invitation. He was a well-set-up man in the late twenties and like his Rector, a bachelor.

Dark-haired, clean-shaven, broad of shoulder, slightly taller than the average, frank blue eyes, and a humorous-looking snub nose, he appeared an excellent physical specimen judged by most standards. He could be faulted, however, with regard to his head. It was of unusual shape and size—a Norfolk head—with a large bump at the back of the skull. But you didn't see Frank Cheam's bump unless you stood directly behind him. A phrenologist would have deduced brains.

"Scotland Yard going the rounds?" he repeated questioningly as he entered the study. "What's this you're talking about, Rector?"

Matthew Hopkins smiled the smile which he fancied was paternal and he placed his finger against the side of his nose.

"A little bird, my dear Cheam! In fact—more than one little bird. Several, in fact. I have my own sources of information."

Cheam laughed again. "After all, sir, why shouldn't you? A working alliance between Church and State—it's not unheard of—you know."

But the Rector pursued the tenor of his way. "It amounts to this, my dear Cheam. This Scotland Yard busybody has called on Parmiter—he's also been to see Tidman. You observe—both of our wardens. Doubtless there are others who have been similarly . . . er . . . treated. I infer from that he'll certainly call on me here at the Rectory—and very probably on you at Mrs. Hicks's. I shall be greatly surprised if he doesn't."

Mrs. Hicks, let it be recorded, was the Rev. Frank Cheam's landlady. The curate looked interested.

"Oh—what's the idea? Checking alibis—or something?"

"Well—I wouldn't say that. According to the chatter of my . . . er . . . aviary, I should say it's more of a general enquiry—a kind of comprehensive discussion—sort of spying out the land. At least—that's how I should be inclined to describe it from what I've been told." The Rev. Hopkins paused, but began to speak again before Cheam could cut in. "For my part, I shall say extremely little—if I'm called upon. And I should advise you, Cheam, to do likewise."

The curate shrugged his broad shoulders. "I don't suppose for a minute that they'll bother me, Rector. If they do, I'll take your advice, sir. Now I'll tell you what I've come to see you about."

The Rector sat back in his chair and put his finger-tips together. He was just a little annoyed with Cheam! Cheam didn't seem to pay sufficient attention to what he himself had just stated with regard to the activities of Scotland Yard. After all—it wasn't exactly a commonplace matter and Cheam should have been grateful for his advice. Some of these young men! Can never be *told* anything. That was the worst of them. He would show Cheam he was annoyed by frowning . . . not an ugly frown . . . a kindly one.

"It's like this, Rector," the curate was saying, "I saw Edmund Gosling last night and he asked me to come along and have a word with you first thing this morning. That's why I popped over so early."

The Hopkins frown developed to considerable proportions. "Why? What's Gosling want? For you to see me about? Can't he come to me direct?"

"It's to do with the Cottage Hospital people. Their funds are low it seems. That is to say—lower than usual. They want the Dramatic Society to put on a show for them—on Wednesday and Thursday fortnight. They'll take *Nothing But the Truth* and they'll absolutely guarantee the audience from their own people. Gosling seems quite satisfied with the suggestion—there'll be no financial liabilities whatever on the Dramatic Society even if the show proves a 'flop'. The Hospital crowd will take over the entire monetary responsibility. Gosling wants you to agree, Rector, before he gives the O.K. to the Hospital crowd to go ahead. He says you couldn't have a better 'cause'."

For some reason, however, the Rector of Wavering hummed and hawed. "H'm—in the circumstances, Cheam, I don't know that I'm too pleased. Is it . . . er . . . seemly?"

Cheam checked a sudden impulse to be violently impatient. "It's for the Hospital, Rector. Surely that fact alone covers a multitude of objections. The sick—and the dying—"

Hopkins persisted. "So it may be. I scarcely need reminding, my dear Cheam. But it occurs to me that there are other considerations. What about poor Vera Ferris? Wasn't she in the cast? On the occasion of the previous performance?"

Cheam grimaced at the Rector as the latter half-averted his face. "She was—but in only a small part. Certainly not one to worry about. Gosling says he can replace her without the slightest difficulty."

"Well then," said the Rector acidly, "if you and Gosling and the Cottage Hospital people have already settled the matter, as you certainly seem to have done between you, why bother to ask *my* permission? I confess, Cheam, that I'm just a little nettled. And I think most justifiably. After all—courtesy costs nothing."

Cheam resisted several acute temptations. But he turned and said: "Gosling couldn't get you last night. I understand he telephoned you twice during the evening but you were out on each occasion. So that you can scarcely accuse him of discourtesy—justifiably."

The Rector retreated in bad order. "I have no wish to discuss the matter any further, my dear Cheam. What's done cannot be undone. I see your point of view. Because—as is my invariable habit—I do my best to. You evidently cannot or will not see mine. If Gosling wants this show on behalf of the Hospital—by all means let him go ahead with the arrangements. I fear, however, that in the circumstances I shall be unable to see my way to be present. Not that that's of any consequence. That's my final word on the matter."

Cheam's eyes glinted angrily—but the Rector was looking the other way. Cheam rose to go.

"Very good, Rector. I'll let Gosling know. I'm sorry you feel as you do. Not my fault I assure you. I'm merely Gosling's messenger."

"My dear Cheam," began the Rector

Before he could say any more, the door-bell rang for the second time that morning. There seemed something ominous about the ringing. Curate and rector faced each other and listened. They heard Mrs. Hodgson's heavy footsteps on the way to the door. They heard voices at the front door—that of Mrs. Hodgson dominant. Then they heard the sound of Mrs. Hodgson coming away from the door. Yes—the Rector, listening intently, realized that she was on her way to the study. Mrs. Hodgson tapped on the study door.

"What is it, Mrs. Hodgson?" asked the Rev. Matthew Hopkins in something like a flutter of excitement.

"Gentleman to see you," announced the housekeeper gruffly.

"Er . . . who is it?"

"The one you were expecting, of course," returned Mrs. Hodgson. She handed the Rector a visiting-card.

"Dear me," squeaked the Rector—"er . . . show him in here, if you please, Mrs. Hodgson. No—don't go, my dear Cheam . . . you stay your ground . . . you can render . . . me your . . . er . . . support. Safety in numbers is proverbial. Despite what has also been said with regard to exodus."

4

Anthony Bathurst allowed Mrs. Hodgson to escort him to the Rector's study.

"You're to come this way," said the housekeeper en route, "the Rector says so himself—so it should be all right. But he's not alone—let me tell you—the curate's with him. Don't suppose you'll mind."

Anthony, in her wake, murmured appropriate conventionalities.

"Come in," he heard the Rector say when he reached the study door— and Mrs. Hodgson pushed it open for him to enter. He was conscious immediately of a certain hostility in the atmosphere. The Rector was very much on his dignity.

"Er . . . good morning . . . this is my curate . . . the Rev. Frank Cheam . . . er . . . Mr. . . . . I'm sorry . . . I scarcely took in your name . . . let me see . . . your card's here." The Rector held up the visiting-card and fumbled generally. "Bathurst. Anthony Bathurst."

"I'm sorry to trouble you, sir. Especially as you have Mr. Cheam with you." Anthony bowed to the curate. "Although I have, unhappily, excellent reason. For as you know I come 'clad in the armour of a righteous cause'." Anthony proceeded to amplify the reason behind his visit. "If either of you gentlemen can give me any help whatever in the matter of the deaths of these two poor girls," he concluded, "I shall be eternally grateful."

The Rector fluttered but Anthony thought that Cheam looked a trifle bored. The Rector came forward. He shrugged his shoulders and spread out his hands.

"What help *can* we give you?"

Anthony knew that it would have to be flattery. That there was no other way. "From many points of view, sir, you're the most important man in Wavering. As the Rector of the Parish. Who knows the families in the Parish as well as you do, *with the intelligence* that is yours? These two girls who have been so brutally murdered were members of your church. You knew their history, their upbringing, their interests, their personal circle . . . can you think of any detail in connexion with *either* of them that might assist the police to bring their killer to Justice? Sometimes, you know, the vital clue may be in a spoken word, in a gesture . . . in a trifle that may seem at its birth merely insignificant?"

Anthony, as he finished speaking, looked from the Rector to Cheam. It occurred to him, in the first sensibility of the glance as it were, that Cheam had grasped his meaning more clearly and more quickly than the Rector. Cheam looked across at Anthony and shook his head slightly.

"Although those two girls were connected with St. Simon's, we are as much in the dark as you people at Scotland Yard," he said. "If the Rector were able to help you in any way, he would do so at once. So would I. But there is nothing that we can tell you. Somewhere in Wavering there is a murderer. We know that—just as well as you know it. *Show us how* we can help you—and you won't find us hesitate. We'll do it like a shot. But if you don't indicate to us what it is exactly that you wish us to do . . . or to tell you . . . well—"

Cheam broke off suddenly and shrugged his shoulders. Anthony realized that he must grasp the nettle.

"Thank you," he replied, "perhaps I see your difficulties more clearly than you imagine. At least as plainly as you see mine. I'll try to justify my coming here. Mr. Cheam has just stated that somewhere in Wavering there sits a killer. That's only too unhappily true! Let's think of him as a malevolent spider. Two flies have already been lured into and are dead in his loathsome parlour. The time will come when he will begin to think of a third. He will not be content with two. That is almost certain. Killers of his type seldom are. I can almost say 'never are'. And it may be sooner than we think. Everyone of us . . . police and public alike . . . must do his or her best to prevent at all costs another life being taken. It is almost a sure thing that it will be a young life again . . . one that we can least afford to spare."

The Rector waved his arms. He endeavoured to convey an impression of his helplessness. "But . . . after all . . . what is there . . ." he started—and suddenly ceased lamely and ineffectually.

The curate stared into space, stepped a half pace forward and said, almost as lamely as his chief: "Yes . . . but you see . . . how it is . . . situated as we are . . . we can't . . . we aren't able—"

Cheam stopped suddenly and joined his Rector in abortive silence. Anthony thought that he understood.

"I know you'll co-operate," he said—"and many thanks for putting up with me as you have. We must all do what we can."

The whimsical thought came to him that he was almost indecently sharing their verbal gaucherie and their mental futility—that the two conditions must be infectious.

"Good morning, gentlemen," he added . . . "don't bother to come to the door with me, your housekeeper will no doubt see me out."

When he stood on the pavement outside the Rectory some moments later, he wiped his forehead with his handkerchief.

"There was but little," he murmured to himself, "but small as it was— it went a hell of a long way."

CHAPTER 8

1

O n his journey back from the Rectory, Anthony called at the police-station. He found Loder there and surprised the sergeant somewhat, with a sudden question.

"Sergeant Loder," he said . . . "you remember that little search-party of ours? That included Inspector Steadman and finished up on the allotments—by the old pavilion?"

Loder stared at him curiously. "You mean, Mr. Bathurst, when the bodies were brought to light? That time?"

Anthony nodded. "That's the idea, Sergeant. That's exactly what I do mean. You cleared the refuse from the top of the old bath—if you remember?"

"As though it was yesterday, Mr. Bathurst. But what are you after—may I ask?"

Anthony rubbed the ridge of his jaw. "I've been thinking about that refuse, Sergeant. It's been on my mind for some little time now. What was it comprised of—exactly? Do you know, Sergeant? More than once I've tried to remember what there actually was on the top of that bath. I can see you tearing at it now as you turned the stuff over. Let me have a shot at reconstruction. There were three broken bricks right at the top of everything. Then came the yellow basin—the second of Tidman's stolen basins—now what exactly was there after that—before you came to the bodies—can you remember, Sergeant Loder?"

Loder nodded confidently. "Pretty well, Mr. Bathurst. I doubt if I shall ever really forget that moment. There was an empty box—it had contained some form of breakfast cereal—an old watering-can, several pieces of filthy, worn-out sacking, a battered dust-bin lid, some broken wooden slats, a length of perished rubber—part of an old garden hose probably—bits of tank and rusted iron—two long pieces of wood, two old kettles, a number of worn-out electric-light bulbs, and a fairly large-sized piece of coconut matting—very torn and frayed at the edges. There may have been one or two other items of junk that I've missed out, but I think I've managed to remember the main contents. But what's your point, Mr. Bathurst? You've got me interested. Have I covered it or have I slipped up on anything?"

Anthony smiled and shook his head at the sergeant. "Slipped up? No. Not for a minute, Sergeant. Nothing against you at all. Just an idea or so playing hide-and-seek in my flibbertigibbet brain, that's all. I suppose that I'm right in assuming that those various articles that you just ran off so expertly are safely housed at Remsford by this time under the care of Inspector Steadman?"

To Anthony's surprise, Loder shook his head. "No, Mr. Bathurst. They're not at Remsford as it happens. I asked the inspector if he'd be taking them over to Remsford for further examination and he said 'yes'—but that he'd send for them later. Your Chief-Inspector MacMorran wanted to give them the once-over, which he did. I suppose that was why Steadman delayed about getting them to Remsford. Anyhow—I'm still awaiting those further instructions."

When he heard Loder's statement Anthony rubbed his hands. "Arising out of all that, Loder, the question resolves itself—where are they now?"

"They're here, sir. In the room at the back. I thought I'd already made that plain."

Anthony grinned at Loder. "I was just making sure, Sergeant, in case there was a shock waiting for me. Lead me to 'em, will you?"

"Come this way, Mr. Bathurst," said the Wavering sergeant.

2

"If you follow me, Mr. Bathurst," continued Sergeant Loder whistling through his teeth, "I'll take you through to the back room. The stuff you've been enquiring about is done up all by itself. I arranged it in accordance with the instructions given me by your Chief-Inspector MacMorran. And I know where to put my hand on it."

"O.K., Sergeant Loder, that's good news as far as I'm concerned."

Loder, still whistling, led Anthony to the room at the back of the police-station. From a large cupboard in the corner, he took a bundle done up in some sort of new sacking and put it on the floor. There were large stitches round the edge of the sacking. Anthony had seen similar-looking bundles before.

"There you are, Mr. Bathurst," said Loder, "there's the stuff you're after—like a ruddy Persian market. Talk about a pig in a poke! Shall I undo the sacking for you ? Then you can see for yourself what's in there."

Anthony smiled and nodded. "That's just what I'd like you to do, Sergeant."

Loder began to whistle again cheerfully as he took a knife from his pocket and bending down, cut the stitches that held the sacking together. Anthony watched the proceedings with interest. Loder then lifted the loose bundle on to a table and unrolled it in front of Anthony.

"There you are, Mr. Bathurst—there you are with your little lot. And it's a choice collection—I'll give you my word. Gladden the heart of any well-established tot-raker—'where there's moock there's money'."

Loder bent over the table and began to sort out the various articles. He placed them one by one on the surface of the table so that Anthony could see each one without any difficulty. Anthony came to the edge of the table and watched him as he separated them. Loder mumbled the details of an appalling inventory as he laid the pieces down. "Three ha'-pence the lot," he declared, when he reached the last article—"and if you ask me, ruddy dear at the price."

He surveyed the miscellaneous assortment of articles with his head cocked to one side. "Now which of that gaudy lot, Mr. Bathurst, would be the particular article which is engaging your special attention? The choice line in kettles or the—?"

Anthony smiled at the question and shook his head non-committally. "I just wanted to have a 'dekko' at the whole lot, Sergeant. To satisfy a stray sort of idea that's come to me."

"Well—you're having the 'dekko' you wanted. What about it—now it's here? Any real brain-waves?"

"Not sure yet! Don't rush me. I hate being rushed."

Anthony bent over the Loder collection and stared at the assortment intently. Suddenly he jerked his head towards the two longish wooden poles.

"Those two rounded pieces of wood, Sergeant—at the end of the table there—what do you make of them? Are they pieces of a pole—one pole—or what? What's your opinion of them?"

Loder picked up one of the wooden lengths and balanced it in his hand. Then he shook his head doubtfully. "I don't fancy they're pieces of a pole. The same pole that is. They don't feel like it to me."

"What are they then, if they aren't that?"

Loder ran his hands down them carefully. "Seem to me more like *handles* of something. The wood's smooth. As though it had been prepared for handling. Say—broom-handles. That's about the nearest I can get to placing them."

Anthony held out his hand for the two pieces. "Let's feel them, Sergeant. Let me get the weight of them."

He felt the two poles with his hands, as the Sergeant had, before weighing them in the palm of his right hand. "Maybe your idea's the right one, Sergeant, after all. I shouldn't be at all surprised. Now let me look at that piece of old matting that was near the bottom."

"Here it is," returned Loder, "it's pretty rough—I'm afraid you won't get much in the inspiration line out of that. Chief-Inspector MacMorran himself spent some time on that."

Anthony looked carefully at the coconut matting with its old and worn edges. "Thank you, Sergeant," he said eventually. "I think I've seen all I want to see. The antiques may now return to the cupboard."

"Well I'm blest," said Loder in mock ruefulness and running his hands through his hair, "not an offer for any one article! After all that display, too. I should never make my living as a junk merchant."

Anthony grinned at him as he turned away. "Singin' rags, bottles and bones," carolled Loder, as they made their way back.

Anthony stood in the charge-room for a few minutes, looking out of the window. Loder went to his desk and didn't bother him. He saw only too well that Anthony's mind was fully occupied with something of importance. Suddenly Anthony turned.

"Look here, Sergeant—do me a favour, will you?"

"What's that, Mr. Bathurst?"

"Get your Inspector Steadman at Remsford to arrange with the Chief to have that bundle of stuff out there dealt with by all the scientific processes—as soon as possible. Can't think myself why it's been left for so long."

Loder was quick to reply. "I can tell you, Mr. Bathurst. Because your Inspector MacMorran was of the opinion that everything there had only been used to fill up the bath—that none of them had anything to do with the murders. Chief-Inspector MacMorran went through them one by one and was convinced of it."

"He may be right," returned Anthony with a shrug of the shoulder, "but personally, I'm not so sure."

3

Anthony decided to walk back to the 'Nag's Head' after his conversation with Sergeant Loder. As he passed the St. Simon's Church hall and institute, he noticed a man come out of the building with a large white poster in his hands. This poster the man proceeded to affix to a notice-board which stood in the hall grounds. Anthony waited deliberately against the railings in order to see what the poster was all about. It was a home-made affair of coloured inks and had obviously not been turned out by a professional printer. It informed the public that repeat performances of the famous farce, *Nothing But the Truth*, would be given on the evenings of the 23rd and 24th of March in the St. Simon's Church hall by the St. Simon's Church Dramatic Society on behalf of the funds of the Wavering and District Cottage Hospital.

As Anthony read the announcement, Frank Cheam came out of the hall and spoke to the returning caretaker Luck, for it was he who had affixed the home-produced poster to the notice-board. When Cheam saw Anthony at the railings, he waved to him. Anthony waved back. He noticed Cheam turn away from the caretaker and come hurrying out towards him. The curate gestured in the direction of the notice-board.

"This is what I'd called to see the Rector about," he said cordially, "when you burst in on the conference. Can't afford to waste time, you know, with a show like this. Must get on with the publicity angle. Want every seat in the house taken to make anything like a profit." He smiled genially as he made the statement.

"Sorry I interrupted you this morning," said Anthony, "hope nothing went the wrong way—because."

Cheam smiled and shook his head. "Not at all, old chap. As a matter of fact I wasn't at all peeved you came in when you did. The wicket was getting just a wee bit sticky and your intervention came just at the right moment for me. Sometimes, you know, the Rector, well—how can I put it—the God of Moses was a jealous God—and He wasn't—and isn't—the only one. Do you get the idea?"

Anthony grinned and nodded. "Well enough, I think." He jerked his head towards the poster on the notice-board. "So you're putting on another couple of shows?"

"Not me. I'm only a humble figure in the background. Gosling's the man in charge. Though I did knock up that bill. There's one thing—it's in a good cause—you couldn't have a better. That's the side of it which appeals to me."

"I was thinking," said Anthony, "that perhaps people *might* give it the go-by rather—seeing the unhappy history of the original performance. That wouldn't be any good to you, would it?"

Cheam rubbed his snub nose with his finger as he considered Anthony's point. "I know what you mean—but I don't think so. For one thing, the audience for the new shows will come from an entirely new area. The Cottage Hospital people themselves have guaranteed that. And—if they hadn't—do you know, Bathurst, I believe the Wavering people will come along and support the show. Many of them again. You know better than I do what that strange mixture of curiosity and morbidity does for people. It's a dreadful thing to say, perhaps, but I shouldn't be surprised if the two murders associated with the Church, don't make it a case of come early to avoid the crush. In other words, Bathurst—house full."

Frank Cheam's blue eyes glinted with amusement. "You may be right, of course—" began Anthony.

The St. Simon's curate cut in with an interruption. "I'll tell you what, Bathurst, I've a proposition to make. You and your Scotland Yard inspector should come to the show. You really shouldn't miss it. That's an idea, isn't it? On one of the nights at least. Why don't you? You might land on something—you never know."

Bathurst thought over what Frank Cheam had said. There were certainly points about it. And, as the curate had suggested—something *might* stick out its nose.

"That certainly *is* an idea, Mr. Cheam," said Anthony. "You may have got something there. I'll have a word with my colleague, Andrew MacMorran, and see what he thinks of it."

"Good," said Cheam enthusiastically—"let me know what you decide and if you're coming, I'll see about getting you a couple of tickets. Don't leave it *too* late before you make up your minds—because the best seats invariably get snapped up before you can say 'Jack Robinson'."

"I'll bear your advice in mind," replied Anthony, "and many thanks for the offer."

"Pleasure," returned Cheam "and don't forget to let me know in good time."

4

Anthony conferred again with MacMorran at the 'Nag's Head' headquarters. They sat as usual, in the smoke-lounge after dinner. MacMorran was inclined to be a trifle despondent at the way things were going generally. His anticipations that the comparative smallness of Wavering would assist him to a speedy and successful solution of his problem, had been by no means fulfilled. Since dinner, he had been the reverse of talkative and Anthony knew instinctively just how MacMorran was feeling, and also *why* he was feeling like it. Some seconds had elapsed since the inspector had last spoken and he now sat staring gloomily into the fire. Anthony lit a cigarette and spoke through the first puffs of smoke.

"This morning, Andrew, I called on the Church. I went to the Rectory. In a way, I suppose, I was lucky."

MacMorran was stung into immediate reply. "Oh—in what way? Takes a bit of believin'."

More deliberate enticement from Anthony. "Well—I was shown into the Rector and his curate. They were closeted together. The Rector's name is Matthew Hopkins. The curate's is Frank Cheam."

"You *were* lucky—I must say."

"Yes—wasn't I? Turned out nice for me, didn't it?" This from Anthony, with bland insouciance. He paused—for MacMorran to gulp again at the bait. MacMorran gulped.

"Well—what are they like? A couple of murderers? Is *that* what you're waitin' to tell me?"

Anthony laughed. "Oh—they didn't seem too bad. Considering the spot of bother they've had. But the point is this—something arose out of the visit. I'll tell you what it was."

"That's nice of you. What was it?"

"I ran full tilt into the information that the St. Simon's Church Dramatic Society is putting on a couple of repeat performances—same play as they previously produced."

MacMorran, in the act of refilling his pipe, paused. "That's a bit startling, isn't it? Seeing what happened the time before? What's the big idea?"

"Special effort on behalf of the Wavering Cottage Hospital."

MacMorran grunted. "If you want my opinion—not exactly in the best taste. Remembering the little girl—Ferris."

"It's the cause, Andrew. So I am informed. The cause before the taste. 'It is the cause, it is the cause, my soul. Let me not name it to you, you chaste stars! It is the cause. Yet I'll not shed her blood—' "

Anthony stopped abruptly. MacMorran regarded him curiously.

"What was that? Shakespeare? Sounded like it to me."

Anthony nodded. "Did it ring a bell, Andrew? It rang some sort of a bell with me. Yet I'll not shed her blood—funny that! What the hell am I trying to remember?"

MacMorran's glance was still full of suspicion. "Well—what are you? What's the main point about this Dramatic Society business?"

"Well—I've been thinking, Andrew. On these lines. Let me illustrate. Don't interrupt. Wait till I've finished. Supposing my original theory's right? That the sight of Barbara Marsden's yellow frock as worn by Vera Ferris on the evening that the play was first performed, put murder into the killer's mind, for the *second* time? Well listen, Andrew—if the murderer saw the frock worn yet *again*, by a *third* girl—"

MacMorran drew in a sharp intake of breath—"Eh—man—what is it that you're thinking? What is it that you're plannin'? To use a third girl as something like a decoy?"

"Yes, Andrew. I confess that I *was* thinking somewhat on those lines."

MacMorran grunted again. "H'm. I don't know that I like it. Wants verra' careful handlin'."

"It does, Andrew. Very careful. I agree with you all along the line. But I think it has points."

"It would mean takin' certain people into our confidence. I don't like that part of it."

"Need it?"

"Can't see it otherwise. Can you?"

"Yes. I think I can. As I'd plan it, only you and I and the girl would be in the know. She'd have to be sworn to secrecy, of course."

"She'd be something else, too," said MacMorran bluntly, "if I know anything, she'd be ruddy well scared out of her ruddy life. I should be if I walked in her shoes. Doubt if we'd get a girl to accept the arrangement."

Anthony was silent for a moment or so. MacMorran realized it and went on to strengthen his point. "Who is the girl? Do you know that?"

Anthony shook his head. "No. That will be ascertained in a day or two."

"When's the first of these shows for the Hospital?"

"The two performances are booked for March twenty-third and twenty-fourth. There's plenty of time to put the plan into action."

"It's the snags that worry me," mumbled MacMorran—"far too many for my liking."

"I think we can get over them, Andrew. I don't see any reason why we shouldn't." Anthony spoke slowly. MacMorran knew from the tone of his voice that he intended business.

"I don't like dangling young girls in front of murderers"—said the inspector forcibly—"fine position I'd be in if things went wrong. I'd have had it—no two opinions about that."

"No reason why things *should* go wrong. If we were careful and matters were well organized. On the other hand, in my opinion, you'd probably trap your man. And, at the moment, I'll be perfectly candid and say I don't see any *other* way of trapping him. To say nothing of the point that quite probably he'll pull off another murder in the very near future. With us here. Right under our noses, as it were. Which would neither increase your popularity, Andrew, with the Chief Constable, nor enhance your reputation at H.Q. In fact—when I think of what the Commissioner would say—" Anthony paused.

MacMorran swore. He swore violently. For he had recognized the symptoms. He knew without any doubt whatever, that unless he were very obdurate he'd find himself—

Anthony was talking again. "As I'd plan it, Andrew, only the girl, you and I and Steadman, would know what was cooking. Plus the essential bodyguard—of course. But they'd simply act in that capacity, carry out their instructions to the letter—and nothing more. As I see things, the girl could be under our complete and absolute protection *all the time*."

MacMorran was defensive. "And how do you define 'all the time'? From when to what other when?"

"Easy enough. From the moment she wore the yellow frock—until."

MacMorran knitted his brows. "Ay—that's all verra well but until when?"

"Until—the doings. Until it was settled either way. If he came for the bait—we spring the trap. If he disdained it—called our bluff if you prefer me to put it that way—well—there's no harm done, we're no worse off, and to-morrow is also a day."

MacMorran repeated himself. "Ay that's all very well! Very comfortable! Very comfortable—indeed. But there's another possibility you've omitted to mention. And I'll tell it to you. Supposing he comes for the ruddy bait—*and gets away with it*? That's my headache."

"My dear Andrew, are we so hopelessly incompetent—surely we could provide adequate protection all through the piece? For a solid week, if need be? If we can't, well then, we're a pair of prize cissies who've no business whatever to be where we are and there's no point whatever in any further discussion."

MacMorran rubbed the point of his jaw. "And let me point out to you there's the girl as well. To say nothing of Mum and Dad. I doubt very much whether—" he broke off and shook his head gloomily. Anthony held up his hand.

"Just a minute, Andrew. You wait. I've got another idea. Why should the girl know everything? Why tell her of the likelihood of any danger?"

"Ah—that sounds considerably better to my way of thinking. How do you mean—tell me exactly."

"Why—simply induce her to wear the yellow frock in the play. Don't tell her any more. Except perhaps to assure her in a casual sort of manner that no harm shall come to her. No need then for her to worry—or her parents. Mum and Dad, in your words, need not be a penny the wiser."

MacMorran began to nod his head. "Now—that *is* an idea. That's far more attractive to me. I don't mind considering it in those terms. But not the other, my boy—not the other. Not on your life. Too risky. By far."

He bent forward and knocked the burnt tobacco from his pipe. "We must get down to the blue-print of this. Work it out in detail so that I can study it from all the angles. First of all—" The inspector felt in his pockets for pencil and paper. As he did so, a thought seemed to strike him. "I say," he said, "this is going to be a bit awkward, isn't it? Much more awkward than you first seemed to think. If we're to spring the trap properly. Strictly speaking—there are certain people who *must* co-operate—if we're to—"

Anthony shook his head gravely. "No, Andrew. I'm sorry—but that's the very last thing we can do. We *can't* co-operate. We *dare not*. To do so would irrevocably destroy the position that we shall build up. It's just asking for trouble. All our work might be wasted."

"I quite see that," agreed MacMorran, "but what about Mr.—"

Anthony cut in before MacMorran could say the name. "No. Not even him, Andrew."

MacMorran stared incredulously. Anthony grinned at him through a haze of cigarette smoke. The inspector's eyebrows went up.

CHAPTER 9

1

Anthony was troubled. The trouble arose on two counts. Each of the counts was connected with the yellow frock of Barbara Marsden. The first was a plain issue. Resolved—it was this. If Anthony's own theory of the murders *were* the correct one, that the second murder had been inspired by the sight of the yellow frock worn by another young girl, why had the murderer *waited a week* before killing Vera Ferris, the girl who had worn the yellow frock on the second occasion? That is to say, in essential terms, why hadn't he killed the girl *in the frock* and not waited until she was wearing something entirely different? That was the first of Anthony's lanes of trouble. For the reason that it bit hard and effectively into the tissue of his theory.

The second was not so elementary an issue, although it was completely to do with himself. Resolved—it added up to this. Why had he forgotten the point of the first count until now? Why had the murderer delayed the kill, delayed it until the very reason for it had passed, and why had *he*, Anthony Bathurst, missed such a screamingly vital point until the present moment? Various reasons floated along and called upon him as it were, but he would have none of them even though they were decked in attractive garb.

He would have none of them because none was sufficiently attractive. So they were received, examined and one by one dismissed. It seemed to him as he sat in his bedroom at the 'Nag's Head' and thought on these things, that it was like interviewing a procession of clients . . . seekers after a situation . . . a situation which was in his hands to fill . . . and none of the eager applicants was found fit and proper . . . with the abortive result that the post was still vacant. Deep was the pit of Anthony's annoyance and wide the well of his self-criticism. For one thing, there was a grave weakness about his theory and the weakness was now thoroughly exposed. Something would have to be done about it, for otherwise Anthony realized that his theory-edifice must be ill-foundationed. Good order must be the foundation of all good things and the same holds true in reverse.

Suddenly, Anthony saw clearly what he must do. What it was imperative he should do next. It might well be, he reasoned to himself, that out of the visit he was proposing to take, would shine forth the light—that light which, so far, had been denied to him. He must call at the home of the parents of Vera Ferris.

2

Anthony came to the house of James Ferris in Spencer Street, Wavering. He had chosen the time of early evening for the visit—and he had chosen well, for James Ferris was at home. He had gone forth to his work and to his labour, until the evening. Although the evening air was chilly and unfriendly Ferris was in his shirt-sleeves when he opened the door to Anthony's knock. He was a short, stocky, heavy-shouldered man with plump cheeks and dark eyes and there was a pipe in his mouth. The pipe was of similar type to himself. Anthony introduced himself immediately and wasted no time over preliminaries. Ferris, with face hard and set, listened, and nodded.

"Come in," he said.

Anthony judged that he was by habit, a man of few words. He followed Ferris into the house as he thanked him for the invitation. It was small—of cottage property type.

"The missus is out," said Ferris bluntly—"do you mind the kitchen? It's not very big, I'm afraid—but there's a fire—and we shall have it to ourselves."

"Anywhere, Mr. Ferris, will suit me. And the prospect of a fire—I assure you I shan't complain of that."

"Sit down, sir." Ferris gestured towards a large wooden arm-chair at the side of the hearth.

Anthony seated himself. He began to talk. He knew only too well that he was faced with a difficult task. To his relief and satisfaction, however, Ferris was a good and intelligent listener.

"My poor girl's gone," said the latter eventually, "and no human power can bring her back. The missus and me—well—we've got to take it.

But I've listened carefully to what you've said and if I can help you, sir, I will. And if you want to ask me any questions—*do* so. There's no call for you to hesitate. If anything I can do—by answering questions—will help to save the life of some other feller's daughter—or wife—or sister—well then, sir, I'm prepared to do it."

Jim Ferris, having delivered himself of what was probably the longest speech he had ever made, spat adroitly and accurately into the fire and then sat well back in his chair. Anthony thanked him.

"I appreciate that, Mr. Ferris. And it's extremely good of you. I *should* like to ask you one or two questions because I think it's possible you may be able to help me a lot. The principal question you may find rather surprising."

"Let's have it," returned Jim Ferris sturdily.

"Here it is then. Between the night of the Dramatic Society's performance—and the night she was killed—did Vera make any complaint with regard to anything that had happened to her? Either to you or to Mrs. Ferris? Think carefully—please."

"I don't have to think," replied Ferris sturdily," because the answer's 'no'. I should ha' been bound to have heard of it if it had been the other way. No complaints such as you mention ever came from our Vera." Ferris puffed stolidly at his short pipe. He noticed the expression on Anthony's face. "Reckon I've disappointed you, sir. With that answer of mine. Reckon you were expectin' something different. Still there it is—that's the truth."

Anthony nodded. "I *had* hoped for something different—I'll admit. Still—you know—. Now tell me this—was she a communicative girl? Was she one to discuss things with you or her mother? Or did she keep 'em pretty much to herself? Girls are so different—some do one thing—some the other. Especially in their present generation."

Ferris thought over the question before he answered. Anthony could almost see him thinking. Eventually, Jim Ferris began to speak.

"Your questions aren't too easy to answer, sir. Not by any manner of means. In the first place, Vera was our only child. After she was born, my missus was poorly for a long time and at last the doctors said she couldn't 'ave any more. Now in my opinion—only children are a bit funny—if you know what I mean. They're not so easy to sum up as the others. They do a rare lot of things on their own. They seem to be flung back on their own resources. Our Vera was a bit that way inclined. And because of it, I wouldn't say she told either me or her mother very much. Either of what she did—or of what she was thinkin'. But I'll say this—she wrote a lot—always writin' letters she was. Different from me—I can tell you! Now I'm the sort of chap who'll put off writin' a letter as long as I darn well dare. Answer letters on the dot, she would." Jim Ferris shook his head. "No," he repeated—"I wouldn't say she told us much. Kept things to herself—she did."

Anthony took in what Ferris had told him. Up to the moment things certainly hadn't gone his way. The very matter he had come here in the hope of grasping, seemed to be eluding him. If Vera Ferris had been consistently a girl of the type her father had just described, it would mean almost certainly that Anthony would go empty away from this house in Spencer Street. On the other hand, had she been a girl whose habit it was to—.

Anthony slashed suddenly at the winding ribbon of his thoughts and turned impulsively to Ferris.

"Your daughter, Mr. Ferris, she wrote a lot, you say? Always liked putting pen to paper."

Ferris nodded with sturdy confidence. "Always, sir. Ever since she was a tiny slip of a girl, just been taught to read and write, she'd always wanted a pencil and paper. But why, sir? What are you after now?"

"Why—I've been thinking, Mr. Ferris. And an idea has come to me. Did Vera keep a diary? Can you answer me that?"

Ferris smiled for the first time since Anthony had been there—a slow, faint, sad, lingering sort of smile. "She did, sir. I'll say she did. She's kept a diary for years now—started it soon after she went to school. Many's the time her mother and me—have chaffed her about it. You know—pulled her leg about the stuff she was writin' down in it. Talk about solemn! I should say—bein' exact about it—that our Vera kept a diary from the time she was about seven years of age." Ferris rubbed the back of his head and chuckled. "Funny you should have asked me that."

Anthony felt a thrill of excitement. Had his luck changed at last? "And she'd kept it up—you say—all the time? And recently?"

The chuckle was short-lived and the smile had gone now. Jim Ferris's face was back to its normal gravity. He took his pipe from his mouth and nodded.

"As far as I know, sir—right up to the very last. Right up to the very day—as you might say."

Ferris turned away quickly and looked stonily out of the window. Anthony was patient and waited for him. Some seconds passed. At last

Ferris turned back again and Anthony said to him quietly: "Any idea where that diary is now, Mr. Ferris ? Could you put your hand on it, do you think, without much trouble?"

"I could—but—" Ferris was hesitant.

"What is it?" asked Anthony.

Ferris became sturdily and stolidly independent. "Well—look here, sir—I don't fancy my girl's private diary bein' handed out to the police, as you might say. There's something about the idea which upsets me. She's dead—I'd like her memory and everything else about her to be respected—and I shouldn't at all care for—"

Anthony interrupted him. "Mr. Ferris—nobody could agree with you more than I do with regard to that. But the diary need not go out of your own hands. If you don't want me to look at it—I understand perfectly. Were I in your place I should feel much as you do. All I ask you to do for me is this. Get Vera's diary—you say you know where it is. You can find it without any trouble?"

Ferris nodded. "It's in her bedroom. With the rest of her things which we've kept. The missus has put 'em all together."

"Get it then, Mr. Ferris, and bring it down here. Then I'll tell you what to do."

Ferris seemed still to hesitate. It was clear that the idea was distasteful to him.

"We may," continued Anthony, "save another girl's life. Another decent chap's daughter . . . or wife . . . as you said yourself . . . not so very long ago."

Jim Ferris turned on his heel and Anthony could hear him going upstairs.

3

Ferris was away from the kitchen much longer than Anthony had anticipated. No sound had come from the upstairs rooms and as many as nine minutes elapsed before Jim Ferris came back to the kitchen. He had come down the staircase almost silently. When he re-entered the kitchen, Anthony saw that he carried a small pocket-diary in his right hand. The diary was closed. Ferris sat down and looked across the kitchen at Anthony.

"Now, sir," he said, "tell me please. Before I go any further, I'd like to know where I am. What is it exactly, that you want me to do?"

"Turn up," said Anthony, "the space for the fifteenth of February."

Ferris stared at him curiously. "Why—the fifteenth of February?"

"Why—that was the evening of the dramatic performance. Your daughter took part in it. That's the evening in which I'm particularly interested."

Ferris shook his head as though he failed to understand. "But that wasn't the evening when she was—"

"I know it wasn't. We'll come to that later."

Anthony was amazed at the man's strange lack of perception. Ferris nodded slowly to himself, carefully put on a pair of spectacles, and opened the diary. Anthony began to speak to him again—quickly.

"Read it to yourself first, Mr. Ferris—*whatever* you find written there. You see—it may be private. If so—particularly so, I mean—I don't need to hear it. And you can forget what you read. But *you* read it first."

Ferris nodded again and slowly turned the pages of the little dark green book. Anthony noticed him stop and bend down a little to read. Anthony saw him frown.

"Well?" said Anthony, "does the dead hand speak? *Is* there anything there—for me?"

Ferris answered slowly and with some degree of emotion. "Yes—I think there is. I'll read it to you."

Anthony could see from the expression on Ferris's face that he was both puzzled and disturbed by what he had read. The man hesitated for quite a considerable time. He looked up from the diary to Anthony almost as though he were questioning something.

"This is written," he explained, "in the space marked the fifteenth of February. But you must understand, sir, that there isn't a lot of space for each day—and the writing's squeezed up rather. But it's Vera's writing all right—and it's done in pencil—I mean it's rather faint as you might say. Anyhow, I'll read it to you."

"That's the idea," said Anthony.

Ferris began to read—slowly—and far from efficiently. This is what Anthony was able to make of what he heard.

"*Nothing But the Truth* performance . . . good show on the whole . . . house packed . . . self very good (so E. G. said) after the curtain. B. M. frock sensation . . . Police and the Wilkes woman (what a cow). On the way home feel certain was followed by beast of a man . . . ran hard . . . succeeded in getting away from him . . . query 'Green Circle' driver or conductor . . . thought of B. M. and felt terrible . . . dare not tell Dad or Mum . . . there'd be hell to pay . . . they'll stop me belonging to Dramatic Society . . . little V. must keep her mouth shut and be careful—that's all."

Ferris stopped his reading. His expressionless voice ceased and he sat, his fingers still clasping the diary, gazing ahead of him with lack-lustre eyes.

"So she had been in danger before," he said, "and she didn't dare tell us because she thought I'd ha' kept her indoors." Then bitterness came into his voice. "Would to God she had," he continued—"she'd ha' been alive now—she wouldn't ha' paid so dearly for her foolishness."

Anthony waited for him as he had waited previously. Until Ferris turned to him again.

"Well, sir, your idea was a good one. You've heard me read out what my girl wrote down."

"Yes . . . yes. Now please read on, Mr. Ferris—read on for the days that followed that entry. See if she's made any further—"

Ferris put the diary into Anthony's hand. "You read it, sir. I'd rather it was that way. Read it for yourself. I'll be content to trust you with it."

Anthony thanked him and read on. From the 16th of February onwards. But there was no mention of Vera Ferris having suffered any further trouble or unpleasantness and there was no additional reference to the incident of the 15th February. The entries in the diary, subsequent to that date, were as normal and indeed as trivial as those to be found in hundreds of diaries kept by people similar to Vera Ferris. Eventually he closed the little book and gave it back to Jim Ferris.

"Thank you, Mr. Ferris. There doesn't seem to be any more. The only entry that interests me is the one that you read out to me. Now I'm going to ask you to help me once again."

"Guessed it 'ud come to that," said Ferris. His face was set and his tone hard and grim.

"When you read that to me—what did you understand," queried Anthony, "by the reference to 'Green Circle'?"

"Why—the 'Green Circle' buses, of course. It's a local bus and coach service. Runs all round this part of the country. As far as Norland—through Remsford and Wolsey and Chippenchurch. There's a company garage here in Wavering. Not far from the church and the company's got an office as well just off the High Street."

"Not far from the church," repeated Anthony—"that means then, not far also from the old hockey-field allotments."

Ferris nodded. "That's quite right, sir. The same thought struck me."

"Tell me then, exactly, what do you understand from the entry in the diary?"

Ferris was quick to reply. "That's easy, sir. On the night of the play-acting, Vera was followed by a man—between here and the institute. It would have been on her way home. He frightened her . . . she remembered what had happened to Marsden's girl . . . but she was too quick for the chap and got away. He was in some sort of uniform, I should say, which she took to be 'Green Circle'. That's why she says the chap was either a driver or a conductor. They wear a light green sort of uniform . . . the 'Green Circle' chaps with a peaked cap."

Anthony nodded. "I remember—I've seen them. But I didn't know that the company had a garage so close to the church."

Anthony rose from the arm-chair. "Yes, Mr. Ferris. I add it up much in the same way as you do. And it seems to me we've got somewhere at last. Time will tell. It's on the cards I may come here to see you again."

"In that case, sir," replied Jim Ferris, "I'm sure you'll be very welcome—I'd like you to meet the wife."

CHAPTER 10

1

Anthony went back to the 'Nag's Head' and tossed the 'Green Circle' into MacMorran's lap. He supplied him with full details of the significant entry in Vera Ferris's diary.

"There you are, Andrew," he said, as he concluded his story. "You've heard of a vicious circle—there's another one for you—to keep it company. Green's proverbially unlucky. You can't say you haven't a springboard now."

When he heard the news Anthony had brought him, MacMorran was critical. His language approximated the unparliamentary (old style).

"Why in the name of ruddy thunder didn't the girl tell her people? It might have saved her own life and us a month of running about. We'll go down to that 'Green Circle' office first thing to-morrow morning. That O.K. with you?"

Anthony made no actual reply to the direct question. "I'm wondering, Andrew," he said, rather dubiously, "how much Vera Ferris could have seen of the man who followed her. To be able to see, I mean, what his uniform was like. The time of the incident I should say, would be somewhere between eleven o'clock and midnight."

"Might have been an exceedingly light night."

"Still—light green as a colour—at night—worn by somebody from whom you're running away—shouldn't imagine it would be too—" Anthony broke off suddenly.

"There's a big calendar in the saloon bar. I remember seeing it there. I'm going to have a 'dekko' at it. May tell me something."

He slid quickly out of the room and was back again almost before MacMorran had appreciated his absence.

"There *wasn't* plenty of light, Andrew. Far from it, in fact. The moon was in its first quarter."

MacMorran grunted at the receipt of the news. "May be something in what you say."

Anthony took possession of his chair again. "Yes. Can't altogether ignore it. If the distance weren't too great, Vera *might* have spotted a coloured uniform. On the other hand—"

He sat quite still in the arm-chair, thinking hard. When, after a time, he began to fidget, MacMorran knew that something was worrying him.

"So difficult to move, Andrew," he said eventually, "in a place like this without showing your hand to somebody who might be the very last person in the world who should see it. That's going to be our worst headache. One needs the most subtle combination of woman's instinct and man's intuition."

MacMorran grunted again. "Much the same thing—if you ask me."

"I'm not—and they're not." Anthony grinned as he spoke. The thrust seemed to have restored his equanimity.

"Well—you know what I mean," returned the Inspector.

"And you know, too, what I mean, Andrew. That we can't be anything like certain whom we can trust and whom we can't."

"Can we ever? In cases of this kind."

Anthony smiled. "There *have* been occasions in the past when we've known a little more than we know now. You're aware of that just as much as I am."

A further period of silence ensued. Again it was Anthony who broke it. "Another strange thing, Andrew. Just occurred to me. Doesn't do my theory any good either . . . unless. . . . Let's suppose this 'Green Circle' shadower of the Ferris diary *is* the bloke we're after. For the two murders. As far as we're aware—he first follows Vera Ferris on the evening of the fifteenth of February—that is to say on the evening of the show. *If* the reason he follows her—as I've been thinking ever since I first formed the theory—is because she's worn the first murdered girl's yellow frock—*he must have been present in the hall—at the show*. Because that's the only place where he could have seen Vera Ferris *wearing* the blasted frock! She didn't go home in it—that we do know. From the action Loder took in conjunction with the Wilkes woman. See where it's leading us to, Andrew?"

MacMorran showed unmistakable signs of incipient excitement. "Ay! Well enough! It means the murderer must have been at the show! *In his 'Green Circle' uniform!*"

Anthony lit a cigarette and spoke through the smoke. "Certainly looks like it, Andrew. Easy to check. That's one thing. Like looking for a haystack round a needle. But—and don't forget this—it all depends on my yellow frock idea. If I'm proved wrong with regard to that—" Anthony shrugged his shoulders.

"Wait a minute." MacMorran spoke slowly. "How long would there have been between the fall of the curtain and Vera Ferris walking home? There was the Loder-Wilkes interlude—don't forget. Our man *might* have had time to pop home and change his clothes if he didn't live too far from the hall."

Anthony nodded.

"That's possible, Andrew, I admit—but I don't think I should regard it as likely."

"Even then," went on MacMorran, "it's still a comparatively simple matter. All we have to do is to find out the names of the 'Green Circle' staff who live near St. Simon's Church."

"Hold hard, Andrew. Why *should* he?"

"Why should he what?"

"Why should he rush home and dress himself in such a manner as to call attention to himself? Eh—Andrew ? There's something wrong there—as I see it. Do you know, I'm beginning to think we're on to something. Just a minute while I work this one out."

"I'll tell you something else that's suggested itself to me," said MacMorran, "and that's this. The night of the dramatic performance—the night we're discussing—you say the moon was in its first quarter. Am I right?"

"Yes. That's right. I checked it on the calendar that's hanging in the saloon bar. Don't you remember? I went out there to do it. There was a new moon on the eighth."

"Right! Well—Vera Ferris dodged him that night. That's something we know. From the diary. But a week later—when you had the moon at the full and you would think there was much less chance of the killer taking her by surprise because she could *see* him better—he gets her! That puzzles me rather. I just don't get it."

Anthony shook his head. "Depends, Andrew. So difficult to gauge. More than one factor. How did he strike? Where did he strike? How did he stalk? Was there any lure? Was there any lure—bait—enticement that she fell for?"

"What enticement could there be? To a girl of that type?"

Anthony shrugged his shoulders at the question. "How can one say? Without knowing so many facts. *Quot virgines, tot blanditiæ.*"

The inspector frowned. "Meaning?"

"To every maiden—her own temptation. Or good enough." Anthony suddenly changed his tone. "Do you know, Andrew—you've caused me very furiously to think."

"Glad I'm of some ruddy use," smiled MacMorran—"although, of course, with no pretensions to being a detective."

Anthony furrowed his brows. "How come, Andrew? I don't get that."

"How can I be?" responded the inspector, "seeing I'm neither alcoholic nor incontinent. I can see you don't read the best fiction."

2

Anthony sat up that evening for some time after MacMorran had sought the seclusion that the bedroom granted. He knew that the time had come for one of his exercises in intensive thought, for the main reason that there were several matters causing him grave concern. He began to think of the diary of Vera Ferris. The diary which Vera Ferris's father had read from and then taken back to the girl's bedroom.

Anthony fished his fountain-pen from his pocket and on the back of an old envelope, he wrote, from memory, the actual words which Vera Ferris had used in her diary, to describe the incidents which had taken place after the performance of the 15th of February. He reproduced them verbatim. Anthony then read them through carefully three times. Was there anything that Vera Ferris had written in that diary which contained *more* than he had at first read into it? Could he read anything into them that was not plain on the face of things? Anthony read the words over once again—and then referred suddenly to his own diary. In size and shape it was a little larger than Vera's. Anthony contrasted the two books and then made certain comparisons. He was ready to admit that what Andrew MacMorran had said earlier in the evening had made a big impression on him. Anthony then referred to different portions of his own diary. He went assiduously through the ninety or so days devoted to the first three months of the year. January, February, and March.

Then suddenly he remembered something and checked himself. MacMorran would be following up the 'Green Circle' clue in the coming morning. Certainly at the offices of the Company and perhaps at the Garage as well. Much would depend on how that enquiry went. Anthony began to think things out again. If the theory, with which he had started seriously to toy, were of any worth, the waters of the crimes were deep indeed. He knew beyond the shadow of a doubt that neither he nor MacMorran could afford to take the slightest risk. And yet—Anthony felt convinced 'that the play's the thing'. If he *could* contrive to deal the cards of the play on the evening of the 23rd of March—as he fully intended to do by hook or by crook—then he dared not leave the slightest loop-hole or leakage. Which meant—amongst other things—that the girl who took the part originally played by Vera Ferris could on no account be . . . .

Anthony paused again. There was Sergeant Loder—of course. With his co-operation, the affair which Anthony was beginning to envisage *might* be engineered with regard to the trimmings. But even with this difficulty successfully disposed of, there still remained the main problem. The attitude of the girl herself. To surmount that was going to be far from easy. In fact, the more Anthony looked at it, the less he liked it and the lesss confident he began to feel about overcoming it. It was absolutely impracticable—he was convinced of this—to *contemplate* possible confederacy from anybody within the inner circle of St. Simon's. More than that even—it was suicidal! Which was almost tantamount to admitting that successful confederacy was impossible. Always with the exception of Loder. And Loder's superiors. Loder was necessary from more than one point of view. There was the yellow frock itself. It must be obtained from Steadman, and the best way in all probability would be via Loder. If Loder could be persuaded to attempt to persuade Steadman—it was precisely at that moment that Anthony had his brain-wave.

The girl to wear the yellow frock for the third time in the St. Simon's Church Hall need not be a member of the Dramatic Society's cast! She need not take any part in the play. As long as she wore the frock, and so conspicuously that she could be seen constantly and continuously by all the members of the audience . . . and others . . . Anthony felt that the conditions which he desired would be fulfilled. The more he thought of this new idea, the more his heart warmed to it. It held advantages on almost every count. Instead of the girl being chosen for him by Edmund Gosling, he could do the choosing himself! And instead of the girl appearing in the dramatic performance for two or three odd moments—Anthony remembered that Vera Ferris's part in the play had been but a minor one—she could be on view in the hall for the entire audience to see for long periods of time. In other words, she could be a programme-seller! She could go from row to row, from seat to seat, in Barbara Marsden's yellow frock . . . and the murderer could gaze his fill at her! So much so, that—

Anthony almost chuckled at the thought. Because he knew that if Steadman and Loder provided the frock, he would be able to supply the girl to wear it. She would be Helen Repton of New Scotland Yard. The girl who had worked with him and MacMorran in the past. The girl who had never let them down!

3

Anthony broke the news of his decision to MacMorran at breakfast on the following morning. The inspector, at the time, was looking dubiously into the bowels of an egg from which he had just removed the top shell.

"It may interest you to know, Andrew," said Anthony, "that I sat up rather late last night while you were engaged in 'enticing the dewy-feathered sleep'. I sat down here wrestling with principalities, powers, and our own little problem. Actually, I was here long after 'the iron tongue of midnight had tolled twelve, until 'twas almost fairy-time'."

"This egg," said MacMorran, "if you ask me—"

"Don't eat the demnition egg, Andrew! Mortify the flesh. Discard it for the homely honey on its bed of toothsome toast. Also—please listen to me."

MacMorran pushed away the offensive egg and reached for the honey-jar. "What is it you want to say?"

"This, Andrew. That early this morning, ere I found my bed, I sat down here and came to a decision. In the matter of the yellow frock of Barbara Marsden and who shall be the next to wear it."

MacMorran grunted impatiently. "I thought that we'd agreed that it must be the girl who is chosen to understudy—"

Anthony waved away the point MacMorran was about to make. "So we may have. But I had a brain-wave, Andrew, and that's all over. I've thought better of it. My new idea has everything to recommend it. As you'll soon see for yourself. It will be *our* girl, Andrew, not *theirs*, who'll 'come unto that yellow frock'! Think of the advantages that must accrue."

MacMorran stared at Anthony across the breakfast-table. The stare was almost a frown. He was plainly puzzled.

"Our girl? Who the heck's our girl when she's at home? If you ask me, you'll have a long way to go before you'll persuade any girl to—" The inspector stopped midway in his sentence and spread honey on his toast. He saw that Anthony was shaking his head.

"By 'our girl'," said Anthony, "I *mean* our girl, as it happens. I don't refer to another girl from the St. Simon's Dramatic Society selected by the producer, Gosling, to play the part that Vera Ferris played. That's just what I don't mean. No—Andrew, I'm thinking of somebody in terms of the 'Yard'. Somebody 'known' as opposed to 'unknown'. What about Helen Repton, for instance?"

MacMorran whistled with surprise as Anthony flicked the name at him.

"Could be worked all right, Andrew—couldn't it?"

MacMorran shrugged his shoulders. "No difficulty about working it—but do you think the lassie would care about the job? I wouldn't describe it as her usual cup of tea."

"Don't be wet, Andrew. You know Miss Repton as well as I do. Has she ever let us down on a job yet? Has she ever shown the slightest disinclination towards a job that we've put into her lap? *Any*? You know what the answer is to those two questions, you old scoundrel!"

MacMorran made no answer. For the eminently sound reason that he knew Anthony was right. He pretended to be turning the matter over in his mind.

"All right," he said eventually, "I'll put it up to her—if that's what you're wanting. And I wouldn't be surprised if she says 'Yes, Inspector MacMorran' when all the time what she's really meaning to say is 'Yes, Mr. Bathurst, your coat is so warm'."

Anthony grinned at the thrust. "I'll tell you what to do, Andrew. 'Phone the 'Yard' directly after breakfast. Get on to her sectional chief and get her permission for Helen Repton to come straight down here. Special duty. Then we can meet her at the station, bring her along here and discuss everything with her. What's already happened, what we've discovered since we came here and our intended plan of campaign."

MacMorran nodded. "I was thinkin' much on the same lines myself. I don't think we can do better than that. I can see what you're after—you want something like a closed shop. Ah well—I can't find it in my heart to disagree with you."

Anthony nodded back. "Yes—and with the exception of Sergeant Loder, a 'closed shop' is what we'll get doing it this way."

"Loder?" MacMorran spoke queryingly.

"Yes. The frock. I don't see quite how we can—"

MacMorran waved away Anthony's doubt with a pontifical hand. "Leave all that to me. Who the heck's Loder? *Scrub* Loder."

CHAPTER 11

1

J ust over an hour later, MacMorran sought Anthony in the smoke-room. "That's all fixed," he said. "I've been on to the 'Yard' as we arranged at breakfast. The Repton girl will report to me here, to-morrow morning. She'll be on the eleven-forty-four train from Liverpool Street."

"Good. Any trouble?"

MacMorran grinned. "None that I wasn't able to dispose of. I had to speak pretty straight once or twice—but after a time it was more or less plain sailing. They could see I meant business. All the same—that woman who's in charge there—she's a tough nut and no mistake. Her way's the only way. Also—which makes it a damn sight worse—she's ruddy well spoiled by the 'Powers-that-Be'—that private room of hers has the best view of the river in all Scotland Yard. Wouldn't *I* like it! Makes my blood boil every time I see her looking out of it."

MacMorran emitted a haze of tobacco-smoke, perhaps to give point to his remarks. The haze was so thick that the inspector himself was hardly visible through it. Anthony, lounging in the arm-chair, looked at his watch.

"What's your programme for this morning?" enquired MacMorran—" 'Green Circle' with me—or are you going off on your own? If you're coming with me—you'd better get cracking. I shall be moving within a matter of ten minutes."

Anthony hesitated before replying. When he eventually did answer, he said: "I think I'll paddle my own canoe this morning, Andrew, if it's all the same to you. I've a mind to call upon a lady."

"A lady?"

"Ah-ha! A lady of some repute in Wavering. Was hers the hand that left unlocked a thousand 'skips'?"

MacMorran looked at him suspiciously. "Are you referring to Mrs. Parmiter, by any chance?"

Anthony laughed pleasantly. "Good for you, Andrew. You've holed in one. Mrs. Parmiter is the name. Wife of Mr. Vernon Parmiter and mistress of the Wardrobe to the St. Simon's Dramatic Society. In accordance with information supplied by Mr. Edmund Gosling—producer to the self-same body. I have an idea that the excellent Mrs. Parmiter will beguile me with the sweet music of speech. With comely speech—with—"

MacMorran cut in and closured Anthony's poetic fancy. "Why Mrs. Parmiter—in particular?"

"My dear Andrew—I ask you!" Anthony looked up in some surprise. "Consider the chain of relativity. Mrs. Parmiter—the Dramatic Society—Vera Ferris—the yellow frock—the unlocked skip—Mrs. Parmiter again. Behold the links are complete. There's the reason for my interest. Who knows what Mrs. Parmiter may tell me?"

"May not's more like it—in my judgment. Especially if old man Parmiter has already sounded the warning."

Anthony nodded. "That's not impossible, Andrew, I agree. But even that might be eloquent in its own fashion. However—we shall see."

MacMorran became severely practical again. "Where will you lunch? Here—or in Wavering somewhere?"

Anthony considered the question. "Here, I think—that is if you intend coming back, too. I'd like to hear the latest 'Green Circle' bulletin."

"O.K.," replied MacMorran. "I'll be back, then, round about one o'clock and I'll expect you somewhere about the same time."

"Rely on me, Andrew," returned Anthony.

2

With regard to his projected call upon Mrs. Parmiter, Anthony boxed clever. Indeed, he gave the matter a considerable amount of thought before he actually decided on the details of his plan of campaign. First of all, he 'phoned Vernon J Parmiter at his place of business. Parmiter frowned when he heard who it was telephoning to him. The frown developed rather than dispersed as he listened to what Anthony had to say. He drummed nervously on his table with his fingers all the time Anthony was talking.

"Well," he said at length, "I suppose I've no valid objection to your seeing Mrs. Parmiter . . . I can't have . . . though what you can find to worry her about . . . I really haven't the foggiest idea . . . but there is just this. I'd like to make plain before it becomes *un fait accompli* . . . I feel I'd like to be present at the interview. After all, my wife is a gentlewoman . . . not used, by any means, to anything in the nature of your suggestion and er . . . well that's how it is, Bathurst, I'd like to be there."

The frown returned to his forehead as he waited for Anthony's reply. "No objection whatever, Mr. Parmiter. In fact I should welcome it. You can 'vet' the interview from both sides. Also, I'll ask you to fix your own time. As long as you can make it sometime to-day. I'd certainly like it to take place not any later."

Parmiter leant forward over his table so that he could see the details on his desk-diary.

"Would before lunch suit you, Bathurst? I think I could manage—"

"What time would that be exactly?"

"Well—say—eleven-forty-five at this office. How's that?"

"That will suit me excellently," returned Anthony, "at your office then—eleven-forty-five ack emma. Very many thanks for the kindness."

Anthony rang off and replaced the receiver in its cradle. He scratched his cheek. 'Now I wonder,' he thought, 'why he's bringing his wife to the office. Why didn't he go home?

3

Anthony presented himself at the solicitor's office in the High Street with about two minutes to spare for the actual time of his appointment. He looked enquiringly at Parmiter's clerk as he entered and the latter nodded to him assuringly.

"Mr. Parmiter said I was to show you in directly you arrived, sir, so will you please come this way?"

Anthony thanked the clerk and followed him. Outside Parmiter's office, he could hear the sound of slightly raised voices. One clearly was a woman's—Mrs. Parmiter, evidently, had already arrived. Vernon Parmiter himself opened the door and ushered Anthony into the room. '

"Mrs. Parmiter's already here," he announced.

He motioned towards a distinctly attractive woman of middle age, seated on a chair by the side of Parmiter's own table.

"This is Mr. Bathurst, my dear. My wife."

Anthony said good morning to the lady and bowed. He was surprised by her appearance. For one thing, she was considerably younger than he had anticipated for Parmiter's wife, with an attractiveness and a distinction that were, to say the least of it, unusual. When she returned his 'good morning', he heard that her voice was most agreeably pleasant, he saw that her eyes were blue and dancing, her dark hair only just beginning to change colour, her features regular and delightful, and her entire manner generally charming and vivacious. As he took the seat next to her, which Parmiter offered him, he congratulated himself on the fact that he had engineered the interview. Something told him inwardly that he was not wasting his time, from whichever angle you chose to look at it.

Vernon Parmiter seated himself in his customary chair. "Bathurst wants to ask you one or two questions. Actually, you aren't compelled to answer them, but he and I have had a preliminary chat about it and I've told him you'll naturally do all you can to help him."

"Oh—don't be stuffy, Vernon," replied Angela Parmiter, "of course I'll answer anything Mr. Bathurst is pleased to ask me. And please remember, my dear Vernon, that you aren't in the Courts now."

The blue eyes looked rather mockingly into Anthony's grey and challenged them in a definitely non-hostile kind of manner. He began to wonder, and then to speculate, what the raised voices that he had heard upon his entrance could have been about. He smiled at Angela and the lady turned her head somewhat provocatively. Parmiter had noted the exchanges and looked down his nose. After that, he coughed.

"Mrs. Parmiter," said Anthony, "two murders in Wavering. Nice girls. Both known to you. One—a member of the same Dramatic Society. Chief Detective-Inspector MacMorran is down here, as doubtless you know, from Scotland Yard. I'm trying to help him. Please try to help me." He stopped and smiled again. "I won't say any more—to begin with."

"There's no need to, Mr. Bathurst. Is it about the frock you wanted to ask me? Barbara Marsden's frock?"

Angela Parmiter spoke with spirit. Before Anthony could reply, Parmiter had intervened. He addressed himself to his wife.

"There is no need, my dear, to put questions into Bathurst's mouth. He knows what he wants to ask you perfectly well without you making suggestions to him." Parmiter's tones were prim and precise.

"Shut up, Vernon," said the lady emphatically, "and don't interfere. This is between Mr. Bathurst and me—if I want your valuable assistance at any time, I'll call for it. If I don't—then you be like the little boy—seen and not heard."

"My dear Angela," fumed Parmiter.

"Skip it," said the wife of his bosom—"I'm waiting for Mr. Bathurst to answer my question." She turned impulsively to Anthony: "Is it about the frock, Mr. Bathurst?"

"Partly, Mrs. Parmiter. Not altogether. At the same time, though, if it hadn't been for the frock, I probably shouldn't be talking to you at this moment. I must admit that." He paused—but went on again almost immediately. "It's really like this. I'm told that you're in charge of the St. Simon's Dramatic Society's wardrobe."

"Who told you that?" she flashed back.

"Gosling. Edmund Gosling—the producer."

"Good Lord," she said gracelessly. "I'm glad he admits it! Sometimes in the past, I've found myself wondering whether the man even *realised* it. Well—we live and learn."

Parmiter began to cough again. The cough sounded critical and censorious. Suddenly, it seemed to irritate Angela. Somewhat petulantly she said to Anthony: "Please go on from where you were—that I am wardrobe-mistress of the St. Simon's Dramatic Society. And that I serve the members of that Society in a purely honorary capacity. What's the next question? Why did I leave the 'skips' unlocked? If it is—the answer's because I always do—because I always have done."

Anthony smiled at her again. "No—that wasn't going to be the question as it happens. Let's get Barbara Marsden's frock over first. Had you any occasion to look inside the 'skip' before Vera Ferris found the frock and decided to wear it? On the evening of the latest performance?"

"No, Mr. Bathurst. The last time I looked inside that particular 'skip' was at a rehearsal some days previously. I didn't have any reason to go to it on the evening of the performance."

The tone of Angela's reply was bright and breezy. "I see. Now tell me—if you can—was the frock there, in your opinion, on that rehearsal evening?"

"In my opinion, Mr. Bathurst—no. I can't be *absolutely* sure—but I am—almost. I'm practically certain that, had it been there, I should have noticed it—and perhaps even wondered about it. Because—at that time, you see, I knew Barbara Marsden was missing. On the other hand, of course, I *may* have missed seeing it."

Anthony nodded. "Yes—of course. Your real point is, had you seen it, you would have almost certainly realised its rather dreadful significance. Many thanks, Mrs. Parmiter. Now let's leave Barbara's frock and come to Barbara herself. Had she, to the best of your knowledge, any connexion of any kind whatever, with the Church Dramatic Society? Have you ever noticed anything, seemingly, perhaps, of the most trivial nature, which would lend any colour to the possibility that I've just asked you about?"

Anthony heard Parmiter move uneasily in his chair. After a time, Angela Parmiter shook her head.

"No. I can't say, truthfully, that I've ever noticed anything of what you suggest. Barbara was not a member of the Dramatic Society and as far as I know, was not particularly interested in any one of the members. I think, if she had been, I should have heard something about it."

"You knew Barbara well, of course?"

"My husband has already told you that, Mr. Bathurst," replied Angela demurely—"I know that he has—he told me all about your previous call upon him."

Anthony looked at her quickly and saw the sparkle in the blue eyes. "Now, Mr. Bathurst," continued the lady, "any more questions?"

"One or two," returned Anthony imperturbably, "and we'll leave Barbara Marsden out of it from now onwards. When the yellow frock was pushed into your 'skip'—in all probability by the murderer—the 'skip' received an unwelcome addition to its resources. That is so, is it not?"

Angela Parmiter flashed a quick look at him as though she were a trifle uncertain as to his meaning. Anthony was conscious of this—but went on.

"Have you ever noticed, Mrs. Parmiter, by way of contrast, when you have had occasion to go to the 'skip', that anything has been missing? That is to say, instead of a frock having been pushed in, something similar had been taken out?"

Angela was silent for some little time. "No," she said eventually, "I can't say that I have. At the same time—"

She stopped rather abruptly.

"Thought of something?" questioned Anthony.

"No. Not that. What I was going to say is that I'm not the best person in the world to answer that."

"Why? Who would be better? I find that statement rather surprising."

Angela laughed at Anthony's question. It was a gay, tinkling laugh. Anthony confessed to himself that he liked it. He liked it so much that he wanted to hear it again.

"Who would be better?" asked Angela, repeating his words. "Why—one or two people connected with the Dramatic Society—Edmund Gosling, for one—most *certainly* Edmund Gosling! It's true I have charge of the 'skips'—perfectly true—but I haven't the burning interest in their contents that Edmund Gosling has—anything like! Believe me—he's got the whole thing at his finger-tips. It's not an *interest* merely with him—it's much more like a consuming passion."

"And yet he didn't know the yellow frock was there?"

"But that's *different*," asserted Angela heatedly—"can't you see it's different? The yellow frock wasn't a Dramatic Society asset—it didn't belong to the Society—it was an intruder—so Edmund Gosling *mightn't* know about it. But he'd jolly well soon know if any of the Society's things had been *taken out* of a 'skip'."

Anthony saw Vernon Parmiter begin to nod in evident approval of what his wife had just said. He also saw Angela's point himself. Of the conversation she had certainly taken the honours. He admitted as much to her.

"I take your point, Mrs. Parmiter. It is well and truly made. I must ask Gosling what I just asked you. I can see now that he would be the best man. Now—one last question before I take my leave and we all go to lunch."

"And what may that be, Mr. Bathurst?" Angela was dead sure of herself.

"Vera Ferris—the girl that, unlike Barbara Marsden—*did* belong to the Dramatic Society—anything to tell me with regard to her? Any attachments—entanglements—interests? You probably had her under your eye a good deal on rehearsal evenings. Did you ever notice anything?"

Parmiter began to cough again. He also made great play of flexing his arm and looking at his wrist-watch. Angela ignored the gestures and began to answer Anthony's question.

"Vera was a very quiet girl, Mr. Bathurst—a very quiet girl indeed. So quiet and so self-contained—so entirely reserved—that more than once I've said to myself about her—still waters run deep—I felt sure somehow that with Vera Ferris there was—" But Angela Parmiter paused and then said: "No, Mr. Bathurst, honestly I've nothing to tell you. There wasn't *anything*—and it's no use my coming over all mysterious and hinting that there was."

Anthony could see clearly that he would get no forrarder. "In that case then, Mrs. Parmiter, I won't detain you or Mr. Parmiter any longer. I need hardly say how much I appreciate your kindness in granting me the interview." Anthony rose preparatory to departure. "By the way," he said casually, "what's the name of the young lady who'll be playing Vera Ferris's part in the next show? Any idea?"

Angela turned her blue eyes on him: "Same answer as before, sir. Apply E. Gosling, Esquire. Whatever he says—will go."

Vernon Parmiter turned round quickly. "Why on earth do you ask that, Bathurst? Are you trying to hint that she'll be the next girl to be murdered?"

The solicitor's face was flushed. He seemed either annoyed or angry. Anthony shook his head.

"No, Mr. Parmiter—on the contrary, I rather fancy that she's the girl who *won't* be murdered."

Anthony waved a genial hand and slid out of the room.

"Good gracious," said Parmiter—"what an extraordinary thing to say!"

4

Anthony arrived back at the 'Nag's Head' just after half-past one. One of the white-aproned waitresses smiled at him by the door of the dining-room.

"Your friend either couldn't or wouldn't wait, sir. He's already started his lunch. Said he was terribly hungry and he wasn't altogether sure what time you'd be back, so he'd start having his. If you go in, sir, I'll bring yours in, too."

"That's all right," replied Anthony—"and thank you very much."

He entered to a disconsolate and disgruntled MacMorran who was just finishing his soup. "You're late," growled MacMorran.

Anthony grinned. "Not so much as you'd notice it, Andrew. Besides, from the point of view of strict time, I haven't exactly been my own master."

He put his head on one side in mock assessment of his companion.

MacMorran argued. "All the same—and that may be—but you're still late."

"My dear Andrew," responded Anthony, "there is a certain what-is-it in your voice, and to quote Bertie Wooster, I can see clearly that if not actually disgruntled you are far from being gruntled."

He took his seat at the table opposite to MacMorran. The inspector said nothing.

"What's happened at the old 'Green Circle'?" enquired Anthony. "No luck?"

MacMorran thawed a little. "You've said it," he answered curtly. "In fact—you couldn't have put it better."

Anthony knew that he must wait for the MacMorran revelations. Gradually and in direct proportion to the rate of disappearance of the inspector's lunch, they began to come.

"I went along to the Company offices," he said, "and eventually reached a gentleman who rejoices in the description of Branch Superintendent of staff. To begin with—he made several serious errors of judgment. Didn't seem to possess an elementary appreciation of who I was or whom I represented. It fell to my lot to instruct him."

"Which you did?"

The light of battle reappeared in MacMorran's eye. "Which I did. I flatter myself—rather effectively. In less than five minutes, let me tell you, Mister Branch Superintendent of staff was singing a very different tune. So much so that he was almost eating out of my hand." The inspector paused, demolished the final morsel of potato and pushed away his plate. "We eventually got right down to business," he continued. "I told him exactly what I was after and what I wanted him to do for me. But to cut a long story short, I drew a complete blank. The grandfather of all blanks. You may be surprised but there isn't a single employee of the 'Green Circle' Company with an address in Wavering. Not one! Every man Jack and woman Jill of 'em resides either in Remsford itself or somewhere the other side of Remsford, Norland, etc. That's the position."

"What did you do then, Andrew?"

There was a silence—the waitress brought Anthony's lunch and the inspector waited for her to leave before he replied.

"I did something then that I've had it in my mind to do for some considerable time. I routed out the caretaker of the St. Simon's Church Institute. He's a chap by the name of Luck. He would have that name, wouldn't he? So ruddy appropriate? He was on the door, taking the tickets on the evening of the dramatic performance. You can guess the question I put to him."

Anthony nodded. "I know the chap by sight. I saw him with Cheam, the curate, once. What did he have to tell you?"

MacMorran deliberately chose the words of his reply. "These are the replies he gave me to my questions. He asserts emphatically that (a) he was on duty that evening at the entrance door all the time the doors were open; (b) that nobody came into the show without him seeing him or her; and (c) that no person was present at that performance of *Nothing but the Truth* who wore the uniform of a 'Green Circle' driver or conductor, *at any time* during the evening. Luck swears that he was either on the door or at the back of the hall all the ruddy time! So there you are and now you know."

Anthony grinned. "Far be it from me, Andrew, to add to the measure of your disgruntlement—but you've told me just what I expected you would."

"That maybe," countered the inspector surprisingly mildly, "but it had to be checked, hadn't it?"

"Agreed. And to an extent we've cleared the air. Because I'm convinced that the 'Green Circle' uniform possibility which Vera Ferris noted in her diary was not *quite* what she imagined it was." Anthony rubbed his hands. "Anyhow—we shall know more about that later. Time, my dear Andrew, will do his ancient task of telling."

The inspector who had by now finished his lunch, pushed his chair away from the table. "I don't know that I follow you. It was either a 'Green Circle' uniform that Vera Ferris saw or it wasn't. If it were—there's a screw loose somewhere and we've got to find where it is. If it weren't—I'm wasting my time reading the Riot Act to ruddy Branch Superintendents."

Anthony finessed. "There are, I suggest, *other* uniforms? In addition to those worn by the staff of the 'Green Circle' line? It may even have been blue. Blue can be very like to certain shades of green—especially at night time."

MacMorran looked at him curiously. "You think the girl may have mistaken the colour?"

"Let me put it like this. Vera Ferris—the eyes of Vera Ferris—were accustomed to seeing 'Green Circle' uniforms in and round about Wavering. I don't suppose, if we come to weigh things up properly, that there was ever a day in the year when she *didn't* see them. Drivers and conductors. On the buses and off them. They were constantly within the range of Vera's sight. The result was—or so I think—that when she saw *any* uniform that wasn't hopelessly dissimilar, she immediately recognized it or connected it with that of the 'Green Circle' line."

MacMorran nodded. "Yes—I can see there's something in that."

"Well—there you are then. That's why I wasn't surprised at your drawing blank this morning."

"H'm. How did you get on with the Parmiter woman?"

"Very much as you did with the 'Green Circle'. By the way, have you met the lady?"

"Not I. Why?"

Anthony laughed. "She's an attractive number. Very different from what I expected. Considerably younger than her husband."

"Nothing unusual about that. Especially if he's well breeched. Most of the sex know where to fix themselves up. Particularly in country places like Wavering. I found that out very early in my career."

Anthony laughed again and lit a cigarette. "The next move, I suppose, is to meet Helen Repton? To-morrow morning, isn't it?"

"That's it. I arranged to pick her up at the station." MacMorran paused and then suddenly changed his tone. "Tell me," he said, "I'm more worried over this case, I think, than I've ever been. *Have* you anything like a clue?"

"At the moment, Andrew," returned Anthony cheerfully —"not half a clue. Not even a decimal part of one."

"Pretty grim outlook," muttered MacMorran.

"But that's not to say I may not have one in a couple of days' time. Cheer up, Andrew—to-night I'll buy you some beer. You'll feel a different man after the second pint."

CHAPTER 12

1

A NTHONY and MacMorran met Helen Repton at the station. The 11.44 East Coast Express from Liverpool Street came into Wavering in reasonably good time—being less than a quarter of an hour late. Helen was in mufti as she alighted and she spotted Anthony and the inspector on the platform immediately. She had worked with them many times in the past and her admiration for Anthony was terrific. It was not confined to her side. To him, she was a girl of singular beauty and outstanding intelligence and never once had he regretted bringing her into action as an auxiliary.

She had been attached to the Women's Branch at the 'Yard' for some years now, although her father was a Fellow of History at Oxford. Helen, herself, had a London degree in Economics and had abandoned what was almost certain to be a distinguished academic career, for police work at Scotland Yard. She was tallish, thin, and dark, and her violet eyes had to be seen to be believed. She grinned as she shot out her hand to Anthony and MacMorran.

"It's a long time," she said, "since Sir John Wynyard died at High Fitchet."

"It is, Helen," he answered.

"Too long," said Miss Repton.

"Too long," repeated Anthony, smiling, "but my dear Helen, who amongst us shall measure time? 'They are not long, the weeping and the laughter, Love and desire and hate.'"

"Not before lunch—if you don't mind," growled MacMorran—"and let me be remindin' you—the girl's down here on a job of work."

Anthony dropped an eyelid in Miss Repton's direction. "Quite right, Andrew. The reprimand was deserved. We'll take Miss Repton back to the 'Nag's Head' with us and over the luncheon-table we'll give her the 'gen'."

"That's the idea," said MacMorran. "We'll push off at once."

They reached the market-place and turned off along the Remsford road. Every now and then, Anthony noticed that Helen Repton was realizing certain abnormal conditions. At the clock-tower in the Remsford road she said: "Extraordinary number of police about. For a county town like Wavering, I should think it's a record."

MacMorran heard the remark and hastened to interpret. "It's all part of Steadman's plan. I agreed to it, naturally. The boys have been drafted in from Remsford, Norland, and Cranchester. As a special protection squad. To-night, when the ordinary population abroad has thinned out a bit, they'll show up even more. Ah well—they won't do any harm." He grinned at Helen Repton. "You wait, my girl," he added, "you wait until you hear what's in store for you."

Helen grimaced to Anthony on MacMorran's blind side. "Why?" she questioned, "what have you got cooking for me?"

"Ever heard how they catch tigers in India?"

"Yes. What about it? One way's to tether a kid and leave it in the open all night. When the tiger scents the bait—"

MacMorran patted her on the shoulder. "Well—there's one thing—you've brought your winter woollies—no doubt—so that as far as being in the open's concerned—"

"Gertcher"—said Helen—"you're an old 'flesh-creeper' and you won't put the wind up me, with all your—"

"Far be it from me," said Anthony, "to interfere wantonly with this truly delightful exchange of ideas, but this imposing edifice confronting us is the 'Nag's Head'."

2

Helen Repton poised a spoon over Anthony's coffee. "There doesn't seem to be any coffee sugar. How many lumps, Mr. Bathurst?" She gave him a soft, comradely sort of smile.

"One only, Helen—if you please. Then you can empty all the rest in Andrew's cup. He's not a greedy man—he merely has a liking for plenty. A question of nationality—actually. Cigarette, anybody?"

Anthony busied himself in lighting three cigarettes. Over the flame of the match, he watched the deft fingers of the girl from Scotland Yard. Helen handed cups to the two men. Anthony looked full at her. What he saw gave him heart. There was no fear in the dark blue eyes. Helen drew cigarette-smoke into her lungs and slowly exhaled.

"Now I'm ready to hear the worst," she said quietly, "so please tell me the whole story."

Anthony turned to MacMorran. "You give Helen the 'gen', Andrew, up to the fall of the last wicket. When you reach that stage, I'll take over."

MacMorran finished his cigarette and began to fill his pipe. "How much do you know, lass? Already?"

"The bare facts only. Two dead girls, their names and ages and how they died. Nothing more than that. I didn't even know that you and Mr. Bathurst were down here. Till you tinkled the section."

"I see." MacMorran got his pipe going. "Well—I'll fill in the details for you—and then you'll be able to see just how and where we stand."

The inspector proceeded to give Helen Repton the necessary information. The girl listened to him without interruption. When he had finished, there was a period of dead silence. Anthony lit another cigarette and offered his case to Helen. He broke the silence and spoke through the first puffs of smoke.

" 'Murder most foul as in the best it is; But this most foul, strange and unnatural.' "

Helen looked at him. There was curiosity in the look. "The inspector has reached the stage," she said, "where you're due to take over."

"You're telling me," returned Anthony.

"Like that, is it?"

Anthony nodded. "Somewhat, I'm afraid. Anyway—here's the rest of the doings. If you have fears—prepare to shed them now."

3

Helen leant lazily over the table as Anthony began. "I have a theory," Anthony said quietly, "that the second murder was inspired by the sight of the yellow frock. I don't care for the word 'inspired' in this particular connexion, but you know what I mean. And its the *nearest* to what I mean. Also—I don't think that the theory is *too* fantastic—either. What do you think yourself, Helen?"

The girl nodded. "I can accept it—as a possibility."

"Good. You can also see, I'm certain, the main difficulty that we're up against. With regard to the identity of the murderer." Anthony paused and waited for Helen Repton's reply. It was not too long delayed in coming.

"You mean," she said slowly, "that the entirely crazy pattern of the crimes, the complete absence of reasonable motive—as far as the ordinarily intelligent person can see—postulate that the murderer may be—well—*anybody*? Am I right?"

"My dear Helen," said Anthony, "I couldn't agree with anybody more. Your reasoning is excellent. The murderer may be—anybody—as you say. He may exist under the most respectable of callings and with the most excellent of reputations—the possessor of the most guileless of features. More than that even—he probably *does*!"

MacMorran grunted as he puffed at his pipe. Helen nodded. "Yes. I'm definitely with you—I can see exactly what you mean."

"Right. With that fact established in our minds, then, it seems to me that our friend the murderer must be trapped into *giving himself away*. Otherwise, we may be compelled to—"

Helen interrupted him. "Red hands? *In flagrante*? That the idea?"

"Red hands—exactly."

"He's a lunatic, of course?" Helen's question to Anthony suggested that she herself wasn't quite sure. He challenged her.

"Tell me what you think yourself."

"Well—to my mind, practically everything points that way. Of course, I've only just got to know the details. But having regard to the stolen fat from the butcher's, the wounds on the cheeks, and the two deaths from manual strangulation—well—I deduce a killer who kills without any real reason, just for killing's sake. Which all points to mental instability. Is that what you expected me to say—or isn't it?"

"More or less what I thought you'd say. And more or less, too, what I *think* I think myself."

Helen nodded with gratification. "Good. Now perhaps I can short-circuit what you are going to say. May I try?"

"You may, lady."

Helen smiled at him and Anthony smiled back. "You're thinking on these lines. That if a third girl wore the 'murder' frock there might very well be an attempt at a third murder. How do I go with that one?"

Anthony's smile broadened. "So well—that you can go on from where you got to. We're both waiting anxiously to hear. Agree, Andrew?"

"Ay! You can count me in on that." MacMorran nodded with an air of profound wisdom.

"Well," continued Helen Repton, "it's fairly obvious that the question now arises as to the selection of this third girl. And when I remember Chief Inspector MacMorran's interesting reference just before lunch to tigers and India—and kids being out best part of the night—need I go any farther?"

"You need not, Helen. And many thanks for the short cut. You've saved me a task that was going to be far from pleasant. How do you feel about it yourself? *Really* feel about it? Queasy—or qualms?"

Helen Repton grinned. "Not on your life. When's the dirty day?"

"Next week. *That's* been fixed—for us. I had no hand in arranging that."

Helen knitted her brows. "How come?"

"Listen, lady. On Wednesday and Thursday of next week, the St. Simon's Church Dramatic Society puts on *Nothing but the Truth*:'

Helen intervened with a sharp exclamation. "The same play as before?"

"The same play, lady. These two performances of which I now make mention are on behalf of the funds of the Wavering Cottage Hospital. Vera Ferris's part will be played by another girl."

"Who'll wear the yellow frock?"

Anthony shook his head. "No—that's not the idea." He spoke extremely slowly. "We don't know the girl, you see. As far as we're concerned, her identity is completely unknown. Gosling, that's the Dramatic Society's producer, will find a girl for the part—but that's all we know."

Helen Repton looked puzzled. "Where do I come in, then? I don't think I quite see that part. I take it that you *do* want me to wear the yellow frock—publicly—and with a metaphorical flourish of trumpets ?"

Anthony nodded. "We do! The Chief here has set his ancient Aberdonian heart on it."

"Well, then—as I said before—how come?"

Helen wrinkled her forehead. Anthony grinned. "There's an excellent historical precedent. Poor Nelly wasn't an actress, exactly. If my memory serves me correctly—"

"Poor Nelly? Should that ring a bell? Because if it should—"

"Mistress Eleanor of Old Drury, whose oranges were invariably the most juicy, the most tasty—"

"But she *sold* oranges—*I* can't sell oranges! Or chocolate! Or cigarettes! Sweet Nell must have functioned in the days of Tory misrule!"

Anthony shook his head to show he was in agreement with her. "No—you can't. How right you are. You can't even sell 'Biscuit or Banbury'. As you point out—under the diabolical influence of a Socialist government—" He broke off and grinned.

"But—" Helen Repton cut in again. "As far as I can see there's *nothing* I can sell. So why drag in Nell Gwyn?"

Anthony waved his finger at her. "You wait a minute, lady. Exercise the quality of patience. Andrew and I have thought of something you *can* sell."

"Not saveloys or something absolutely foul like that?"

"There is no place in my cast for the 'hot dog'. Cerberus, perhaps, but not his torrid poor relation. If I thought that—"

Helen put her arms across the table. "What is it, then? What *do* I sell?"

"Programmes, lady. The humble printed sheets which I always think on occasions such as that under notice should give the names of the cast in the order of their disappearance. One could then, perhaps, enjoy certain exercises in delectable anticipation. Whereas, under normal conditions—"

"Programmes," said Helen musingly—"now as an idea that's not so dusty. Who thought of it?"

"Modesty," returned Anthony, "forbids me to—"

"I might have known," countered Helen Repton.

4

"What about the yellow frock?" Helen frowned as she put the question.

"What about it?"

"Where does one lay hands upon the article?"

"I'm seeing about it this afternoon," replied MacMorran, "leave all that to me."

"Is it by way of being an atrocity?"

"I like that—I must say," said Anthony in mock indignation, "it's just your colour—you're dark. And it's in the very latest Wavering fashion. Just as though we'd ask you to—"

"*Le dernier cri*—eh?" smiled Helen. "How you two love to pull my leg. And I suppose once I'm garbed in the saffron and I've hawked my programme wares for the half-hour that precedes the rise of the curtain—it's all going to be plain sailing. *N'est-ce pas*?"

"We hope so," responded Anthony.

"We haven't the details of the plan cut and dried yet," added MacMorran, "but you'll know all about them in good time."

Helen meditated. "There is *one* thing," she said after a few seconds. "I don't know whether you've quite realized it. I shall be a stranger in a foreign land. Don't you think that fact alone may cause people to regard me with a soupçon of suspicion?"

"You mean?"

"Well—don't you think it will be something like my wearing a label? Said label reading—'warning to all present —this girl is exotic—she doesn't belong here—she is just a piece of cheese in the mouse-trap'. For 'mouse'—read 'murderer'."

Anthony looked grave. "I think you've got something there, Helen. The stranger in the land! The Amahagger put hot pots on the heads of strangers. What do you think, Andrew?"

MacMorran chuckled. "It's your plan. You thought of it. You're not passing the buck now. The girl's right—undoubtedly. You could do with some of her brains."

Anthony became quiet. When he spoke again, he said: "We shall have to chance it. For the main reason that I don't think we shall be able to hit on anything better. Also—we've gone too far to draw back. Our mad murderer may not know the face of *every* girl in Wavering. Actually, I don't suppose he does for a moment."

"You made a mistake meeting me at the station. Supposing he's already seen us together? If he *has*, that's torn it."

Anthony nodded rather gloomily. "I think you're by way of being right again, Helen. Although the odds are heavily against us having been seen together—in that short space of time. Unless he's watching us all the time—absolutely dogging our very footsteps. All the same, during the week that's coming, I can see that our best plan will be to keep apart as much as we possibly can. It's certainly a point to you.'"

MacMorran sought to alleviate the position. "There is this about it. You'll look so very different, my lass, when you're got up to sell those programmes. It's astonishing what make-up and lipstick—"

"Heavens!" cried Helen, "I was afraid you were going to say when I was got up 'to kill'. I was realizing with horrid insistence that there might be two meanings attached to the phrase and the cold shivers were coming."

She lit a cigarette and leant back in her chair. "Well—how far have we really got?"

"You know the main outlines of the position. Inspector MacMorran will arrange the business of the frock. He'll see that you have it in your possession as soon as possible. After that, the three of us can go into the matter more thoroughly and fix up the details."

"I see. Well—that's that. And what do I do in the meantime?" Helen looked from Anthony to MacMorran.

"I think," said the latter, "that if you knock about on your own, generally, in Wavering itself and round the district it wouldn't be at all a bad idea. From more than one point of view. You might even manage to pick up something that has eluded us."

"That will suit me very nicely—especially if the weather keeps dry and moderately sunny."

"Good—and this afternoon I'll get on to Inspector Steadman at Remsford and see about those glad rags of yours."

Helen pretended to shiver. "It's all a bit on the eerie side, isn't it? To think that somebody may soon look at me and almost—lick his chops!"

"You have a disgusting mind, Miss Repton," said Anthony.

CHAPTER 13

1

Macmorran was as good as his word and the frock that had
been worn by Barbara Marsden and Vera Ferris was in Helen
Repton's hands on the following afternoon. He and Anthony
had returned to the 'Nag's Head' in the early evening to hear if she had
any further comments to make on it. Helen came into them half an hour
before dinner was due.

"*No bon*," she announced simply.

"Why not?" questioned MacMorran, "don't drive me to drink by
saying it's not your particular shade."

Helen grinned at him. "Worse than that, great Caesar. The darned
thing doesn't fit. It's miles too small for me. With which incontestable
fact, kind sir, I fear there's no argument."

MacMorran grunted dismally and looked across at Anthony. "Your
move," he said curtly.

Anthony looked at Helen Repton. "Absolutely impossible?" he
queried.

"Absolutely. Not a hope. As the thing is at the moment."

"H'm! Definitely not so good. Well—you're a girl, you're used to
frocks, buying them and trying them on—what's your suggestion? Could
it be altered in the time?"

Helen shook her head. "Not half a hope! It's *miles* too small for me.
The only thing I can suggest is to have one made for me exactly like it.
Is that a reasonable proposition?"

Anthony turned to MacMorran. "There's this local woman," said the
inspector. "I don't know that she wouldn't be the best bet. What's her
name? Wilkes, isn't it? I wonder whether she might be able to—"

Anthony cut in. "Julia Wilkes, you mean. The local dressmaker in Shelford Row." Then he began to shake his head opposingly. "I don't like it, Andrew. It's doing the very thing, after all, that we've so strenuously tried to avoid. To an extent, it's going to let her in on the ground-floor."

"She needn't know—*all*" countered the inspector.

Anthony made no reply for some seconds. "No—I admit that. She needn't know *all*. But what she must know—is very nearly all. Unless the woman's plain daft—which we know she isn't. Her intervention in the case already gives ample proof of that. Is there any alternative? What do you think yourself, Helen?"

Helen Repton was quiet for some seconds before she answered Anthony's question. "You've got to think of this. The frock I wear must look exactly like the original. And there aren't bags of time for us to play with. This local woman may have the material, the trimmings, the kind of sequin—or she may know where they can be quickly obtained. On the whole, I'm inclined to agree with Chief-Inspector MacMorran—that this Wilkes woman's our best bet."

Anthony heard the judgment of Helen, as delivered, and was silent again. He was, seemingly, weighing the various considerations against each other. MacMorran was content to wait for him. The only sound in the room came from the ticking of the clock on the mantelpiece.

"All right," he announced eventually—"you win. I surrender the pass. What do you think, Chief? When Miss Repton presents herself to Julia Wilkes—shall you or I go with her, do you think—or shall we let her go alone? Which is the better proposition in your opinion?"

"Let her go alone," answered MacMorran, "it will give Julia Wilkes less to think about and also to talk about. What the eye doesn't see—you know the rest, both of you." He paused—to continue at once. "Besides that, I've considerable faith in Miss Repton's acumen. I know perfectly well that she'll play her cards as adroitly as possible."

"O.K., Chief! Leave it to Helen—eh? Leave it to her and hope for the best? Very well then—we'll arrange it like that."

Helen looked at the clock. "I'll go round to Shelford Row and interview Julia Wilkes," she announced firmly—"directly after dinner. Whichever way we look at things, there's no time to be lost."

2

"I think that I'll accompany you," said Anthony, "as far as the turning of Shelford Row. I'll risk it at this time of the evening. Perhaps I might even come a little nearer. We'll see how things are when we get there."

"Don't tell me *you've* got cold feet," returned Helen, "after such an excellent dinner, too."

Anthony winked at the inspector. "Good people are scarce. And I'm taking no chances."

"Give me two minutes to powder my nose," said Helen, "and I'll be ready. It'll be pretty dark, won't it?"

"Not too bad. There's something of a moon. It's in its first quarter. I'll wait for you just outside the entrance to the saloon-bar. Don't hurry. Take your time."

Helen joined Anthony in under five minutes and they set out together. Anthony nodded down to the parcel she was carrying.

"That the frock?"

"That is. How far's the destination?"

"About half a mile from the cross-roads. Not more, I should think. We want the centre of the town and then we turn left. How long do you think you'll be with the lady?"

"Well—I shouldn't be too long, should I? I mean—it's either one thing or the other, isn't it? She'll say either yes or no. We shan't argue about it."

They came to the High Street. "Plenty of police—do you notice? *And* civilian patrols in a good many of the side roads. There may even be something of the sort functioning in Shelford Row."

"All the better for yours truly. I don't think I've ever been so well looked after. I assure you it's an entirely new experience."

"Turn left here," said Anthony, "and then, I fancy it's the first on the right. Either the first or the second."

They came to the first turning. "Bartlow Row," said Helen—"it must be the next turning."

They came to the next turning—Shelford Row. "There's a brass plate at the side of the gate," Anthony informed her. "I saw it one afternoon when I was having a look round. And it's on this side. About half a dozen houses down. I'll hang about in the vicinity until you reappear."

"O.K.," returned Helen. She shifted the parcel containing Barbara Marsden's frock from one hand to the other.

"Good hunting," called out Anthony, as she walked away from him.

3

Helen Repton walked slowly down Shelford Row. She kept her eyes on the gates as she came to them. She wasn't obliged to walk far. There was the brass plate as Anthony Bathurst had said. It bore the words: 'Julia Wilkes, High Class Dressmaker'. Helen pushed open the gate, walked up the garden path and rang the bell. The house was dark and for a time her ring elicited no response. Helen rang the bell for a second time. Then she thought she heard a dragging sort of footstep somewhere at the back of the house. She was tempted to ring the bell for the third time but she resisted the temptation. Then she heard the footsteps coming towards the front-door and she was glad that she had not been too impatient. She heard the click of a light switch and a burst of light filled the passage. Slowly the door opened and Helen saw a middle-aged woman confronting her.

"What is it?" asked the woman, "what is it you want?"

"Are you Miss Julia Wilkes?" questioned Helen.

"Who else should I be?"

"Oh—good," said Helen with a light-heartedness she was far from feeling. "I'm so glad that I've found you at home. May I come in?"

"Well," returned the dressmaker rather grudgingly—"it's late for me—but—is it about a dress or something?"

"Yes."

Helen slipped into the passage and Julia Wilkes slowly closed the door.

"Come into the front-room," she said.

Helen followed her into a well-furnished and extremely comfortable front-room.

"Now what's your business?" said the high-class dressmaker.

Helen put the parcel on the table in front of her. "I'm sorry I'm late—but I want you to make me a frock. You've been recommended to me very strongly by several people in Wavering."

"You aren't a Wavering girl," said Julia Wilkes sharply.

Helen looked at her and smiled her sweetest smile. It came right out of the top drawer.

"I'm staying in Wavering," she answered—"that's why I want you to make me the frock. And that's why, too, I've come to the best dressmaker in Wavering."

"Poppycock," replied Julia bluntly.

Helen gestured towards the parcel. She ignored the dressmaker's curtness.

"I'd like it made just like that one—the one in there. That one's not my size. It's much too small for me."

Julia Wilkes took the parcel and began to undo it. Helen's eyes wandered round the room. Over the mantelpiece hung a large oil-painting. Of a man. An elderly man. It was like Julia, probably her father, thought Helen, or it might even perhaps, go back yet another generation. As Helen looked at it she saw that there was something strange about it. Her mind sought the strangeness. Where was it exactly? The answer to her questing came almost immediately. The strangeness was in the man's eyes. To Helen Repton, as she stood there and looked at them, they seemed like great pools of emptiness. It occurred to her as the thought registered, that she had never seen eyes quite like them.

Julia Wilkes opened the parcel and took out the yellow frock of Barbara Marsden. Helen watched her intently. Julia gave a sharp intake of breath as she saw the frock and recognized it for what it was. It was almost a hiss.

"So," she said, slowly and deliberately, "*that's* why you've come to me. You knew that I made the frock."

Her eyes bored into Helen's face. They were full of doubt, suspicion, and mistrust. Helen thought that they looked even cruel. Julia flashed a question at her.

"How did you come by this? Tell me. I like straight dealing—not hole and corner business. How did you come by this frock?"

Helen decided to fly her colours—it seemed to her, as a quick decision, it was the best thing that she could do.

"You should know," she replied, "what my possession of that frock implies. It should tell you . . . many things."

"What do you mean, young lady? Please explain yourself more fully."

"You recognize the frock?"

"I do. Who should recognize it better?"

"You know who wore it?"

"I do. *And* who wore it for the second time. When I also recognized it."

"Well then—doesn't that explain matters to you? You know where the frock went—after it was worn on that second occasion . . . you know into whose hands it passed. Surely there is no need for me to explain more?"

Julia Wilkes was silent as she weighed the import of Helen Repton's words. She rose from the chair into which she had sunk to undo the parcel and came across to Helen. She put her hands on Helen's shoulders and once again her sharp eyes bored into the girl's face. Suddenly, such was Helen's imagination, the face of the dressmaker seemed to become the face of the old man in the portrait. Helen steeled herself to say no more, to stand perfectly still. Slowly, Julia Wilkes removed her hands from Helen's shoulders.

"I see," she said. She spoke the words as slowly as she had moved her hands. "I see. So that is the explanation. Yes, young lady, I should have seen through that at once. Julia Wilkes was slow!"

"I am glad," returned Helen, "glad that you understand why I have come to you and why I am in the position to ask you to make the frock for me. It is always a good thing when people understand each other quickly. But let's be practical. Can you make the frock for me? In a week? Because I need it for next Wednesday. To wear next Wednesday."

A cunning crept into Julia's eyes. "Yes. I can make the frock. I have enough of the yellow material left over."

"It must be exactly the same. The trimmings, the sequins— everything."

"Don't worry," added Julia—"I can do the job. I have—everything." She began to declaim. " 'Yellow and black and pale and hectic red, Pestilence-stricken multitudes: O thou who chariotest to their dark wintry bed—' Didn't know I loved poetry, did you?"

"Shelley, isn't it?" asked Helen, knowing full well that it was.

"That's right. What you young girls come to nowadays—to be sure! Now you stay in here like a good girl while I go and find my measuring tape. I can see you're a good deal bigger than the girls who wore this frock before. Stay here and I'll pop back in a minute."

Julia bustled from the room like a busy housewife and Helen heaved a sigh of relief. Anthony Bathurst would be pleased there was going to be no difficulty about the frock—after all. As she waited for the dressmaker's return she looked up again at the oil painting of the old man. Those eyes! Extraordinary! Full of emptiness. If the cliche that the eyes are the windows of the soul were true.

At that precise second, Julia Wilkes came bustling back. Her hands were full. "Now, young lady," she said in a brisk business-like way, "stand up there and I'll take those measurements of yours. By the way, you didn't tell me your name."

Helen hesitated. "Call me Mademoiselle X," she answered.

"Shrouded in anonymity—eh?" remarked Julia. "Is that the idea?"

"We'll call it that, if you like," replied Helen, "because I'd like you to regard this visit of mine as entirely between you and me. Actually, if you only knew it, you're being paid a particularly high compliment. Things wouldn't have gone like this—with any dressmaker."

Julia said "humph" and grunted. She began to measure the girl in front of her. Suddenly she laughed.

"What are you laughing at?" enquired Helen.

"Oh—at just the way it goes. When I sat down in my arm-chair this evening, I little thought I should be doing this before the morning. I wanted to watch the cabaret on the television programme—but of course Mademoiselle X has to come along and upset all my arrangements. So l laughed. That's better than crying, young lady. No guts in the girls these days. Different from my time. I should say so!" She pushed the tape under Helen's arm-pit. "You're a bit bigger than you look, my lady. Deceptive. Some girls are. I'd say they are. In more ways than one. I say though—the thought's just come to me. You'll have to watch your step. When you wear the new frock. Have you thought of that?"

Julia's face was curiously inquisitive as she bent over to do her work. Inquisitive and cunning.

"Have I thought of what?" countered Helen.

"Well," laughed Julia Wilkes, "there have been two murders, you know. Two girls have been strangled. Wearing the frock I made for Barbara Marsden." More work with the measuring tape.

"Is that strictly true?" demanded Helen.

"Is what strictly true?"

"What you said. Was the second murdered girl wearing the yellow frock?"

"Oh—I don't know. Perhaps she wasn't. You can't go by everything you hear in the street, on the corners, and over the fences. Just bend over a little to the left, young lady, it you don't mind."

Helen obeyed the request. "All the same," continued the dressmaker, "you'll have to watch *your* step—same as I said you would. You don't want a murderer's hands at your pretty throat." Julia began to laugh again. "I bet he'd catch a fox if he tried any fun and games with you. You'd deal with him good and proper. Serve the beast right, too. Hanging 'ud be too good for him. We're a lot too easy with them. No doubt about that. What we want these days is to restore some of the old-time punishments. Like those you read about in books. What's the good of being namby-pamby with beasts that prowl about killing young girls and treating them like a lot of cissies when you catch 'em! No sense in it. They want something they can *feel*. They ought to leave it to me'. I'd make 'em jump about. A good red-hot poker up their you know where—that 'ud be more like it."

Julia chuckled, either at savoury reminiscence or delightful anticipation. She stood back from Helen for a second or so and then jotted a line of figures on the back of an old envelope with the stub of a pencil. Julia slipped the envelope and the pencil on the table.

"Now turn round the other way, will you please, young lady? Let me see what you're like across the shoulders."

Helen dutifully turned round and the dressmaker busied herself at the back.

"Yes," she said, "I made that frock on the table there for Barbara Marsden. Just before Christmas. She little knew what it was going to mean for her. Still—all her life she wasn't too bright. If she hadn't been what she was, she'd never have come away from the Parmiters. Good place she had there. Not a better one in the whole of Wavering. Just hold that right arm of yours straight out, will you? Straight out. That's right. I don't want the frock to pull under the arms. Which is the fault of so many frocks. Now—let me see—what was I talking about? Oh—I know, about Barbara Marsden leaving the Parmiters. There's only one person in Wavering who knows the real reason she left. And I'm not telling, my dear. Not on your life. Wild horses couldn't drag it out of me. I may be a talkative woman—I don't admit that, mind you—for an instant—but I know when to keep my mouth shut and when not. Oh—yes—I wasn't born yesterday. There are no cradle-marks left on my—you can guess where I mean."

Julia Wilkes grabbed her envelope and pencil-stub again. "Another thing," she said very quietly, but at the same time, very insistently—"I don't really know who you are, do I? I mean—I don't know your name. Not your real name. To me you're Miss X—that means you're an unknown quantity."

Helen was at a loss as to what to say. She took, therefore, the course that she considered the wisest. Like the dressmaker fumbling at her body, she also would keep her mouth shut. Suddenly, Julia Wilkes changed her tone.

"I shall require you for a fitting," she announced.

Helen thought that a note of triumph sounded in it. "When shall I come?"

The dressmaker pursed her lips at the question. "Well—suppose we say Saturday? Saturday evening—eh? That suit you?"

"Yes—I think so. I can manage Saturday."

"Very well, young lady. That's fixed, then. Saturday it shall be."

"What time? Morning, afternoon or evening?"

Julia Wilkes cocked her head to one side. "Well—if it's all the same to you, Miss X, suppose we say the same time as you came this evening? I don't mind sacrificing my television again on behalf of a good customer. Or even shall we say, on behalf of a very *interesting* customer." There was a wealth of meaning in Julia Wilkes's words.

Helen nodded. "Very well, then, Miss Wilkes. Saturday evening—same time. I'll be here punctually—never fear."

"It's a good time to come," said the dressmaker musingly, "the streets are quiet. Or at least these side-streets are. The majority of Wavering people will be indoors."

"On Saturday evening?" queried Helen, "surely not? Saturday evening's the time when people are out. More than any other time. What about the cinema and the various locals?"

Julia wagged her forefinger. "In normal times—yes—I might be disposed to agree with you. But times have changed. There's a killer roams the streets of Wavering. A killer who's killed twice! Although the police are looking everywhere for him! Don't you see—the killer makes all the difference?"

She bustled Helen to the front door. "Till Saturday then, young lady. It'll be a quick job for me—but never fear—I shan't let you down. Julia Wilkes always delivers the goods. Telegraphic address—'Reliability, Wavering'. Good night, my dear."

"Good night," returned Helen, "and very many thanks."

The front door of the dressmaking establishment closed behind her. Julia walked back to the yellow frock on the table in her room. She picked up a pair of scissors and began to use them. The sequins came off, one by one. And as she dropped them into a small box, Julia Wilkes began to sing quietly to herself. She sang in a rather rich contralto and the words were the words of Tosti's 'Good-bye'.

CHAPTER 14

1

In the meantime, Anthony Bathurst had waited for Helen Repton's return, at, or near, the turning into Shelford Row. Once or twice, two men had come close to him and in his opinion, looked at him rather suspiciously. He knew, however, that they were almost certainly private patrols so that their concern did not worry him. It must be confessed, however, that he felt somewhat relieved to see Helen coming towards him up Shelford Row. Anthony was quick to join her.

"Well, lady—and how fared my ambassadress? I'm not denying that I'm glad to see you."

"I'm a sight for the blepharitic, am I? Ah, well—it's nice to be that sometimes. I'm not denying either that I'm not sorry to be with you again."

Anthony shot a sharp glance at her. "Why—what do you mean?"

Helen shook her head. "It's difficult to put into words."

"Can't she make the frock?"

"Yes—the frock's O.K. She's making me a new one. I've had my measurements taken. You have no cause to worry in the matter of the frock."

"What's the trouble, then?"

Helen laughed. "No trouble at all. And please don't jump at conclusions. All that I was trying to convey was that Julia Wilkes, dressmaker of Wavering, is by way of being a bit of a character. I don't think she'd be everybody's cup of tea—by a long chalk."

"Tell me," said Anthony simply, "and don't leave anything out. The full story, if you please, Helen, with nary an omission. I assure you you'll never have a more attentive listener."

Helen Repton took up the challenge and gave Anthony a detailed account of the incidents connected with her recent visit to the dressmaker. Upon occasion, Anthony interrupted with a sharp question, but generally speaking, he gave her her head until she'd finished.

"Anyhow," said Helen, as she concluded her recital of facts, "the old girl's eccentric. That's how I'd describe her."

"A card—eh, Helen? Would that description fit, too?"

"It would. She's a proper card, all right. In the meantime, and what is most important to me, are *you* satisfied? Do I find favour in my lord's sight? Is my task well done and do my accomplishments find lustre?"

"It is, Helen, and they do. After all, the main object of the visit was to fix up about the dress and that you've done successfully."

"Good. Your satisfaction is my reward. Going back to Julia, however, what do you think of the Parmiter reference? In relation to Barbara Marsden? What do you think Julia Wilkes really meant?"

"I think, Helen, that in vulgar terms, she was showing off. That she was trying to impress you, whom she knew to be a stranger to Wavering, that nothing went on *in* Wavering, that *she*, Julia, didn't know the ins and outs of. In other words, that if you need an authority on Wavering and all matters appertaining to Wavering, you must go to Julia Wilkes and Julia Wilkes only. It's a form of village pride and conceit that I've run across before in my experience."

"You think, then, that it was a form of conceit that dealt in exaggeration? That Barbara Marsden left the service of the Parmiters, whoever they are, for quite an ordinary everyday reason and that Julia Wilkes, when she hints at things mysterious, is just a liar and a highly sensational one at that?"

"Yes. That just about sums up what I do think. I've met the Parmiters—more than once. In fact I had a rather special interview with the lady the day before you came down. Parmiter is the Wavering solicitor, also a churchwarden at St. Simon's Church, and his wife holds office—quite honorary, of course—in the Dramatic Society attached to the church."

Helen became critical. "They rather impinge on the main problem, don't you think?"

"I suppose they do." Anthony began to think over what Helen had said. "Maybe I'll have another look at them from the Barbara Marsden angle. Your point may be a good one. Where there's smoke, there's usually some form of fire at least. When did you say you were due at the Wilkes's again?"

"On Saturday. Same time as this evening."

"Did you fix the day or did Julia?"

"Julia fixed it. She suggested Saturday before I could make any choice. For one thing she says the streets will be clear. Because of the murders."

"Should doubt it myself—Saturday evening. All the same I'm quite prepared to learn that the murders have made a difference."

Helen Repton shook her head. "For a time, perhaps. But I'll guarantee that state of things won't last very long. You see if I'm not right. People have surprisingly short memories. In about a week from now, I should say things'll be normal again."

"Unless—"

"Unless what?"

"There's a third murder. If that contingency should arise—and God forbid that it does—the streets'll be clear of a night then! And they'll stay like it for some considerable time. Think of Jack the Ripper."

Again Helen shook her head. "Don't worry. There isn't going to be any third murder, I'm certain of that."

"For what reason? Please enlighten me."

"No reason," replied Helen, "no reason at all. Just put it down to my womanly intuition."

2

"I'm going to Remsford to-day," announced MacMorran, "for another conference. With Steadman and the Chief Constable wallah—I'm always tempted to call him Sir Kempton Park. I shan't be back, probably, until the late afternoon."

"O.K.," replied Anthony, "that suits me. My programme is mapped out too. My time will be fully occupied."

"What is it this time?"

"I'm calling on Gosling again. For one thing I want to arrange about Miss Repton for those two evenings next week. I think he'll be the best man to see."

"You mean about her being a programme-seller? I suppose you *must*?"

Anthony nodded. "Afraid so, Andrew. I'll get Gosling to agree. I don't anticipate any difficulty, but I'm afraid I'm bound to mention it to somebody. Much as I dislike it."

"There shouldn't be any difficulty. With regard to the girl—I think it might be better, from all points of view, if she disappeared from Wavering until Saturday evening. I think I'll send her back to town. The less she's seen about the place the better. What do you think yourself?"

Anthony considered the question. "Perhaps you're right, Andrew. All right, then. Let her come back on Saturday and go along to that dressmaker in the evening. Will you tell her?"

"Yes. Before I go out. I'll 'phone that female atrocity who commands her comings and goings. There'll probably be a basinful of abuse on each side—if I know anything. Makes me wish I knew some new words."

Anthony grinned. "Perhaps she'll oblige you with some."

MacMorran growled. "I'll go along and have it out with Miss Repton now. See you later."

3

Once again Anthony was lucky. He found Edmund Gosling at home. The latter looked surprised to see him.

"Oh come in, Bathurst—do. I hope you haven't brought me any bad news."

Anthony followed Gosling in. To the same room they had used on the occasion of their first encounter.

"Sit down," waved Gosling—"and tell me the worst."

Anthony shook his head. "Nothing like that. I come *(a)* suppliant and *(b)* inquisitive. In other words, I need your assistance on two counts."

"Command me," said Edmund Gosling.

"Thank you. That's very charming."

"Smoke?" said Gosling. He pushed a silver cigarette-case in Anthony's direction.

"Thank you," said Anthony again.

Gosling supplied a lighter. Anthony accomplished his hat-trick of 'thank you's'.

"Now tell me, please," said Gosling, "what it is you've come to ask me. If it lies in my power to help you—I shall be only too pleased."

"That's good of you. Inspector MacMorran of Scotland Yard and I hope to be present at your show next week. Actually—we've been invited."

Gosling's face was a study in impassivity as he listened. "By whom, may I ask?"

"Well—to tell the truth it was Cheam, the curate, who suggested it to me. I told MacMorran. We thought it over and the inspector and I have decided to come."

"What . . . er . . . exactly . . . is the idea? Surely not interest in the drama as portrayed by amateurs ? And not . . . er . . . quite the leading flight of amateurs at that?"

"Well—you never know, my dear chap. I think Cheam's idea was that we might pick up something . . . seeing what happened on the occasion of your previous performance. He was definitely out to help us. Anyhow, MacMorran and I are chancing our arm."

"Very good," replied Gosling tersely, "although I can't see much in the idea for my part." He shrugged his shoulders in affected resignation.

"Well," said Anthony, continuing, "this is where you come in. I take it you're more or less in charge of the show ?"

"You can call it that, I suppose."

"Good. Now listen. There will be a third representative of Scotland Yard there—in addition to the inspector and me. But I'm not sure yet in what particular capacity."

Gosling wrinkled his brows. "How do you mean? I'm just a trifle puzzled."

"Cunning must be met with craft," replied Anthony. He produced a slip of paper from his wallet. "Stick your monicker on that for me—and you'll be doing the cause of Justice a great favour."

He handed the slip to Gosling. Gosling took it, frowned, read it, and then frowned again.

"All right," he said, after a pause of some seconds, "you know what you're doing, I suppose."

He felt for his fountain-pen in his waistcoat-pocket, unscrewed the top and put his signature to the bottom of the slip of paper. Then he gave the paper back to Anthony.

"You don't feel like being any more explicit?"

Anthony shook his head. "I'm sorry but in the circumstances, I can't very well. I'm not the only one concerned, you see. I'm sure you understand. Also—keep it absolutely under your hat, will you?"

"All right." Gosling smiled back—"as far as I'm concerned—mum's the word. I presume that concludes your suppliant act? Now for the next item on the programme. What about the inquisitive?"

"That's what I'm coming to now." Anthony replaced the slip of paper with Gosling's signature in his wallet. Gosling waited for him. "Going back to the matter of the Dramatic Society's 'skip'—and the responsibility therefore of Mrs. Parmiter—which you'll remember we touched upon in our previous conversation—I've had an interview with that lady and I put certain questions to her. I went for that specific purpose. The upshot of our interview was that she referred me to you."

The frown had reappeared on Gosling's face. "Oh," he returned rather snappily, "and why was that, may I ask?"

"Your knowledge, so she stated, was much greater than her own."

"H'm. Compliment, I must say—and from a totally unexpected quarter. May I have the details?"

Anthony smiled. "You'll recall the incident of the yellow frock that found its way into the 'skip'?"

"How can I ever forget it?"

Anthony ignored the somewhat dramatized exaggeration. "Well, from the reverse angle, can you tell me if anything is *missing* from the 'skip' ? Has anything been taken away from it?"

Gosling looked a trifle bewildered. "I can't answer that here and now. Can I? It means making a thorough examination of the present contents of both 'skips'. You can see that for yourself, surely?"

Anthony nodded. "Yes, that's true. I take it from your answer, that you haven't actually missed anything? Up to the present?"

Gosling answered slowly. "No—I can't say that I have."

"You have no actual knowledge that anything is missing ?"

"No. Definitely not."

"There's no inventory, I suppose, of the 'skips" contents?"

Gosling took a little time to answer Anthony's question.

"There's no complete inventory. Or anything like one. Too much like a rag-bag for that. *Olla podrida*—absolutely. But there are certain lists in existence. I can remember seeing one of them sometime ago in the larger 'skip'."

"Lists? What lists would they be—exactly?"

"Well—supposing we had say half a dozen or so costumes made for a certain production, there would almost positively be a list compiled of them."

Anthony nodded. "I see."

Gosling went on. "But you can quite understand, Bathurst, that without checking the contents, I couldn't for the life of me say that anything was missing from the 'skips'. And it would be a hell of a job to do. Take hours!"

Anthony was thinking. That word 'lists' had not fallen on stony ground. There was a definite chance here.

"Would you mind if I came with you and had a quick glance at some of those lists you mentioned just now?"

Gosling seemed perturbed. "Tell me what you think may be missing. Then there is a chance of my helping you."

Anthony hesitated—and then played for safety. "I wish I knew, old chap. If I did know, my path would be considerably smoother. All I'm doing is to pursue a theory which at the moment is rather on the nebulous side and distinctly wraithlike. But if we *could* go along and—"

Gosling glanced at the clock on the mantelpiece. "I can't manage it this morning, I'm afraid. I've an appointment in half an hour's time. Which will take me well into the afternoon."

"What about this evening? Could you manage to find time for me, then?"

Gosling scratched his cheek. "Well—as a matter of fact—there's a rehearsal this evening. I don't know whether—"

Anthony cut in impetuously. "Oh—excellent! I take it you'll be down there? I could meet you. You rehearse, presumably, at the institute?"

"Oh—yes. On the stage. And, of course, I must be there. Very well then—I'll see what I can do for you when the rehearsal's over."

"Name the hour and I'm your man."

"Say about half-past nine then. But my dear chap, take a friendly warning—don't expect too much. I should hate you to be disappointed."

Anthony laughed. "That'll be my headache," he replied.

4

"Did you see that producer chap?" enquired MacMorran.

"Yes. He was at home, luckily."

"Was he co-operative? No trouble?"

"Yes—to be fair to him—I think he was—on the whole."

"You don't seem to be sure about it," growled the inspector.

"Well—I was ca'canny—I was careful not to commit myself too fully. Almost at the last moment, I decided not to give the game away too thoroughly. Actually, I got this out of him."

Anthony opened his wallet and handed MacMorran the slip of paper bearing Edmund Gosling's signature. MacMorran frowned as he read it.

"St. Simon's Church Dramatic Society. Performances of *Nothing But the Truth* on behalf of Funds of Wavering Cottage Hospital, March 23rd and 24th.

Please enrol the bearer in the capacity of ....

(Signed) Edmund Gosling."

"What's the idea?" demanded MacMorran.

"From the way I put it, Andrew, Gosling will be expecting a man. I said 'a representative of Scotland Yard'. Ten to one on it."

"He can easily find out. All he has to do is to—"

"You wait and see. It may not be quite as simple as you think. I've more than one card up my sleeve and it depends how I play them. Anyhow—I hope to have him guessing for *part* of the time at least. Don't forget *one thing*, Andrew! This show next week is not a *normal* show as far as the Dramatic Society is concerned. It's for the Hospital."

"Well—what about it? How does that matter?"

"How does it matter? In this way. The members of the audience, and I've no doubt some helpers, too, will be drawn from the Cottage Hospital circle. In the ordinary way, for a normal show, they'd all be Dramatic Society connexions, and Gosling would be familiar with practically all of them. But because there are Hospital people concerned on this occasion, there will be, I haven't the slightest doubt, many people in the hall on the two evenings who will be perfect strangers to him. *Now* do you follow my line of reasoning?"

MacMorran rubbed his jaw. "I can see that it may make a certain amount of difference. And you *may* get away with it. On the other hand—" The inspector broke off and shrugged his shoulders.

"How did you get on at Remsford, Andrew?"

"Much talk and little wool. In fact the only wool knocking about was the amount the Chief Constable kept on losing. Steadman's patience under fire was extraordinary. Much in advance, I'm afraid, of what mine would have been, had the attack been directed on me. I told them both that the murderer, in all probability, was a chap in a 'bowler hat, who smoked a pipe, carried an umbrella and his daily newspaper, who looked exactly like many thousands of others—"

Anthony cut in. "They must realize that, Andrew, if they think at all. Still—take courage, *mon ami*, I'm beginning to have hopes."

"I'm pleased to hear it—it's more than I am."

"Yes," continued Anthony, "I'm beginning to toy with a theory. To-night will help to show whether I'm on the right track or not."

"To-night? What's on to-night?"

"To-night," replied Anthony, "I'm attending a rehearsal of the St. Simon's Dramatic Society. My theory will undergo a testing."

"I hope it keeps fine for you," returned MacMorran.

CHAPTER 15

1

Anthony stood at the back of the hall and watched the rehearsal for some time. The standard of the performance was mediocre—as he had anticipated. But Gosling, on the other hand, as producer, seemed to him a man that knew his job thoroughly. His general suggestions, comments, and orders were intelligently conceived and quietly given. His sense of grouping, moreover, was sound and well thought out. Anthony waited for the rehearsal to finish. As soon as this came about, and the players left the stage, he strolled quietly down to the chair in front of the 'foots' in which Edmund Gosling was seated. The producer jumped up when he saw Anthony at his side.

"Ah—here you are then. You don't mind waiting for a few minutes, do you? Let the cast get clear before we do anything. I told them to buzz off home as quickly as possible because I wanted the dressing-rooms to myself for half an hour or so after the rehearsal."

"Thank you," replied Anthony, "a good move on your part."

"We've been honoured this evening," continued Gosling.

"Oh—in which particular direction?"

Gosling smiled. "With the presence of the Rector. It isn't so very often he comes to a rehearsal. But he was a trifle 'stuffy' over the way this show was arranged—I fixed it up really before I got the O.K. from him—unthinkingly—and he took the huff over it. But he's a decent bloke at heart—and I suppose he's relented. This is his way of healing the breach and declaring peace."

"I've met him," said Anthony. "I called on him soon after I came to Wavering."

Gosling shot him a quick glance. "I'm afraid I didn't get very far with him," elaborated Anthony, "but perhaps I can understand that—on the whole."

"He's done a good deal for St. Simon's," said Gosling, "and I get on very well with him. I always like to speak of people as I find them." He looked at his watch. "It should be O.K. by now. The cast should have cleared off. So we'll stagger along to the dressing-rooms and see what we can do with this job of yours."

Gosling turned on his heel and Anthony followed him. As the producer pushed open the first dressing-room door, Anthony heard voices in conversation. Gosling half-hesitated but then, with a quick toss of the head, he entered the room with Anthony on his heels. In the dressing-room were the Rector and his curate. Each of them registered surprise at Anthony's appearance. Gosling was quick to explain.

"You've met Mr. Bathurst, Rector, I think—and you, Mr. Cheam."

"We have—both of us," said the Rev. Matthew Hopkins smilingly—"but I for one certainly didn't expect to see him here this evening. All the same, that fact won't prevent my welcoming him."

The Rector and Frank Cheam shook hands with Anthony. Gosling essayed further explanation. The Rector began to shake his head.

"I'm afraid that I shouldn't know very much about that," he declared, "Cheam here would know more than I do. He *has* taken part in one or two productions, whereas my own debut in the histrionic art is still delayed. But, of course, you're the man yourself, Gosling, to help our friend. The very man! Who knows as much of the inner workings of our Dramatic Society as you do?"

"That's all very well, Rector. But I'm afraid the job isn't such a simple affair as it sounds. You see—both 'skips' are in use again. Costumes which were out for cleaning have been returned. Still—we can but try. Let's start on the 'skip' in this room. I fancy there may be a few of those lists I spoke about in here."

Gosling opened the 'skip' and knelt down in front of it. He busied himself for some time and then rose to his feet again.

"There are three lists in here. No—four. Now let's see what they are. *Pirates of Penzance*—that was when we were operatic *and* dramatic— *Good Losers, Officer 666,* and *Caste.*"

Anthony shook his head. "I don't think I need bother you with regard to any of them. Still—may I glance at them for a second?"

"Certainly." Gosling passed over four pieces of cardboard with typed details on them. Anthony ran his eye quickly down the particulars before returning the cards to Edmund Gosling.

"Any more?" he enquired.

The Rector and Cheam stood watching the proceedings with interest.

"Not in here, I'm afraid. There may be some in the other 'skip'," said Gosling. He took off his spectacles and wiped the glasses with a silk handkerchief.

"What is it you're actually looking for?" said Cheam—"perhaps I might be able to help."

"Don't actually know," grinned Anthony—"if I did, I'd tell you like a shot. Something that isn't here. Or that *may* not be here. Which, when you come to think of it, is a funny thing to look for, isn't it?"

The Rev. Matthew Hopkins burst into high-pitched laughter. "My dear fellow, I ask you! Like treading on the stair that isn't there—or so it seems to me."

"The other 'skip's' in the farther room," announced Gosling, "the one more recently purchased—you know the way, I think."

Gosling moved off and Anthony and the cloth followed a few paces in his rear. Gosling opened the second 'skip' and after some quick handling of the contents found a number of cards.

"Six of them in here," he said, turning round quickly to the others, "and they're all of them in the sere and yellow. One or two before even your time, Rector. *Beggars in Hell, The Jacobite, What Every Woman Knows, Romance on Wheels, The Middle Watch*, and *The Admirable Crichton*. Any questions ?"

Anthony held out his hand. "May I look—please?" One of the titles that Gosling had mentioned had caught both his ear and his imagination.

"Which one?"

Anthony boxed clever. "*The Middle Watch*."

Gosling passed over the card. "Nothing missing there," he said, "I can tell you that at once. Because we hired the lot. All the uniforms used in that show were returned to the costumiers. Which is the case more often than not for a show of that kind. The card tells you that if you look at it. It deals only with props."

Anthony saw the entries and realized that Gosling was right. "You see," went on Gosling, "we should only keep the odd stuff in the 'skips'. Where, for example, a costume has been specially made for us—or in the case of a uniform, lent or given to the society. As a rule, anything lent us for a particular show ends up as a gift and stays in the 'skip' for possible future use. That's a pretty safe bet. You see the difference between this kind of stuff and costumier's stuff—don't you?"

"Oh—yes. It's more or less what I should have expected. But, of course, I couldn't be absolutely sure until I had it from you." Anthony continued to box clever. He continued: "And, of course, I see your main point. That you can only establish a definite deficiency by going through and checking everything. Which, naturally, would be no light job and which would take, necessarily, an enormous amount of time. Now, if for instance, I asked you whether—"

Whatever Anthony may have intended to say, was negatived somewhat abruptly, by an interruption from Frank Cheam. The curate suddenly said to Gosling: "May I see those cards, old chap? Those you mentioned to Bathurst a few moments ago?"

"Certainly," replied Gosling—"they're all yours." He passed the cards over to the curate.

"Ah—I thought so," exclaimed Cheam, "here's an example, Gosling, of the point you were making to Bathurst. This card I'm looking at is in relation to the show entitled, *Romance on Wheels*. There were a couple of costumes used in that which we scrounged from somewhere. One was a nurse's—there was a hospital setting in the last act, if you remember — and the other was a kind of bus conductor's. Neither of them, to the best of my belief, came from any costumier's." Cheam turned to the Rector. "Do you remember the show, Rector? The daughter of a rich man falls in love with a bus conductor, who eventually turns out to be—"

"No—I'm afraid I don't," said Matthew Hopkins hastily. "I don't think I could have seen it. It certainly doesn't rouse any memories as far as I'm concerned."

Gosling came in to Cheam's support. "That's quite right," he said, rather impatiently, Anthony thought. "I remember the show. And the two costumes used in it do illustrate what I was saying just now. They certainly didn't come from Benjamin's as most of ours usually do— and they were no doubt kept by the Society against possible future requirements. What does the list say? Any remark against either of the costumes as listed?"

"Can't see any," returned Cheam. He showed the card to Anthony. "Look—see for yourself. Notice the two entries?"

Anthony looked and nodded. "One costume (nurse) and one uniform (bus conductor's). Good. Now I presume these two costumes are still in the 'skip' somewhere? That's your point, isn't it?"

Gosling nodded. "That's the idea. Shall I turn 'em out for you so that you can have a look at them?"

"If you would be so good," answered Anthony.

Gosling took off his glasses and polished them again before smiling at the two clergymen.

"There's one thing about Bathurst—I'll say this for him —he sees a thing through to the bitter end."

Gosling replaced his glasses and turned again to the 'skip'. "The uniform was a blueish-grey in colour to the best of my recollection," he remarked, "although it's some time since I actually set eyes on it."

"Quite right," confirmed Frank Cheam—"it was almost what you'd call Air-force blue. It had a sort of blue braid-edge."

"I wouldn't know," chirped Matthew Hopkins.

Gosling was taking various articles and costumes from the 'skip'. He stacked them on the floor at the side of it. Anthony watched the proceedings with the keenest possible interest. After a time, Gosling straightened himself, stood back from the 'skip' and pushed his fingers through his hair.

"Makes my back ache," he grunted—"not so young as I was. Gets me right across the back muscles."

Gosling took a breather for about half a minute before bending to his task again. Suddenly they heard him give an exclamation of satisfaction.

"Here we are, gentlemen. Here's the nurse's costume. Nicely folded and apparently all in order. Now for the uniform. Shouldn't be far away."

Anthony saw Gosling turn more things over and put some of them on the floor. Then he saw the producer shake his head—twice. "The darned thing's not here," announced Gosling . . . "and that's a solemn fact. I don't know whether it's one of Bathurst's hunches or not . . . but the darned bus conductor's uniform is certainly not in this 'skip'." He emphasized the last four words of his sentence.

"Are you sure, my dear Gosling," said the Rector, "that it's not in the other 'skip' ? You didn't examine it thoroughly, you know. Seems to me that can easily have happened. Somebody—Mrs. Parmiter, perhaps—may have come along and—"

Gosling closured him. "There's no reason for moving it, Rector, that I'm aware of. And if it *had* been transferred, for any reason or purpose—the card and the other costume should have been moved with it. And we *know* the card and the nurse's affair were in this 'skip'."

"You can easily test the Rector's suggestion," remarked Anthony—"why not do so at once? It will settle the matter."

"O.K.," said Gosling rather churlishly, "but I think I should have seen it, if it had been. We'll beetle back to the other room and take away the number we first thought of. I'm all for friend Bathurst and his bitter ends. Enthusiastic isn't the word."

Gosling led the way back to the first dressing-room. He threw back the lid of the 'skip' and started to wade through the contents again. There was a long period of absolute silence, as Gosling fulfilled his task. The Rector went and stood by the side of the 'skip' and looked down anxiously at Gosling's kneeling figure. Cheam also watched with interest. Anthony waited to hear Gosling's final declaration. Eventually it came. The producer raised himself from the 'skip' and turned to the three men who had been watching him so intently.

"Not here," he announced firmly—"same as before. The uniform's gone. And I'd like to know who the blazes has pinched it!"

Neither the Rector nor Cheam spoke. Anthony looked across at Gosling.

"I hope to be in a position to answer that within the course of the next few days. In the meantime, my dear sir, and to you gentlemen as well, my very best thanks for your help and assistance. At last, I'm beginning to make progress."

The Rector seemed perturbed at the turn things had taken. Several times he shook his head as though he were facing a problem of dismal shape and ungainly proportions.

Frank Cheam, however, put into words what the others were thinking.

"All the same," he said, "there is this about it. We owe Bathurst our congratulations. I don't know whether it was a long shot or not—"

Anthony interrupted him with a smile. "*Not* a long shot, by any means. Something much, more like an odds-on favourite."

2

The rain lashed the pavement with an almost indecent fury. Anthony buttoned the collar of his mackintosh tight to his chin. With his other hand he held an umbrella gallantly over the head and hat of Helen Repton.

"The elements, my dear Helen, are most certainly unkind."

"So was my wretched train," answered Helen, "over twenty minutes late. But you don't need me to tell you—seeing you've been waiting for me."

"To be exact, lady, twenty-two minutes late." He sniffed appreciatively.

"What is it?" asked Helen.

"Merely that I like your perfume. May I enquire what it is?"

" 'Angel's Kiss.' It's new. From Recamier's. I'm so glad it's approved. I liked it myself. Now I shall like it even better. I say, though, what a perfectly foul night."

Anthony guided her deftly round an awesome and ever-widening puddle. She gave him a critical glance.

"Any progress since I last graced Wavering with my presence?"

"Yes. Decided progress. The hunt is almost up. By either Wednesday or Thursday of next week, I'm hoping that we shall delete 'almost'."

"Like that, is it?"

"Yes—definitely like that. Ouch!"

"What was that?"

"Drops from an exalted umbrella. Down my neck."

"I'm frightfully sorry."

"Don't worry. It's all in a good cause. Nothing really—compared with what Sir Walter Raleigh must have suffered."

"Was it quite on the same plane?"

Anthony laughed. "About six feet higher, I should say. Taking your point absolutely literally."

"Where are the watch-dogs this evening? To my eye, on our journey so far, there's a distinct thinning of the ranks."

"The ardour of the citizen-army is quelled—or perhaps quenched is the more appropriate word—by our sister, the rain. Can't say I blame 'em myself. The citizens, I mean." Anthony took her arm. "We cross here. Don't you remember?"

Helen stepped from the kerb into a gully of swirling water. "This is, I suppose," she said, "an example of Spring in Wavering."

"I'm afraid you're right. But I've more than half a notion that on this particular Saturday evening it may be equally atrocious in Park Lane. The rain, you know, falls on the just and the unjust alike. It's possible that we twain represent the two categories."

"I think you're being rather optimistic."

"I'd prefer you to have said pessimistic. But your sex invariably wears rose-coloured spectacles. Know where you are now?"

Helen circumvented an umbrella point and looked round. "Yes. Turn left and then the second turning on the right. Am I correct, sir?"

"Beautifully. And the adverb is comprehensive."

"Would you mind telling me exactly what I am this evening? A Scotland Yard executive or a merely pleasant companion ?"

Anthony smiled but the umbrella intervened and the smile wasted its fragrance on the Wavering air. "For a period of approximately two more minutes a charming and delightful companion, for the period that will then ensue—duration unknown—er—what you said in the first place."

"I think," said Helen, "that we have reached Shelford Row. What will you do? Wait like you waited before?"

"I'm afraid not. For one thing I shall become appreciably wetter."

"You know what I mean," returned Helen severely.

"Take it as read," said Anthony. "My watchword will be 'I serve'. If only for the very good reason that I shall also stand and wait."

Helen halted at the turn. For a brief second Anthony moved the umbrella. Then he handed it to her.

"Now showing," he said, "for positively the first and last time in Wavering, the stupendously successful picture—*The Return of Mademoiselle X*."

3

Helen Repton slid quickly round the wind-swept and rain-driven corner. Anthony turned away, dug his hands well into the deep pockets of his mackintosh and cast his eye around for something which might even masquerade as shelter. A few yards ahead he spotted a narrow doorway. The shelter it promised would be but scanty but anything, so Anthony reasoned, would be better than nothing, so he walked quickly towards it and flattened his back against a wooden door. In this way he contrived, to a certain extent, to prevent the rain from beating directly on to him. The street seemed utterly deserted and Anthony could hear no sound of running vehicle or moving footsteps.

He stood there for a period of about five minutes, nursing the fervent hope that Julia Wilkes would possess the swiftest fitting technique of all the world's dressmakers. From time to time he slid back his cuff to check the hour by his wrist-watch. The hands, to his way of thinking, had never before travelled so slowly. Suddenly, as he stood there, he heard the sound of footsteps. They were approaching. And whose ever they were—that person was running! Running fast! With acutely concentrated effort! The footsteps came nearer and a few seconds later, the runner came into Anthony's sight. It was a girl. And although her shoes were light they beat on the pavement with an energy such as is parented by panic. She flew by at sheer speed.

Anthony, flattened against his doorway and silent in the shadow, waited, almost in fascination, until the flying figure, drenched and devastated, passed him. But he saw the girl's face clearly and plainly. Her face was ashen with the terror of fear, her arms and legs jerked convulsively as she ran and quick, soft sobs came from her. Anthony saw her tear into the curtain of rain and disappear into the distance.

He stood there—thinking hard. What had the Gods of Sheer Chance delivered into his lap? Anything or nothing? But if ever he saw the agony of frantic fear—

His thoughts were suddenly disrupted by the sound of other footsteps. Quick, sharp-sounding steps this time. Steps that seemed to be made with a definite fixity of purpose, they approached him from the same direction as had the running girl. Anthony pressed himself against his door and, as he did so, his ear caught the notes of a soft whistling. A man was coming towards him. In a familiar-looking grey overcoat and cap. The collar of the coat was turned right up and the fellow's shoulders were hunched against the onslaught of the rain. The whistling grew louder as the man came nearer, Anthony recognized the tune. It was 'Lily Marlene'. Anthony stood motionless against the doorway. The man passed on the very edge of the pavement entirely oblivious, seemingly, of Anthony's proximity. His head was bent to escape the full force of the wind and Anthony was unable to see his face. The man passed the door and all that Anthony could see of him now was his back. There was something strangely familiar about it. Something in the manner in which the shoulders were carried was distinctly reminiscent. Anthony lashed at his memory for the answer he so badly needed. For a time, the revelation eluded him—but then, very suddenly the necessary reminiscence came to him—and Anthony knew the identity of the man who had whistled 'Lily Marlene' as he walked past him. It was young Norman Ferguson.

4

Helen Repton lowered the umbrella that Anthony had handed on to her and rang the bell of Julia Wilkes's house in Shelford Row for the second time during that week. On this occasion, however, the response to her summons was prompt.

"Come in, my dear," said Julia, "but what a night you've picked! If it had been anybody else but you that I was expecting, I should have said that they wouldn't turn up. But I knew *you'd come*." Julia giggled.

The emphasis on the final words was unmistakable and Helen was allowed to have no illusions concerning it. She decided to treat it lightly and returned, therefore, a flippant answer.

"Oh—and why was that, Miss Wilkes ?"

Julia almost leered at her with cunning suggestion. "Because you're *different*, my dear. Different from the ordinary rank and file of people. But give me your mac and that umbrella! Good gracious, the water's simply pouring off it. I'll put it in the sink in the kitchen—it'll feel at home there. Just wait here a minute for me."

Julia disappeared into the recesses of the house with Helen's umbrella and mackintosh and Helen waited for her in the passage. Her first listening impression was that she could hear voices, but on second thoughts, she was by no means so certain on this point. It occurred to her as she stood there at the foot of the staircase that it was Julia whom she could hear and that the dressmaker was talking to herself. Suddenly, however, the door of what was evidently the kitchen opened and Julia Wilkes reappeared, a strange bright spot showing in each of her otherwise pale cheeks.

"In here, my bright young thing," she said, "the room in which you were before."

Julia turned the handle of the door and ushered Helen into the room of the oil-painting of the old man. Julia switched on the light.

"By the way, young lady," she asked, "are you in a hurry? Or have you plenty of time at your disposal?"

"I'm afraid I haven't, Miss Wilkes," replied Helen, "in fact—it's very much the other way. So that if you *could* make it short and snappy—

"H'm. Pity! Sorry to hear you say that. I'm fond of companionship. Congenial companionship. You see—I'm a lonely woman. Nobody left to me in the world to love." She laughed harshly. "Still—you know your own business best."

Julia, having delivered herself of this statement, stood with her back against the door and deliberately looked Helen over from head to foot. Helen Repton began to feel distinctly uncomfortable under the searching scrutiny.

"You're a nice trim figure," declared the dressmaker, "making a frock for you isn't like swaddling a quartern loaf—which I'm called upon to do more frequently than perhaps you'd imagine."

"How's the frock progressing, Miss Wilkes?"

The dressmaker assumed a look of infinite wisdom. "It'll be ready for you, don't you worry about that. Julia Wilkes doesn't let her clients down. I call them clients—my old father would have called them customers. But that's the march of time. If every son and daughter thought as their fathers and mothers thought—there wouldn't be any progress in the world at all. That's what I always say."

"I think you're right," nodded Helen as brightly as she knew how, and contriving at the same time to steal a glance at her wrist-watch. Julia Wilkes saw the quick look and interpreted it.

"But there—I'm letting my tongue run away with me—and that won't suit your book, Miss, will it? Now you just stay in here and I'll go and get the 'creation' for your fitting."

The dressmaker laughed her harsh laugh again and darted out of the room. Helen began to think things over. On the whole, she concluded, she felt an intense dislike of Wavering and all that Wavering stood for. If it weren't for Anthony Bathurst—the door opened again to admit Julia with pins in mouth and in her hands a frock in being. She put the pins on the table.

"Here you are, my dear. Here's what you require. Just what the doctor ordered—eh? Now let's see where we are with it. Just slip your things off, will you? If I'm any judge, it won't need very much in the way of alteration."

Helen prepared herself for the test. Julia made play with innumerable pins, smoothed folds, prodded Helen's shoulders, cosseted her ribs and then stood back to inspect *la toute ensemble*.

"Very nice," she declared, "although I says it myself. Just requires finishing off." She rubbed her hands and a knowing look came into her eyes. "You'll look very attractive, my dear. The men'll be after you. Or . . . perhaps . . . a man—eh? Ha-ha—that's a good one. When do you want it?"

"Could I have it by Monday? By Monday evening, say? I'll call here for it."

Julia cocked her head to one side. "That's not giving me too long—but I'll do it. Seeing it's for you, my dear."

Helen donned her discarded clothes. Julia brought umbrella and mackintosh and accompanied her to the front door. As Helen stepped out, Julia began to giggle.

"After all," she whispered, "it's the wrong colour, you know! Sprats aren't yellow—or anything like."

"Sprats?" echoed Helen, puzzled at the remark.

"Yes, my dear," returned Julia—"sprats—they use 'em, don't they, to catch mackerel?"

As the door slammed behind her, Helen Repton could still hear the dressmaker's harsh laugh.

CHAPTER 16

1

To Helen's relief, when she found herself on the pavement of Shelford Row, the fury of the rain and wind had abated considerably. It was still raining, it is true, but the lashing onslaught of the early evening had given way now to a much more normal fall. To her further relief, she picked out Anthony's tall figure, waiting on the corner. As she approached him he moved forward to meet her.

"Well," she said, as they joined forces, "there are, I suppose, dressmakers and dressmakers. But this one of your introduction, Mr. Bathurst, is one right out of the bag."

"Why? Has she gone back on you? Don't tell me that."

"No—it's not that. It's the woman herself. She reminds me of something out of *Arsenic and Old Lace*. She's a character, I can tell you."

"*Arsenic and Old Lace*, eh?—Well—as a dressmaker—the latter half isn't an incongruity."

Helen laughed at the Bathurst quip. "No—when you come to think of it—I suppose it isn't. Perhaps it's partly my fault—I'm not used to these country places."

Anthony laughed with her. "I'll tell you what it is, Helen. You aren't prepared. 'to talk statistics of *crime passionel* in rural districts'."

Helen wrinkled her nose before shaking her head. "But Julia Wilkes isn't a widow in a by-street—she's much more like a frustrated spinster."

"Not bad. I accept the correction with abject humility. But tell me— what of the singing and the gold—the yellow and the sequins?"

"Oh—that's O.K. Quite a decent frock, considering everything. Ready for me on Monday evening. I'm calling there for it. But . . . er . . . Mr.

Bathurst . . . I'm convinced that Julia has cottoned on to the idea that it's far from an ordinary order. Flies don't crawl on Julia. She wasn't born the day before yesterday."

Anthony was silent for a second or so as they turned into the High Street. "No. I agree. I hardly expected to hoodwink the lady. I had to take a chance. But if my judgment of the lady is only moderately sound—things shouldn't turn out too badly. I'll try to explain something of what I mean by that statement. Julia Wilkes, dressmaker, has been something like a *dea ex machina* right through the story of the Wavering murders. As, to a certain extent, you yourself know. She made the frock that Barbara Marsden wore. She alone recognized it when it was worn by Vera Ferris. And now, she's been called upon to make a similar frock when Scotland Yard moves in a mysterious way. Now—if my assessment of Julia's psychology is anything like accurate—she's a person addicted to vanity. She's flattered—distinctly flattered—by being in a position of centre stage right through the show, as you might say. If she run true to form—and I think she will—she'll hug that flattering unction to her soul—and keep a still tongue in her head. I don't fancy that she'll move in any way until the game's been played to a finish. I may be wrong—I may be taking too much for granted—but that's how I see our mutual friend Julia Wilkes."

Helen Repton half shook her head. "You don't agree with me?" said Anthony.

"Not exactly that," replied Helen. "I think I'm merely wondering whether the word you used just now—dea, wasn't it—was altogether appropriate? Anybody less like a goddess —I can't imagine."

Anthony grinned as he manipulated the umbrella. "Don't forget the context that went with it. That makes a difference, surely? And here we are again at the 'Nag's Head'. Let's hope there's something palatable for supper. Possibly a dainty fillet of something akin to sausage-meat—possibly even—"

Helen cut in . . . almost viciously. Her thoughts hadn't travelled as Anthony's had: "To me—she's a rather repulsive woman—and nothing else."

"My dear Helen—really "

"Yes—really, Mr. Bathurst. To my mind she becomes *de plus en plus dégoutante*."

2

"The yellow frock, my dear Andrew, that might adorn a programme-seller on the evenings of Wednesday and Thursday of next week," said Anthony, "is, so I understand, O.K."

MacMorran grunted with satisfaction. "All I hope is," he declared, "that it may lead to something. Personally, I'm doubtful. Very doubtful. Nothing like so hopeful as I was. Things have been quiet here ever since we arrived."

"May be the calm, Andrew. That precedes the storm. It does happen like that, you know."

"May be something quite different."

"Such as?" enquired Anthony provocatively.

"The killer may have cleared out. Left the district."

"Fresh woods and pastures new? That the idea? Well—if that's the case—no doubt we shall get to hear of it. In due course."

"When he breaks out again—you mean? That's all very well. But it means that we shall have to start all over again. And candidly—that's exactly the size and shape of my present headache."

Anthony shook his head. "I disagree with you, Andrew. I'll lay you a guinea to a gooseberry that either on Wednesday or Thursday evening next, there'll be a recurrence of the Wavering horror. That is, if you can spare one of your gooseberries."

MacMorran regarded him sceptically. "What makes you so ruddy confident? Or is it one of your so-called hunches?"

"Partly, perhaps. Partly not. The science of deduction has no small share in the vaticination. Anyhow—it's a case of wait and see."

MacMorran proceeded leisurely to fill his pipe. "Where's the girl?" he demanded, "haven't seen her since she had her grub."

"Gone to Uncle Ned, Andrew—she's tired for one thing and for another—she's got a mind full of Julia Wilkes, Wavering's leading dressmaker."

MacMorran stared at Anthony, "And what exactly is that remark intended to convey?"

Anthony smiled at the inspector. "Merely, my dear Andrew, that the afore-mentioned Julia is by no means one of Nature's gentlewomen. Definitely—*not* everybody's beaker of Orange Pekoe."

"That may be so," rejoined MacMorran, "she certainly struck *me* as a quaint sort of bird—but I shouldn't have expected her to get *our* girl down. From what I've seen and from what I know of Miss Repton in the past. She's always been so remarkably cool-headed. Can't quite make that out." MacMorran shook his head as though he were plagued by doubt.

"You never know, Andrew. Some people are sufficiently misguided to be allergic to oysters. And they'll never know the extent of my sympathy."

"Oysters—my foot," returned Andrew MacMorran.

3

When Anthony went to his bedroom that evening he felt that the time had come again for another of his exercises in 'intensive thought'. He found the most comfortable chair, saw that he was equipped with cigarettes in plenty and settled down to concentrate on the essentials of the Wavering problem just as he had so many times in the past when called upon to tackle similar riddles. In a cloud of cigarette-smoke, he took fountain-pen and a sheet of note-paper and proceeded to make the following notes:

(1)   Barbara Marsden strangled January 24th. Body hidden in old bath back of hockey pavilion on allotments. Possibly before that—in theatrical 'skip'—query. Wore yellow frock to Church Social. Frock made by Julia Wilkes. Traces of fat on shoulders and also on wickerwork of another 'skip'. Knife slash on cheek. Fat stolen from Tidman. Dead girl had been employed by Parmiter. But left his service suddenly—query. Parmiter and Tidman both churchwardens. Coincidence! Boy friends—Norman Ferguson and Sid Rolleston—R.A.F. and R.N. Query—demobbed.

(2)   Vera Ferris strangled February 22nd. Body hidden in bath as in case of Barbara Marsden. Wore same yellow frock in dramatic performance a week previously. Frock taken by her from Dramatic Society's 'skip'. Frock recognized during performance by Julia Wilkes. Traces of fat same as B. M. Again, fat stolen from Tidman by same method as in first instance. Diary of V. F. mentions that she was followed on her way home from dramatic performance by man in 'Green Circle' uniform. But Andrew M. is satisfied that he has established the fact that no G. C. staff reside in Wavering. Query—'Green Circle'. Uniform may have been something else. No boy friend in case of V. F.

(3)   Significant fact—'blue-grey' bus conductor's uniform missing from Dramatic Society's 'skip'. According to the curate Cheam—colour suggestive of 'air-force' uniform. Query—N. Ferguson—and running girl.

(4) Two wooden broom-handles (? *inter alia*) found with bodies of the murdered girls. Fantastic theory—perhaps —can they have any connexion with the 'wooden poles' carried by performing bear that did his stuff outside Tidman's shop last' November ? Strange how this theory came to me early on and persists in 'whanging back'. Query—'claw'-mark on girls' cheeks.

(5) Conclusion—if any! Murderer—if *human*—probably anybody. Insignificant, common-place, ordinary, entirely unsuspected. Smiles by day—and kills at night. But *possibly*—one of say, about a dozen people—who keep popping up now and then and here and there. *Ultimate* conclusion—wait and see what next week brings forth—despite somewhat disconcerting pessimism of Andrew M. I can't *really* get an identifiable suspect!

Anthony sat back in his chair, carefully read the notes he had just jotted down, folded the sheet of paper and placed it in his wallet. Try as he would, his mind refused to dissociate itself from the stolen fat and the knife-slashes on the dead girls' cheeks. Surely—it persisted to him in its argument —there must be vital significances herein, if he were only able to grasp them? But what were they? That was the question. The question to which he *must* find the answer. And then—at that moment, Anthony thought of something else. His mind went back to the earlier part of the evening and the waiting period he had spent in the rain and wind while Helen Repton was in the house of Julia Wilkes. He could hear again the sound of the running girl's footsteps, her quick-breathed fear and the whistle of the man with the hunched shoulders who had followed her down the street.

Anthony furrowed his brows. Could he be really certain that the man was Norman Ferguson? *Was* it the man himself? His walk? After all—he hadn't done much walking when Anthony had interviewed him. What clothes had he been wearing? Anthony tried hard for the reminiscence of the association but it was strangely fugitive and persisted in eluding him. But Ferguson had *mentioned* that he had been called up for the R.A.F.! Backwards and forwards Anthony's thoughts rioted, churning at the various data which were his mind's consideration. With the invariable result that he found himself concentrating on the knife-slashes on the cheeks . . . on the fat applied to the feet and shoulders of the two dead girls . . . each girl had been treated in the same sinister manner . . . was this fact an expression of sadism . . . or was there something deliberately methodical about it?

Anthony shook his head. It was so unusual . . . so apparently meaningless . . . so bizarre . . . it seemed to him, though, the more he dwelt upon it, that there was something like definite and deliberate method attached to it. He gnawed and worried at this bone of an idea for a long time in the hope that something tangible would come to him out of it. Struggle against it as he might, he was unable to rid himself of the mental suggestion that the slash on the cheeks was part of some obscure and obscene ritual. Something to do, so his mind continued to tell him, with the *blood* of the victim. The cheeks had been slashed because the murderer . . . his worrying became more acute and more intense . . . something darted into his brain and conjured up in his thoughts, practices akin to those of the Black Mass . . . similar to those associated with the infamous cult of diabolism . . . and then . . . very suddenly, Anthony sat up in his chair . . . of course . . . the poles . . . the knife, the fat, the poles! There was the connexion! They all three fitted!

How blind he had been not to see this damning fact before! Anthony felt a thrill of elation course through him. He began to rub his hands . . . slowly but deliberately. If he didn't know 'who', he was beginning to think that at last he knew 'why'.

"And in the twentieth century," he muttered to himself . . . "well . . . well . . . well."

CHAPTER 17

1

L ate in the afternoon of the following Monday, Anthony provided Helen Repton with something very much like a surprise. Actually, the incident occurred just before tea.

"I'm not exactly looking forward to this evening," she said . . . "and do you know, it's altogether a new experience for me—to admit anything like that."

Anthony gave her a shrewd, calculating glance. "What do you mean . . . exactly?" he asked.

"I'm alluding to the fact that I call for my frock this evening," she answered with an assumed lightness of tone, "and try as I may, I find it impossible to regard a visit to Julia Wilkes with any emotion other than extreme distaste. Sorry, Mr. Bathurst, and all that—but that's just the way it goes."

Anthony allowed his glance to dwell upon her. What he saw on her features occasioned him some amount of mental disturbance. Helen's face was white and strained. In all his previous experience of her assistance to him, he had never seen her in anything like the condition in which she was now.

"What is it the wretched woman does to you?"

Helen shivered. "Just gets me down—that's all. It's nothing, of course, and I'm just being crazy over it. Please forget it. I'm being absurd. I ought to know better."

Anthony shook his head at her. "You'd rather not call on her this evening? Is that it?"

"Of course not," defended Helen sturdily—"I must go. It's my duty to go. Don't take any notice of me."

"I don't know that you must, Helen. All that has to be done is to call for the frock and take it away. Anybody can do that. Now I come to think of it—I don't see any valid reason why I shouldn't call for the frock myself. It might give me an opportunity of improving my acquaintance with the formidable Julia. Do you know, the more I envisage it, the more attractive I find it—I think I'll do it. Will that suit you?"

Helen Repton shook her head. "It *suits* me all right. But it's all wrong. It's pandering to my weakness. I'm behaving like an hysterical schoolgirl—you mustn't do it. Please let me—"

Anthony's words cut into hers. "Not a bit of it. You've got it all round your neck. I'm doing it to suit myself. At this stage of our problem, nothing would afford me greater pleasure than a closer walk with Julia Wilkes. Please divest yourself of the idea that I'm considering you. Nothing of the kind, my dear, I assure you. For one thing—entirely subversive to discipline—and you know what a stickler I am for that. Nobody ever stickled more stickily."

Helen Repton realized that she had contested a losing battle. She shrugged her trim shoulders and smiled at Anthony.

"It's very sporting of you—and I suppose I must give in—but I have no illusions about it. I know *exactly* why you—"

"Sit down," said Anthony, with a wave of the hand, "and scribble a note to Julia. To give me the authority for collecting the yellow frock on your behalf. She may be awkward over it. It may then develop into a case of 'stickler v. stickler'."

Anthony grinned. Helen went to a table, found note-paper, and wrote. After a time, she half-turned and looked towards Anthony over her shoulder.

"She knows me as 'Mademoiselle X'," she said, "so I've signed this note with that signature. Will it do?"

Anthony nodded to her. "Excellent," he declared—"I can't think of a better." He rose from his chair and chuckled. "When she opens the door to me this evening, Julia *will* be surprised! And perhaps not only surprised. May be a trifle disappointed as well. I know that I should be were I in her circumstances. I wonder how she'll react to disappointment?"

2

It was at precisely half-past seven that evening when Anthony rang the bell of the dressmaker's house in Shelford Row. The response came almost immediately. Anthony heard the sound of feet hurrying to the front-door. The door opened to reveal Julia Wilkes. Anthony could almost hear her face fall.

"Who are *you*?" she exclaimed suspiciously, "and what do you want here?"

"Merely a messenger, madam," replied Anthony—"the letter will explain."

He handed over Helen Repton's scribbled note. Julia Wilkes tore the flap of the envelope and read the letter, her eyes full of distrust and resentment. He noticed that she held the note close to her eyes.

"Don't like it," she snapped, "don't like it at all. The girl said she'd come along herself. Why hasn't she come? Doesn't say anything here as to why she hasn't come. Don't like substitutes—any more than I like strangers. Besides—what about my account? Who'll settle that?"

She glared at Anthony inquisitively and critically. "The lady in question cannot call on you this evening, madam, because she is compelled to be elsewhere. With regard to the matter of the bill—I shall be pleased to do the necessary."

"That's all very well," grumbled Julia Wilkes, "I don't like it. Like people to keep their own appointments. Then you know where you are. All fair and above board. Can't stand people that don't keep their word. Breach of faith." She stopped talking and looked him over appraisingly. "Don't know that I altogether like the look of you. Look like a copper to me. Different from Loder and his like—but a copper all the same. Once a copper—always a copper. It's your feet, I suppose, that give you away. Big and ugly. Still—we can't stand talking here—I suppose you'd better come in. Although it's against my better judgment to let you."

Julia stood back from the door and grudgingly yielded Anthony entrance. Then she piloted him into the room to which Helen Repton had been shown previously. Like Helen, Anthony saw that it was comfortable and well furnished.

"Sit down," said Julia with curt directness, "and I'll bring you the famous frock. Or should I have said 'infamous' ?"

She started a high-pitched laugh which rather startled Anthony and which he could hear persisting for some time after she had left him. As he sat there, he began to understand better why Helen Repton felt as she had said she did. At that moment, his glance took in the portrait of the old man over the mantelpiece. Strange eyes! Extraordinarily strange eyes. Something began to tick in Anthony's brain. He had heard something about a man in the family of Julia Wilkes. Now who was it had told him? The answer came to him promptly. It had been Tidman, the butcher in the High Street. Julia's father, once a successful corn-chandler, had gone 'funny' in his advancing years. 'Nuts' had been Tidman's colloquial description. That in itself would account for this oddity in the eyes of the man in the oil-painting above the mantelpiece.

Anthony rose from his chair in order to take a closer look at the portrait. There was a likeness to Julia. Round the mouth and the line of the jaw. Anthony began to sort out one or two matters that had been troubling him. In a country town of the size and general calibre of Wavering, one would have thought, that all things being equal—he heard the sound of Julia's footsteps approaching again and he slipped quietly back into the chair. The door opened and Julia entered with a brown-paper parcel.

"There you are," she said, with an ugly twist to her mouth, "there's what you've come for. All ready and finished. I'm one of the people who keep their word. Pity there aren't more like me. Hope it will please your little lady-friend. Funny if *she* got strangled in it."

Again the high-pitched laugh from Julia to finish her statement. Anthony judged it politic to make no immediate reply. It seemed to him that comment would be indiscreet.

"Thank you, Miss Wilkes," he said eventually, "and now, please tell me how much I owe you."

Julia cocked her head to one side. "Would seven guineas hurt you? Seeing what an important commission it is?"

"Whatever you say, Miss Wilkes. I'll pay you now." Anthony's hand went to his wallet. He counted out the currency notes and found the appropriate amount in silver. "There you are, Miss Wilkes. The exact money—no bother for you to find change."

Julia Wilkes counted the notes and the coins with an avid meticulousness. "Quite right—but only just."

She took the money to a side-board and Anthony heard her open a drawer. Suddenly she wheeled round to him. "Well, Mr. Policeman, aren't you going? Because you're not welcome here, I can tell you. There's nothing more to see—or hear. So you needn't wait another second."

Anthony leant back in his chair and smiled. Then he indicated the bill on the table. "The receipt, Miss Wilkes, if you please."

The dressmaker snatched at a pen from her side-board, leant over the table and scribbled her signature across the bill. She jerked the paper towards Anthony with an impatient gesture. As she saw him examine it, she burst out: "Well—and what's wrong with it?"

"It lacks a twopenny stamp," replied Anthony quietly.

The dressmaker grabbed the bill back and suddenly both her manner and her tone of voice changed.

"I beg your pardon, I'm sure. Please don't think I'm not a business woman. I should positively hate you to think that." The manner was almost gentle—the voice quiet.

"On the contrary," said Anthony, "I have the greatest respect for your business ability. To say nothing of your natural acumen."

Julia Wilkes grinned as she did the needful with the receipt-stamp. Anthony heard her begin to whistle. She was still whistling as she saw him off the premises. But he had walked at least a hundred yards before he realized that the air Julia had whistled fitted the words of 'Who's your lady friend?' There were certainly no flies on Julia . . . even though she rubbed Helen Repton the wrong way . . . funny how suddenly her manner had changed just now . . . almost as though she had felt herself under a new influence . . . and then, with a surge of excitement, Anthony found himself almost feverishly feeling for his diary.

3

Wednesday evening came. It was a beautiful evening of early spring. The moon, almost at its full, rose early and hung over the little town, laden with its white fire. Anthony and Andrew MacMorran made their way to the institute separately from Helen Repton. Helen travelled her own road, by no means displeased that the yellow frock with its sequins, which she wore under her coat, suited her reasonably well and fitted her remarkably well. For a country town dressmaker, thought Helen, Julia Wilkes wasn't so dusty!

In recognition of the requirements and urgent needs of the local Cottage Hospital, anybody who *was* anybody in Wavering, seemed to be present. Frank Cheam had been right in his prophecy. The people flocked to the show on account of the excellence of the cause.

When Anthony and MacMorran arrived, Cheam failed to conceal his delight. "Oh—good for you," he exclaimed when he saw them coming up to him—"I'm delighted to think that you're using those tickets after all. You'll find I've scrounged you a couple of really good seats."

Anthony thanked him cordially and the curate of St. Simon's bustled off to greet other arrivals. Anthony saw, either seated or in the foyer, the Rector, Owen Tidman, Vernon Parmiter and his wife, and the ubiquitous Julia Wilkes. Once, too, he saw Edmund Gosling come through the swing-doors which communicated with the dressing-rooms. Gosling, he thought, looked anxious and worried and several times mopped his forehead with a handkerchief.

Anthony spoke to MacMorran. "Sit here, Andrew—and I'll nip along and arrange my programme racket."

MacMorran nodded. "O.K. I've seen to all the other arrangements. Told Steadman what we want and he has been most helpful. I've a soft spot in my heart for our girl and it would hurt me considerably if any harm came to her. So there won't. Take that from me and go ahead."

"Thank you, Andrew. I'll start the ball rolling, then." Anthony slipped through the connecting-doors that led to the dressing-rooms. He was on the look-out for the programmes 'H.Q.'. It didn't take him long to spot it. A beaming, stout, effusive lady was evidently in charge. She donated packets of programmes to a number of nymph-like creatures who clustered round her, with the air of a goddess who had walked to glory and run to fat.

Anthony pushed Gosling's authority into her hand. He had completed it appropriately before leaving the 'Nag's Head'.

"Programmes, please," he said cheerfully.

The stout lady scowled at the slip of paper which Anthony had given her. Still scowling, she transferred her glance to Anthony himself. He returned smile for scowl. Expansive and ever-widening.

"I don't know," she said to herself—"who are you? What's your name?"

"Smith," returned Anthony cheerfully, "initials A. A., Alfred Albert. Perhaps you know my cousin Tom Smith—better known by his nickname, 'crackerjack'—Mr. Gosling told me to see you."

The stout lady grumbled loud and long. "Too many fingers in this pie to-night. Wherever you go. Too many cooks by far. I don't like it." She began to count programmes. "There you are, Smith—er—Mister Smith. At threepence each. Fifty. I'll book them out to you. Take the rear of the hall on the left-hand side."

Anthony lifted the pile of programmes. "Too many of you Hospital people," said the stout lady, "shan't know where we are if I'm not careful."

Anthony smiled again. "Good cause," he said as inanely as he knew how.

"Glad you think so. Too many people interfering."

Anthony essayed further inanity. "More the merrier—eh what?"

"The more—the muckier," returned the stout lady almost venomously—"that's how I feel about it. And for two pins I wouldn't hesitate to tell Mr. Gosling so."

Anthony turned and disappeared. He knew that Helen Repton would be in the place of his instructions. He moved quickly towards the spot. A young man almost collided with him as he passed through the connecting-doors. Anthony looked up at the near impact and saw that it was Norman Ferguson. His head was down and he seemed to be in a violent hurry. Anthony watched him as he made his way to a seat near the front. Ferguson, evidently, had not seen Anthony, because he sat down without giving even the semblance of a glance in Anthony's direction. Anthony found Helen Repton in the path outside the hall as he had told her to be. He pushed the bundle of programmes under her arm.

"Here you are, lady. Fifty at threepence a time. You ornament the rear of the hall on the left-hand side. Bring the proceeds to me when you've sold 'em as I'm on the books, not you. Name of Smith—me. Alfred Albert. 'Igh class. Very 'igh class. Now nip into the ladies' 'cloaks', get rid of your coat, smooth out the creases of the Wilkes's creation—and get cracking. Let Wavering gaze its full on you. O.K. ?"

Helen nodded. "Yes—that's all understood. Where shall I settle this programme lark with you?"

"Here. Same spot. At the end of Act Two. You nip out here with the doings and I'll meet you and relieve you of it. Till then, lady, keep your eyes skinned and good-hunting. Now go and do your stuff."

Helen Repton slipped away into the shadows.

4

Anthony joined MacMorran in the auditorium and Helen began in her role of programme-seller. She found no barrier to her performance of Anthony's directions. She took off her heavy coat, accepted the check for it from the ancient crone on duty as attendant and, at a convenient moment, sidled unostentatiously into the hall with her stock of programmes.

There was another girl on the left-hand side of the rear of the hall, bent evidently on similar employment. This pink-clad girl made no attempt whatever to conceal her resentment at Helen's appearance.

"I'm here," she announced in an aggressive whisper.

"So am I," returned Helen brightly.

"I wasn't told you were coming here."

"I wasn't told *you'd* be here."

The pink girl pouted. "I wouldn't cry over it if I were you," said Helen, "it isn't worth it—believe me. You take the left of the aisle—I'll take the right."

"*You* aren't in the Dramatic Society," said the pink girl suddenly, "I've never seen you before."

"Quite right, my dear. I'm Cottage Hospital. That's why I'm helping. Several of us are. *Now* do you understand?"

"Suppose I've got to," returned the pink girl, "but all the same I'd like   —"

She broke off abruptly in the shadow of prospective customers. "Programme, sir? Programme, madam? Threepence each. Thank you, sir."

Helen gave thanks for the benison of the interruption. She moved a few steps up the aisle and took better stock of the people around her. She saw no face that was familiar to her. Then a rush at the doors—a bus-load in all probability—kept her busy selling programmes for some minutes. A light touch on her arm brought her to the turn. A man in clerical clothes was standing by her. His eyes smiled.

"I say," he said, "are you one of the Hospital helpers? I'm just checking up. The Rector spotted you and asked me to. My name's Cheam—I'm the curate here, you know."

"Yes—I'm Hospital—as you imagined."

"Thank you so much. No end good of you to help. Very much appreciated. I'll tell the Rector."

The curate smiled once more and passed on. Helen breathed again. She looked at her wrist-watch. Still a quarter of an hour before the curtain. She must remember Anthony's instructions and 'exhibit' herself as prominently as possible. Another clergyman passed by her and, as he passed, he looked at her rather longer than he should have—that is according to the canons of courtesy. To say nothing of the courtesy of canons. He was much older than Cheam—Helen supposed him to be the Rev. Matthew Hopkins—the Rector.

She was conscious of many people brushing by her, men and women. And many other men and women purchased programmes from her. Some of the former seemed to linger unnecessarily over the purchase. Thus the minutes passed until the curtain went up—and Helen sold her last remaining programme and slid noiselessly into an unoccupied seat at the back of the hall. To her surprise she found that she was sitting next to the young person in pink.

"Oh"—said the latter petulantly—"so it's you again."

"It's both of us," replied Helen.

"Fancy that now," said pink.

"I don't," returned Helen.

CHAPTER 18

1

The moment that the curtain descended on the second Act, Helen retrieved her coat from the clutches of the crone and made speedily for the obscure corner of the path where she had rendezvous with Anthony. He was waiting for her when she arrived.

"My," she exclaimed, "but you've travelled fast."

Anthony grinned. "My feet were shod with lightning, lady. As a wingèd messenger of—"

Helen poured coins into his cupped hands. "Sold out, sir. Twelve shillings and sixpence there. Fifty at threepence a time. Are you going to count it?"

Anthony dropped the coins into his overcoat pockets. "Not on your life. Know your skill and honesty. How do you think you went?"

Helen smiled. "I paraded to the nth degree. Did you happen to notice me? I almost embroidered the chair-rows with pieces of myself. I festooned myself in postures and poses all designed to lure, intrigue, and attract. Not altogether, I fancy, without a measure of success. Several pairs of masculine eyes have fastened, fixed, and feasted. Now tell me— the other part. You know—the part that really counts." She shivered just a little as she spoke.

"Cold?" inquired Anthony.

"Just a bit. Try not to be too long."

"I won't. Now listen carefully. When the curtain falls, don't get away from the hall too quickly. Let the crowd get well going before you begin to make a move. If the bait has been taken, there's no doubt you'll be watched all the time—right from the final curtain. Then—when you've re-collected that coat you're wearing—you can take your time over this to your heart's content—saunter away casually in the direction of the

Remsford side of the town—that is to say, the side where the allotments are. That's all for you. Leave the rest to us. Oh—I know—if nothing happens, give yourself ten minutes' easy walking exercise and then we'll pick you up. Revolver O.K.?"

Helen nodded. "I'll say it is. And don't worry—I shall be all right. But tell me one thing—please—before you go. Where exactly will you be? Because—"

"In a private car, never more than a couple of hundred yards behind you. Sounds warm and comforting, doesn't it?"

Helen nodded again. "It certainly does. All right! I'm clear. Nothing else, is there?"

"No. I've given you the bundle. You can buzz now—and I'll run along and pay in your ill-gotten gains. Oh—if it *should* come to a show down— play your fish skilfully—don't be in too much of a hurry and let it jump the rod."

"I'll do my best—you know that."

"I do. All the best. We'll be with you."

Anthony saw Helen running back to the hall. He thought for a moment and came to the decision to pay over his programme-receipts there and then. There would still be time for this, judged by his experience of amateur productions.

The curtain was still down when he re-entered the hall. He made, therefore, a bee-line for the communicating-doors. As he passed through them he found himself face to face with Tidman, the butcher. In almost the exactly corresponding position he had previously encountered Norman Ferguson. Tidman looked a trifle startled. His face suggested that he was endeavouring to 'place' Anthony, but that his brain wasn't ticking right.

"Good evening, Mr. Tidman," said Anthony, "you're quite right as it happens—we *have* met before. The encounter took place, actually, on your own territory."

Tidman's face cleared. "Of course! I've got it. One of the bloodhounds of crime. Couldn't think where it was I'd seen your face."

Anthony smiled. "Glad I've rung a bell."

But Tidman seemed curious. "But what are you doing here? Don't tell me you're looking for a murderer at an amateur dramatic entertainment! My dear chap! The setting's all wrong—just haywire."

"I expect you're right. But you never can tell. Murderers have been known to turn up in the most unlikely places."

"Yes—I know—but my dear chap! Have a heart. Rectors and curates, churchwardens and the like—come—you're pulling my leg—I feel sure."

"There are others present, Mr. Tidman. Even butchers and bakers—and possibly—tucked away somewhere—even an odd candle-stick maker. I shouldn't be surprised at anything."

Tidman shook his head. "No—it won't do. You're all wrong. I shall have to come and give you a hand—that'll be the end of it. Still—can't stay jawing here. I expect I shall run into you again somewhere."

The churchwarden nodded and pushed open the doors to admit him into the hall. Anthony stood thinking. A burst of laughter told him that the curtain for the third act was up at last. Anthony's fingers caressed the ridge of his jaw. He began to wonder what MacMorran was thinking. The inspector knew what to do if Anthony didn't return to his seat before the end of the show. Anthony moved swiftly forward, therefore, towards the farther dressing-room, presided over by the goddess of programmes. The stout lady was still there. An almost seraphic smile pervaded her countenance. She was counting money! Anthony stepped into the room.

"Smith's the name. Initials A. A. And you can trust any member of the great and noble Smith family to bring the mill its further grist."

He poured coins on to the table. "Twelve shillings and sixpence, madam. Or in other words, fifty programmes at threepence a time. Sold out—no returns. What salesmanship!"

"Thank you, Mr. Smith. Thank you, indeed. As far as I can see up to the moment, the programmes have gone excellently. *Much* better than usual."

"That's very complimentary, madam. Much appreciated—assure you. Good evening."

"Shall we be seeing you to-morrow, Mr. Smith?"

Anthony paused by the door. It occurred to him that it was strange that he couldn't answer the stout lady's question with any certainty. He tiptoed back to the table.

"Perhaps," he answered—"and then again—perhaps not. We Smiths are unpredictable. Good evening to you again, madam."

2

Anthony and Andrew MacMorran waited for the car. Happily there was no delay. It came up behind them and stopped by the kerb—a good hundred yards from the hall on the Remsford side. Anthony saw Steadman seated inside and a liveried chauffeur at the driving-wheel. Before they got in, Anthony spoke to MacMorran.

"Good show," he said quietly, "nobody would take this outfit for a police job. It's just right. Couldn't be bettered. I must congratulate Steadman."

"Don't be too confident," came MacMorran's warning—"there's a long way to go yet. This is only the beginning."

Steadman leant over and opened the door for them. Anthony and MacMorran slipped inside.

"Good work, Inspector," said Anthony to Steadman—"just what the doctor might have ordered."

"Thank you, Mr. Bathurst. I think it's the goods—although I say it myself. Now what about the young lady? I take it she knows exactly what to do."

"Yes. That's all right. You can rely on her absolutely. She's not out yet. She'll take her time—on my instructions—and she'll come this way."

"What do we do before we sight her? I don't want to hang about here too long."

"Turn the car," said MacMorran, "and run slowly in the other direction. Until we meet her." He glanced at his watch. "Judging by the time now—we'll meet her for certain. Then your chap can run on a little distance farther and turn again. Coming back we can keep the girl in sight all the time. Everything's laid on and we can take it all as quietly as possible."

"O.K.," said Steadman. "I'll tell Pooley."

The Remsford inspector lowered the glass and spoke quietly to the driver. Pooley said something which Anthony was unable to catch. Steadman turned round again.

"He says what's the young lady wearing?"

"Brown tweed coat," answered Anthony, "tell him you'll tap on the glass directly we spot her."

Steadman relayed the instruction and Pooley turned the car and began to cruise back. Anthony watched the pavements carefully. Just as they reached the hall, he saw Helen Repton stroll casually away.

"O.K.," said Anthony quietly, "get cracking."

Steadman leant forward from his seat and tapped on the glass of the centre window for Pooley to hear and to understand. The car ran on for some little distance before turning again. By the time it faced the direction of Remsford again, Helen was about two hundred and fifty yards ahead. Anthony, for one, was able to see her brown-coated figure almost on the corner, by the church of St. Simon's. He was in one of the rear seats, and on the same side as Helen Repton was walking. She was sauntering quite coolly and almost casually, her hands thrust deep into the big pockets of her tweed coat, exactly as he had prompted her. There were several other people in close proximity to her, many of whom, undoubtedly, had just left the church hall.

"Can you see anybody besides our girl, Andrew?" he asked MacMorran. "I mean anybody in whom we might have more than an ordinary interest."

MacMorran's eyes never left the range of pavement.

"Nobody I can pick out," came the reply, "we must wait a little while until they sort themselves out somewhat."

The car proceeded slowly until they saw Helen actually take the turning that led to the allotments and the old hockey pavilion.

"Now watch carefully," said Anthony.

"Too many people about," growled MacMorran—"too many of 'em going the same way home. That's the trouble."

Anthony's mouth was set in hard lines. He realized that the 'Yard' inspector had hit the nail on the head.

"Just a minute," said MacMorran, a second or so later, "I rather fancy that there *is* a figure that seems to have detached itself from the rest of them—many of the people have crossed over the turning. We shall be able to see more clearly when the car turns the corner."

The inspector's words electrified the others. There was a dead silence inside the car as Pooley turned the driving-wheel. Was it a man—or a woman? Or was it—

The car took the turning . . . slowly. . . .

3

Helen Repton waited for the cloak-room to be more or less clear before she claimed her coat from the bent figure of the crouching crone on duty. She donned her coat, patted a stray tendril of hair in place in front of a cracked and discoloured mirror, powdered her nose and let her hand assure herself that her coat-pocket contained her revolver. About to turn to make her way out, her blood ran cold as a hand gripped her shoulder.

"I smell the blood of an Englishwoman," a voice hissed in her ear.

Helen completed the turn that she had started to make—to see Julia Wilkes behind her. The dressmaker laughed discordantly. "Ha-ha," she exclaimed, "that gave you a start, didn't it? Still—never mind, young lady—it's only me. No need to get scared. I'll tell you what I wanted to say to you." Julia Wilkes came quite close and whispered in Helen's ear. "I don't want anybody else to hear me say this. But your frock looked very nice, my dear. Most *attractive*! Perhaps 'fetching' would be the word. I'd like you to give me the name and address of your dressmaker."

Before Helen could reply, however, Julia dashed out of the cloak-room as though hounds from hell were at her heels.

'Nice cheerful start,' thought Helen, 'and well in keeping.'

Consigning Wavering and its entire population to a place of darkness, she made her exit from the little room and stepped out into the night. She walked down the roughish path and came to the pavement.

"Now for it," said Helen—"I wonder if I resemble in any way an alluring morsel of cheese?"

4

Obeying Anthony Bathurst's instructions to the letter, she turned right and strolled nonchalantly (or so she flattered herself) in the Remsford direction. She soon noticed what MacMorran was observing from the comfort of the car. That the pavement was moderately thick with people.

'Grateful and comforting,' she thought, 'but no good from the point of view of the human mouse-trap.'

She began, therefore, to walk even more slowly—in the hope that the High Street would soon begin to get less congested. Her hopes were realized. The farther she walked, the more the groups of people began to thin. Most of them were, doubtless, returning from the entertainment. Helen began to think on similar lines to MacMorran. Everybody, or almost everybody, who had witnessed the dramatic performance, seemed to be going home in the direction of Remsford. If anybody *were* actually trailing her, she wouldn't know about it yet awhile. Probably not until she had rounded the corner by the church itself.

She came to the corner and slowly took the turning with a devout prayer in her heart that Anthony and his car were not too far behind her. Anyhow—there was nothing else for it now—she summoned all the resources of her courage and walked on. In the direction of the allotments . . . and the disused hockey-club pavilion . . . where two girls before her had come to their deaths. She strained her ears to hear footsteps. *Was* there anybody actually following her—now? Now that she had left the main stream of people? A strong and almost irresistible inclination came to her to look round. The temptation was terrific. But she resisted the urge and actually permitted herself to smile. There was *one* thing that wouldn't happen to her. Even though it wasn't of any particular comfort. She wouldn't be turned into a pillar of salt!

She strained her ears again. She couldn't hear *anything*. She couldn't even hear the sound of a car. She was a good hundred yards down the road by now—almost abreast of the 'Green Circle' garage. There were two 'single-deckers' drawn up in the yard outside the main building. But she saw no sign of any staff—either in uniform or in mufti. As she walked past the out-buildings, she decided to accelerate her pace. To do this might tell her what she so badly wanted to know. Had the bait been taken or was she just wasting her time? She quickened her pace appreciably and as she did so, she glanced at her wrist to see the time. What she saw occasioned her surprise. It was just three minutes since she had left the hall cloak-room. Good lord, she thought, it seems more like three hours. Shows you what nerves can do with your judgment. She could see the desolate-looking stretch of allotment land. What a place to walk out to—at this time of night. What a mercy the moon was so bright!

She heard a train whistle a long way off and, even farther away, the sound of a clock chiming. That must be a quarter-past eleven. But both the train whistle and the clock chime were friendly sounds—better to her ear than the sound of sinister, implacable footsteps. Helen walked on and on. Until she was able to distinguish clearly the outlines and general shape of the old pavilion. She looked at her watch again. Thank goodness, Anthony's margin of ten minutes was almost up. She halted in her tracks and listened. Her ears failed to detect the slightest sound. She might have been alone in the world. The gauntlet which Anthony had thrown down had been ignored by the killer. Helen half-turned and as she did so, a car drew up almost as it were, by her elbow. A door opened and she saw MacMorran's weather-beaten face.

"Jump in, lass," he said, "and we'll take you for a ride."

Helen stepped briskly into the car. "For this relief," she said jauntily, "much thanks."

Steadman leant over towards her. "Nothing doing—eh? Nothing at all?"

"Nothing," replied Helen—"and I'm not sure yet whether I'm glad or sorry."

Anthony sat silent at the back of the car. "We thought there was early on," continued MacMorran, "just before you turned the corner by the church. There was a figure well on your tail. We all thought we spotted somebody whose wrists might fit a pair of bracelets. But it seems we were wrong."

"I've seen and heard nothing," returned Helen, "but naturally, I shouldn't. I just walked on and didn't look back."

Steadman rallied Anthony. "You've barked up the wrong tree, I'm afraid, Mr. Bathurst. Point is—where do we go from here?"

Anthony shook his head. "Ah—that's something I'd give a lot to know myself."

He relapsed into silence again. The car was making speed now towards the 'Nag's Head'. Suddenly Anthony gave a sharp exclamation and his hand went to his pocket. Steadman saw him open a small book.

"Don't tell me," Steadman said facetiously, "that you've the killer's name down in your diary, because I shall find it difficult to believe."

Anthony smiled—for the first time since Helen had entered the car. "My dear Inspector," he said, "not the killer's name. But something, perhaps, almost as valuable. With regard to this evening—I must take all the censure you choose to give me. I deserve it. The miscalculation was mine.

The car was stopping. Pooley turned it round and pulled up outside the 'Nag's Head'. Anthony, MacMorran, and Helen Repton alighted. Anthony lingered for a second and spoke to Steadman through the space of the lowered window.

"Same arrangements to-morrow evening, Inspector Steadman—if you will be so good."

Steadman was startled by Anthony's request. "To-morrow evening, Mr. Bathurst? Same again?"

"Same again," replied Anthony gravely.

"Why? Do you really think that it may—"

"I have high hopes," replied Anthony.

Steadman whistled. "You mean—same in every detail?"

"Same in every detail, Inspector. It is always a matter well worth remembering—that to-morrow is also a day."

Steadman accepted the inevitable. "Very good, Mr. Bathurst. That shall be done. Rely on me." Steadman put the window up, waved to the others and the car made off.

"You've done the right thing," said MacMorran, "I'm in entire agreement with you. To-morrow gives us another chance."

Helen Repton, who had been a few paces ahead of them, retraced her steps. "What was that you arranged with Inspector Steadman?" she asked.

"You heard, Helen," said Anthony grimly—"I'm sorry, my dear, *but you heard.*"

CHAPTER 19

1

Inside the 'Nag's Head', Anthony went straight to the telephone, and dialled a number. It was some little time before the connexion was made. When he heard the answering voice, Anthony said: "Is that you, Sergeant Loder? Oh—good—it's Bathurst this end. I've been just a trifle anxious—as you may guess. What happened?"

"Nothing. Not a sound, not a glimmer, not a glimpse. Just a complete nothing."

"I was afraid so."

"I guessed you would be. What happened with you?"

"Same as you, Sergeant—only perhaps more so."

Loder clicked his tongue at the other end. "Not so good —eh?"

"Definitely not so good. Still—we aren't done with yet."

"I should say not—good lord—no. What did the inspector say?"

"Which one?"

"Remsford. Have a heart, sir. I wasn't referring to the Chief."

"Oh—he wasn't too bad. Considering everything. I'm afraid he's gone home just a little surprised—perhaps."

"Surprised? How do you mean, sir?"

"Well—before we parted company, I laid it on again for to-morrow night. The Dramatic Society's at work again to-morrow evening, you know."

"You laid it *all* on again?"

"Yes. The whole bundle. Why not? No earthly use if you don't do things properly. Half measures never got a man anywhere. Excluding, of course, milkmen and licensed victuallers."

Anthony heard Loder chuckle. "When you say 'all', Mr. Bathurst—I take it you're including my crowd, again?"

"I am, Sergeant. Repeat performance for all ranks. With identical arrangements as to the details. If you should click, you know exactly what to do. And if you *could* give me the tip well in time—well I needn't say any more. It would strengthen my hands. All the same—I know you can't do impossibilities and I certainly don't expect them."

"O.K., Mr. Bathurst—I'll do my best—as you know."

There was a pause. "Anything more for now?" asked Sergeant Loder.

"No—I don't think so. You're on top of everything. Oh—there *is* one thing I wanted to ask you. Was there any sign of the other gentleman concerned?"

"The other—?" Loder seemed mystified.

"Yes. You should know whom I mean—the—"

Loder cut in. "I get it. The name on the front, you mean, don't you?"

"That's the idea, Sergeant—that's what I did mean."

"Thought so. Came to me gradually. No—never showed up at all. The whole place seemed to be in absolute darkness all the time I was on my little job. Is it important, do you think, sir?"

"Don't know, Sergeant. Maybe—maybe not. Anyhow cheero for now and good hunting."

Anthony replaced the receiver in its cradle. He stood by the telephone for some seconds—thinking hard. Then he began to whistle and went up the staircase to his bedroom—two steps at a time. He had bungled the case ever since he had started on it—and its pattern was only just resolving itself in his mind. So much to do, he thought, and so little time in which to do it. To know 'why' is but half the problem. If he could only clasp the missing, elusive thread and know 'who'! Until he knew 'who', his way was beset with difficulties. He came to his bedroom door and turned the handle. Suppose the killer had but recently— Anthony stood beside the dressing-table and began to toy with the nucleus of an idea . . . a nucleus that grew and developed . . . until it became an idea on its own. Anthony untied a shoe-lace and kicked off a shoe. Perhaps there would be time even now!

2

At nine o'clock on the following morning, breakfast was in progress in the little dining-room of the 'Nag's Head'. The surroundings were charming—majestic trees stood in their sovereignty in whichever direction the eye of the beholder chose to travel. It was a quiet breakfast on this particular March morning—even though more than the mere promise of spring was in the air. Helen Repton sat between Anthony and Andrew MacMorran. It was she who broke the silence.

"I detect," she said, "an entire absence of *joie de vivre*. understandable. But at the same time regrettable. I think I shall go for a long walk in the woods. As a preparation for the 'high-spots' of the evening. The *possible* 'high-spots'."

"Not a bad notion," said MacMorran with an approving nod of the head, "efface yourself."

Helen gave him a mock bow over the breakfast-table. '"Thank you, Chief. *Moritura, te saluto.*"

Anthony's grimness melted into a grin. "Come off it, Helen. Don't make the damned business sound worse than it really is. My 'willies' are numerous enough—in all conscience."

Helen smiled at him. "That's the first time in my chequered career that I've heard *you* talk like that."

"Only shows you," replied Anthony.

"Right down in the depths?" she questioned quizzically.

"Oh—no—nothing like as bad as that. 'Sicklied o'er by the pale cast of thought.' "

"Finding a way out?"

"Going to look for one."

"Where?"

"I've a mind to try the library—the place of books."

Helen affected surprise. "Is there such a thing—in this superb hole?"

"A small branch affair—next door, I fancy, to Vernon Parmiter's. Administered, I should say, by the County."

Helen shrugged her shoulders. "The County! Just hark at the man. How long has optimism—"

Anthony broke into her question. "I know. I'm acutely aware of the full-flowing generosity of general County administration. But who knows—it *may* be my lucky day and I may find a stray shelf tucked away somewhere and there may even be a row of books nestling thereon. Anyhow—I'm going to have a bash. You, Andrew, can stay here, stretch your legs in that arm-chair you always hog, and refresh yourself with long and repeated draughts of the wine of the country."

MacMorran shook his head. "That's what you think. Actually, I'm meeting Steadman again. At Remsford."

"Conference?"

"Ay—you can call it that."

"Feet cold?"

"A wee bit. Certainly getting that way. If things misfire again to-night—" the inspector broke off with an expressive gesture.

"I know," said Anthony—"it may well be that we shall toil two nights and catch nothing. Not so good!"

"It may mean one of several things," went on MacMorran, "and they're what I must see Steadman about."

"Yes," said Anthony—"I suppose that is so."

3

Anthony mounted the short flight of stone steps that marked the entrance to the Wavering branch of the County Council library service. He walked through the small newspaper-room and tapped quietly on the counter at the far end. Above this counter could be seen the sign, 'Reference Library'. He tapped quietly and lightly, but it must not be assumed that there was a song in his heart. A white-faced, bespectacled girl came rather tardily to answer him.

"Reference Library wanted," said Anthony—"have you anything in the nature of a catalogue that I might glance at?"

The girl mumbled something unintelligible and moved off. Anthony waited patiently for revelation. The interval that elapsed tested both his patience and his endurance. Eventually, the pale girl returned with a volume conspicuous for dilapidation.

"There's this," she said apologetically, "but I wouldn't claim that it was up-to-date."

Anthony thanked her and retired with the ancient volume to a near-by seat. He turned to the index and looked up the references in relation to the letter. 'W'. "Witchcraft," he said to himself, "or even perhaps 'witches'. Possibly 'Witches' Sabbath'. Ah—here we are. There is one book mentioned. *The History of the Witch in England*, by Clarence Sandys. That should give me something, at least, of what I'm after."

He returned to the enquiry counter. The pale-faced girl with the spectacles was on this occasion ready and waiting for him.

"Would you be good enough," said Anthony in his most charming manner, "to permit me to glance at this book for a few interesting moments ?"

He indicated the desired title with his finger on the ancient catalogue and repeated it to her: "*The History of the Witch in England*, by Clarence Sandys."

"Yes," said the girl at the counter in a voice that matched her complexion. "I'll get it for you. Please wait here."

Anthony waited. He went on waiting. He also served! More than once he looked with a mixture of irritation and impatience at his watch. Good lord, he thought, where in hell's name has the wretched girl got to? He could hear voices. Their general tone suggested somewhat pertinently that on this particular morning neither was God in His Heaven, nor was it all right with the world. Then Anthony heard the word 'witch' emerge plainly from the distant altercation. The voices began to die down and at long last, he saw the anaemic-looking assistant approaching him again. Anthony looked at her expectantly. His optimism, however, was ill-founded.

"I'm sorry, sir," she said, "but you can't have the book you wanted."

"Present tense," said Anthony, "the book I want."

The girl flushed a little. "I'm sorry," she repeated.

"May I enquire the reason I can't have it?"

The girl hesitated. "It's not here," she asserted. Her voice, Anthony thought, lacked conviction.

"Do you mean, rather, that you can't find it?"

She shook a head of mouse-coloured hair. "It's not here."

Anthony seized the animal's horns. "In that case," he said pleasantly, "I'd like a word with the librarian. Or—with the person in charge."

"I've seen him," said the assistant.

"Very likely. But I haven't."

The girl hesitated again. "I'm afraid I must insist," said Anthony firmly.

She looked into his eyes—assessing chances. She beheld neither help nor hope.

"Er—then—will you please come this way?"

Anthony needed no second bidding. He went that way.

4

They came to a room of eminently depressing externals. On the door was a small wooden tablet. It informed the world that within was housed (under certain time limitations) no less a person than Rollo Bone, Librarian in Charge.

"Just a minute, please," said the pale girl. She stepped into the room and incredibly quickly, stepped out again. "Mr. Bone will see you, sir," she chirped.

"Thank you," said Anthony—"the nearer the bone, of course "Heslid round the ugly door and into the room.

Its interior was, if possible, even more depressing than its outside appearance. A tall, thin, lank-looking figure, rose to his entrance. His eyes protruded ominously and he spoke in a throaty voice. His collar waged constant war with his Adam's apple.

"Good morning. Are you a ratepayer of Wavering? That is to say, have you a Borrower's Ticket for this library?"

Anthony smiled and shook his head. "Neither a borrower nor a lender. Or—if you prefer it—I am not—and I haven't."

Mr. Bone threw off a cloak of inky apprehension and embraced undisguised relief.

"In that case, then, I'm afraid that even if the volume you desire to refer to, *was* forthcoming—"

Anthony shook his head again. He presented Mr. Bone with a visiting-card. Mr. Bone's eyes protruded even more unmistakably.

"This, of course, makes a difference. I . . . er . . . had no idea . . ."

"I was afraid that was the case."

Mr. Bone glanced up quickly but the face of the tall man with the grey eyes, was impassive. Mr. Bone made strange noises in his throat.

"Unfortunately the book you require is missing. Both to me and to my staff . . . the . . . er . . . defection is inexplicable. I presume it's of some importance to you?"

"Yes. To my investigations. Shall we say . . . valuable books stolen from libraries? May I hear the details of this loss that you fear your library has sustained?"

Mr. Bone beamed. "Of course. I begin to see. Certainly . . . certainly." He leant forward in his chair and picked up the telephone-receiver.

"Come in, Miss Pain, will you, please? And bring with you the Reference Library Issues Register . . . yes, that's right . . . the one you showed me a few moments ago."

'So her name's Pain,' thought Anthony, 'well, well!' The delay was but short. Miss Pain entered with a largish book.

"Now . . . er . . . Mr. . . . Bathurst," said Bone. "Here you will see the somewhat unfortunate situation with which we're faced."

Mr. Bone opened the book. "What was the date that you mentioned, Miss Pain?"

"Early in January, Mr. Bone. Somewhere about the third or the fourth, I think it was."

"Good. Ah—here we are." Mr. Bone found the appropriate page and the desired entry. He turned the book round so that Anthony could see. "On that date in January," continued Mr. Rollo Bone, "our copy of *The History of the Witch in England* was requested for reference. Now a book issued in that manner, should never be taken from the Reference Room. It is signed for, when issued, and another entry made by the assistant when it is returned to the shelves. You will observe that there is no such 'return' entry. I cannot escape the unhappy conclusion that the person who asked for the book in question . . . er . . . walked off with it in his pocket. . . Most . . . er . . . regrettable."

" 'Convey'—the wise it call," said Anthony, "but there—you seem to be minus a book. Now help me again, please—what do you make of the signature of this unscrupulous student of witchcraft?"

He handed the register back to the librarian. Mr. Bone inspected the signature for many seconds. "Er—it's not very plain, is it? . . . It looks to me like . . . er . . . Macdonald . . but I should have to guess at the initials. Er . . . Miss Pain . . . what do *you* make of this name? Is it Macdonald—do you think?"

The pale girl examined the writing fastidiously. There was a further interval before she could screw her judgment to the deciding-place.

"ln my opinion," she said eventually, "it's Smith."

Mr. Bone seemed annoyed. The throat again underwent internal combustion. Anthony smiled. Bone came back to the practical. "What do you think yourself, Mr. Bathurst? I should be most interested to hear."

Anthony shrugged his shoulders hopelessly. "My guess is as bad as yours—or Miss Pain's. Personally, I should incline to the Chinese. Shall we say, Ming Ling Mung? A signature by any other name—would—you know the rest."

A silence ensued. Anthony thought hard. He was undesirous at this juncture of giving away too much. He decided to question Miss Pain.

"Would it have been you, Miss Pain, who issued the book? In January?"

"Yes, I do all the Reference inquiries."

"Any memory of this particular case?"

Miss Pain consigned herself to thought. "It *wasn't* me," she said, semi-triumphantly—"I was away sick that week. I had 'flu. I've just remembered. You remember, too, don't you, Mr. Bone? We had that temporary girl here. Came from the Labour Exchange."

The librarian nodded. "That is so, I *do* remember. A Miss Blenkinsop— or some such name. A rather dowdy person."

Anthony groaned inwardly. He had no time to spare to chase fugitive and dowdy Blenkinsops. He played his last card. The thought occurred to him.

"Can you tell me the name of the publishers? Of this book of Clarence Sandys?"

Mr. Bone's second beam appeared. "Oh—certainly. There will be no difficulty about that. The name of the publishers will be shown in our stock records." He turned to Miss Pain at his side. "Get that information for this gentleman—will you please, Miss Pain?"

"Certainly, Mr. Bone." Miss Pain vanished.

Mr. Bone attempted to make further conversation. "I suppose this is a pretty serious case—that you're engaged on ?"

"I'm afraid it is."

Mr. Bone shook his head. "Extraordinary! I never recall such a thing happening here before."

"Only shows you, doesn't it?"

"It most certainly does. Dear-dear . . . er . . . extraordinary. Ah—here we are."

The door opened to admit Miss Pain. She sat down primly by the side of her Chief. "Messrs. Puckeridge and Barrett, Paternoster Row."

The librarian began to shake his head again. The degree of the shake suggested that all was indeed lost.

"Most unfortunate," he said, "most unfortunate!"

Anthony sought elucidation. "Why is that, Mr. Bone—may I ask?"

Mr. Bone spread out his hands with a gesture of despair. "Puckeridge and Barrett, alas, are out of business. A very old and respected firm—with a reputation second to none—but now alas—gone! They found themselves unable to compete with the pace of modern business—especially from the publication angle. They put their shutters up."

Bone shook his head sadly. He seemed to have made it an almost personal matter.

Anthony heard what the librarian said. It occurred to him as he listened that ever since he had come to the case the tide had steadily flowed against him. He stood up.

"Many thanks for your assistance. I must do the best I can with the information you've given me." Mr. Bone appeared pleased to hear this—despite the problem of his missing book. He shepherded Anthony to the door with a great deal more fuss than was necessary.

"Thank you, Mr. Bathurst. I'm truly sorry I haven't been able to help you more. Good morning to you."

Mr. Bone closed the door of his room. He went to his table. He spoke to Miss Pain: "I remember that Blenkinsop woman," he said, with a far-away look in his eyes; "there was a certain body odour. . . ." Miss Pain had fled!

CHAPTER 20

1

Anthony stood on the pavement outside the Wavering branch of the County Library Service lost in thought. So far away was he indeed, that he failed to see Vernon Parmiter pass in front of him. Parmiter gave an involuntary start when he saw Anthony, but for reasons best known to himself, he omitted to disclose his identity.

Anthony looked at his wrist-watch. The time showed at half-past ten. So short a time for the so much that he had to do. His own fault, of course. Why hadn't he concentrated on the witchcraft angle directly the idea had come to him? Instead of merely finessing with it? Now that he had made more or less certain of his ground, he could hear, mentally, the striking of the eleventh hour. Suddenly he thought of something. Or rather, of somebody. He whispered a name under his breath. Dennis Quinn! Dennis Quinn—who had been contemporary with him at Oxford—and who now had made something of a name as a student of the occult. Anthony had read several articles that he had written. Was there the chance—the thin chance perhaps—that Dennis Quinn's peculiar erudition extended to the realms of witchcraft?

Anthony debated the matter silently for a few moments and then moved swiftly across the road. There was a telephone box outside the main post-office—it seemed to him that it might, perhaps, give him his last opportunity. As he walked towards his objective, he tried to remember where Dennis Quinn lived. It was comparatively near London—he knew that. Somewhere south of the Thames—somewhere—he had it—Dulwich! Should be plain sailing for him then.

Anthony came to the telephone-box and thanked his lucky stars that he found it empty. *And*—there was also a London Directory on the shelf in the corner. "Thank the Lord it's Quinn—and not McDonald." He turned the pages. "Can't be many." Then he saw the point and smiled to himself. "Should be five, of course—and no more."

He found Dennis Quinn's number and dialled. Eventually it was a man's voice which answered. Anthony sought identity, congratulated himself and embarked upon explanation. The voice came back.

"Good lord—it's you, Bathurst? I wondered who you were . . . where did you say . . . Wavering . . . yes . . . I remember the affair . . . certainly if I'm able to . . . only too pleased, old chap. Now tell me the worst."

Anthony unloaded. Quinn came again. "Witchcraft . . . eh . . . well I'm blest . . . don't tell me you're taking that on . . . oh yes . . . I've given it a reasonable amount of study in connexion with my other stuff."

"Oh good. That's another load off my mind. May I put two or three questions to you?"

"Certainly—go ahead. That isn't to say, of course, that I'm a cert to answer them. Anyhow—fire away."

Anthony put his opening question. To his complete satisfaction, Dennis Quinn had no hesitation with regard to the answer.

"Oh—yes—certainly. They were extremely fond of fat in their rituals. Usually the fat of a murdered child. The witch would anoint her feet and her shoulders with fat of this kind before mounting her broom-stick for the rendezvous of the Witches' Sabbath. What? The other way round? How do you mean . . . the fat? No—no—your particular witch must be unusually daft if that's the case."

Anthony came over with his second question. Quinn's reply was immediate. "Oh—yes. That is so. Broomsticks, distaffs, or even household rakes. They were the common methods of transport. All nationalized now—of course."

"That's very nice of you, Dennis. Now for my third and, I hope, my last question."

"What is it, old man?"

Anthony put his third question and waited for Quinn's answer. "By Clarence Sandys? Oh—yes . . . I know the book pretty well. In fact, I'm fairly certain I've a copy of it here somewhere. What's that? No . . . nothing outstanding about it. . . it was written, I should think somewhere about seventy years ago. Yes—that's right—Puckeridge and Barrett. Very old people. Disappeared now. What? Oh—it deals mainly with the 'witch-finders'—the people who travelled through the country hunting out witches or so-called witches. The eastern counties were among their favourite hunting-grounds. Somewhere about the middle of the seventeenth century. One of the most famous of these fellows is reputed to have hanged sixty-odd in one year—in the county of Essex I fancy it was . . . that's a coincidence . . . where you are now . . . he worked on what they call the 'water' test. What was that? Why—a test that was eminently simple and equally direct. The suspected 'witch' was chucked into the nearest river. If she floated, she was declared a 'witch' by the waterproof—and subsequently hanged. If she didn't float—well I needn't go on, need I?"

Anthony heard Dennis Quinn chuckle at the other end of the telephone. Before he could interject, Dennis had gone on.

"There's a rather good story attached to this particular 'witch-hunter' described in Clarence Sandys's book—in the end he was unfortunate enough to be hoist with his own petard. What? Why—in this way! He played his cards badly and managed to get himself 'suspect'—so they decided to test him with a dose of his own medicine. Either luckily or unluckily—have it which way you like—when they chucked him in the river, he floated! With the result that he went the same way as his sixty or so victims. Poetic justice—what? I've been trying to think of his name for the last few minutes and it's just come to me. The fellow's name was—"

Dennis Quinn spoke both Christian and surname and was amazed to hear Anthony almost yell into the sound of the spoken words.

"What," yelled Anthony, "what was that name you mentioned? Say it again, for the love of Mike."

Dennis Quinn repeated his previous words. "Dennis," said Anthony gravely, "you've done me an inestimable service. Ringing you up was a stroke of genius on my part. It sure is my lucky day—yes, sir!"

"Good," returned Dennis Quinn, "if that's how you feel, buy me a beer next time we run into each other."

"Make it two," said Anthony, "and I'm your man."

2

The atmosphere at lunch was distinctly different from that which had prevailed at breakfast. MacMorran, who had returned from Remsford, failed to notice for some time the new look which showed on Anthony's face. When Anthony and the inspector sat down at the luncheon-table, Helen Repton was absent. Anthony mentally noted the fact but made no comment. The defection had occurred before and on that account, he paid no particular attention to it. MacMorran was full of himself and his activities at Remsford that morning.

"How did you find Inspector Steadman?" asked Anthony, "under the weather or full of beans?"

MacMorran shook his head rather gloomily. "I wouldn't say that he was either—really. Just a little peeved with Life and things in general. But not too bad. All the same—I don't think he's quite got over last night."

"You don't say," remarked Anthony—"bad job about him."

MacMorran shrugged his shoulders. "Well—you can't expect him to be waving flags—can you? After all—he's only a poor ruddy copper with nothing much to look forward to—beyond a measly pension and a shack in the country. He can't afford to make *too* many bloomers or else he may find himself—"

Anthony put down his soup-spoon. "Good lord, Andrew—what's come over you all of a sudden? Give my kind regards to your long-suffering partner in sleuth and tell him the tale about triumph and disaster. Anybody would think from the way you talk, Andrew, that *I'd* stood him up! Gertcher!"

But MacMorran was impervious to the advice. "That's all very well. He's not a bad bloke, Steadman—I've worked with plenty worse. My impression is he's got a headache now because he *expected* too much."

Anthony eyed MacMorran enquiringly. "Expected too much? How do you mean, Andrew?"

"Last night. I've had last night in mind all the time we've been talking. Steadman—you see—"

Anthony waved a table-napkin at the 'Yard' inspector. "Forget it, Andrew. And listen to me. The case is solved."

He spoke abruptly—on purpose. He achieved the effect he desired. MacMorran was jolted.

"What the heck do you mean by that remark? How is the case solved?"

"Well—as good as. All over bar the tumult. If you'll promise to forget Steadman for the matter of a few minutes—and listen to me, I'll tell you something."

MacMorran looked at him suspiciously. "Where have you been this morning?"

"Same where I told you I was going. Library—place of books."

MacMorran became a changed man. He knew his Bathurst and he knew from the look in Anthony's grey eyes that there was no flippancy now.

"And you—got somewhere?" asked MacMorran.

"Yes, Andrew," replied Anthony quietly, "I got somewhere. Maybe I got all the way. The link that we needed so much, Andrew, to complete our chain—turned up at last."

"Certain of it? Absolutely—positive?"

"Quite certain, Andrew."

"That's good enough for me, then. What is it?"

"Witchcraft, Andrew. Neither more—nor less."

MacMorran's equanimity was shocked. "Now I can't—"

Anthony intervened. "That's where it started, Andrew. Witchcraft is the basis. The killer, in other words, is bent on stamping out witchcraft. That is to say, young girls are condemned as witches in this killer's diseased mind—and wiped out. Pretty dreadful, isn't it?"

There was a silence. Anthony pushed away his plate. MacMorran seemed too dazed to eat. When he spoke, the words came from his lips—almost singly.

"And you *know* now, who this beast is? You are quite certain as to . . ."

"Listen, Andrew—and I'll tell you some more. Then you'll be in a better position to judge. Somewhere about the middle of the seventeenth century, there was a special 'witch-hunt' in East Anglia. Note the district, Andrew. It was quite a gala affair—a much bigger job than was usual for these doings. East Anglia had the best witches and the hunter wanted them! He is said to have hanged over sixty in Essex alone. Note the county, Andrew!"

Anthony paused again. By this time, MacMorran was staring at him, curiously . . . as though held by a strange fascination.

"Ultimately," went on Anthony, "this 'witch-hunter' came to a sticky end. To the same sticky end, in fact, as he had sent so many of his helpless victims. It still keeps pretty grim, doesn't it?"

MacMorran nodded. "But I don't see," he said, "how you can be so sure of things . . . all this you've told me about, happened three hundred years ago . . . I can't see why it should have anything to do with what's happening now . . . I can't see how it *can* have . . ."

Anthony lit a cigarette and spoke to MacMorran through the flame of the match. "Merely this, my dear Andrew. You might be interested to hear the name of the gentleman who was in charge of the 'witch-hunt' in the seventeenth century. I was. Extremely so. In fact—I can assure you that when I heard it—it made me sit up and take notice."

"What," asked MacMorran slowly—"*was* the name?"

"Matthew Hopkins," replied Anthony quietly.

"Good God Almighty," whispered MacMorran—almost reverently—and then, "it may be only a coincidence. After all—there must be—"

MacMorran stopped. Anthony was shaking his head. He replied as quickly as before.

"It must be the answer, Andrew, to our problem."

As he spoke, he heard the sound of the door closing. Looking up, he saw Helen Repton coming towards the table. In her hands she carried a profusion of yellow primroses and fragrant wood-violets.

"Sorry to be so late for lunch—but I wandered rather farther than I had intended. Aren't these lovely?"

3

There was an unusual edge to her voice that caused Anthony to look up sharply. He watched the girl as she placed the flowers on a newspaper at the end of the table. Helen's head was down. Anthony was unable to see her face clearly. When she eventually did look up, Anthony spoke. "What's the trouble, Helen?"

She shook her head gently as the waitress brought in her lunch. When the girl had gone, Anthony repeated his question. He knew that Helen Repton's face was white and strained. She answered quietly:

"I'm as certain as I can be, that I was followed to the woods this morning—and watched—pretty well all the time. Got me down rather while it lasted."

MacMorran took in what was being said. He added his anxiety to Anthony's. "No protection, I suppose? No 'Loogue' with you?" She shook her head again. "No. I left it in my drawer upstairs. Not too bright, am I?"

"Put us in the picture, Helen," said Anthony, "please."

"Well, I walked towards the woods—as I told you I was going to—it was a perfectly gorgeous morning—and when I got there and saw all the lovely spring flowers, I thought I'd pick some. I've never seen such wizard primroses. Look at them and judge for yourselves." She gestured towards the flowers on the table.

"Go on," said Anthony, semi-severely. Helen grinned.

"Well—I hadn't been there very long when I fancied I heard the sound of a car. Close. Then it stopped—suddenly. For a time I paid no more attention to it. Went on picking primroses. I suppose ten minutes went by. Perhaps it was even longer. Until I was almost certain that I heard the sound of footsteps. *Stealthy* footsteps. Like somebody walking very carefully—as though the owner of the steps didn't want to be heard. *Stealthy*! I tell you—it didn't appeal to me at all. Then I heard a cracking sort of sound—behind me—as though someone had stepped on a piece of wood. I turned quickly and I'm positive that I spotted a dark shape that seemed to vanish between trees." Helen Repton paused. "I didn't know what to do. For a few horrible seconds, I'm ashamed to confess that I panicked. It was all so quiet and deserted—and, of course, knowing what I know—" She shook her head again and stopped.

Anthony and MacMorran waited for her. "Gradually, I cooled down . . . and began to think . . . really . . . think intelligently. I decided to make a bolt for it. I'd make for the nearest spot of cover—and then 'leg' it as hard as I knew how. Away to my left, which was the road side, there was a clump of bushes. I knew if I could make them, they would screen me . . . nobody could possibly see me if I could once get into them. So I 'hared' for them like a shot, stayed 'put' for a few moments and then ran hell for leather for the road. I made it," she concluded simply.

"See any sign of the car?" asked Anthony.

"No. None."

"Parked away somewhere," said MacMorran.

"When you eventually got to the road," asked Anthony, "anybody follow you then?"

"I didn't see anybody."

"This figure you saw in the woods—what was it like?"

"Just a dark—almost black shape. Nothing more than that. I got no more than a glimpse—behind trees."

Anthony looked at MacMorran. "This settles it, I think, Andrew. Agree?"

"You mean—the bait's been—?"

Anthony nodded. "Exactly. To-night's the night."

"Thank you very much," said Helen Repton, "thanks for those kind words."

MacMorran left his seat at the dining-table and went to stand by the fire-place. "Now tell her," he said to Anthony, "tell her what you told me just before she came in."

He took out his pouch and began to fill his pipe. Anthony told Helen. She listened to him—white-faced. When he had finished she smiled ruefully.

"Interesting. And . . . rather frightening. Well—we live and learn. I've never fancied myself as a witch—although at times I admit I've been called something very much like it."

MacMorran smiled a grim, frosty sort of smile. "Now, listen," he said, "with regard to this evening . . ."

CHAPTER 21

1

It was at 2 p.m. precisely that an envelope fell on the mat just beneath the Rectory letter-box. The Rector, who had heard it fall, picked it up quickly, glanced at it—and then took it to the kitchen. He handed the envelope to his house-keeper, Mrs. Hodgson. "This . . . er . . . missive . . . appears to be for you, Mrs. Hodgson."

Mrs. Hodgson frowned, fumbled for her spectacles, looked uncompromisingly at the name and address on the envelope and tore up the flap.

"Now that's very nice of somebody, Rector," she said gushingly—"two tickets for the show this evening." She examined the tickets. "And good seats, too. Reserved Row D." She peered into the recesses of the envelope. "And there's nothing to say who's sent them. Fancy that now! Some good Samaritan, I suppose."

The Rector coughed. "You have friends, evidently, who mask their goodness with anonymity. People who prefer to do good by stealth. Very charming of them—very charming. You'll take advantage of the offer . . . doubtless?"

Mrs. Hodgson wiped her hands on her apron. "I should like to, sir—if it's all the same to you. Will you be able to manage, do you think? According to the ticket, it starts at eight o'clock—and the seats are reserved."

The Rev. Matthew Hopkins smiled. "Certainly I shall be able to manage, Mrs. Hodgson. By all means go to the dramatic performance and enjoy yourself. It will do you good. All work and no play, you know."

The Rector rubbed his hands and departed. As he walked up the hall, Mrs. Hodgson heard him humming a hymn tune. She strained her ears to catch what it was. It came to her—'All Glory, Laud and Honour'—

the Rector of Wavering always prided himself upon his flair for the appropriate. At twenty minutes past two, Mrs. Hodgson heard another voice in the house. She recognized it as that of the Rev. Frank Cheam, the Rector's curate. Listening at the kitchen-door, she could hear him in conversation with the Rector. She must not be misjudged on this account. It was not her habit to listen in this way. On the present occasion, she listened because she wanted to catch the curate before he went out. For this reason. Mrs. Hicks who 'did for' the Rev. Cheam was an 'old china' of hers and they often hunted in couples and took their pleasures together. Inasmuch as Mrs. Hodgson had been the fortunate recipient of two tickets for the show that evening, what then could be more natural than her desire for Mrs. Hicks to accompany her? "After all, my dear, they're buckshee, you know, and there's nobody I'd as lief have near to me as you, Matilda."

2

As a result therefore, of this flight of desire, Mrs. Hodgson waited for the opportune moment for her pounce. Eventually, she heard the preliminaries of Cheam's departure. Whereupon she crept quietly up the hall in the direction of the front door. The Rector was shaking hands with his subordinate. Mrs. Hodgson pounced.

"Oh—Mr. Cheam—please excuse me—but would you be good enough to do me a favour?"

Frank Cheam smiled. "Certainly, Mrs. Hodgson—if you'll tell me what it is you want."

Mrs. Hodgson could see the Rector smiling at her benevolently. "Well, sir," she continued, to Cheam, "it's like this, somebody's sent me two tickets for the play this evening. And I thought as how your Mrs. Hicks would like to come with me. Would you be so good as to ask her with my love—and give her this ticket, sir? Tell her I'll meet her outside at five minutes to eight. The seats are reserved, you see, sir. If she can't come, tell her not to worry—it doesn't matter."

The curate beamed at the Rector's housekeeper. "Certainly, Mrs. Hodgson—only too pleased. I'm going back to the house now—I'll give Mrs. Hicks your message and the ticket. I can't say, of course, how she's fixed for this evening—but I expect it'll be all right." The curate bestowed the ticket in the breast-pocket of his overcoat.

"Thank you very much, sir," said Mrs. Hodgson.

3

At 7.30 p.m. Anthony handed Helen Repton her stack of programmes. "Same arrangements, Helen, as yesterday evening," he said. "I'll take the cash in the same way, same time, same place. O.K.?"

"Yes. Shall be glad when it's all over."

"Glad—or relieved?"

"Both—car all fixed?"

"You bet. Just as before. Don't worry. Keep cool—and both eyes open. Got everything?"

Helen nodded. Anthony looked down at her from his six feet plus.

"Those violets of yours look exquisite. On that yellow. Very fetching, lady."

Helen shuddered. "Don't like the word. Don't fancy it any way."

Anthony looked at her anxiously. "Feeling all right, aren't you?"

She managed a grin. "Fair. Not waving flags."

"You'll be O.K. We shan't stand you up—don't worry. Listen—and I'll tell you."

Helen listened. When Anthony had finished she said: "Sounds O.K.— but he *must* be a cunning devil—and you never quite know how cunning can break out."

"How do you mean?"

"Different methods. He might play his hand in a different way. Then where should I be?"

"Don't think so. Even then you can always play the ace as a last resource. Besides—this evening—MacMorran'll be on his tail at the other end."

"All right. See you later then."

"You will," said Anthony.

He walked round and entered the hall from the back. On the threshold of the men's dressing-room he encountered Gosling. The producer was engaged in argument. His *vis-a-vis*, evidently, was a member of the cast. Gosling was speaking with emphasis.

"You can argue as much as you damn well like, Rogers, there was almost a full tin there yesterday evening. I saw Bradley actually using it. He was cleaning off a few minutes after the 'rag' was down. So the ruddy stuff *can't* be far away. Have another look—for the love of Mike."

Rogers, still grumbling, sheered off. "Some of these chaps get my goat," said Gosling, turning to Anthony, "if a thing isn't under their ruddy noses, they scream for help."

"What's the trouble this time?"

"Wants to put into me that there's no coco-nut butter. When I know damn well there's almost a full tin in there somewhere. Talk about helpless and hopeless."

"Too bad," murmured Anthony—but a thought had danced into his brain. Fat! Grease! On the feet and the shoulders! As the thought registered, he heard another voice. He turned quickly and saw Frank Cheam.

"Message for you, Gosling—from the Rector. He asked me to tell you that he can't come along this evening. Not feeling too good. Some sort of chill which he's afraid may turn into 'flu. Apologies and all that, he says."

"Right-o," replied Gosling, "many thanks for coming to tell me."

"Pleasure," said the curate.

Anthony broke away from them and made for his seat. On the way, he caught sight of Parmiter and his wife. Actually, his eyes met Parmiter's—but the solicitor didn't appear to recognize him—for there was no response. Just as Anthony found his seat, the curtain went up.

4

At 9.42 p.m. Anthony slipped out of his row of chairs to collect Helen's cash for programmes. He made his way through the connecting-doors to the outer door that opened on to the grounds. To his dismay, he was unable to open it. The door was locked—and there was no sign of the key. Anthony cursed under his breath. Then he cursed *coram publico!* As he tugged at the handle of the door he continued to curse. For Gath to hear and for the echo to reach the streets of Askelon. Why on earth was the door locked at this particular moment? It had always been unlocked. As he asked himself the question, a chill premonition struck at his heart and his forehead beaded with sweat. There was only one thing for it—he must return and go through the hall. There was just the chance that the curtain was still down. But as Anthony dashed back—he knew that he had squandered several precious minutes. And a great deal can happen during that time!

CHAPTER 22

1

At 9.40 p.m., or two minutes before Anthony moved to the locked door, Helen Repton picked up her coat from the cloak-room crone, collected her cash and unsold programmes, and went out to keep her assignation with him. The moon was at its full and its brilliance gave the condition almost of daylight.

As she rounded the corner of the institute, in the natural expectation of seeing Anthony there, she noticed with some surprise a small car parked at the side of the path. Its origin looked obscure but its ancient lineage was there for all to see. Helen half-halted and as she did so, she was just conscious of a uniformed figure ranging herself at her side. She turned involuntarily . . . and the sky fell on the back of her head. But the blow had been neither timed nor placed as effectively as the assailant had intended.

2

At 9.45 p.m. two plain-clothes men, on duty within the old hockey pavilion, broke into conversation. This conversation was authentic.

"Don't know what you think, Bert," said Constable Sarson, "but if you ask me, it's flippin' cold."

His companion in vigilance growled an assent. "You've said it, Fred, flippin' cold it is. And also I'm afraid a flippin' waste of flippin' time. May be wrong, of course, but that's my flippin' opinion. I'd sooner have been with the 'sarge' at the back of the butcher's shop."

Sarson shrugged his shoulders. "They don't hand you your pay-packet, my lad, to hold opinions about policy. Or with regard to tactics. Those things are for them what's higher up. The police force, to which you and me have the high honour to belong, exists, in the main, for the prevention of crime. Not for the apprehension of the criminal. My first 'sarge' used to drum that into me. Never walk into trouble, he used to say. Walk round it, away from it, but never flippin' well *into* it. If you had to walk into it, he said, and there was no possible way of avoidin' it, be a flippin' tortoise—never a flippin' hare. He reckoned he got his promotion because of his record. Absolutely flippin' clean. Went nine years without a charge. Clever feller he was—and no mistake."

Constable Smollett made no reply. Sarson went on. "And don't forget something else, Bert—the criminal has a habit of returning to the scene of his crime. Flippin' well nearly always. Got a gasper?"

"I shan't have," answered Smollett, "if you keep on smokin' 'em."

He proffered the packet with smouldering reluctance. "What are they?" asked Sarson—"I didn't notice."

"Freeman's," replied Smollett curtly.

Sarson took a cigarette and cupped his hands round the flame of a match. Smollett pushed the packet back into his pocket. Sarson walked to the door of the pavilion.

"Look at that old moon up there—doin' 'er stuff. Might be flippin' daylight."

Smollett saw him suddenly lean forward. "Thought I spotted something," said Sarson—"behind that heap there."

Smollett joined him. "Where?"

Sarson pointed.

"Your flippin' imagination," said Smollett.

"There's something there," persisted Sarson, "work round the side towards it and have a 'dekko', will you?"

"What—me?" said Smollett, "in my state of 'ealth?"

3

At 9.46 Helen Repton came back to something like consciousness. That is to say, she opened her eyes and tried to think. And immediately fear mocked her senses and dried her mouth. But she became aware of two things. There was a horrible pain somewhere at the back of her head—and she was lying on the floor of a car. The car was moving. Her fear increased—but with a terrific mental effort she began to pull herself together. She knew that she must—that herein lay her only chance.

Her hands and feet were free. The killer evidently thought that she was 'out' for some time. She would, whenever necessary, simulate unconsciousness. She felt in her coat pocket for the gun . . . furtively. It had gone! And now fear gripped her tightly! The car was moving but slowly . . . how far had they already gone? If not *too* far, could she possibly help towards her own salvation? Could she convey to Anthony in any way—she propped herself up a little from the floor and gently and noiselessly lowered the already open window a matter of another inch. Then she plucked a handful of violets from the bunch she wore and let two flutter from her fingers through the aperture. A few seconds later she repeated the action and then again . . . and again. All the time she watched anxiously the hunched and huddled figure at the driving-wheel. So far, so good . . . the driver had seen nothing.

The car turned a corner and Helen's fingers fluttered again. Violets, she thought hazily. Violets, violets all the way. There was a movement from the sinister figure by the driving-wheel. Helen sank back upon the floor of the car . . . her eyes closed . . . her body stiff and inanimate. The car was stopping. The car stopped. There was no movement from the driver now. Just stillness and absolute quiet. What was he waiting for? The answer came to her comparatively quickly. Her captor was making sure that the coast was clear. Stealthily, Helen pulled more blossoms from her corsage . . . with the hand that was the farther from the driver. She clutched the tiny flowers in her clenched hand. If she were going to be taken into a house . . . or into anywhere . . . she must drop another. . .

4

At 9.48 p.m. Anthony hastened through the hall and came out into the grounds. He rounded the corner, as Helen had, some eight minutes previously, with his heart in his mouth. When he saw the programmes and coins scattered on the ground, all his worst fears were realized. Then he saw the marks of the car. Anthony began to run . . . and he ran to the gate which led to the street. As he ran, he cursed . . . he flagellated his blundering . . . and his impotence . . . and MacMorran . . . and everything! There was none that had done good . . . no—not one. In this way he came to the High Street.

CHAPTER 23

1

At the kerb he halted. What the hell had MacMorran been thinking of to let—? Anthony caught his breath and clapped his hand to his head. For a blinding flash of revelation had come to him and had illuminated his darkness. He remembered the circumstances of the uniform stolen from the property-basket. He remembered his little investigation of the incident . . . what had transpired therefrom . . . he recalled what young Ferguson had told him . . . he turned suddenly and began to run again. To run hard . . . and he ran in the road . . . for he was running where a car had travelled but a few minutes previously. He had run but a few paces when he saw the first violet . . . in the moonlight . . . almost on the crown of the road.

2

Anthony knew what the violet meant and he began to hope. He ran harder and faster. And, as he ran, he came to his first hand-clasp from Fortune. For a car flashed by him, tangented to the kerb and waited. Anthony saw it, knew it for what it was, and gave thanks from the profundity of his heart. This car might well mean Helen's salvation. As he drew abreast of the car that waited by the kerb, Inspector Steadman's head was poked through the window. His enquiry was terse.

"What the hell do you think you're doing?"

Anthony tore open the car door, yelled: "Drive like blazes," and hung half of himself out of the window.

"The killer's got Miss Repton," he gasped as the car began to make speed, "just drive on and leave the rest to me."

Steadman's mouth opened in an amazement which was amplified as Anthony gestured towards the roadway. "Violets," he cried, "look for violets."

The time now was five minutes to ten.

3

Steadman exclaimed triumphantly: "There's one."

Anthony nodded—but said nothing. His eyes were grim, hard and unyielding and they never left the road. It was a question of time and time only. There was the business of the fat and the poles—and—it would take some minutes, at least. . . .

The car swept on . . . implacable and relentless. It reached the corner where the first car had turned and Anthony saw the little emblem of colour where Helen had dropped it.

"Turn left," he shouted, and the chauffeur swung the car with swift and smooth precision. "Not long now," cried Anthony, "the car must be outside somewhere. There's been no time for anything else."

The chauffeur nodded and pointed away to the left. "There it is, sir. Outside a house."

"Drive like blazing hell," yelled Anthony. Then he saw the last little flowers.

4

Steadman and Anthony jumped at the first possible second, tore up the path and hurled themselves at the door. It was stout and stood firm against the assault. Steadman stood back from the barrier before giving it the full weight and impetus of his broad shoulder. Anthony hurled himself at it for the second time and the door yielded abruptly to the onslaught. He and Steadman entered together but Anthony took a slight lead at the first turn. Certain obscene noises and a scream—neither very far away—were eloquent advices. Anthony and Steadman threw themselves against another door which gave no trouble and then they burst headlong into the room.

Anthony saw Helen Repton prostrate on a bed and another figure with the strange fierce light of madness in its eyes crouched in a corner. On the floor, close at hand, could be seen a knife. . . . uncouth sounds came from the figure's lips . . . sounds that started as words before trailing off into the nothingness of gibberish. As Steadman moved swiftly in for the capture, the figure raised its hands menacingly . . . and Anthony saw the strength and the malevolence in the powerful fingers.

"Hit him," said Anthony curtly. Steadman cracked home a beauty right on the front of the jaw and the uniformed figure of the Rev. Frank Cheam toppled helplessly . . . and crashed to the floor.

Anthony took Helen in his arms. "What did I tell you," she said with a funny little quaver in her voice—"didn't I say that it might go another way? You can never tell with—"

"You win," replied Anthony . . . "and don't forget to remind me of it—any time you feel like it."

CHAPTER 24

1

Anthony drove the Bentley through the streets of Wavering. "Take your last look at the dear little place," he said. MacMorran and Helen Repton groaned in unison. "And when I open my big mouth," went on Anthony, "just whisper the name of this charming little burg—will you? It will be both effective and salutary." He nosed the car on to the main London road. "Every time I think of the darned place I get cold shivers."

"What about me?" said Helen—"what do you think I get?"

"The most remarkable feature of the wretched case was this. I wasn't actually certain of the identity of the killer until his hands were on Helen's throat . . . as you might say."

"Keep on," said Helen, "don't mind me."

"Well—that's a fact—and I must admit it."

MacMorran contributed confirmation. "That must be so," he declared, "because on that last evening I was wasting my time keeping the Rector under close observation. And Helen herself thought it was Hopkins we were after. I shouldn't have parked myself on his tail if we hadn't thought the case was open and shut . . . no . . . sir."

"Supposing," said Helen Repton quietly, "that I hadn't dropped the flowers? Supposing I hadn't been such a bright little girl . . . could you have found me, do you think?"

Anthony checked the car at traffic-lights. "Yes," he replied, "as a matter of fact—I had already started to run in the direction of Cheam's place. The truth had come to me in a flash. It was heaven-sent, of course."

"Tell me how," said Helen.

"Well," said Anthony as the car re-started, "when I found the door outer locked against me, my suspicions were aroused. When some minutes later I saw the programmes, etc., lying on the ground—I guessed pretty well what had happened. *And* I saw the car marks on the gravel. *But*—what I *couldn't* understand as I stood there was the Andrew angle. He was looking after Hopkins. How had the Rev. Matthew Hopkins given Andrew MacMorran the slip? Andrew had been on his tail for some hours. I was flabbergasted! Stupefied—for some seconds. I began to ask myself the question—had we, after all, put the tail on the wrong man? You see—it had been only Clarence Sandys's book which had clinched it for us with regard to the Rector. And then, as the question developed—the truth suddenly catapulted itself into my mind. I remembered the occasion when I called on Edmund Gosling to test my theory that a uniform might have been stolen from the St. Simon's 'skip'. I remembered the exact details of what had taken place."

"What were they?" asked the inspector.

"Why the only man who could remember the existence of the bus conductor's uniform was the curate, Cheam. At the time, I thought it a legitimate effort of memory on his part—but as I stood there by the kerb wondering what the hell to do—there flashed into my mind the *real* reason why Cheam had remembered it. And I recognized the touch of audacity which he had used to tell me about it. Other things fitted, too . . . amongst them, the hiding of Barbara Marsden's frock in the 'skip' . . . and when these remembrances did come to me . . . I knew the truth at last. God —what a mess I nearly made of it!"

They saw Anthony shake his head in self-deprecation.

"He's mad, of course," said MacMorran, "mad as a hatter. That's been established. Have you ever noticed that large bump at the back of his head ?"

"Many a time, Andrew."

"Well—I've ascertained that was caused by a heavy tree-branch which fell on him one day in a gale when he was a child. Well—that was the beginning of it all—no doubt. Ever since then, the poor fellow's been up against it."

Anthony waved on an on-coming car. "He's not always 'dippy', Andrew. That's the extraordinary feature of him. He has these homicidal attacks, which, incidentally, are of quite recent outbreak—at the full moon. That was one of my first clues to the wretched business. Don't you remember my sudden interest in the calendar? Barbara Marsden, Vera Ferris, and poor old Helen here were all three attacked round the full moon. I worked on that all the way through—or at least ever since I cottoned on to it. The yellow frock at the full moon was the first incitement. The bait, if you like. I refer, of course, in the main, to the first murder."

"You'll pardon me," said Helen Repton, "don't steal my thunder, please! *I* was the bait."

Anthony grinned. "The one thing I *can* take a pat on the back for, and about the only thing, was my witchcraft deduction. But even that, you see, turned out to be unlucky. Because it led us in the wrong direction."

Helen furrowed her forehead. "How do you mean, exactly? Surely it—"

"Why—in this way. In my attempts to *confirm* my witch-craft deduction, I ran slap into the Matthew Hopkins street—as I've already told you. Not only did I find witch-craft, young girls, blood drawn from them, fat used in the ritual, East Anglia, Essex—all these—bang in the picture, just what the doctor ordered—*but also a gentleman by the name of Matthew Hopkins.* Naturally I lapped it up and fell—not only 'for it'—but ruddy well 'into it'. Once again, you see, the luck was dead out." Anthony paused.

"I take it," said MacMorran, "that the curate pinched the book from the local library, got the witchcraft idea from it and the next time the full moon was turned on, the pot started boiling. Is that the idea?"

"Almost, Andrew. Not quite. The Rector himself was the innocent instigator. He already knew about his witch-hunting namesake, having read Sandys's book. Unfortunately *after* he I had read it, he told Cheam about it—in the course of ordinary conversation one day. Cheam wanted both to read and to keep the book—so he stole it—and as it turned out, the anticipation of a modern witch-hunt was the last straw as far as he was concerned. The unhealthy excitement engendered by the reading caught hold of the poor fellow's already abnormal brain and unbalanced it. The first full moon, subsequently, with Barbara Marsden in the yellow frock, sent it flying. He must become the new Matthew Hopkins! He must smell out a witch and kill her! That was how he saw Barbara Marsden—dark-eyed and black-haired. You know the method he employed to kill her."

Anthony swung the Bentley round an island. Helen craned her head for the sign-post.

"Not long now," she said gratefully—"I can do with a spot of home sweet home."

2

"I'm beginning to see," said MacMorran, "a month later, of course, there were the yellow frock again, the moon and—the dark-eyed, dark-haired Vera Ferris."

"Precisely, Andrew. And the burning desire to destroy yet another 'witch'. The yellow frock at the show fanned the flames. The full moon again made the blaze. That was the pattern exactly."

"And it would seem, knowing what we know now, that the girls were *not* strangled on the allotments. Agree?"

"One for, one against. In the case of Barbara Marsden, I should say she was killed on the institute premises after the Social was over. That's why the body was first of all pushed into the empty 'skip' and the frock left in the other one. He disposed of the other clothes. Later on, the body went to the allotments—in the car. It seems he hired a car upon occasion from a tenth-rate garage. In the case of Vera Ferris, I think she was strangled on the allotments. Knocked silly probably and then shoved in the car. In that last attempt he decided to use the house. That meant ensuring the absence of Mrs. Hicks, the landlady. I told you how he worked that, didn't I?"

MacMorran nodded. "The tickets—you mean? Mrs. Hicks and her buddy, Mrs. Hodgson? Yes, you told me."

"Mr. Bathurst," interposed Helen, "how was it that you were able to deduce witchcraft? I don't think you told us that."

"No—I didn't—you're right. I was going to—but I switched off. Well—I think I arrived there by degrees. The fat, the *stolen* fat was, of course, the clue that first set me off thinking. I worried and gnawed at that fat for days on end. I was convinced that there was something there, which, if I could only dig it out, would prove immensely important. Then, my mind went from the fat to the poles. Those poles found with the bodies of the two girls. I couldn't get the idea out of my head, that they looked like broom-handles. The next thought-transition was both natural and inevitable. Broom-handles were succeeded in my mind by broomsticks. Broom-sticks connected with fat! Then a bell rang somewhere. Broomsticks suggested witches and at the back of my mind somewhere, was the faint belief that fat was part of a certain witch-craft ritual. Just as the drawing of the victim's blood. That, of course, was why the cheeks were knife-slashed. You can discern therein, the tortuous working of the diseased mind. The broken poles for the brooms, the blood from the cheeks, and the fat *on the victims* . . . the killer was just dabbling with things he didn't understand."

"Tell me," said Helen, "why did he leave that yellow frock in the 'skip', after the first murder? When he moved the body?"

"Like you—I've considered that point. He may have made a mistake—forgotten it. But I fancy that from his knowledge of the 'skip', and of the Dramatic Society generally, he thought it would lie there for months . . . as safe as houses. It was sheer accident that Vera Ferris took it out and wore it."

"Yes. I see. I think you're right."

Anthony nodded. "I don't think there's much doubt about it. And also, from that, I conjecture something else. Would you care to hear it?"

MacMorran smiled. "He won't be happy till he's told us. Get it off your chest."

"Well—I was referring to the conductor's uniform. I'm moderately certain that wasn't used when Barbara Marsden was strangled. I should say in that case that he made an appointment of some kind with Barbara at the New Year's Social. It may have been anything . . . come to my place and I'll lend you a book . . . wait behind until the others have gone . . . you know the kind of thing I mean. . . .

Barbara was flattered by the attention . . . seeing who he was . . . and she fell for it. But when he saw Vera Ferris wearing the yellow frock . . . which he knew should have been in the 'skip' . . . and the second murder began to suggest itself when the full moon came a week later . . . the association of the 'skip' suggested the employment of this uniform which he knew was in there. It would serve as an adequate and generally accepted disguise."

"Generally accepted? Why do you—"

"Because a uniform something like the one he wore was a common sight in Wavering—*and* near the allotment site."

"It looks to me," said MacMorran, nodding his head, "that Vera *was* strangled down there—not at the house."

"Yes—I'm afraid so, Andrew—as I said." Anthony half- turned. "Any more for the 'Skylark'?"

Helen Repton shook her head. "I don't want to hear any more, please. . . . I hate and loathe Wavering . . . and I hope I never set eyes on the beastly place again . . . why *anybody* ever goes there, I can't possibly imagine."

Anthony swung the car round a corner. By the side of the road, another car was parked. A man came from it and signalled to Anthony. Anthony slowed down and stopped. The man who had motioned to him, looked in the 'Bentley' and spoke to Helen.

"I'm so sorry to trouble you—but I'm not quite sure of my way. Is this the right road for Wavering?"

"There isn't one," replied Helen, "but this will take you there."

"Can I do it by twelve o'clock?"

"You should—but whenever you arrive, it'll be too soon."

The enquirer looked puzzled. "Er . . . thank you," he said as he backed away.

Anthony chuckled as the car re-started. "Spite," he remarked, "sheer, blind, unreasoning feminine spite."

Helen Repton pursed her lips. "I'm not playing," she said primly.

"About a hundred yards down the road, on the left-hand side," said MacMorran, "there's a little pub. . . ."

THE END

Printed in Dunstable, United Kingdom

65743185R00147